instagram.com/samanthaleehowe

Also by Samantha Lee Howe

The Stranger in Our Bed

The House of Killers

Kill or Die

KILL A SPY

The House of Killers

SAMANTHA LEE HOWE

One More Chapter
a division of HarperCollins*Publishers*
1 London Bridge Street
London SE1 9GF
www.harpercollins.co.uk

HarperCollins*Publishers*
1st Floor, Watermarque Building, Ringsend Road
Dublin 4, Ireland

This paperback edition 2021
First published in Great Britain in ebook format
by HarperCollins*Publishers* 2021

A catalogue record of this book is available from the British Library

ISBN: 978-0-00-844459-4

This novel is entirely a work of fiction. The names, characters and incidents portrayed in it are the work of the author's imagination. Any resemblance to actual persons, living or dead, events or localities is entirely coincidental.

Printed and bound in Great Britain by
CPI Group (UK) Ltd, Croydon CR0 4YY

In memory of Jack Harman,
lost to the world too young and too soon.

'They yearn for what they fear.'

– Dante Alighieri, *Inferno* (tr. by John Ciardi)

Prologue

TEHRIN

Tehrin Kozem smooths back his shower-wet locks, then walks into the bedroom with a towel slung around his hips.

'Morning babe,' he says.

His girlfriend Kara is sleeping still, covers pulled around her as she tries to hold onto the dream she's having. She hasn't heard his soft greeting and doesn't respond. She's like this every morning and Tehrin finds it endearing how reluctant she is to wake.

For months now he's been living in London with Kara. She has an expensive apartment in the Docklands, and Tehrin knows he's fallen on his feet in every way. Kara is smart, beautiful and has personal wealth.

They met six months ago when he was visiting relatives in London, and it was a shocking whirlwind that he still hasn't quite got his head around. Though she's white and his parents didn't approve, he just had to be with her and so he didn't return to his home in Syria. Instead Tehrin came to live with Kara, turning his back on everything he'd always known.

Every day he receives an email from his mother begging him to return to his rightful home, and to marry a fiancée he's never met. But Tehrin has found love and nothing, not even his considerable inheritance, will entice him back to take part in a life he no longer believes in.

Thanks to his English mother, he has dual nationality. He also has a trust fund, that neither of his parents could keep from him. Not since he turned 21 and his grandparents' money came into his own control – all four million pounds of it. Though his father had tried tying up his inheritance in court – as an attempt to pull him back in line – this only succeeded in making Tehrin more determined to live as he wished.

Tehrin dries himself and then, naked, goes to Kara's side of the bed. He looks down at her lovely sleeping face. Such pure skin. So white and smooth next to his warm brown flesh, and those beautiful blue eyes that never appear cold. Tehrin's heart swells with pride until he almost imagines it bursting from his chest. How has this happened? He is so fortunate. Allah was smiling on him the day they met. He is the luckiest man in the world.

Kara moves and groans as though she objects to his intense scrutiny, but she doesn't wake and so Tehrin pulls on some boxer shorts and goes out to make his strong aromatic Arabic coffee, while she holds on a little longer to sleep.

The apartment is large and open plan in the main living areas. It reminds him of the TV shows Kara sometimes watches on home improvements. It's clean and modern, no character at all, except for the slight touches of feminine glitter here and there.

He's never asked her about her style but now, as he waits for the small metal pot to bring his coffee to the right temperature, he thinks about the home they will one day buy together: when he finally persuades her to marry him.

The pot begins to boil, and Tehrin takes it off, pouring coffee into a miniscule cup. He adds sugar and then, sitting at the breakfast bar, sips the hot drink.

From the bedroom he hears Kara's mobile phone ring and her half-grumpy response as she answers. *Probably her mother,* he thinks. Kara is close to her, and they often talk on the phone. Tehrin has yet to meet his future mother-in-law, but Kara says she's happy for her daughter nonetheless.

Life is good. Tehrin has everything he could ever want and he's never been happier.

His own mobile phone is charging on the kitchen counter. He switches it on and begins to wade through his emails, pushing aside the pleading ones from his mother. He sees one from his solicitor asking him to call. Then he receives a notification for voicemail.

He calls the message service and listens.

'Tehrin, I'm afraid your payment didn't arrive. Can you call me? This account is a little overdue now.'

Tehrin frowns. He set up the BACS payment himself, ready to go yesterday. He opens his bank account app and logs in.

The account opens and Tehrin is shocked to see the balance of his account reduced to zero, and a message from the bank telling him his account will be closed now that he's moved his money to another bank.

'Father! Damn you!' he says, but this is irrational. His father *couldn't* touch his money, that would be fraud! He can't believe he'd resort to that.

'Is that coffee I smell?' Kara says.

'Yes,' says Tehrin, but he's distracted and doesn't look at her.

'What's wrong?' she asks. Kara comes over to the breakfast bar.

'The money. My inheritance. It's gone.'

'What do you mean, gone?' she asks.

'My bank account is empty.' There's an edge of panic in his voice.

'That must be an error,' she says.

'Yes, of course. It must be,' he smiles at her in an attempt to dispel his own anxiety. 'I'll call the bank.'

He searches for the helpline number and rings it but as his phone connects to the call centre, Tehrin looks up and sees that Kara is holding a gun and pointing it directly at him.

He almost laughs, thinking this is some kind of joke.

'You'd better hang up,' she says. 'I know exactly where your money is. I opened a new account in your name. An account that only I have the access codes for.'

Tehrin disconnects the call. He stares at the gun. A feeling of anxiety replaces the emotion of love and pride that he'd been enjoying just moments before.

'How?' he asks.

'Remember the parcel you signed for last week? You gave your money away in that very second.'

'I don't understand,' Tehrin says. His mind flashes to their loving sex the night before, but this woman, with such coldness in her eyes, does not feel like the same one he made love to.

'Oh Tehrin. It would have been so much better if you hadn't checked today. I was going to take you out somewhere. Now you're going to make a tremendous mess on my rug. Mother won't like that at all. Plus, it means I'll have to bring a cleaner in to dispose of you. Such unnecessary trouble.'

Kara sighs.

Tehrin climbs off the breakfast-bar stool and backs away from her.

'You'll kill me? After all we've meant to each other? All you had to do was ask. My money would have been yours if we married…'

'I don't love you, Tehrin. I can't feel anything like that about anyone. But for what it's worth, I never faked it in the bedroom,' Kara says.

'Kara…'

She smiles and then in a moment of elucidation, he knows: *this isn't even her real name.* His mother had warned him about women like this. She'd known who he was and had gone after him. Everything about her is a lie.

Flight mode kicking in, he turns and runs for the bedroom.

The gun goes off: two near-silent pops. Sharp punches smash into his back. By his own momentum, and from the impact of the bullets, Tehrin is propelled forwards. His legs give under him and he drops hard onto the hardwood floor. He tries to get up but his legs won't work. His arms are weak and he can barely move.

Kara walks towards him.

'You're such a pretty boy,' she says. 'It was fun while it lasted.'

She presses the gun against his forehead.

Fear surges up into Tehrin's chest as he realizes this is the end of his life: 21 and he's barely even seen the world…

He closes his eyes but it doesn't stop Kara from pulling the trigger and plummeting him into darkness.

Chapter One

BETH

Bethany Cane's hand trembles as she turns the key in the lock. The door opens and she enters her home for the first time in weeks. Beth looks over her shoulder at the car posted outside. Her 'new norm' for the foreseeable future in the form of a twenty-four-hour security detail. Beth is grateful for them.

A few weeks ago, she was rescued from a mental health ward. This secure medical facility had been told by her kidnappers that Beth had had a mental breakdown. She'd laid low at the unit, showing no signs of aggression, not knowing if the place she was in was real or fake. It could all be part of some elaborate set-up to make her believe she was in an actual hospital. It turned out she was all along. She'd been trained to avoid being tricked in this way, and she knew without doubt that she had been abducted. Just not why or by whom.

She'd just started to believe that this place was real, and was working on the doctor to try and get him to call MI5, when, much to the confusion of the doctors and nursing staff there, her new boyfriend, the pathologist, Elliot Baker turned up with colleagues to free her. He was a much-needed familiar face given the circumstances.

After they found and rescued Beth, her boss, Ray Martin, had launched an investigation into who had put her there and how this had happened in the first place. All the paperwork appeared to be genuine, even the name of a legitimate police surgeon had been used as that of the person who officially sectioned her. The only problem was, this particular man hadn't even been on call that night. In fact, he'd gone away for a short break with his wife and hadn't even been in London at the time. It remained, therefore, a mystery as to how the kidnappers had arranged the scam with such skill. All they knew was that the Network – a terrifying conglomerate running a lucrative operation involving the kidnap and brainwashing of children – were behind it, and Beth had been taken as leverage to force her colleague, Michael Kensington, to hand himself over to them.

Life changed a lot after that as Beth and Michael were forced into a safe house to protect them both over the next few weeks.

Now they're just trying to normalize, something that in Beth's case has always been easier said than done.

Beth takes a breath and closes the front door. She lives in an end-terrace house, with more garden than most have in the outskirts of London. She looks down the hallway. Just to the right are the stairs leading up to the three bedrooms and family bathroom. To her left is the living room, and further down on the right is a small water closet built in under the stairs. Beyond, and directly ahead at the end of the hallway, is the kitchen. She heads towards it, passing all of the other closed doors.

Beth glances around the kitchen. The room is so familiar and yet it is strange to be back here after all these weeks – almost a month – of being cooped up with only Michael and bodyguards for company. But the kitchen is almost as she left it. She notes the differences. A checked tea towel is folded, and not scrunched as it was before, on the counter top. The mug she'd used for hot chocolate is now washed and left upside down to dry. And the window that had been broken by her assailant has been fixed – all thanks to Elliot.

Beth glances at the back door, wondering if she'll ever feel safe here again as a painful anxiety churns her stomach.

'But of course, I will,' she says aloud in order to dispel the nervousness.

Her voice trembles, giving away the falseness of her bravado. She hasn't been back to work since the first night when they brought her back to Archive's offices, in the MI5 building near Borough Market. Despite insisting she feels well, she'd had to have the obligatory counselling to help her deal with the trauma of a home invasion.

She'd been to see a woman called Mary Blake a few times since.

'Just because you weren't physically hurt, doesn't mean you aren't traumatized,' Mary had explained. 'In fact, this sort of attack can create all sorts of deep-rooted emotions that can have a terrible impact on your mental health. That's why you're here, Beth. To try and make sense of them, talk them through so they no longer have an effect on you.'

Beth had listened, and talked, and shared how she felt, but always remained aware that she really couldn't show any intense signs of anxiety, because this could have a bearing on her ability to do her job. Or at least might be viewed that way by her superiors. Nothing had meant more to her than her position at Archive until recently, not even her two sons whom she'd given up in a divorce agreement. Even now Beth has no regrets about that. How much better it was that Cal and Philip hadn't been there that night. The thought of them seeing anything, or even being taken, was almost too much to bear, and it reminds Beth that she does in fact love her children. She just wasn't the full-time mother sort. Hence she'd allowed her ex, Callum, to have full custody. And now, while she may still be in danger, it is even more important that they stay away from her.

Beth puts the kettle on before taking her suitcase into the utility room. Once there she unloads her clothing into the washing machine. Although the safe house has a machine, this week Beth hadn't bothered to use it, storing her clothing for her own washer as though she knew she had to do something normal when she got home. Now, she sets the machine going, adding detergent, then she takes her suitcase upstairs.

As she reaches the landing, Beth has a momentary flashback. Someone grabbing her from behind, the chloroform-soaked cloth pressed over her mouth and nose. She can still smell that distinctive chemical odour, and her stomach roils with the recollection. She shudders as she approaches her bedroom door.

Then she hears Mary Blake's voice, soft and reassuring, in her ear. 'Take the bull by the horns...'

Beth strides forward and pulls down the handle, pushing the door wide open. She pauses at the door for a split second and then she walks in with forced confidence. She looks over her shoulder, as though she expects her abductor to still be waiting for her and then takes a deep breath.

The room has a smell, she's not sure what it is. She sees the curtains are still closed, and she goes to the window and pulls them aside. Then she opens the window letting in a waft of fresh air. This done, Beth already feels like she has begun to reclaim the room.

The bed is as she left it, bedding kicked back as though she'd just got up. She strips the bedding away, throwing the duvet cover, bottom sheet and pillow cases into a pile on the floor. Then she goes back out onto the landing and retrieves her spare set. After remaking the bed, she feels more in control. But the room where her attack took place still doesn't feel hers. There is black dust on all of the surfaces, where forensics had dusted for prints. Going into the ensuite, Beth gets a disinfectant spray from under the sink. She uses it on all the tops and sides of her furniture, removing the murky smears. After that she starts to feel better about her bedroom. The cleaning is an important process, in helping to settle her nerves as she wipes away the memory and fear of the attack with her cloth and spray.

She does the same in the bathroom. And then she spends the afternoon cleaning every room in the house.

By tea time Beth is feeling tired, the house is fresher. She's thrown out all the turned food from the fridge, and cleaned the inside ready for when her shopping delivery arrives the next day.

As she puts away all of the cleaning products, there is a knock on the front door.

Beth goes out into the hallway and stares at the door.

'Hey Beth. It's me!' calls a voice from the other side of the door, though she isn't sure who 'me' is.

She takes her phone from her pocket and looks at it. There is a text from Elliot, saying he's planning to call after work. Beth goes to the door. She puts the chain on before opening.

Elliot is standing on her doorstep.

'Hi,' he says. 'Can I come in? I brought take-away.'

He holds up a bulging white plastic bag.

Beth removes the chain and lets Elliot in. He hugs her, giving her a light kiss on the lips.

'I've missed you,' he says.

Though Elliot was with MI5 when she was released from the psychiatric ward, they haven't seen each other since that night. They've shared texts and phone calls, but that is all, since it was impossible to continue their relationship while she was at the safe house: a place even Elliot wasn't allowed to know the location of.

Beth is pleased to see him, but there's also an underlying stress with this unexpected meeting. He's been here and fixed things for her, at her request, but they'd never been together in her former family home before. It was something she had been avoiding and hadn't planned on. At least until her divorce was finalized. In the circumstances though, all of these worries don't matter anymore.

'Come in the kitchen,' Beth says.

Beth indicates the small four-seater table and Elliot places the bag of food on the top. 'Hope you like Chinese,' he says.

'I love it,' she says.

Beth gets plates and cutlery and places them down. Elliot pulls a bottle of Merlot from the bag, as well as several food cartons.

'I didn't know what you liked so I went for some safe options. Sweet and sour chicken, prawn curry, egg fried rice and of course some fortune cookies.'

'Sounds perfect,' Beth says. She puts two glasses down on the table and sits opposite him.

Elliot opens the screw-top bottle and pours the wine.

As Beth removes the lids from the food cartons she bursts into tears.

'Oh God! Sweetheart!' Elliot says. 'I'm sorry, have I gone too far?'

'It's such a relief not to be alone here.'

Elliot moves to the chair next to hers and reaches for her. He holds Beth until the tears dry up. One hand strokes her back, while the other smooths her hair back from her face. When she finishes crying, she looks at him, embarrassment colours her cheeks.

'Feel better?' he says.

Beth nods.

'Here, have some wine and let's eat this food. Then, later, I'm going to take you upstairs and make love to you. Is that okay?'

Beth leans into him, kissing him on the mouth.

'You're amazing,' she says.

'Well, I'm working on it,' he answers.

They eat in silence. Beth sips at the wine and for the first time in weeks she feels safe. She glances at Elliot as he eats the food with a great deal of gusto. She can't believe how lucky she is to have met him.

Chapter Two

MICHAEL

The body is lying in a bath full of water. Wrists cut, precise slices along the veins for maximum damage. The water is red as though every precious drop of her life's blood had drained into it: even after her heart stopped pumping.

She's a young girl, no older than 18, strawberry-blonde hair, stained crimson now on the long tips that float on top of the water.

I see Neva in her. Younger, yes, but it could be her lying there. I turn this thought aside, reminding myself I'm done with Neva as I bring my mind back to my work.

But shaking her from my thoughts isn't as easy as I would like: I see her everywhere. I don't even trust that this girl does resemble Neva. It could all be my mind superimposing her onto the corpse, regardless of my conscious effort to forget she was ever in my life.

Given to the house of killers to be trained as an assassin at the age of 5, Neva was raised by the Network. When I became involved with her, she told me she'd broken her conditioning. She'd enlisted my help to find her birth parents, saying she wanted revenge. At the time I learnt that I too had been under the influence of the Network, trained and brainwashed as a child to become a sleeper agent. Because of our mutual past, Neva and I had a connection. The memory of this still makes me feel sick to my stomach and my heart sore. After months of believing in Neva, thinking we had something, I'd struggled to let go of that belief until enough proof was put before me and I couldn't deny it anymore. She'd been stringing me along. A thought that was never too far from my mind especially when I was alone. Then, I'd go through stages of unfettered emotions. Anger. Regret. Denial. Sadness. All of which left me drained and miserable and culminated into one main emotion: grief. I mourned her loss despite the knowledge that I'd been tricked.

Every night, unable to distract myself, my mind went through scenarios of where she might be, what she was doing. She was, I believed, working with her mother. An assassin we knew only as Annalise, who had taken over the running of the Network after my father, and chairman of the committee running the Network, Andrew Beech, had been killed at the house in Alderley Edge.

It is harder than it should be to stop thinking about Neva as I try to focus once more on the girl in the bath. Even so I sink my mind into the work at hand, and the distraction is a relief, however brief, from my obsessive thoughts.

Normally this kind of case wouldn't come our way, but

the local police have called us in because my boss Ray had sent out a request to alert us of any unusual death. Despite appearances, this is no suicide. The killer hasn't even tried to make it pass as one. The knife or blade used is gone and it is impossible to slice more than one wrist like this yourself because the cutting of the first arm makes your hand useless to do the work on the second. But of course, MI5's very efficient pathologist, Elliot Baker, will confirm this all for certain.

As I wait for Elliot, I slip back to thinking about Neva. Where is she now? Did she flee the United Kingdom to Amsterdam as once we'd both been set to do? Half of the time I hope she'll contact me, the other half I pray she won't. I'm lost without her, though I hate to admit it. I feel that void left inside me and I probe it as I remain solitary at this bloody crime scene. Neva's absence is the phantom left by a lost limb. Part of me has gone with her, and I feel the shadow of my missing part lurking out of reach, but niggling still to be scratched.

I am alone: broken. They say time will heal but I can't see how I can ever recover. Or how I can pull the fragments left by her betrayal back together to make me whole again.

Now MI5 are looking for Neva in connection with the brutal murder of an air stewardess called Angela Carter, as well as the timely death of Solomon Granger – a hacker that we think Neva worked with to hijack a plane, killing many innocent people in the process. Granger was found hanged in his cell while in MI5 custody. Suicide. *Or was it?* After Neva had told me that no one was safe, even in our care, it is probable that she killed him.

My emotions spike, my face flushes and an intense rage surges up inside me at the thought of Neva slipping into our secure facility unseen and taking Granger's life. Granger is silenced now, and his testimony, though recorded, had little value on his death. His demise stopped us from getting retribution. We can't put Neva in a line-up and have him formally pick her out. There will be no trial brought forward by the Crown Prosecutor for Angela's horrible death. This is the worst tragedy of all and something that often frustrates me about my job: the guilty rarely get punished even when we solve a case.

But what Solomon had told us, had at least given some leads that we could follow up.

'Security Agent Kensington?' says a voice behind me. 'Is it okay to come in?'

I turn to see Security Agent Elsa Stevenson standing by the door. She's wearing her crime-scene suit, and her dark-brown bobbed hair is tucked in under the hood. Everything is in order. I nod to allow her permission to view the scene.

I'm surprised at Elsa's formal address of me, but then the two of us do not have an easy working relationship. Not since she tried to follow me for my boss, Ray Martin. At the time Ray had placed me in an RAF base in Lincolnshire, and Elsa came along at a convenient moment to 'help me' off base in her car. All to give me the chance to head back to London and to Neva. Just as Ray knew I would do if the opportunity arose. The thing is, as a result, I don't quite trust Elsa, and she has made no secret of the fact that she doesn't trust me either. But since Beth's abduction, and now medical leave, Elsa has been brought into our offices and so I'm forced to work with her regardless. Despite all this, I'm actually glad to see her and her presence goes a long way to bringing me back to the present and taking my mind away from my dark thoughts of Neva.

'God she's young,' Elsa says.

'Yes,' I nod. I glance at her and see her eyes linger on the knife wounds. Her expression is guarded, though her vocal reaction reveals that Elsa is shocked by the sight of the corpse.

'This is Neva's M.O. isn't it?' she says.

Hearing her name spoken by Elsa makes my heart leap in my chest. The respite of not thinking about her is taken from me. I see her again dancing behind my eyes. Sleeping beside me. Reaching with loving arms to pull me to her. I shake the images away.

'Wrist slitting? Killing for no apparent reason? Definitely *not*,' I say.

'But the knife…'

'A lot of the Network's operatives use this type of blade. It's standard issue. That's why we've been brought in. This is no ordinary murder. And they need someone like me to study it,' I hear the bitter tone in my voice as I snap out the words. I'm sure that Elsa knows all about my profiling skills and my history with the Network, but I feel like putting her in her place a little more. But as I meet her shocked expression I rein myself in. Arrogance is not usually one of my failings. This girl just brings out the worst in me. Or is it just her casual reminder of Neva that has thrown me over the edge?

'Do you… put yourself into the mind of… the killer?' she asks.

I pull myself together. Yanking back the irritation and anger Elsa has reared in me. I half nod, half shake my head before saying in a softer tone, 'In a way, but not really. I analyse behaviour by the way the murder is committed. I can't really *think* like the killer does, but the detail gives me insight to what sort of person he or she is. How little empathy they show is interesting too.'

Elsa looks relieved and embarrassed as if she understands my antagonism towards her and recognizes how hard it was for me to moderate myself because of it. 'Was there any empathy for this one?'

'Depends,' I say.

'On what?'

'Whether she was conscious or not when her wrists were cut and she was placed in the bath. And only the toxins in her blood will tell us the answer to that,' I say.

'But… you have an idea already?' Elsa prompts trying to smooth over the earlier awkwardness by getting me to talk about my methods.

'I think she was drugged. There's no sign of a struggle,' I say.

Elsa looks again at the girl. She frowns and I know she's trying to see what it is that I see. Not everyone can do it. I recognize the signs by experience and instinct as well as all I learned taking my profiling degree.

'Look,' I say trying to show her something tangible. 'Her eyes are closed. She was sleeping. She didn't feel a thing, but nor could she save herself.'

'You really are good at this,' Elsa says, her eyes slightly narrowed.

I don't respond to the compliment but it makes me feel like a prick for my arrogance and moodiness when she first came in.

To allay any further tension I leave the bathroom, and Elsa, to look around the other rooms of the apartment. This is a short-term rental for tourists. When the girl didn't check out as planned, housekeeping found her and called the police.

In the bedroom the girl's case lies open on the bed, half packed. Not something you do if you plan to take your own life and this only reinforces my initial opinion that she didn't intend any such thing. The other room is a lounge diner. There's bread in a toaster, popped up, toasted, but left unbuttered and uneaten. There's also a cold mug of tea on the kitchen worktop.

Someone came in while she was making her breakfast, but there was no apparent struggle, unless the assailant tidied up afterwards. I begin to wonder if she knew the person. Or was she overcome after being drugged? That would require much more stealth. The drink could have been spiked while she was in the other room getting ready to leave. But how did the perpetrator get inside if they weren't invited?

I sniff the contents of the mug. There's no unusual scent. That doesn't mean anything though.

On the side is also the girl's handbag. With gloved fingers I remove her wallet and find her identification. Her name is Sinead O'Brierley. And she's just turned 18 according to her driving licence.

'Hi Michael!' I come out of the kitchen to find Elliot Baker, fully suited, like Elsa and myself, in crime-scene gear. Mask, gloves and hood all in place so that we avoid cross-contamination of the scene.

'Hello, Elliot. I have a feeling the girl was dosed. Probably the half-drunk mug of tea in the kitchen,' I say.

Elliot nods, smiling over his face mask. 'I'll be sure to save the contents for analysis,' he says.

I realize I'm being a bit of an arse telling the good doctor what to do. That's twice in one day that I've been full of myself. And neither Elsa nor Elliot deserve this from me. He's one of the best, and often his opinions expand, or reinforce my own observations. I give him a self-conscious nod then move away and leave him to do his job.

Elsa loiters near the front door as Elliot and his team move through the flat, photographing, bagging and tagging anything of interest. The girl in the bath is dealt with last, once moving her isn't going to affect any of the evidence elsewhere.

Elliot spends a long time in there with her. Photographs are taken and fingerprints are found around the bathroom. Only then is the water in the bath drained away through a sieve and the body lifted out. She's placed in a body bag and put onto an ambulance trolley to be taken out to the mortuary van. I watch one of Elliot's men wheel her away as I stand outside the apartment, my role there merely to observe, and take away anything I can that will help me build a profile of our killer. This one is not going to be easy because it seems random. Yet, I know it isn't. I believe she is linked somehow to our ongoing investigation of the Network, Neva and her peer assassins. I don't have any proof, just a gut feeling, and someone, somewhere must have believed it too, otherwise the police would be taking care of this one and not us.

When Elliot is finished the flat is cordoned off with crime-scene tape. We'll keep this place off limits even to its owner for a while until we are sure we haven't missed anything.

I pull off my PPE and stuff it into a black bag with the forensics team's suits to be disposed of later. For every new crime there's always a new suit. No risk of contamination that could ruin a future case.

'Well that wasn't pretty,' Elsa says beside me at the lift.

'Death never is,' I say.

Chapter Three

NEVA

Six years ago

She looks a lot like me, Neva thought as she watched her target through a pair of binoculars. Talia Bukowski was her name. She was similar in age to Neva; around 20 years old. The girl was tall, slender and strong, a well-trained operative and Neva, never one to take the easy hit, decided she wouldn't just kill her at a distance, she would get closer and learn more about her intended victim.

She wondered what the girl had done. *Curiosity kills.* Neva had been a full-time assassin for over three years and she'd never questioned her orders. But she looked into Talia's past and discovered no scandal. She'd been a model student, recruited by the FSB in her early teens, and as a result was given the best education. Neva became somewhat fascinated with her. Like herself, Talia had excelled in everything she put her mind to. So why did she deserve to die?

Against her orders from the Network, Neva followed Talia for several days. Talia was a creature of habit and Neva soon learned her routines. On the fourth day, Talia left the Kremlin as usual and made her way west into the Alexander Garden. Not learning anything further of interest, Neva had decided she'd finish Talia that day.

She followed the girl, snapping pictures, and behaving like a tourist, until she saw someone approach, stopping Talia in the centre of the park.

Neva recognized the man. He'd been pointed out to her once and she knew he was a senior figure in the FSB. A general with a certain reputation as a sexual predator. Something most of the female operatives who worked in the Kremlin were forced to tolerate.

Neva heard the heated argument between the two but could not make out what was said. She saw Talia tearing herself free from the man's brutal grasp and the rage on the general's face.

Neva made a decision then that she wouldn't kill Talia until she'd talked to her after all. She didn't understand why she wanted to do this, and it was against protocol. But she didn't like the general, and she suspected he was behind the call to retire this talented girl. It was something of a waste in Neva's eyes.

When the general stormed away, Neva left the distraught Talia in the park and headed off to the girl's home.

Talia's apartment was in a dilapidated building not far from the Moskva River, which ran south of the Kremlin. Neva broke in. She walked through the place, noting the sparse furnishings and abject poverty that Talia lived in. In the kitchen she saw a pan half filled with water on the cold stove. Talia couldn't even afford a kettle. Why was an agent working at the Kremlin so deprived? It didn't make sense.

She searched the apartment looking for evidence of others who lived there. But there were only signs of Talia, which made Neva's presence less complicated because she wasn't likely to be disturbed.

When Talia arrived home, Neva slipped into the bedroom unseen and took her Glock from her pocket, screwed on the silencer and waited.

Talia opened the door. She came into the room and began to remove her jacket.

Neva closed the door, blocking Talia's exit and only then did the FSB agent realize that she wasn't alone.

Talia swallowed and looked at Neva steadily.

'He told me someone would finish me,' she said in Russian.

'I have been hired to kill you, yes. But I don't know why,' Neva said back to the girl in perfect Russian.

'He *wants* me. I said, "no". He didn't appreciate that. I suppose you will kill me now?' Talia said.

'Not today,' Neva said. 'But sometime soon.'

On the roof of a building 800 yards from the Kremlin walls, Neva was ready. As she looked down the Schmidt and Bender telescopic sight attached to the AX308 sniper weapon, she focused on the main staff exit where Talia would be leaving from.

Right on time Talia exited. She paused in the doorway and lit a cigarette, before strolling away. A short time earlier, Neva had used a Kestrel weather meter and ballistic calculator to estimate the movement of wind. She knew she was in range and her target was hers for the taking. A red dot appeared on Talia's chest as the laser rangefinder centred on its target. Then Neva fired two shots in rapid succession. The bullets plummeted into Talia's chest; blood blossomed on the front of her white blouse and Talia slumped to the ground. Blood bubbled on her lips and she gasped for breath. Around her screams for help took up. A tourist ran to her side, and called an ambulance from their mobile phone, babbling in German.

On the rooftop, Neva removed a 4mm hex key from the cheekpiece of the gun, then she loosened the screw on the Quickloc barrel release. The barrel came away and Neva stowed it in a holdall. Next, she folded the stock right over the bolt handle, reducing the weapon by a further ten inches. She placed all the parts into the bag.

While an ambulance collected Talia's body, Neva disposed of the holdall down the building's garbage shoot, before exiting and walking away to the next street to collect her car: a racing-green Mini Cooper. It had GB stickers and a British licence plate and screamed 'tourist'. Neva opened the door, climbed inside and started the engine. She pulled away from the kerb and drove out of Moscow.

On the outskirts of the city was an abandoned

warehouse. The huge delivery doors were wide open and Neva drove the Mini inside and parked. She sat in the car until a short time later an ambulance arrived. The vehicle approached in silence: no siren to draw attention to its location.

'Your life doesn't need to be the end,' Neva had said a few days earlier. She held Talia's eyes with her own and lowered the gun.

Talia had looked at her, her eyes shining with unshed tears; she didn't dare hope for clemency. She'd disobeyed her superior, she knew what would happen. She should have just slept with the pig. But something inside Talia refused to bend. She'd done everything anyone ever asked, but she couldn't tolerate the general. Neva wondered if she would have done the same in this woman's position. But then, no one would ever dare put her in a corner that way. And Neva's superiors were interested in her talent for death, not her sexual prowess. No, she would never experience this, she wouldn't allow it.

'I'm no executioner for a pervert,' Neva said. 'And I have need of a body double.'

'What do you mean?' asked Talia.

'We are around the same height and build. We could be made to look the same if you changed your hair,' Neva explained. 'And from time to time, I will need to be in two places at once.'

Talia shook her head, confused by the offer as she tried to understand what Neva wanted from her.

'You want me to be… you?' she said.

'Sometimes. Yes.'

'But how? They will want to see me dead,' Talia said.

'And they will,' Neva said.

Neva got out of the car and opened the back doors. Talia was sitting up. The white blouse she was wearing was covered in red, but Talia was unharmed. She wiped away the smear of faux blood from her lips.

Neva held out a bag for Talia. The girl took it and looked inside. There was a change of clothing, a sweater and a pair of jeans – very westernized – for her to change into. Neva talked to the ambulance driver and paramedic while Talia removed her stained clothing.

Once she was dressed, Talia climbed out of the back of the ambulance and joined Neva.

'The general will want to see my dead body.'

'And he'll see one,' Neva said.

She handed over a briefcase to the ambulance driver. A white van drove into the warehouse and pulled up beside the ambulance. Two men got out of the van, and opened the back. They pulled a body from it and transferred it into the ambulance.

A woman, the same height and build as Talia, with two gunshots in her chest, precisely where Talia had 'appeared' to be shot.

'You killed someone to save me?' Talia said.

'This is a prostitute who died last night of an overdose,' Neva explained. 'The body wasn't logged into the mortuary thanks to my friends here who were on the lookout for a suitable replacement for you. Come with me.'

They got into the Mini as the ambulance drove away. The ambulance driver switched on the siren again as he left.

Neva followed at a safe distance. Then parked up near the hospital car park. From a holdall in the back seat, Neva pulled out a wig and handed it to Talia.

'Put this on,' she said.

Talia took the wig and stuffed her own hair up into it until the wig lay neatly on her head, and looked natural.

A short time later, Neva received a text.

'It's time,' she said glancing at the screen.

They both got out of the car and walked around the back of the hospital. There, a mortuary attendant met them at a back door. He hurried them both inside and led them down a long empty corridor.

In the mortuary, the dead body of the prostitute was being stowed in one of the fridges by the ambulance driver and paramedic that Talia had already met.

'Strip,' said Neva. 'Just the top half.'

Talia looked confused.

'Don't worry, they've seen it all before,' Neva said.

She told Talia to lie on the mortuary trolley and then Neva covered her up to her shoulders with a white sheet. She spent some time applying make-up to Talia's face.

'Be still, I have to take a photo. This is our proof.'

Neva took a photograph with her phone.

'Get dressed,' she said to Talia.

Talia got up and dressed again. She put the wig back on so that she wouldn't be recognized leaving the hospital.

'Look,' said Neva.

She held out the phone showing her the photo. Talia's face had been made pale, and she looked newly dead.

'You better wash that off now,' Neva told her. She held out a packet of face wipes which Talia took, and proceeded to use.

When she looked normal again, Neva and Talia left the mortuary the same way they entered. The mortuary assistant followed and locked the door behind them.

Back in the car, Neva sent her photograph to her source.

Payment sent, came the reply.

'It's done,' Neva said. 'You're officially dead.'

Talia looked at her, the enormity of her new freedom dawned on her. She could go anywhere. Do anything. No more Kremlin rules. No more ownership of her mind and body. She could be herself at last.

'But. Where do I go?' she said.

'I've taken care of that,' Neva told her. 'This time tomorrow you'll have a new passport and we'll be flying out of here.'

'Where to?'

'Switzerland first. There you'll be near me, so that I can… train you.'

Talia let this sink in. *Yes.* She'd agreed to be Neva sometimes and this was a small price to pay for her liberty, but what did this all really mean? Talia didn't know, but she didn't fear it either.

'Why did you help me?' Talia asked.

Neva had turned the car away from the hospital. She kept her eyes on the road. A plan was forming in the back of her mind. She didn't know why she needed Talia herself at that point. It was one of those spur-of-the-moment decisions Neva had made, at a time when she'd been used to always taking orders. If the Network found out what she'd done, she'd be retired. Talia was, therefore, dangerous to her. But Neva didn't concern herself with thoughts of their anger. She'd been unafraid, unfeeling, unbroken. What she was doing was somehow logical. She didn't like how they constantly monitored her life anyway and it would be convenient to be off the grid sometimes when they didn't know about it.

She hadn't seen this as a rebellion, though on some level she had always known it was. But there had been something about Talia that had inspired Neva to save her instead of destroying her. She reminded Neva, perhaps, of herself. Controlled and moderated always by others, and if she couldn't yet see the need to escape that, she could at least give Talia some autonomy.

Deep down Neva's saving of Talia hadn't been all that altruistic: one day she may have need for a corpse body double herself and it would be convenient to know where to find one. The next day, Neva and Talia (now renamed Janine Beaujolais) flew from Moscow to Switzerland.

Neva set Janine up in her first apartment and began paying her a retainer. Her only job was to learn to be Neva.

'How did you manage all of this?' Janine asked.

'Money. You can get anything you want if you can pay for it,' Neva explained.

'Who *are* you?' Janine said.

'They call me Neva.'

Chapter Four

MICHAEL

Present day

I'm in my office, just off the open plan central workspace that Beth has always occupied and where she would have several computers running, doing various searches at once. Ray had told me she would be sharing this with Elsa when she returned to work. Confirming that Elsa was here to stay for the foreseeable future.

'There was flunitrazepam in the tea,' Elliot says as though he can't wait to share this information with me.

I look up from my computer and see him at the door. I wave him into my office.

'Take a seat,' I say.

'How did you know by looking at her?' Elliot asks sitting down on the other side of my desk. 'Only the drug doesn't have any smell and doesn't leave any physical marks. I also found traces in the urine that was still in her bladder which confirmed that she'd definitely had some.'

I tell him my observations as voiced to Elsa before he'd arrived on the scene. Elliot nods, and I know it's because he understands this as well as I do. He has also been trained to observe and theorize. The difference between us is that he can prove his findings with science, and I rely on him to back up the theories I make with medical evidence. Or from a psychological viewpoint, a similar case that confirms my ideas.

'Was she… raped?'

'No,' Elliot says. 'And there was no sign of her fighting off an attacker, or any bruising to show a struggle.'

I frown as I picture her again in the bath. 'She was staying in the apartment alone, travelling from Ireland. Then she was targeted by our killer. But I'm having difficulty finding a motive. None of it makes sense.'

'She hadn't met up with friends?' Elliot asks.

'Not that I know of. The Irish Garda have taken it up over there. But I may need to fly over and examine the girl's computer. Apparently her sister said she was talking to someone online and she thought she'd gone to meet them,' I explain.

'That's odd. Possible grooming but no sexual motive,' Elliot says.

'Unless the death was sexual enough for the killer,' I say.

Elliot shrugs. 'Your department, not mine.'

'Have you seen Beth?' I ask changing the subject.

He looks sheepish, 'Yes. Last night. I was worried about her being alone in the house. Especially the first night.'

'Good,' I say. 'I was concerned too. But I think she was sick of my company at the safe house.'

'Well there's nothing like your own home, is there?' Elliot says. 'Anyway, I just wanted you to know what I'd found. The full report will be emailed across later today.'

Elliot stands up and goes out. A few seconds later Beth comes in.

'Oh, you're back!' I say. 'Elliot didn't tell me you'd travelled in together. Now it makes sense why he came into the office and didn't just call me.'

Beth blushes. 'Yes, well. The shrink has given me the okay to return,' she says.

'How do you feel?' I say.

'Like… I *need* to get back to work,' Beth says. 'I just met Elsa…'

She lets this hang in the air waiting for me to comment. I don't.

'Well, it's nice not to be the only girl around here now,' she says. 'And our workload has been crazy recently.'

'It's good to have you back, Beth,' I say.

Beth goes out. A few moments later I hear her showing Elliot out.

I turn back to the pile of papers and folders building up on my desk. More cold cases have arrived this week than usual. We are still looking for links to the Network. But it is good Beth is back. Elsa is still so inexperienced and although having her around is better than not, she has a lot of training to do before she will become really useful to us.

I open the top file and see the face of a little girl looking back at me. The picture is black and white. A very old case – fifty-five years ago. This is a 5-year-old girl called Zaphire D'Aragon who vanished from her family estate in Toulouse,

France. I can tell she has fair hair but not the exact colour. I study the child's face. She looks like any child of that age, and the file doesn't tell me much about her except… she was a twin. *Interesting.* The twin sister remained safely with the parents, but Zaphire was never found. If Zaphire was taken by the Network, it's possible that one or more of her parents was involved with Beech. Which means they willingly gave over their daughter. Power and money are great motivators. I make a note to send this information over to our counterparts in Interpol to investigate further.

I shut the file and stare at the wall of my office, filled as it is with Post-its and photographs of all known Network agents. There is only a computer-generated photofit of Neva but I find my eyes drawn to it.

The assassin in me rises and that uncontrollable rage surges up once more as I look at the picture. I can't shake how stupid this all makes me feel. Let alone the utter squirming embarrassment I continue to experience whenever discussions with Ray, Leon or Beth lead back to Neva. I can feel their eyes on me sometimes. I almost hear the unspoken questions that hangs between us like accusations. *How could she have duped you, Michael? How could someone of your skills not know what she really was?*

I should have seen it coming. But Neva is not just a good spy, she is probably the best. But this knowledge doesn't stop me feeling a great deal of self-loathing. It doesn't prevent me thinking I'm a failure. Or from imagining I would kill her right now if I could get my hands on her.

My hands clench into fists. My jaw sets and I glare at the picture, imagining my hands around her throat, stifling her breath as well as her treacherous and seductive words. But the thought of ending Neva doesn't give me any satisfaction. It just compounds my misery: I regret she's gone, even though I now know the truth about her.

'Hey,' says Beth from the door. 'Penny for them?'

She follows my gaze to the incident board. 'We'll get her Mike,' she says. 'We'll get them all.'

I uncramp my hands and nod, straightening my tell-tale expression. How can I possibly explain my thoughts to Beth? They are so confused, even I don't understand them.

I wish I had Beth's confidence.

I've taken to wearing my Glock 17 full time now, as Beth and I, and perhaps everyone else in Archive, are no longer safe. Neva has learned too much about us.

'Anyway,' says Beth. 'I came in to tell you, your sister Mia is on the secure line. Want to come and talk to her?'

'Yeah. That'd be great.'

When I finish my call with Mia, I feel a little better. Mia is the one anchor in my life that remains constant. I would sacrifice anything for her and my beautiful niece, Freya. And, indeed, I had lost everything I had thought I wanted because of my loyalty to her.

A few weeks ago, Neva and I rushed to Mia's side in a bid to protect her from the Network. I thought I was defending my sister, but there I learned all about the double life of my brother-in-law, Ben Cusick. A further blow and betrayal to us both. Ben had shown his hand when he thought I'd been triggered again by the Network. He revealed he had been working for MI6 and had lied to Mia for years. The revelation was a shock to both Mia and me and had almost crippled their marriage. But now they are working on it and Mia, Ben and their daughter Freya have been given new identities. Even I don't know where they are but Mia is allowed a weekly call to a secure line in MI5 so that I can at least know they are safe and well. A situation that is very hard on us both. I'd sworn to protect Mia and Freya and now that task had been taken away from me. I'm dreading the day when the calls will have to stop because Mia will have to transition fully into her new life, without further contact with me. I'll never be able to see or speak to her again and I'll never see my niece grow up.

There is a rising panic inside me as I anticipate the approaching end of our small contact, and worse still that I will have to go through the rest of my life trusting that they are both safe, but never knowing for sure if that's so.

Even so, I have to accept it is important that Mia disappears because once we both belonged to the Network, and now they want to call in their assets. Mia doesn't know this. Or at least not all of it. She has been told some truths. Like the fact that the couple that brought us up weren't really our parents. But she doesn't know that Will and Annie Kensington are dead – executed by Neva. I chose not to tell her, just as I didn't want her to learn that I was a trained killer, and that she might have been groomed as a breeder for the Network's kill house.

Since Mia, Ben and Freya would be starting a new life, it wasn't necessary to burden her with more. After I'd outed

Ben, he told me privately that Mia had been suffering with anxiety that Freya would be taken from them. It's likely to be caused by some deep-seated memory that she was drawing on from the conditioning. She is sheltered now, and the Network can't find her. So, I hope my sister will never have to experience the trauma of giving up my niece to the house of killers.

But even as I tell myself Mia is safe, I regret her lack of full knowledge about our past. Forewarned is forearmed, after all. And one of the issues that stopped me leaving with Neva and going to Mia's aid instead was that Mia didn't know she was in danger.

For that reason, I didn't take the decision to keep all of this extra baggage from her lightly. Mia's marriage was on a precipice, more knowledge might be the burden that could tip it over the edge. Even so, it means that Ben can't come clean about everything he knows either. An added pressure on him, though after spending six years lying to her already, I doubt he will find it that difficult now. There is always the fear though that Mia will learn he is keeping more from her. All of which isn't good and she may see it as further betrayal. Can their marriage recover from more deceit and lies? I don't know. All I can hope for is that they can rebuild their lives together and that Ben is strong enough to keep my sister and niece safe, no matter what.

But Mia's call had been reassuring on that front. She'd talked about Ben and Freya and it appeared that they were getting back to normal. I hoped so anyway. They need to be united now more than ever.

Chapter Five

LIZZIE

'Wild-haired Lizzie' her friends used to call her, and she'd been pretty back in the day before she met and married Barry. But marriage and several failed years trying to conceive had transformed Lizzie into someone less wild, more staid. Barry, bored with their life, had eventually succumbed to the charms of his much younger secretary. Like everything else in their life, this scenario was a cliché. Lizzie hadn't even cried when he told her, the same day he moved out to be with the girl. In fact, Barry's departure was a relief. It signified that Lizzie no longer had to try. No longer had to be a wife. No longer had to please anyone other than herself. Barry had been difficult to satisfy at times. His expectations of her, their marriage, the potential children – that in the end weren't possible – it had all been too much, and for the last few years she'd been miserable anyway.

She had signed the 'quickie' divorce papers – what was

the point of dragging it out and making him wait two years to marry the girl? Lizzie wasn't the vindictive sort anyway, it took too much energy, and gained you nothing but more stress. Besides, Barry had been generous because she hadn't been difficult and because he felt guilty. She'd ended up with the house, and a nice lump sum in the bank to keep her comfortable. She didn't have anything to complain about.

Two years off 40, Lizzie wanted each day to slow down. It had taken her a few months of going to work, coming home and being alone at night, to consider what she wanted to do with the rest of her life.

'You need to look after yourself,' her friend Vicky had said after Lizzie voiced concerns about getting older. 'There's no reason to just give in to nature. You have to do everything you can to make time stand still. I mean… don't you want to meet someone new?'

I'm not 'past it' by any means, Lizzie had thought. *So maybe it's time to get back out there.*

Her red hair, always a sign of her once passionate nature, had faded down: a more golden and less red colour, that someone once called strawberry. The truth was that her vibrant red had just been diluted by oncoming white but certain photographs still made her look somewhat Nicole Kidmanish.

Vicky had been encouraging and had taken Lizzie to see her beautician. Botox, fancy nails and a great new colour and cut, made Lizzie feel better than she had in years. The colour was balanced out and she took some selfies as Vicky suggested.

'Looking good!' Vicky had said. 'Time to get online…'

'What do you mean?' asked Lizzie.

'Dating site, silly!'

It was just a bit of fun at first. Lizzie chatted to a few people and was invited out on a couple of dates. She never took them up on it, but the online flirting was exciting. Then Lizzie started getting some flattering comments from one person. It made her feel attractive, even though they weren't her type. She was *curious* though, and more than a little lonely. But she didn't admit this, even to herself.

They chatted sometimes on Messenger, but Lizzie wouldn't do FaceTime calls as it worried her. Even so, the friendship grew over a few months. Lizzie found it easy to express her feelings to this anonymous friend, though she'd never been good at that before. But typing your emotions just wasn't as challenging as speaking them and her friend was never judgy and was always sympathetic.

The relationship went to a new level when the occasional chat turned into regular exchanges, from weekly to daily, without Lizzie realizing.

I'd love to meet up one day, her friend typed.

Lizzie replied with, *Wouldn't that be nice?* But she never really considered that they could meet. Her friend lived in Europe, and it was a good excuse to keep things the way they were.

Then she got a message that her new friend was in town, along with an invitation to meet for a drink. Lizzie wasn't sure and made a few excuses not to go. But at the last minute, and after some very persuasive texts, she decided it couldn't do any harm to meet. Especially in public.

The pub her friend suggested wasn't too far away from her home, just a twenty-minute walk and so Lizzie had finally agreed.

It was a nice warm evening and Lizzie enjoyed the exercise. Even as she made her way there, she thought of how Barry would hate this: he wouldn't walk anywhere, and it reminded Lizzie how much she liked being able to do what she wanted. Like this spontaneous meeting with someone she didn't really know, even though the calls and texts made her feel like she did.

She went through the scenario of what it would be like to meet this friend face to face. Could they be as comfortable in person as they were online? She hoped so. Then she blushed at the thought of this leading somewhere else. Where could it go? After all, Lizzie wasn't like that.

Lizzie almost turned around and headed back home when she saw the pub ahead. She stopped at the traffic lights but didn't cross the road.

What am I doing meeting a total stranger?

She received a text then: *Looking forward to it, but I'm a little nervous.*

Of course, Lizzie thought, *we are in the same boat. It will be weird for us both.* Yes, it was a little scary but that added to the excitement of the adventure, didn't it?

She crossed the road and went into the pub. Inside she saw her new friend waiting with a bottle of wine and two glasses already poured. They'd talked about putting the world to rights with a good bottle of red. She walked in feeling more comfortable now. They could be friends, even if Lizzie wasn't ready to take it further than that.

There's a moment of confusion when Lizzie wakes. She doesn't remember coming home, and certainly can't recall coming to bed. Her mind flutters around the evening. Some remembered laughter, but the rest is a bit of a blur. She feels a bit dizzy now, and nausea burns the back of her throat. *How much did I drink?*

She groans and tries to get up as the prospect of vomiting becomes a reality. That's when Lizzie discovers that she's tied up.

Her arms are splayed apart, wrists secured to something she can't see. It's pitch black, and she can't tell where she is. It's not home. It can't be. Her bedroom curtains never block the street lights out this well.

'Hello?' she croaks and then she turns her head and pukes to the side. The acrid smell of vomit lingers near her head.

'It's all right,' says a quiet voice beside her. 'It's normal after Rohipnol.'

'What's going on?' Lizzie says. She's scared now and still feels so very sick. 'Where am I?'

It feels like she is lying on a bed of leaves. She tugs at the bonds that hold her down, it feels as though she's tied to four wooden stakes, hammered into the ground. She tries to move her legs but they too are spread and attached on each side. She is helpless.

'Look, whatever you've done…' she says.

'I haven't done anything to you,' the voice says.

'Please. Let me go… I won't tell anyone…'

Sharp pain silences Lizzie as something moves across her thigh. It takes a moment for her to realize that it was a knife. The cut pulses and throbs. Her inner thigh grows damp as blood pumps from the wound.

'Why are you doing this?' Lizzie says. Already she is light-headed from loss of blood. She tries the bonds again, but nothing gives and then the real panic sets in. She is wounded and she's going to die.

Tears spill from Lizzie's eyes. What has she done to deserve this?

She hears her attacker move away, and then light pours in as a door is opened. She sees a beech tree beyond the opening and she realizes in a rush that this is her garden shed. All she has to do is scream and her neighbours will come running. But the blood is still pouring – no, *gushing* – from the wound and her strength ebbs away with every pulse. She doesn't have the energy to speak, let alone scream.

She struggles again, moving her arms and legs, but they are held tight. She can feel the glutinous warm blood pooling under her thigh. The wound throbs in time with the beat of her heart as her life drains from her.

She drifts off as the blur of sound fades into unconsciousness but then the shed door closing hurls her out of the darkness.

She is left listening to her own breathing.

Her eyes close once more.

The tears of fear dry on her cheeks. Her muscles start to tense and her head aches as her brain struggles to keep her alive.

Her pounding heart slows.

Each beat grows further apart and then Lizzie slips back into unconsciousness, never to wake again.

Chapter Six

NEVA

Neva wakes. For a moment she forgets where she is. Then the memories rush back in, changing her perspective of how this day will go. She is unhappy and frustrated.

It is a few weeks since she fled the Tower Bridge Hotel, and Solomon Granger threw his accusation her way. At that point she knew it was all over with Archive, before her work with them had even begun. A disappointment she hadn't been prepared for because she'd wanted to work with Michael. She'd wanted to help them to bring down the Network.

As usual she disposed of anything that they could use to track her, like her phone. But first she sent Michael a text, telling him that she was being set up.

You've been playing me, he'd said by reply.

She had stared at her phone for a while, wondering what she had expected him to say. She was no expert in relationships, after all, for she had never felt anything like this before. Michael was her strength and her weakness. Being cut from his life left a gaping hole that Neva had no idea how to fill.

She went through a scenario of conversation in which she tried to persuade Michael to believe in her. Each time she saw him turn his back. It was disappointing that he didn't give her the benefit of the doubt at first. But in the end, she didn't try to change his mind. What was the point? Michael now believed she had been lying to him and Neva really couldn't blame him. She was a child of the house and by the nature of their training, taught to lie with perfection.

Michael's rejection hurt though. Even as Neva took the sim card from the phone, water leaked from her eyes: tears she hadn't shed since the early days spent in the house.

She forces herself to go to ground because old habits die hard. When in doubt she retreats to safety.

Burner phone gone, passports that Michael had known about still need to be disposed of: Neva now has to find a new life when she had begun to believe for the first time that she had a chance at some form of normality.

She stares at Michael's passport photo for a while, and then tears it in half. What a fool she was to ever believe they could be together, let alone be a married couple.

Neva berates herself for her weakness and her inner voice is that of Tracey Herod, her one time handler. *You're pathetic.* It takes her a few days to even begin to function again.

Despite the ongoing shock of Michael's mistrust, she sets the wheels in motion to establish a new identity, with the plan to leave London via the Eurostar. While she waits, her mind is in turmoil, she can't concentrate properly. She feels lost.

After a week she realizes that she can't go on like this. She has to talk to Michael. She has to tell him her side and somehow try to convince him that Granger lied. What possible motive he had for that, Neva doesn't know. But she isn't who he claims. At least… she doesn't *think* she is.

Life, post-kill house, is sometimes confusing. Neva can't be sure that she hasn't been coerced, just as Michael once had been. He'd been a sleeper agent for the Network, raised and conditioned to live a double life. There is always the possibility that something is lurking inside her too, still waiting to be triggered. That something may well have been set in motion and she now has no recollection of it. No one knows better than her how the Network play with your mind and so she picks around her memories again, trying to see if anything was off. The thought horrifies her: after all the work she's done on herself to break free.

Six months of Neva's life had been in hiding during the time that Granger claimed she was acting as a double for the stewardess, Angela Carter. Neva recalls everything she's done in that time and none of it involves a plane hijack. Or so she believes. But she can't help thinking – *what if it was me? What if I did these things and just can't remember them?*

She wants to get Michael back on side until they can learn the truth. Sometimes, she toys with the idea of letting Archive take her in, doing a polygraph. Proving she doesn't know anything about Carter. But capture would just make her a sitting duck. The Network will send someone after her, and they will come in strong. It wouldn't matter where they put her – the Network has allies everywhere. This is not a realistic or sensible option, no matter how much she misses contact with Michael.

She returns to Michael's apartment block. She hangs out in the street in the hope that she can catch him alone. She doesn't want to run until she has that one last chance to see him again.

During the wait for Michael's return, Neva sees Janine's apartment invaded by MI5: Michael has told them about her. They find nothing: Janine ditched that location and identity as soon as Neva had left the apartment with Michael. It is standard practice once a location is revealed to an untrusted party – in this case Michael. Janine never trusted Michael even when Neva had. Neva now concedes that Janine was right too: Michael has betrayed them. There is no doubt on that score. And it tears her up inside: he was the one person in her life that she truly believed in. When the truth dawns on her that he's given her up to Archive, she wants to yell and shout at him. Perhaps even punch him in the face for it. She even imagines herself on her knees, begging for forgiveness for something she doesn't think she's even done. She hates feeling this way. All these irrational emotions make her weak when she has to be stronger now than ever. What good are feelings to someone like her anyway?

Despite her rational mind chewing away at the stupidity and futility of her turbulent heart, Neva can't stop herself from riding this terrible rollercoaster. She has no one to talk to about it. No one to help straighten her out, or put things in perspective. She may be a mature killer used to dealing with the harsh reality of death, but to her relationships are new and confusing. Neva doesn't know how to process this abject sense of loss or how to mend the hole inside her that it's created.

Since MI5's raid on the flat, Neva has avoided any contact with Janine, even though they can reconnect through the web at any time. Like Neva, Janine has bolt-holes all over Europe. She doesn't know where Janine has fled to anymore than Janine knows where she is. Even so, there's comfort in knowing she's out there, ready to be called back should Neva want her. For once Neva imagines talking to her associate on a girl-to-girl level. But what would she tell her?

'Janine, I'm in love…'

Neva gives a harsh giggle at the thought of saying such a thing to Janine. All they ever talked about was assignments. They are not friends, not really. Neva explores what she feels about Janine, but the pain of losing Michael blocks out all other emotions.

With her new identity in her hand, Neva can no longer use it as an excuse to stay. She says goodbye to London and, subconsciously, to any chance of speaking to Michael as she boards the Eurostar to Amsterdam.

She thinks about Janine briefly when she's settled. Neva has no use for a double now. the last thing she needs is to be 'seen' anywhere. She has to remain hidden. At least until she knows for sure that she isn't a sleeper agent. *What will I do if I am?* A chill shivers up Neva's back followed by a whirl of paranoia. *If it's me then I'll have to deal with it.*

To convince herself that she is in control, she takes to recording and monitoring her movements in the apartment she now lives in. Every few days she skips through the footage. So far, nothing out of the ordinary has occurred, as she sees herself doing exactly what she remembers doing. But still she doesn't feel secure.

She calls herself Mila Jansen. This identity was a real person once, except that Mila Jansen died at the age of 8. The death record, however, has been expunged and Mila was 'reborn' a few years ago with a new life. A life that Neva had occasionally dipped into. She'd done this frequently to free herself from her handler, Tracey, using Janine in her stead. On such occasions, Janine, armed with Neva's phone, would live in an apartment in London and she'd also take on hits that came in during that time. Neva would take 20 per cent off the top and Janine would get the rest for doing the wet work. It was a situation that profited them both, and it also gave Neva the opportunity to be free of the Network's control. When Janine wasn't working for Neva, she worked freelance, taking jobs that were being farmed out, or which she gleaned from the dark web. Neva didn't know, or care, how Janine spent her down time. What she did care about was that Janine disguised herself. Neva had trained her well, and trusted that she did. Neither Tracey nor Beech ever got wind of her exploits, and none of it ever came back to Neva, and so for a few years Neva and Janine had a good arrangement.

On paper, Neva's new personality is a student and as

such she dresses the part. Casual jeans and sloppy slightly grungy tops. Make-up-less for the most part, she ties her hair back in a scruffy bun. She doesn't hang out in the student bars and she is quiet. So, her busy neighbours don't pay too much attention to her. She is, as always, hiding in the plain sight of normality because she knows this is the best way not to be noticed.

After showering and dressing, Neva checks her security footage, sees nothing unusual, and then she packs a small holdall. In the bag she stows a Glock 17 with several cartridges. On her wrist she has her usual knife holster, ready with a mere flick of her hand to use when needed.

After weeks of waiting, her hacker source Elbakitten has at last sent her a very important lead which is the only reason she would take a risk now to venture out of Amsterdam. Crossing borders is risky, but to catch up with Beech's former chauffeur, Eldon Fracks, the danger is worth it. Last time she had a lead on Fracks, the Network had set a trap for her in Brighton. Even now she doesn't know if Fracks was ever genuinely there and had somehow skipped away before she arrived and before Network operatives had tried to capture her. She thinks of this as she prepares for her mission now. She will be extra vigilant, just in case he's been used to lure her in again.

Packed and armed, Neva leaves her apartment and sets off on her journey to face Fracks. She pushes down the dancing excitement that tries to surface, forcing herself back into the coldness that an assassin of her calibre has as a default setting. But after all she's experienced, going back into that stark cold place once more isn't easy. She stops trying to quell the anticipation. Letting it lift her up and out of the constant sadness she's felt since leaving London. It's not the thrill of a potential chase that makes her adrenaline surge, but the thought of something tangible to aim for after weeks of inertia. Or the thought that she might learn something that could redeem her in Michael's eyes. Wouldn't that be the ultimate prize?

Chapter Seven

MICHAEL

The woman is in her own garden shed, staked out on the wooden plank floor as though she is sunbathing. The only difference is that she's tied to four posts which have been driven through the floor, and that she's under cover. Her femoral artery has been sliced, and it's clear that she's bled to death. The end would have been quick, no more than ninety seconds, judging by the depth of the wound.

'How long has she been there?' Beth asks over my shoulder.

'Judging by the smell, anything up to a week,' I say.

We both back away as Elliot and the police forensic team approach the shed, having traversed the front garden and travelled around the side of the house.

It's dark and electricity hasn't been fed through to the shed from the house, and so they set up several battery-powered lights on tripods inside. The garden is cordoned off, but I see a man watching from the upstairs window of the house next door. The heavy police presence in the street and around the front of the house will keep most of the curious away. Already a news van has arrived and one of the homicide detectives is dealing with them. On the face of this, it appears as though they are in charge of this investigation but in reality, MI5 is running the show. It's unusual, but so is this murder or we wouldn't have been called in.

I go into the house and find PC Parker in the kitchen, making a cup of tea.

'Who raised the alarm?' I ask him.

'Work colleague and friend of the victim. She's in the living room, Sir, if you want to speak to her.'

'Is that tea for her?' I ask.

Parker nods, then after stirring in two spoonfuls of sugar, he hands the mug to me.

I go into the living room where the victim's friend waits to be interviewed. She's a very attractive woman in her late 30s. Long brown hair that curls in such a way to look casual but actually takes a lot of work to do. Her clothing is expensive and stylish and she is, overall, very well groomed.

'Security Agent Michael Kensington,' I say, introducing myself as I give her the mug of tea. 'You're a friend of…'

She takes the tea and sips it, grimacing when she tastes the sweetness of the sugar.

'For the shock,' I say.

'Lizzie,' she says as though she's just processed my first comment. 'Her name was Lizzie. Elizabeth Seacroft.'

'Can I take your name please?'

'Victoria Johnson. Everyone calls me Vicky,' she says.

'How long were you friends with Lizzie?' I ask.

'We went to school together,' Vicky explains. 'And worked for the same firm. Lizzie is… *was* a graphic designer. I work in the accounts department.'

'And Lizzie hadn't turned up for work for a few days?'

'That's right. She's always so reliable. She loves her job and she didn't call in sick so, I got worried. I rang and texted her, but got no response. I knew something was wrong.'

I ask Vicky about Lizzie's personal life and learn she is recently divorced.

'But it was amicable,' Vicky explains.

I make a note of Barry Seacroft's name and address for further investigation. But I already know it isn't Lizzie's ex that killed her. No, this was done by someone with a precise knowledge of murder.

'Was Lizzie seeing anyone?' I ask.

Vicky shakes her head. 'She was on a dating site, but she told me it was just flirting. She wasn't really ready for dating yet. She was just, you know, having fun and building her confidence.'

'So, she didn't discuss meeting up with anyone?'

Vicky frowned, 'No. She'd have told me if she was going to do that. We were always in touch. Every day. That's why I knew there was a problem.'

'What's the dating site she was on called?' I ask.

Vicky gives me the name and I make a note of *Yin and Yang*. I question her a little longer but don't learn much more. I let her go after taking all of her details for future contact.

When she's gone, I pull on my gloves and do a cursory search of Lizzie's house. In the sitting room I observe that Lizzie liked her house minimalist. There are no photographs or ornaments on the window ledges or the mantlepiece in the living room. Not even family photographs that you'd normally find in a home.

I find a photograph on the wall going upstairs. Lizzie's ex-husband is laughing as he peels off the garter from his wife's thigh. Lizzie is turned away from the camera as though someone had just asked her something and drawn her attention away so I can't see her face properly. It's odd to see pictures of a couple in the home after one or other has left and it could mean anything that Lizzie hadn't removed this one. Was she still in love with her husband? Or it didn't bother her that their life together was over, and so the photo didn't offend? I recall again that Vicky said the split was 'amicable'. If this was really the case then Lizzie was lucky indeed. At least until she met her killer.

I look around the bedroom, it's neat and tidy, like the rest of the house: the bed is made. Not everyone does that in the morning. It says a lot about Lizzie. She worked full time and yet managed to keep her home perfectly in order. She was not someone to break her routine, nor someone likely to take a chance on meeting up with a stranger. So, what had happened? How had Lizzie been led astray? Or was her death a random attack?

I give a brief glance into the other bedroom and the bathroom and then I go back downstairs. In the hallway I spot Lizzie's handbag. It's dropped at the door, almost forgotten. It jars with me that it's there like that, but I'm not sure why. I pick the bag up and open it. Inside is her wallet, holding credit cards and a little cash. I look for her mobile phone but realize it isn't there.

The phone could tell us who Lizzie was last with and its contents are therefore very important. I look around the house, checking the plug sockets to see if the phone is on charge anywhere, but I don't find it.

I look back at my notebook and find Vicky's number. I ring her. The call is picked up right away and Vicky, her voice thick and tearful, asks who's calling.

'It's Michael Kensington. I'm sorry to disturb you. Can you give me Lizzie's mobile phone number please?'

Vicky's voice echoes as she rattles off the number and I realize she's on a hands-free device in her car. I don't keep her on the phone.

After I hang up, I call Lizzie's phone hoping it will ring and give away its location but instead it goes straight to voicemail. Not a good sign. If the phone is switched off locating it won't be easy. I hang up.

I go back outside, just in time to see Lizzie's body being loaded onto an ambulance trolley. They wheel her around the side of the house then put her into the mortuary van.

When Elliot has finished his search of the shed and his forensics team are still bagging and tagging possible evidence, I follow him to the front and to the van.

'Thoughts?' I ask.

Elliot removes his mask but keeps the crime-scene suit and gloves on.

'I'll do the autopsy this afternoon and let you know what I find. The first thing I noticed though… well this could be a serial killer,' Elliot says.

'How do you deduce that?'

'She looks like an older version of the other one. The girl we found in the hotel.'

'Sinead O'Brierley?' I say.

Elliot nods. 'They could be sisters, or mother and daughter if this girl had given birth to her very young.'

I hadn't seen Lizzie's body properly before Elliot arrived but now I want to take a closer look.

'But the killing was different?'

'I suspect it was the same knife used, but yes. This one seemed… crueller.'

Elliot leads me to the mortuary van where Lizzie's body is now stowed. The driver stands by the back doors: they lie open as though waiting for us. We climb in the back.

Elliot unzips the top of the body bag and I see Lizzie's face for the first time. There are streaks of black mascara running down her rot-bloated cheeks, which suggests she'd been crying seconds before she died.

I'm shocked and breathless as I study Lizzie's face. It's like a glass of cold water is thrown over me. Yes, I see the resemblance to Sinead. I also recognize another likeness to someone else. I push the thought of this away and try to focus on the evidence that will help me develop the growing profile of the killer.

'She was possibly awake and very scared when she was cut,' I say.

'We'll see what toxicology comes back with,' he says. 'But I think so too.'

Elliot zips up the body bag and we get out of the van. The driver closes the doors locking Lizzie's body inside. I find myself staring at the back of the van, lost in my own thoughts. I see Lizzie's face behind my eyes and I superimpose another face over it. I shudder. Can this really be happening?

'You can take her now,' Elliot says to the driver.

The man goes around to the front and gets in the van. I watch as the vehicle pulls away.

'I'm going to get back and start my examination,' Elliot says before removing his crime-scene suit and gloves, throwing them into a black bag in the boot of his car.

I remove my gloves and wait while he closes the trunk.

'You okay?' he asks.

'Just mulling over what I've seen today,' I say.

'I'll be in touch,' he says, climbing into his car.

As Elliot drives away, I return to the back garden and find Beth speaking to PC Parker.

'I'm waiting for the ex-husband to come and secure the house,' Beth says. 'I've told him we'll want to speak to him.'

'He has keys?'

'Apparently they were still friends,' Beth says. 'But we'll be looking at him very closely anyway.'

I leave Beth and PC Parker and look around the garden once more. Elliot's team are just finishing up searching the whole yard and one of them points out some footprints behind the shed. It's a female pathologist who I haven't met before but she appears to be leading the search.

'Size 11,' says the woman behind her mask. 'So, someone the same height as our constable there.'

I glance at Parker, my eyes sweep over him down to his uniform boots. 'Or… our constable himself… look at his shoes. Come on people! We're on a crime scene!'

Parker's size 11 boots are covered in mud. I shake my head at the sheer naivety of the constable.

Once I've pointed out Parker's contamination of the scene, it changes the ballgame for the team. The pathologist is embarrassed that she hadn't noticed.

'We'll have to take a print of his footwear to prove it's his,' she says trying to cover the slip.

'One other thing,' I say. 'Did anyone find the victim's mobile phone?'

The pathologist shakes her head. 'Not out here. But we'll look when we have a proper search of the house.'

I tell her about the handbag in the hallway, explaining the phone's absence. Then I leave them to do their job, knowing they'll be very thorough now. She takes Parker inside the house to remove his shoes.

'Stay here and make sure all protocols are followed,' I say to Beth. 'That was a bit of a rick with Parker's shoes.'

Beth rolls her eyes and looks back at the house. I follow her gaze. We can see Parker and the pathologist through the kitchen window. The body language isn't as professional as it should be.

'I'll speak to Elliot about her,' Beth says. 'You've got to keep your head in the game no matter who you work with.'

'I'm going back to the office to do some digging,' I say. 'I'm going to search for Lizzie's profile on this dating site and see if anyone in particular has commented on her pictures.'

'Right. I'll crack the whip around here now and read them all the riot act,' Beth says.

I know the crime scene is in safe hands as Beth can be a real – and the only word that suits her is an Americanism – bad ass, when she's riled.

'How're you getting back?' she asks because we came in her car.

'I'll call an Uber,' I say.

'See you back there,' Beth says. She walks away and back into the house, her voice fading as she enters. 'Okay, can we have a bit of professionalism in here?'

I smile as I walk back around the side of the house and to the front.

When the taxi arrives, I head back to the office to start my initial work on profiling the murderer. Already my mind is racing ahead because Elliot's assumption that we have a serial killer on our hands is sure to be right. As with any new case, I'm excited by the prospect of finding out who that killer is and where it will lead. But one thing is for sure, I can't help thinking this is somehow connected to Neva. Not just because of the obvious resemblance of the victims to her, but also because, if Elliot is correct, of the very specific knife used on both victims. I'm sure we have a Network assassin here. But who and why would they be killing innocent women with no other connection to them than a passing resemblance to their most wanted rogue agent?

Chapter Eight

ELDON FRACKS

Eldon Fracks orders a continental breakfast and strong, black coffee to help wake up his wine-befuddled brain. He is a creature of habit, and this particular coffee shop has become a favourite haunt.

Coffee in hand, Fracks reflects on how his whole life has changed. At first, he thought this was a disaster, but now Fracks sees that his life has made a dramatic turn for the best. As the former chauffeur of the head of the Network, Fracks was privy to a great deal of information. All of which he'd managed to keep to himself. Like everyone else, he'd feared Mr Beech, but Fracks had been an expert on 'making like' the three wise monkeys: though he saw and heard everything, he never spoke of the Network's evil. For this he'd gained the unquestioned trust of Beech and his associates.

But now Beech was gone: shot down by a task force who brought his private assassin training house down around his ears in the process. And Fracks had been able to avoid capture, all because Beech had sent him off the property on some petty errand. Fracks didn't even recall what it was that Beech had requested, he only knew, as he drove away from the large mansion, standing in several acres of land in the heart of Alderley Edge, that there were helicopters and army trucks heading directly towards the house. He saw them, just as he made the decision to turn left instead of right, and he passed the assault team as he did. There was no way he would complete the task Beech had given him because he was not going back to the house.

He'd contemplated calling it in, but Beech might have demanded his return. Fracks reasoned that the outcome would be whatever it would be, no matter what he did. So, he decided not to intervene and kept on driving, eventually ditching Beech's limo and heading off towards Manchester airport.

He heard about the raid on the radio app through his phone which was tuned to a local station. Beech wasn't mentioned by name but enough was said to let Fracks know that his employer was dead. It was, as he'd suspected, time to get out of Dodge.

As he always kept an overnight bag and his passport in the boot of the limo, along with a holdall stacked with cash that Beech used as an emergency fund, Fracks had jumped onto the next flight to Germany. There, using Network contacts he'd heard of, but never revealed he knew about, he obtained several new identities. Everything was easy when you had money. At the time he'd just planned to lie low until the organization regrouped, but it wasn't long before he realized how privileged he was to have escaped unscathed not only MI5, but the Network itself. This could be a whole new opportunity. A whole new life. A clean slate, leaving behind the Network and all it stood for. A rarity for anyone who had dared to become embroiled in their machinations.

But Germany was not a safe place for Fracks, since it was a Network stronghold. The grapevine revealed that someone was looking for him, and so he did the only thing he could to avoid detection: Fracks travelled. Never staying long in any one location, he kept on the move. It helped that the Network, having lost their illustrious leader, were thrown into total chaos. Fracks had banked on this too, understanding more than most just how much control Beech had over the other committee members.

But there was one assassin who'd aspired to be more and had set out to move up the ranks. When Fracks heard that Vasquez was looking for him, he went to ground as low as he could get.

That's when he ended up in Belgium.

In Brussels he hired a cheap studio apartment. He wasn't flash with money, and made every effort not to be noticed. He lived very simply. The money he had from Beech's stash – a mere £250,000 – wouldn't last if he was too frivolous and he had no legitimate way of earning more. He accessed his own savings, transferring further funds to a Belgian bank called KBC to use when he was certain they'd given up looking for him. Then he heard that Vasquez had 'disappeared'. Fracks breathed a sigh of relief at this news. Rumour had it that the upstart assassin had been erased by the Network's committee. Fracks didn't enquire any further for fear of drawing attention to himself.

After that he stayed in Brussels. As time went on, he stopped checking on the dark web platforms for signs of his name being mentioned. With confirmation of Vasquez's death, he was sure that no one would remember or care about Beech's driver. What was he in the scheme of this great machine that controlled governments, and destabilized economies? *Nothing.* Not even a cog anymore.

Walking back from the coffee shop, his stomach rounder from his newfound pastry addiction, Fracks is relaxed and happy. The thing that had once frustrated him now pleases him. Who among those he'd driven around would even remember the face of one chauffeur? He'd been like a piece of furniture to them all, even Beech, which was why they hadn't been careful around him. And now he is anonymous. He is free. And he can leave those awful people behind.

He stops off at a little bookstore on his route home. Here the owner has imported books in English to loan for a small price. Fracks chooses from some of the new arrivals. He likes history and drama but he avoids thrillers – it's too close to the life he once led and his reading is for pleasure.

The bookstore owner packages up the books, wrapping them in tissue before putting them in a bag.

'Three weeks to return,' he says in pidgin English.

Fracks nods, pays him and takes the bag.

Reaching the small block of flats where he lives, Fracks walks upstairs to his studio apartment. He's never lived anywhere so small before, but the lack of possessions is freeing, and he has no urge to buy anything that isn't essential anymore. Sometimes he thinks back to his nice apartment in London, the full cabinet of fine brandies and whiskies that he opened on special occasions. The expensive furniture that populated the rooms and the superking bed that he'd slept on – at times with someone else he'd picked up for the night. But all of that is shallow and he's learned to appreciate the simple things, which, more than anything means that he remains hidden.

He opens the apartment door and goes inside. As he expects, all is quiet. He fixes himself a coffee, after lunch the wine will be opened, but for now, Fracks' retirement also means time to read and relax.

He sits down in his favourite chair by the window and watches the world go by.

He drains his coffee mug and then reaches for the bag of books. Yes, life is good, and Fracks will enjoy losing himself again in the fictional historical dramas he loves so much.

Chapter Nine

MICHAEL

I find myself looking at Neva's photofit picture as I compare her to Sinead and Lizzie. The two women are similar but not really like her. Even so, the strawberry-blonde hair is striking in its resemblance to Neva's natural colour – rarely seen in her case as she often disguises it. While I look at the pictures, I try to be analytical. The two dead women seem to have their appearance as their link to each other, though they were at different stages of their lives. Sinead was an 18-year-old and single, whereas Lizzie was 20 years her senior and a divorcee. I'm sure this is not a coincidence. We have a serial killer on our hands.

But how are they somehow associated with Neva?

I close my eyes and try to push thoughts of her away but find I can't. The betrayal and lies sit inside my stomach like a stale lunch badly digested. It hurts sometimes and make me furious at others. Sometimes I yearn for the days of forgetfulness granted by Beech's conditioning. Maybe then I could spare myself thoughts of her. Haunted as I am by her memory in every detail of my life. Not least in my working days. No matter how much I tell myself to forget her though, I can't.

I open my eyes again and look at the dead women once more. I'm sure I'm designing Neva connections with Lizzie and Sinead that aren't there. Only time and the autopsies will tell. But two deaths within weeks of Neva's escape doesn't feel like a coincidence.

But who is doing it, and why?

It's probably nothing to do with her, I think. *A fluke!* But deep down my gut says otherwise. Not that I feel I can trust my instincts that much right now. I had thought I was right about Neva, and how wrong I was.

I rifle through the lives of Sinead and Lizzie. So different from each other, but there must be something that draws them together, or brings them into the sightline of our killer.

I open my notepad and read again the interview I'd done with Lizzie's friend, Vicky. *There.* The dating site. *Yin and Yang.* I open the browser on my laptop and search the name. I come up with Wikipedia and Urban Dictionary entries for the meaning of the phrase. Then I find the website: *Yin and Yang: Opposites Attract!*

The site is closed unless you open an account and so I can't just browse the member profiles. I weigh up what to do for a moment, before I send Ray an email, explaining that I'm setting up an account on the site in order to look at Lizzie Seacroft's profile, hoping to find a lead. I don't want him to think I'm using the work computer for anything other than official research. Though we are generally trusted, such things would be frowned upon and I'm still wary that any of my actions might be misconstrued. Even so, none of this will be necessary if we find Lizzie's phone – assuming she has the app on there, it would hopefully link us to her account, any messages received, and an opportunity to browse to see if Sinead was on the same site.

Before I continue on the site, I look up Lizzie's number and find out who her service provider is. Then I set in motion the requests required for information on who Lizzie spoke to last. It is just a matter of formality to get warrants for a murder victim's phone records but it can take time. I also send the information to Beth to see if she can trace the location of the phone when she's back in the office. Though, if it's switched off, this will prove difficult.

I receive an email response from Ray about the dating site.

Good plan! Let me know what you find out.

Happy that my boss knows what I'm doing, I open an account under a pseudonym, using one of our 'safe' credit cards to pay the subscription, and then I search through the female profiles until I find Lizzie's. She calls herself 'Wild-Haired Lizzie', but her photos show her with salon-groomed locks. She boasts of her newly coloured and coiffured hair on one of her statuses and there is a swarm of men responding to her, chatting her up, and suggesting they have a 'private' chat. This, I learn, is done in the form of 'rooms' rather than a private message and both parties have to agree to enter the said room. The site's terms and conditions boast of this as a feature to stop unsolicited private messages being sent to another person – it helps to keep things 'above board'.

Looking at Lizzie's public posts and the comments below, I make a note of all of the men's names, placing a star against each name every time I see a comment from them on Lizzie's page because the frequency of their communication may flag something or someone.

Then I look for Sinead O'Brierley. It takes another forty minutes wading through female profiles before finding Sinead. She's using the name 'Nadie O'Brierley' and this is why my specific search didn't find her right away. I look through her selfies and then wade through the comments looking for matches with those remarking on Lizzie's pictures, but there aren't any. The age divide is obvious on the site, and only men around Sinead's age are leaving comments for her. I wonder if this is another rule on *Yin and Yang* as often it's a given that some older men will be looking for younger girls.

Even so, I hope to find one or two of the same names to narrow down the search but nothing shows up. Then I notice something. A photograph that looks familiar. I flick back to Lizzie's page and study the profiles of her admirers again. *There.* A man called Werner, he says he lives in Europe, but is no more specific than that. I check his entry, looking at the other photographs he has there. I open another browser window and lift up Sinead's profile. There is someone there called Stacey. A girl. But she has posted an identical picture of the same Bengal cat that Werner has.

This is not evidence in itself, it could be a coincidence that both people had found and shared the same photo, but in each case, 'Werner' and 'Stacey' claim that the animal is theirs. That *is* suspicious. Could there be two different people pretending they owned an animal that they didn't? Or had one of them taken it from the other's profile?

I'm not that familiar with catfishing but something is awry on *Yin and Yang*, despite the rules and regulations they impose on members. And I'm going to find out what.

A few hours after sending the warrant, I receive the information from Lizzie's phone company. There are several phone numbers listed on her account, but one shows up over and over again. I check it against Vicky's number and see this isn't hers. Neither is it Lizzie's ex's number. When I search for the owner of the phone, I find that this number isn't registered to anyone. That means that the number has been obtained, but never registered to top up with funds. It's probably a burner, or a temporary number that someone has been using. But assuming it is our killer, it confirms that they are no ordinary or random murderer. Lizzie was specifically reeled in and this person made a conscious effort to go after her.

I look up at the photos on the wall again. My eyes fall on Neva's photofit. Every gut instinct in my body is telling me that she and Lizzie and Sinead are connected. I just don't know how or why yet or even if I dare listen to it.

Chapter Ten

NEVA

It's a hot summer's day and Neva is wearing shorts and a strappy top. Big sunglasses hide her face and a floppy hat covers her hair. She's carrying a backpack filled with her essentials and looks every bit like she belongs in Brussels as she rides around the streets on a bicycle.

As Elbakitten had promised, Fracks was at the coffee shop like clockwork every day and Neva is waiting for him to come outside.

He has his coffee and pastry, then Fracks saunters down the street, relaxed and confident. He doesn't believe anyone knows he's here. But the mistake he made first was transferring money from his personal accounts into the small local branch of KBC. All it took to find him afterwards was Elbakitten searching street camera footage back to the day when Fracks had first entered the bank to set the transaction in motion. He'd had to use his real I.D. in order to access his accounts in England, but the man had become complacent over the last two months. Elbakitten had found him several times on different cameras since then, and often at the same time in the same district. This information she'd sent to Neva, and as it had proved valid, Neva planned to use Elbakitten more. Her fees were reasonable too.

Neva focuses on Fracks as he approaches a small bookshop. After going in and browsing, he comes out half an hour later with a bag of books in hand. Neva doesn't move from her spot until Fracks is four hundred yards down the road, then she gets on the bike and follows. Fracks makes a turn at a side street ahead. When Neva reaches the corner of the street, she sees Fracks coming out of a bar, holding a bottle of wine he's just purchased.

A few feet away he enters an apartment building.

Neva rides the bike past the building and then parks and locks it up at the end of the road. Fracks is inside and climbing the stairs to his own apartment when Neva walks back. She studies the building. Then she returns to her bike and takes off again for a ride.

By late afternoon, Neva returns to Fracks's building. After remotely monitoring CCTV nearby, she knows that Fracks hasn't left. At the door she reads the names on the residents' doorbells. The only one not listed is on the top floor. From the research she's done, she knows that this one is a studio apartment. She doesn't press the bell for this flat, instead she calls one of the others and waits for a response.

'*Hallo?*' says a voice in Dutch.

'Ik heb een pakket bezorgen,' Neva says in a bored tone in response. *I have a parcel to deliver.*

'I'm not expecting a parcel,' the occupant replies.

'It's for your neighbour,' Neva responds. 'They didn't answer and I want to leave it by their door.'

'Which one?' asks the woman on the other end.

Neva says it's the top floor.

'Ah. *Him!* Yes, he'll be drunk by now!'

The door buzzer sounds and allows her access. Neva never takes for granted the help of nosey neighbours, but sometimes their information is invaluable. She'd seen the wine, but this woman must have noticed Fracks' return and routine daily. It also means the woman is very observant, which could be a problem for her too.

Neva takes a small parcel out of her holdall and walks into the hallway. The apartment block is basic with no main reception, Neva notes that the stairs go all the way up to the top floor in a spiral. Holding the fake delivery package in her hand, she begins to walk upstairs. On the second floor a woman is standing by her door waiting for her.

'You the delivery girl?' she asks.

Neva nods, '*Dank u*, I have to get this delivered today or they won't pay me!'

The exchange is made in Dutch and the woman nods and goes back inside her own apartment, satisfied that she hasn't let a thief inside. Neva passes by and heads up the next flight of stairs.

When she reaches the top level, she stuffs the parcel back inside her backpack and retrieves her Glock from the bag instead.

At the door to the studio apartment, Neva studies the lock. It's an old mortise, incredibly easy to pick. She puts the Glock in the waistband of her shorts and takes out the lock-pick set from the front pocket of her backpack. She places the bag on the floor then presses her ear against the door.

A loud drunken snoring can be heard from within.

Neva picks the lock and she opens the door. The hinges creak, she pauses and waits, but Fracks hasn't heard her and doesn't wake – Neva sees him slumped and sleeping in a chair by the window, a bottle of French wine stands on the small table beside him, but even from the door she can see the bottle is empty.

She picks up her backpack and brings it inside. Then closes the door.

Fracks sleeps on, oblivious of her presence as she approaches. Neva looks down at him. She waits to see if he will wake, but Fracks is in a deep sleep and doesn't move. Neva looks around. The studio consists of a large loft space: kitchen, living space and bedroom occupy different corners of the same room. The only separate space is the small bathroom to the left of the front door.

Neva walks over to the kitchenette and runs cold water into a jug she finds there. She goes back to Fracks and throws the water over him.

Fracks jerks awake, spluttering as he breathes in the same time the water hits him. He coughs and chokes, coming from his inebriated dreams back into reality.

'Hello, Mr Fracks. I'm Neva,' she says.

'Oh my god!' Fracks says. His ruddy face blanches white as he stares down the barrel of the Glock in her hand.

'You've come to kill me…' he whispers under his breath, and in that instant Fracks is sober again.

'You and I are going to have a little talk,' Neva says. 'And if you lie to me or fail to tell me what I want to know, you are going to die.'

Fracks shivers as though Neva is already stepping across his grave. She pulls up a chair and looks directly at him.

'Beech was very upset when they lost you,' Fracks volunteers. 'He always saw you as some personal achievement. Like his son Michael.'

Neva narrows her eyes and studies him.

'It appears you know as much as Vasquez thought you did,' Neva says. 'Hence his people tried to find you.'

'Did they send you?'

'I work for myself these days,' Neva says. 'I'm here to find the names and addresses of the committee.'

'I don't know where they are exactly. I swear. Committee members move base at regular intervals…' Fracks says. 'Beech didn't even know where they lived. Just areas they covered. They don't trust each other, you see.'

'Pick up that book,' Neva says pointing to the book that Fracks had fallen asleep reading. She pulls a pen from the pocket of her shorts and places it on the table by the empty wine bottle. 'Write their names and those locations in the front.'

Fracks reaches for the book and picks up the pen. His hands are trembling as he opens the cover to the front blank page. He writes:

Kritta (Berlin); Banwick (Cardiff); Subra (Jerusalem); Petters (Oslo); Conor (Edinburgh); Drake (Venice); Armin (Kabul);

Stanners (Loch Lomond); Ruddy (Florence); Aelen (Belfast); Cruik (Madrid).

'But… I heard that some of these were dead. And their locations are generic. Vasquez…'

'What do you know about that?' Neva says.

'Just that Vasquez tortured some of them to find the others…'

'Who was tortured and killed?' Neva asks.

'I heard Aelen and Ruddy are no longer with us…' Fracks says.

'You just told me that none of them know each other's location. So, which is it Fracks? Do they, or don't they?'

'Some of them did, I suppose. The rumour was that Vasquez was fed information by another interested party who wanted in on the committee. Codename: Annalise,' Fracks says. He's breathless and scared as he speaks.

Neva leans forward at the mention of Annalise: she is of interest. The person that Michael said could be her mother. Annalise had been at the Tower Bridge Hotel when shit hit the fan a few weeks ago. Her underling and other committee member, Subra, died that day – killed by Solomon Granger after he learned she was behind the death of his lover Angela Carter.

Yes, the committee are a treacherous lot, and they'd turn on each other at any opportunity. This is proof of it. But it isn't enough, and Neva believes that Fracks knows it. She needs everything she can get from him.

'I know you have more,' she says. 'Where is Annalise based?'

'Ah. Now she never moves…' Fracks says. 'And I do know that. A château in the South of France.'

'If she never moves, then why is she safe from the others?'

'No one will go after Annalise. They are all scared of her, and she has her own network. Beech even suspected her of being the leader of the Almunazama.'

Neva has heard the name of this cabal through various sources. They are a corporation that rivals the Network and could possibly take over their resources if the latter failed to regroup.

'I'd heard that Subra was working with them,' Neva says. 'Did you know Subra killed Armin?'

'I'd heard rumours but nothing was definite and the committee would kill her if they suspect it.'

'Subra is dead,' Neva says. She explains how and why.

'Why are you sharing that with me?' Fracks asks. He looks scared, as though he knows his number is up. 'Look, if you're planning to kill me… I'm willing to tell you what I know but you should understand, I went to ground because I didn't want to be part of the Network anymore. I wanted to be free of Beech, but knew I couldn't escape while he was alive. I took my chance when MI5 raided the house. I won't be talking to anyone about you. I can't or they'll kill me for my desertion. So, you see, they'll never know you found me unless you turn me in.'

Neva studies Fracks. He could be useful as an extra ear to the ground, but can she trust him?

'Tell me exactly where Annalise's château is,' she says.

'And everything you know about her security detail. Then perhaps we can discuss your future.'

Fracks starts talking and Neva's trained memory retains every detail as he describes the location of Annalise's château, in Occitanie, just outside of Toulouse.

'She has her own vineyards,' he says. 'I heard Beech telling someone he'd been once. He didn't stay in the château as even then he didn't trust her, and he had his own security in tow. He said it was a beautiful place and a working winery that produced wine which was popular with locals and which was also exported around the world.'

'What's the winery called?' Neva asks.

'I don't know. Or its actual address. And there are several wineries in the area. But if you go there, I'm sure you'll pick up on which one it is.'

'You've earned the right to live,' she says stowing her Glock back in the waistband of her shorts. 'Don't make me regret it, as I don't give second chances.'

Fracks nods, relieved, but his hands still shake as he holds out the book he's written in and borrowed from the bookstore. The book will have to be paid for in full, but the price will be worth it to save his life.

Neva stands, she picks up her holdall from the doorway where she left it. She stuffs the book inside.

She smiles at Fracks. 'Remember… I know where you live. I know who you are. I know your movements. So don't try anything silly. We wouldn't want the Network to find all that out, now would we…?'

She winks at Fracks, opens the door and leaves.

Chapter Eleven

MICHAEL

'My name is Security Agent Michael Kensington,' I say.

Debra O'Brierley was in London to collect Sinead's body and I thought it best to speak with her face to face and see if she could shed any light on who Sinead might have been meeting on her trip. She has been invited to a local police station so that I could meet with her. We are now in a small and informal interview room.

'You're not the police? You're an *agent*? I don't understand,' she says.

'I'm a Security Agent. I work for MI5. We've been passed your sister's case because it might be linked to another we're working on.'

'What other case?' Debra asks.

'I'm afraid I'm not at liberty to say at the moment. But please be reassured we are doing everything we can to learn what happened to Sinead.'

'Was she… tampered with?' she asks.

'No,' I say.

'Oh thank God! My mother was so worried about that. She was a good girl and…' Tears spring into Debra's eyes.

I wait while she composes herself.

'Why? Why did this happen to her?'

'Sometimes these things don't have a reason,' I say. 'I believe the Garda were given access to her computer. Did you or they find anything that could help us? Perhaps something linked to the *Yin and Yang* dating site?'

Debra shakes her head. 'She was just making friends… you know? It's such a small town where we live. Sinead, she didn't want to just end up with some local boy. So, she was talking to someone on the site. The Garda did look and so did I but I couldn't find anything weird on there.'

'But she came here to meet someone?' I ask.

Debra nods. 'Yeah, but not a man. A woman. They both wanted a girl holiday but had no one to go with.'

'They agreed to meet in London?' I ask.

'Yeah. But her new friend was supposed to share that place with her and ended up being a no show. She sent her half of the rental money though, so Sinead wasn't out of pocket. She was just a little annoyed that she'd been let down. She said, "I guess that's what you get for trusting someone you've met online but don't really know." Anyway, she did the sightseeing alone in the end. And she enjoyed it. But I guess it wasn't the same as sharing it with someone else,' Debra says.

'Were you in touch with her while she was away?'

'She was posting pictures on Instagram, and she sent me a few texts because I asked her to check in because she was alone. That last evening she said she was looking forward to coming home.'

Debra begins to cry again. When the tears lapse, I show her Sinead's profile on my phone.

'Who was the girl she was supposed to meet?' I ask. There are two females that chat to Sinead on the site and Debra looks at them. 'There's Stacey and Romy. Did she mention either of their names to you?' I ask.

'No. I had a look at those accounts. I remember the girl was called Julie… yes that's right! Julie or Jules. She lived in Europe somewhere.'

'Okay. One final thing. Did Sinead ever talk to this Julie directly? Either FaceTime or on the phone?' I ask.

Debra shakes her head. 'I don't know. I assumed she must have but I didn't think to ask her. It all seemed above board.'

I let Debra go and complete the transfer paperwork for the release of her younger sister's body but I'm left with her final words ringing in my ears: 'above board'. Is it a coincidence that this is the same language used on *Yin and Yang*'s terms and conditions? Or am I just reading too much into things?

Chapter Twelve

MIA

'Is this just a temporary safe house?' Mia asks as Ben unlocks the front door for the first time.

'No. This is standard procedure. New build. New life,' Ben says.

They go inside.

The house is an executive five bedroom with a large open hallway and wide staircase. It's bigger than Mia expected, but no less ordinary. Ben goes back to the car on the paved driveway and brings in the one suitcase with their few meagre possessions, taken in a hurry when they'd left their own house to go into hiding. Mia places Freya's carry car seat down in the hallway. Oblivious to the change of location, Freya gurgles and smiles. She's five months old now.

When Ben closes the front door, Mia opens another one inside. This leads to the lounge. Mia's face falls when she sees the furnishings.

'Who in their right mind has a white carpet with children?' she says.

She fights back the urge to cry. The furniture is all show house, she should feel grateful, but none of this is their taste, nor their choice.

'I know this is an upheaval,' Ben says. 'But in a few years, when our identity is established, we can sell up and move where we want. We'll be lost in the system. And you and Freya will be out of harm's way. Life can resume and there'll be no need for paranoia.'

'Sell up? You mean we *own* this place?' she asks.

'Yes. Well… the new us, Mica and Brody, do.'

Ben explains the 'miniscule' mortgage that helps them look real.

'How miniscule?' she asks.

'We'll be clear in the next few years. Financially this family is very secure. I have a guaranteed job. Our credit rating is as good as it gets and we'll be mortgage free a lot sooner than we would have been with the farmhouse.'

He points all of this out with enthusiasm as being the plus side of their new life. Anyone in their right mind would think so too, and Mia knows that. But none of it helps. She may have gained all this, but she's lost everything in life she's ever known. She is grieving and it will take more than the promise of being mortgage free to make that better.

Upstairs she finds a wardrobe full of clothing, all the right sizes for her and Ben – but a little too suburban housewife for her personal taste.

Mia bursts into tears. She sits on the oh-so-white linen on the bed and sobs until Ben finds her.

'Mia. Sweetheart. Please.'

'This is so awful. I hate it Ben. This isn't our home. Or clothes. Or life. I don't know how to be Mica Charter. I'm Mia Cusick.'

'It'll get easier. You'll find yourself in Mica eventually,' he says.

'You don't understand, I don't want to. I want to be me,' Mia says.

She cries again. Ben holds her, but she knows he doesn't know how to make this right.

'What if I get Michael on the phone for you?' Ben says.

'Really?' Mia says.

'If that will help?' Ben said.

'You know it will!' Mia said.

Ben uses a phone that he takes from the suitcase. One that Mia knows is encrypted. Then he calls MI5 for her.

After the phone call Mia is calmer. Michael has always been her touchstone and to have him cut from her life leaves an open and festering wound that no amount of reassurance from Ben can heal.

'One day all ties will have to be cut, or he'll pose a threat for you and Freya,' Ben says. 'You know that, right?'

Mia's mood plummets again.

'Not yet, Ben. I can't cope with all of this. It's too soon.'

Ben nods.

She doesn't ask, and he doesn't tell her, but she knows why they are unsafe. Mia has felt it since the day Freya was born. A dark threat hangs over them: Freya is special. And though these thoughts loop around and around in her brain, Mia doesn't know the answer to why this is happening, or what, other than disappear, they can do to protect Freya from it.

'How long will we have to do this for?' she asks Ben.

'A few years. But I'd say… at least ten,' Ben says.

'Why ten?'

He glances at Freya and his expression, though guarded, is somehow significant.

A few hours later Ben goes out 'to work' but Mia wonders if she'll ever trust Ben again. Despite her promise to try and see past it, Mia struggles to accept his betrayal. He'd lied to her about what he did, when all along he was spying on her for MI6. She still doesn't know the full facts behind this surveillance. It is frustrating and makes her angry at times. But most of all the lack of control makes her afraid.

Mia knows Ben is still keeping secrets from her. Like the fact that his new job really does appear to be the same as his old one. And she's heard him on the phone, taking instructions. What's more, she is sure it was his old boss on the other end of the call: she'd recognize Erik Steward's voice anywhere, and Ben is being very surreptitious whenever the calls come in.

She tries not to think about this now as she feeds Freya some baby rice. Freya is being testy and difficult, spitting out the rice over and over again until Mia gives up, knowing that she's tired and ready for her afternoon nap.

'I wouldn't want this muck either,' she says throwing the bowl and spoon into the kitchen sink.

Mia wipes Freya's face and hands with a soft damp face cloth before picking her out of the bouncy chair. Then she presses Freya to her breast, offering milk and comfort to settle her down.

When Freya finishes her milk, Mia takes her upstairs to the nursery. It's pink. Not like Freya's old room that was a very pale lilac – it's a minor point that irritates Mia – this assumption and choice someone made on her behalf, that a girl's room should be pink. She decides then that she'll go out and buy some paint, changing the colour to make the room feel more like it belongs to them. That at least will make her feel more in control.

She places Freya on the changing table and changes her nappy. Just as she finishes someone rings the doorbell.

Mia puts Freya in the cot for safety and then she goes down to the front door.

There's a state-of-the-art security system installed in the house, and Mia has it on an app on her phone. Taking her mobile out of her pocket, she looks at the camera and sees a young man, maybe 18 years old, standing on the doorstep.

She presses the green button that allows her to speak to the person outside without opening the door. Ben insists they do this as a matter of habit for all callers – just in case.

'Can I help you?' she asks.

'Hi there Mrs Charter,' he says. 'I'm Jack. Jack Harman. I'm here to mow your lawns.'

Mia pauses for a second, unsure what to do. She studies

the boy's face. He looks harmless. He'd also called her 'Mrs Charter'.

'Who asked you to come?' she asks now.

'Oh. Sorry. Your husband booked me,' says Jack.

Mia opens the door. In person Jack looks younger than he first appeared on camera. He's just an ordinary young man, quite innocuous.

'Hi,' he says smiling. 'I live down the street and was looking for part-time work. Mr Charter told me I could help in the garden. I brought my dad's mower.'

Jack beams at her and Mia finds herself smiling back at the charming and somewhat entrepreneurial youth at her door. She likes him and it negates her surprise at Ben booking a gardener when he was partial to doing it himself when they lived at the farm. He'd spent many hours out on the ride-on mower, but now Mia wondered if that was why. An average garden wasn't appealing to Ben now, or maybe he was deliberately fitting in with the norm for their new suburban lifestyle. He was, after all, a spy trained to fit in with any environment. In fact, Ben fitted in here too well. It almost made Mia think that this was a lifestyle he'd been more suited to and Ben was 'undercover' in their old life. All of which wasn't that far from the truth despite what he told her now.

'The grass is looking a little shoddy,' Mia says. 'Thank you Jack.'

Jack sets to work on the front lawn, mowing in neat rows as though he's had a lot of practice at doing this. Then he takes the mower to the back garden and does the same.

When he's finished, Mia offers him a cold drink. Jack accepts a glass of lemonade.

'How much do we owe you?' she asks.

'Don't worry,' he says. 'It's been taken care of.'

Jack gives her a cheeky wink and then he wheels his mower back around the side of the house and out to the front. She doesn't watch where he goes from there. But she's left with the feeling that she's just made a new friend.

Perhaps this is the first step to normalizing? she thinks. But then, he's the first person she's spoken to other than Ben, Michael or Freya in over two weeks.

Chapter Thirteen

ANNALISE

'I'm going to call him Kai,' Annalise says.

She stands over the cot looking down at the baby. He's just over six weeks old and he has soft black hair and a mid-brown smooth skin tone that shows off his mixed heritage. Beside her is a short woman in a nurse's uniform. Her hair is pulled back from her face, and she holds a very serious and professional expression as she gazes down at the child.

'Is he making good progress, Matron?' Annalise asks. 'No defects?'

'He's adorable. And perfect,' says Matron. 'He'll be an excellent asset.'

Annalise nods. In contrast to the plain Matron, her stunning white hair falls over her shoulders like a blanket of pure snow. She's wearing a turquoise kaftan over her athletic, slim frame. 'He must have the best of everything. I think he will even call me "Mother".'

'Of course, he will,' says the nurse. 'They all will.'

The nurse makes no judgement at this request, though she knows Annalise is 60. Because who would ever think this beautiful woman could be such an age with her timeless perfection?

Annalise glances around the nursery. There are seven cots in the room, all with tiny occupants. Three girls and four boys, including Kai. None as old as three months and all from a variety of sources.

'Such a shame the mother of this one didn't survive,' Matron says. 'But the others are providing him with the milk he needs.'

Annalise looks to the door at the side of the nursery. Yes, there on the other side of the building live the six women who supply sustenance for her children. Though willing recruits, they were separated from their children straight after they gave birth. The women are pampered and cared for, extracting daily the milk required to keep all seven children healthy. Annalise has a series of nurses that come in to take care of the babies, as well as Matron, who monitors them all.

The nurturing will be as efficient as always and as they grow, they will come to know Annalise as their 'true' mother. The one person who cares for them most. Not some unimportant biological sack who carried them for nine months.

As the others before them did, they will give Annalise their undying loyalty. And as they mature, they will train to be the best they can be, before becoming part of her small army.

'Rest, little one,' she says to Kai. The baby looks content, having never known any other life than this one.

Annalise leaves the nursing house. A large manor in its own right, built in the 100 acres of land that surrounds the building and which is also the home to her vineyards. She walks across a paved courtyard and enters the north wing of the château. As she passes through the kitchens, the cleaning and serving staff bow their heads but say nothing. It is how she likes it.

Annalise has spent years building this empire. And all through lessons she learned from the Network. Now she is almost ready.

She carries on through the house, passing now to the south side and out again onto yet another courtyard. The property is vast, and another manor lies on this other side. This one contains the school. A huge house, purpose built, with dormitories and classrooms, as well as a gym, a swimming pool and an outside arena to accommodate the training that her students undertake.

She enters the school via the back door and moves silently through the building, looking into classrooms. She's proud of her children – all of them. For they are even now better than those churned out of the Network's houses.

If only Beech had known what I was capable of, she thinks. *How my kingdom will supersede his.*

Twenty-five years ago, Annalise had seen the error of the Network's ways. Led as they were by Beech, who was stuck in the old ways and not open to evolving even then. Beech had taken over the Network a few years earlier. Annalise had hoped he would improve things but what she'd seen, when the committee sent her to examine the schools, was a devolution from the time when she had been taken and trained by one of the finest houses: the French house.

Back then they'd taken some of Mendez's work, but until Beech came along, the houses were free to develop their students in their own style. The houses competed with each other in their push for perfection. It was healthy. And then Beech changed it all when he insisted that all Network houses adopt Mendez's methods fully. By then Mendez had honed his conditioning techniques to create automatons. Beech hadn't wanted operatives. He'd wanted mindless robots.

But none of this mattered to Annalise, not until Tracey Herod had turned up, and demanded her daughter as a tribute for the Network. Annalise had kept her pregnancy quiet but someone had leaked the news to Beech. Perhaps because she'd refused to surrogate Beech's own children a couple of years earlier, Beech had become – she was told – enraged by the fact that she had taken a long-term lover, and had subsequently given birth. Beech demanded her child and at the time, Annalise's stronghold was only a vision she had for the future. She was faced with a dilemma: refuse and lose everything or send the child to the British house as requested.

But which child to send? After all, she had given birth to twins.

Chapter Fourteen

ANNALISE

Twenty years ago

Annalise had greeted Tracey respectfully. She was after all one of Beech's most trusted trainers.

'Can we fetch you some tea?' Annalise asked.

'Does your daughter have your colouring?' Tracey said.

'What do you mean?' Annalise had said.

'Your hair,' Tracey said.

At the time, Annalise's long locks were a luscious strawberry colour which tumbled over her shoulders.

'I'll show her to you,' Annalise had said.

She went in search of the girls. One she'd called Fleur, the other was Fae. They were a few weeks off being 5 years old, born within seconds of each other. Fae was the youngest and yet the toughest of the two. By then the girls had already been taught the basics of combat. Playing together, they learned Judo and Karate, and both were supple gymnasts.

Annalise found them with their tutor, sitting in the garden, drawing animals and flowers like normal children. She studied them both, trying to divorce herself from the position of 'mother'. For the first time she began to appreciate what her own parents had gone through when they gave her over to the French house at a similar age.

Though twins, Fae and Fleur were not identical. They were similar and looked like sisters, but it was easy to distinguish them from each other, especially for her as their mother.

Their father, Valentin, had been killed soon after their birth. A tragic road accident Annalise had thought at the time, but now she considered the possibility that Beech had been behind it. Or someone else in the Network wanting to garner favour with him by teaching her a lesson. It was okay for them to take lovers, but they were not permitted children or long-term relationships unless they were given permission.

Annalise had known she was breaking the rules but the pregnancy hadn't been intentional. She'd been at a clinic about to take care of it when she had a sudden epiphany: her child was special and it had to be born. She hadn't known then that there were two of them growing inside her.

While Tracey waited in the château's drawing room, Annalise had thought back to Valentin and the promise she'd made him.

'Protect our child from Beech,' he'd said before the girls were born.

'I'll always do that,' she'd said.

But at that point, with Tracey there, she knew she had no choice. One of them had to be given over or she'd find her château swarmed with the Network's assassins. If that happened Beech would take them both and Annalise knew she couldn't fight them all off, despite her own, ever-growing, security staff. No, she was playing the long game and she had to remain impartial and strategic. She would have to put aside the feelings she'd developed for the girls – emotions she had thought herself incapable of – and let one of them go for the sake of the other one.

Annalise had looked at her children for a long time, and then, she'd taken Fae's hand and led her away from the garden and into the house.

In her office, she snipped a piece from Fae's hair and placed it in the top drawer of her desk, bound with a piece of string.

'You'll do me proud,' she said to Fae. 'Be strong, fight hard, and *win*. Failure for you is not an option. Remember who you are Fae, though they'll try to take that from you. Do you understand?'

'Yes, Mother,' Fae said.

She stared Fae in the eyes for several long minutes and then she took her hand again and led her to the drawing room. Tracey waited there, sipping tea as though she were a welcome guest instead of an unwanted intrusion.

When Annalise brought Fae in, Tracey stood and walked around the girl.

'She's... *perfect*,' she said.

Tracey had been very happy with Fae, Annalise had noted, and it made her suspicious of the motive behind her visit. It was only later that she learned that Fae hadn't been sent for by Beech. Fae had been a lookalike who filled a place in the house so that Beech never learned about Tracey's failure with another child who had died during the conditioning process. Annalise wondered how many times this had happened before then. How many children had been changelings to cover up the fact that Mendez's process was too harsh and sometimes had devastating effects? Annalise had been furious when she learned the truth, but then she realized what a unique opportunity she had. She now held something over Tracey, something that Beech would probably kill her for if he learned the truth. For operatives and handlers acting on their own was something he would never turn a blind eye to.

So, she contacted Tracey and insisted on an audience with her at the house. Tracey refused at first, giving the excuse that the house's location was on a 'need to know' basis.

'Ah, but of course, and so is the fact that my daughter replaced a child you killed with your process,' Annalise said. 'And Beech knows nothing of this, does he?'

Tracey couldn't argue, but she still fought back. 'He doesn't know you had a child,' she said. 'Perhaps we are both in a precarious position.'

'I have a proposal. One which will bring us both a great deal of power,' Annalise told her.

Intrigued, Tracey had agreed to meet and Annalise flew to England, a small, but strong, security detail in tow, and she had driven from Manchester Airport in a limousine to the house at Alderley Edge.

On arrival, Tracey, who had been running the house then, took her into an office off the huge hallway.

'Tell me your proposal,' she said.

And then Annalise had outlined her idea to build a new conglomerate that would one day take control of the Network.

'But how?' Tracey asked.

'We build our own houses. But we do it better than Beech. We *train* warriors, we don't *condition* them. We give them a purpose and a vocation. Through nurturing we generate love and respect and loyalty,' Annalise said.

'What you're proposing is little better than Mendez's methods,' Tracey had said. 'It's radicalization by virtue of not knowing any different.'

Annalise smiled. 'But so much better that your slaves believe they have free will.'

Tracey's smile grew as she studied Annalise. 'What role will I play in your new order?'

'What role do you want?' Annalise asked.

'I will enjoy the benefits of your power. Money, security – above all no "retirement". When I am put to pasture, I must be trusted to keep my secrets and be allowed to live to the age nature intends.'

'An idea that should be granted to all who serve us,' Annalise had said. 'And yours by right as of this day.'

Tracey agreed. 'Where do we start?'

'Fae must not be fully conditioned. You'll undo whatever Mendez does. She must be mine always,' Annalise told her.

'That won't be easy,' Tracey said, 'and may bring

suspicion on me. If she isn't treated like all the others, then I might be replaced and will be no good to you.'

Annalise thought for a moment. Then she said, 'I've heard that Mendez is using another method on Beech's own children?'

Tracey is surprised that she knows about this and it shows on her face.

'A new method. It might not work,' Tracey had said.

'Partial conditioning. A separation of themselves from the assassin they become,' Annalise says.

Tracey blinks. Annalise feels a sense of satisfaction that her intel is correct.

'He's trying to make sleeper agents,' Tracey admitted.

'Thank you for your honesty,' Annalise said. 'Now let me propose this. Fae is given the same treatment in reverse. You will rename her Neva. Neva will be the dominant personality, acting as Mendez's training would make her. But Fae will be there in the background. And only you and I will know how to activate her.'

Tracey looked down at her hands for a moment and Annalise saw them tremble. She read this as a sign that the proposition excited Tracey.

'It'll be dangerous. She might… break…'

'It's a risk. But… no one knows Mendez's method's better than you. Can you do this?' Annalise asked.

'I can,' said Tracey. 'And I will.'

After forming their alliance, Tracey had allowed Annalise to see Fae. The little girl was not pale and withdrawn as she had expected her to be. No, she looked vibrant and strong. Annalise knew then, she'd made the right decision as to which daughter to give. Whatever happened, Fae would adapt.

'Mother,' Fae said on seeing her. 'I'm working hard, as you said.'

'You're Neva now,' Tracey told her. 'This is not your mother.'

Fae/Neva looked up at Annalise. The expression in her eyes was far more mature than her recent fifth birthday afforded her.

'I'm Neva,' she said. 'You're not my mother.'

It hurt a little to hear the words from her daughter's lips, but Annalise froze her heart and nodded as Neva was led away, back to the dormitory where she would continue her development in the name of the Network.

'I want to see her progress at intervals,' Annalise said. 'I will send you the content that I wish to be programmed into her.'

'Fine,' Tracey agreed. 'But you need to let me work on her for a while. Mendez has made a great deal of progress with Neva already. She's pliable. But I'll have to twist around what he's done already, and it will be a slow process in order to make sure she isn't damaged.'

Annalise accepted Tracey's terms and she left giving very little thought to what they would do to her daughter as she climbed into the limousine and headed back for the airport. Annalise had always seen the whole picture: even as a trainee herself back in the French house. She knew that knowledge was important as well as strength and agility in order to survive the world that she'd been chosen for. All children were assets, hadn't she been just such an asset for her own parents? A twin also, she'd been given over to the Network and she'd excelled while her sister led a pampered life, unaware of the choice her parents had made.

Annalise wasn't placing all of her hopes on Neva's success, however. No, she had another daughter that she would also train using her own experimental methods. It would be interesting to see how that panned out. Fleur would not be pampered. She would be treated as any trainee was. She would be inspired to be the best. Just as Neva would be.

Chapter Fifteen

NICOLE

Present day

Nicole Sheridan switches on the shower before stepping inside the cubicle and pulling the curtain closed behind her. In the changing rooms, she hears the friendly chatter of the other women from the same spin class as she lathers up and washes away the intense perspiration generated by the exercise.

Nicole is shy and she doesn't know any of their names, though for several weeks now she's been on smiling terms with a couple of them. She also caught one of the men giving her an appraising look a few times. But she didn't encourage it: he's not her type.

Shower done, she pulls the towel around herself and goes out, passing another woman who is waiting for a free cubicle. The woman smiles at her and Nicole nods.

Clutching her key in her hand she goes in search of her locker. Still wrapped in the towel she opens it and pulls her clothing free. She dries and dresses under the towel, marvelling at how all the others just throw their bodies out on display with barely a thought of those around them. It isn't as if they all have perfect figures either. Nicole finds it all a little embarrassing and turns away facing the lockers instead of looking into the room. She's self-conscious about her weight – it's why she comes to the gym. She's the sort of person who just has to look at anything calorific and the pounds go on. Her whole life has been a nightmare of diet and exercise to fight the bulge.

'They are frightful, aren't they?' says a voice beside her.

Nicole turns her head to see the woman from the shower.

'Is it just me that likes to keep my privates private?' the woman says.

Nicole finds herself smiling at her. She's in her mid-20s. Pretty with long red hair that's tied back in a ponytail. Taller than average, slim but athletic.

Nicole looks around and notices that the other women, still talking in loud banter, haven't overheard their exchange.

'Me too,' she whispers. 'It's a bit… well… I don't really want to see everyone else's either.'

'I'm Jewel,' the woman says.

'Nicole.'

'Nice to meet you. I've just joined this class. Is it the same every week?'

'Pretty much,' Nicole says. 'Not all of them are here for every class though. I come Tuesday and Fridays.'

'Oh really? That's the days I've booked for too,' says Jewel.

'But you haven't been before?' Nicole observes.

'Just moved into the area. I'll be honest, I don't know anyone here and I'm hoping to make friends.'

Nicole smiles. 'I'm happy to help.'

'I hoped you'd say that!'

Jewel invited her to go for a drink and they sat in the gym coffee lounge to the side of the room while the much bigger group from the spin class took up the opposite side.

'I normally just leave after the class,' Nicole says.

'I'm not surprised, with that lot being so cliquey,' Jewel said.

Nicole glanced at the group. Still being loud as though they all competed for attention from each other as a form of validation – they belonged, though Nicole thought she didn't and therefore never tried to fit in. All she had wanted to do was hold back that inevitable swamp of blubber that her mother had given in to, always blaming baby fat as the issue.

Her mother was the worst for fat-shaming, picking at her for every extra pound that Nicole might store, whatever the time of month. She'd become so obsessed with her daughter being thin that she'd actively encouraged her to puke if she overate. But those days were gone now, and Nicole, with the help of counselling, had been working really hard with her food issues, while learning to recognize that her mother was the one with the problem. Even so, gym attendance was a crucial part of her feeling in control. It was also a source of discussion at her counselling sessions, along with her lack of friends. But she doesn't share any of this with Jewel, who casually talks about her own life, telling her about a recent failed relationship, and her need to take back her life.

'He was always putting me down, you know?' Jewel explains.

Nicole did know. Her counsellor had pointed out the co-dependency issues and why she chose partners that abused her and made her feel worthless. Though she keeps all of this to herself as she listens to Jewel talk.

'You're a good listener,' Jewel says. 'But what's your story?'

'Story?'

'Yeah. We all have one.'

Nicole shakes her head. 'Nothing much to tell. I'm single at the moment. A few failures too. I'm content being alone for the time being.'

Jewel nods her understanding. 'I hear you.'

Nicole smiles at her. For the first time in a while she may have made a new friend.

'I have to go,' Jewel says. 'But, see you Friday?'

'Yes. I'll be here,' Nicole says.

Chapter Sixteen

NEVA

Neva looks at the book that Fracks gave her. It is a hardback copy of a historical romance. Not the sort of subject Neva would have expected Fracks to have found appealing. She opens the cover and looks now at the names Fracks had written on the blank first page. The penmanship is untidy, and Neva recalls the shaking of his hand as he wrote.

Kritta (Berlin); Banwick (Cardiff); Subra (Jerusalem); Petters (Oslo); Conor (Edinburgh); Drake (Venice); Armin (Kabul); Stanners (Loch Lomond); Ruddy (Florence); Aelen (Belfast); Cruik (Madrid).

She takes a pen out of the drawer in her small kitchen and crosses off the names that are no longer valid. She knows that Subra executed Armin and was then killed by Solomon Granger. As for Stanners (the real father of her assassin colleague and of the former head teacher at the

Alderley Edge kill house, Olive Redding), Michael had confirmed that he was dead and suspected Olive of the deed. Revenge no doubt for his part in handing her over to the kill house when she was an innocent child. Neva understood that revenge more than most. She wanted the same thing herself. If Annalise was who they thought she was, Neva wanted her dead too. At least, thanks to Fracks, she has some direction in which to look.

Neva looks at the other names. Which of these did Vasquez take down in his pursuit of a place on the committee? Fracks had said Aelen and Ruddy were gone. Neva underlines these names rather than crossing them off. She will have to do her own research to confirm this is the case.

Neva opens her encrypted laptop and begins another search on onionland. Her contact Elbakitten may be able to shed some light on these characters and, so far, her intel has proved reliable. She sends an encoded message to Elbakitten and then waits for a response.

Half an hour later Elbakitten replies. They go into a private chat room.

I need anything you can find regarding the following names, Neva types.

These are codenames? Elbakitten replies.

Yes, Neva responds.

That information may be expensive, Elbakitten replies. *Should I test one name first?*

Try Kritta since it's the first one on the list, Neva says.

I'll get back to you in 24 hours, Elbakitten says. *I'll message you in the usual way.*

Neva disconnects. Then she looks around the small apartment and frowns. She's tired of hiding out in Amsterdam, but has no desire to go elsewhere. Travelling and crossing borders is still too risky. For this reason, the world no longer feels big and she experiences a claustrophobic resentment of Amsterdam. She wonders now why she came here. There were many other locations she could have chosen. Other identities she could have taken on. But Neva had chosen Amsterdam for another specific reason. She'd told Michael about her bolt-hole here and part of her hoped he would come and find her.

She finds herself thinking of Michael now, as she often does. She's still grieving his loss and her heart feels like it's shattered in pieces. She still wishes he'd given her a fair hearing and toys with the idea of making contact again, knowing she won't: she can't bear further rejection.

What if he doesn't reject you? she thinks.

That scenario passes behind her eyes. She sees Michael now, caring, warm, persuasive.

'Come in and talk,' he'd say, expressing concern. 'Tell us your side.' But she has no side. She didn't do what she was accused of.

Neva stalls again on this thought. *Did she?*

To reassure herself that she hasn't been compromised, Neva looks at her security footage again. She skips through seeing only normal activity.

'I didn't do it,' she says aloud. 'I'm not a sleeper agent.'

But the doubt remains as she resets the recordings and, aware that her own cameras pick up her every move, Neva begins her regular exercise routine.

She runs a mantra – one of her own making and not from the conditioning of the past – over and over in her mind as she works out.

I am strong. I am Neva. I am in control. I'm death for those who deserve it.

Chapter Seventeen

MICHAEL

'It appears that our victim, Elizabeth Seacroft, *did* meet someone in a local pub. One of the bar staff remembers selling a bottle of wine with two glasses to a woman that Elizabeth met up with. He recalls that she had long red hair tied in a ponytail and she wore glasses. Black rimmed. Unfortunately, I haven't been able to corroborate his statement. I pulled up security footage around the area but she doesn't show up anywhere,' Beth says.

'Are we are looking for a woman?' Ray asks.

We are in Ray's office because we always do our main group briefings in this room. There is a large conference table in the centre, and we sit around it, looking at the screen above Ray's desk.

'Not necessarily. The friend she met might have nothing to do with her death. However, the pathology report shows flunitrazepam traces in her bladder. Just like Sinead,' I say. 'Which had to be slipped to her at the pub because it needs time to work. For this reason, it's plausible that someone else could have been watching and dropped something into Lizzie's drink. Or it may well be the friend that she met up with for a drink. Though this seems unlikely.'

'Why do you think it unlikely?' Ray asks.

'Our perpetrator has made a great effort not to be seen, so why openly meet the victim in a pub where there would be many witnesses? It's just not the way an assassin would work. Especially if we believe there is a connection with the Network here. Beth, did you see Lizzie on the cameras in the area?' I ask.

'Yes,' Beth says.

She casts the footage up onto the screen. We see Lizzie leave the pub alone and very much alive. She is staggering a little as she walks as though she's had too much to drink.

'She was on her own all the way. Though there is a break in coverage about two hundred and fifty yards from her house. So, we can't see her approach and go inside the house. However, based on the fact that her handbag… you see she's carrying it there… was in the hallway, it does look as though she entered. How she ended up in the shed later we don't know,' says Beth.

'Was her mobile ever found?' I ask.

'No,' says Beth. 'No sign of it.'

'Then the perp took it with them,' I say.

'But why would they do that?' asks Ray.

'There had to be something incriminating on it,' Elsa chips in. 'There's no other reason.'

'Possible communications from the killer, or it could be photographs on Lizzie's camera,' I say.

'Do we have a list of Lizzie's last telephone calls and any text messages?' Ray asks.

'There was one number she'd rung and received calls from that was unregistered. Could be our perp. We've tried to trace it but it's switched off, so if it was a burner, it's been ditched. Lizzie didn't make or receive any calls that evening though. It would suggest that this person she met arranged it some other way. Through the dating site or some other social media platform. All of which we have no knowledge of or access to without Lizzie's phone. She didn't have a home computer and only used her phone to communicate with other friends. And we've drawn a blank on Facebook as she appears not to have it.'

'No social media?' Elsa says. 'Who doesn't have Facebook this day and age?'

Beth shrugs, 'Well none of *us* do…'

'That's obviously for security reasons,' Elsa says. 'But who… *normal*?'

'I have a friend who's a teacher and she detests social media. She uses WhatsApp though,' Beth says. 'Maybe we can see if Lizzie had an account there. I'll check with her service provider to see we can get access to her account. See what apps she downloaded. It will confirm at least if she had a *Yin and Yang* account on there. Or any other apps that might be used to communicate.'

I fill them in on my interview with Debra O'Brierley. 'Debra said her sister had planned to meet a female to holiday with. She'd met her on the dating site and they had become friends. Just to be clear, Sinead wasn't gay – it was purely platonic. It appears that at the last minute though, this person let her down. Though Debra says Sinead told her she still paid for her half of the accommodation.'

'Do we know how she paid?' asks Beth.

'I'm assuming the money was sent to her bank by BACS,' I said. 'Or possibly PayPal.'

'Let's check on that,' Ray says. 'It could be a lead, but might just help us rule out this person.'

'I'll look into it,' says Elsa.

'One more question Beth. Do we have any footage of this red-haired friend of Lizzie's arriving at least? Perhaps if we get a screenshot of Lizzie's other friend, Vicky may recognize her. She might be the last person to talk to the victim and may know something that can help.'

'I looked, but didn't see anyone entering the pub who looked like that,' Beth says.

'Where's the footage focused near the pub?' Ray asks.

'There's some on the street, and one directly on the main door. But the problem is there's another door at the back that leads into the pool room and bar at that side. The woman could have come in that way,' Beth says. 'There's no cameras on that side.'

'Can we check CCTV all around that area? Especially on the other side?' I ask.

'I have, but I'll cast the net wider and see what I come up with,' Beth says.

'I can help,' says Elsa. 'That's a lot of footage to look at for one person.'

'Thanks,' says Beth.

Beth finishes the briefing with more information from the autopsy report. The evidence does appear to point to the same killer for both victims. Elliot is certain it's the same knife.

'Okay. Thanks everyone. That's all for now,' Ray says. 'Michael… if you could just stay behind for a minute.'

I remain in my seat as Elsa and Beth leave.

'I wanted to be the one to tell you; Leon has moved over to MI6. He's replacing your brother-in-law. It's a promotion so I couldn't object given that he only filled your job on a temporary basis. It is, therefore, the perfect opportunity to reinstate you.'

After all that's happened, I'm more than a little surprised by Ray giving me my old job back, which means extra security clearance. And basically I'll be running the department as his second.

'I don't know what to say.'

'Say you're glad to be fully restored,' Ray says.

'I am of course. But why?' I ask.

'You deserve your life back and shouldn't be punished for things you aren't responsible for. Plus, the shrink is satisfied that your conditioning has been fully deactivated due to the hypnosis you agreed to. At every turn you've done the right thing.'

'Thank you,' I say even though I know this in no way gives me my life back. That can only happen if Neva is part of it.

'Elsa seems to be fitting in. But she needs some guidance and you and Beth will be perfectly placed to give that.'

'Right.'

'Now, any thoughts on how we might track Neva? There

was a possible sighting in Brussels. Then she was off radar again,' Ray says.

'As you know she didn't share with me the locations of her bolt-holes – except the one in Kingston. But she's partial to using holiday let sites. The only issue is we have no idea what identity she might use. Perhaps put a flag up for single women travelling alone?' I say.

'But she had mentioned going to Amsterdam with you?' Ray says.

'Yes, but not any particular address. It could be a let, and if so, we are looking for one that is long term but was taken around the time Neva fled. Unless of course she did already have somewhere – which was my impression.'

'If you remember anything else…' Ray says.

'Naturally, you'll be the first to know if I come up with anything. Or if she tries to contact me again. I've kept that last burner active, just in case,' I say.

'Good,' Ray says.

I leave the office but I'm uncomfortable with the exchange that has just happened. Did Ray give me back my old role just to test if I knew more about Neva than I'd previously admitted? I walk back to my office frowning as I worry away at the idea. I can't blame Ray for holding back his full trust, I'm not that confident in myself these days either.

Still frowning, I walk into the central office and find Beth and Elsa at opposite ends of the room looking at their computers. They don't exchange any friendly chat and I'm aware as I go into my office just off theirs that Beth isn't that happy about having a new arrival. I wonder if Elsa's sex has more to do with it than her abilities. Beth, despite her declaration that it was nice to have another woman around, always liked being the only one in our group. Now that she isn't, does Beth see Elsa as a rival?

I'm determined to keep a close watch on both of them now that I'm back in charge. I'll have to head off any competitive behaviour if I see it, though I actually don't care to have Elsa around myself. There's something about her that makes me edgy.

Perhaps it's because I know that she'd been working with Ray for some time before I'd ever met her.

It reminds me, I suppose, that Ray has his own secrets that sometimes Beth and I aren't privy to, and knowing that keeps me and Beth on our toes.

Chapter Eighteen

MIA

They live on a new-build estate of large executive houses. With the welcome pack – probably devised by the person who decorated and furnished their new home – Mia has learned that there is a large park in the centre of the estate. Placing Freya in her pram, Mia goes out for a walk to explore the area. Even though she's nervous to go out, Ben has reassured her they are safe where they are: no one knows they are here. She forces herself out, trying to establish some normality she can live with.

Where she and Ben lived before, Mia had an acre of land to potter around on. She enjoyed gardening when she hadn't been working. But her new smaller garden didn't interest her as much as the larger one she'd had. She'd loved the wild flowers and mossy grass – less than perfect but as nature intended – much more than she cared for the immaculate lawns here.

On this estate every house is picture perfect, every

garden is neat. They are also all the same. The normality doesn't feel real. Just like the sunny day. It's all too flawless.

Mia craves her lost life and former innocence. She looks back on it with new eyes – how was she so unaware? Mia recalls her parents with a feeling of distance. Hadn't she always known the cookie-cutter life they'd created wasn't real at all? It is clear now how detached they were. Their mother's perpetual baking. The smudge of flour always on her cheek as though part of her daily beauty regime. It was so ridiculously 1950s that it should have been obvious.

She found herself wondering if her parents were even lovers. Or what they actually did when Michael and Mia weren't home. She tried to imagine them doing anything other than what she'd witnessed and couldn't. They were too good at appearing normal. And in a way, Mia and Michael had taken them at face value. Like most children, they had paid very little real attention to the lives their parents had, accepting that they were just a normal boring couple when really nothing could be further from the truth.

They are dead now and she can't ask them any questions. Michael didn't tell her how it happened, instead he said they were missing. But Mia suspects what really went down.

As she pushes the pram closer to the playground, she finds herself thinking about a TV series she once dipped into. A perfect family, all assassins. All robots. She can almost imagine now that her parents hadn't even been human.

Where was the genuine affection? she thinks. She and Michael became detached from them as soon as they both left for university. And it hadn't been difficult. There was little interaction between Mia and her parents during those years, and Mia and Michael moved out, never going home again after they graduated, except for one time when her parents moved to Cambridge.

It was odd, but Mia can't even remember the regular phone calls she had with her mother. Unlike her university friends, her parents weren't desperate to hold onto her. They never made her feel guilty for not visiting. But there were calls, and the occasional meet-ups with Uncle Andrew. She just can't remember what they talked about.

Huh! Beech… their real father! What a total mindfuck!

Mia's mind skirts around the whole idea of it. She can't focus on the important questions and so skitters away to think instead about the grass or the sunlight. The truth – when you look at it – isn't all it is cracked up to be when it destroys your peace of mind.

How much does it matter anyway?

Mia glances down and smiles at Freya. The little girl is slowly drifting off to sleep with the movement of the pram.

She pauses at a road crossing. The playground is just ahead and Mia can see a few mothers with toddlers using the swings and slides. Being outside makes her feel better and she pushes aside the looping study of her past life interspersed with random and distracting thoughts of other things as she crosses the road.

There are no crazy drivers speeding through the estate. Even so, there is an iron fence all around the play area and Mia passes through the gate, closing it behind her. She wheels Freya towards a bench and she takes a seat, watching the other children running and playing over on the park.

Freya makes a tiny sound, as though objecting to the sudden stillness of the pram. Mia looks at her, but the little girl is merely mewling in her sleep.

'Sleep my little one…'

Mia freezes.

Her mind whirs and stalls. She has heard that before. Where has she heard that before? Her mother. It must have been. But no matter how hard she tries to remember she can't recall her mother ever saying this to her or Michael. It's not her voice she can vaguely hear in her head. It's someone else… but who? She's distracted by a child on the swings. Back and forth they go. Back and forth. Mia forgets what she was trying to think about.

Freya whimpers again.

'You're safe,' Mia says.

She looks around at the other mothers and children in the park. Over by the swings, two women cast her a casual glance. By the slide, as a little boy of three climbs the ladder and slides down, another woman – possibly the boy's grandmother – looks long and hard in Mia's direction. Mia casts her eyes around the playground. She feels exposed and observed. It's the oddest experience she's ever had. Is it just curiosity that a new family have moved onto the estate? Or are they all spying on her? Reporting back.

She finds herself looking around, beyond the park, over to the other houses beyond the railings and across the road. Was that a glint of glass catching the sunlight from a top bedroom of the house directly opposite? Perhaps binoculars. She squints at the window, but the anomaly doesn't happen again.

I'm paranoid, she thinks. *No one knows we're here. This is just silly.*

But the sensation of being observed won't dissipate and Mia stands up, and releases the brake on Freya's pram. She walks out of the playground and heads back to the safety of her new house.

Halfway home she finds herself looking over her shoulder. The street is empty, no one is following and yet she doesn't feel alone.

A car passes, and Mia watches as it heads away. Was it driving too slowly?

As she reaches her cul-de-sac, she sees Jack Harman mowing her next-door neighbour's lawn. Happy to see a familiar face, she waves to him as she passes. He smiles back at her.

There's a sense of relief as she reaches the front door of the house. This new build might, after all, be a haven of sorts.

'Are you all right, Mrs Charter?' Jack says, wheeling his father's mower past her front gate.

She looks back at the young man, his eyes show concern for her and Mia realizes she had been hurrying up the driveway to the front door as though something was chasing her.

'I'm fine, thank you, Jack,' she says.

Jack nods. 'Okay, but I'm around if you need anything.'

Mia thanks him again and goes inside the house. Once the door is shut behind her she gives into a terrible trembling. Despite Jack's offer she feels even more concerned. It was as though he were waiting for her to return and the mowing of the lawn next door was just his cover… He could be a spy. He could work for the Network. Anyone could.

'What's wrong with me?' she says.

She rests her back on the door as though barricading the world out. She takes a deep breath in and tries to regulate her breathing. She feels vulnerable, not an experience she's ever had before. She looks back at the sleeping baby and an intense fear clutches at her chest. *Is Freya safe?*

Afraid to let the baby out of her sight, she pushes the pram into the kitchen. Then she runs the cold water tap and fills a glass. Still shaking, she sits down at the breakfast bar and sips the water. Her hand shudders and she sloshes water onto the worktop.

She can't rid herself of the thought that Freya might be in danger. She reflects on this concern – a very real apprehension after all, hadn't they been put into witness protection for this very reason? She decides that she needs to speak to Ben when he returns later. She's sure he's hiding the full facts from her. Without the full story, Mia grasps at shadows and fears unknown phantoms.

I have to know what's really going on, she thinks. Only then can she truly deal with the change her life has taken. Only then will she know what to do if someone comes after them.

Chapter Nineteen

BEN

At least the weather's held, thinks Ben as he pulls up in a spot by the kerb just down from the pub where he had agreed to meet his boss.

Ben locks the car and heads into the pub. It had been agreed that Ben shouldn't come into the MI6 offices in London for fear of being spotted and followed back home, and so when he has to report to Erik Steward, his boss, they arrange to meet in this somewhat out of the way and random rural village. The place is called Bassingham and it has a great little pub called the Five Bells which is on all sorts of 'best of' lists. It's an hour's drive away from their new home in the Lincolnshire Wolds and Ben sees it as something of a treat because it allows him to dip back into his old life. The place is lovely too: all ivy-covered outside, and wooden beams inside all interwoven with hops and *objets d'art* like stuffed animals, old books and firearms.

Ben takes a seat at their pre-booked table and waits for Steward who arrives a short time later.

A young waitress comes over and out of habit Ben and Steward order tapas to share and soda water to drink.

'You weren't followed?' asks Ben. Although he knows that Steward would have made sure, he still worries.

'It's safe,' he says. 'How are you getting along?'

'Okay. Mia isn't very happy in the new house. But it's probably just a period of adjustment,' Ben says. 'She was happier once we allowed her contact with Michael.'

'We have him under full surveillance,' Erik Steward says.

'What have you learned?' Ben says.

'The woman Neva hasn't tried to make contact with him. And Ray Martin gave him full security clearance again,' Steward explains. 'We have Martin's office tapped, thanks to Leon.'

'Tchaikovsky is now working for you?'

Steward nods. 'He was happy to help.'

'Is there anything I can do?' Ben asks.

'For the moment you need to lay low, but if Michael leads us to Neva, we may well get access to the Network's committee and bring them down in one swoop. If that happens, maybe you and your wife will be able to return to your old home. If it doesn't, however, then you might have to accept this as your new normal.'

'I can do some research and paperwork for you at least,' Ben points out.

'Of course,' says Steward. 'But, back to your brother-in-law. Ray is convinced he's now deactivated and the Network can no longer coerce him to act for them. The conditioning he experienced as a child was pretty intense though.'

'You believe he's still a danger?' Ben asks.

'We can't know for sure. With regards to Mia…'

'Mia is off limits, Erik. You know that,' Ben says.

'Naturally. But you haven't seen anything unusual in her behaviour that might be cause for concern?' Steward says.

'No. And as I said, she's not part of *this* discussion.'

Steward takes a sip from his soda water.

'The thing is, we need to talk about her. Is she coming apart, Ben? I have to know,' Steward says.

'Of course not. She's upset though. And scared. She's been pulled away from everything she knows. How can you expect her not to be? She doesn't understand the extent of what was done to her and Michael and honestly, I don't want her to. Why shatter her illusions even further?'

Steward nods.

'She'll be fine eventually,' Ben continues. 'It's a big change for us all.'

'I don't doubt that,' Steward says.

'But less for me than Mia. I, at least, still have contact with my old life and job. Mia can't even tell her friends where we are, or ever see them again.'

Ben stops talking as the waitress arrives and deposits a two-tiered tapas stand onto the table. It's a house sharing platter with various starters and a favourite of the two men when they meet up.

'Thank you,' says Steward to the young girl.

When she's gone, they help themselves to a portion of food from the top tier: chicken liver pâté with ciabatta. They appear to anyone who cares to look at them, like any two friends meeting for lunch.

'What else have you learned from your spying on Archive?' Ben asks.

Steward laughs. 'Office gossip… Bethany Cane is sleeping with the pathologist, Elliot Baker. They have a new girl on the team. She was on the radar for MI6 a few years ago, but for some reason she wasn't recruited. Perhaps because Ray had already called dibs on her. Anyway, Elsa Stevenson is her name. She's got a lot of potential as an agent, though they aren't giving her much responsibility.'

'Is she fitting in?' Ben asks as if he already knows the answer. Steward gives him a sideways glance.

'Not sure, Michael isn't that warm with her and neither is Beth. The latter I understand, as Beth's nose could be put out of joint with her sudden appearance. Michael's problem I just don't know.'

'Is Michael still in a safe house?'

'Yes. And Beth is on permanent security detail for fear that the Network will try to take her again. All in all, Archive is currently quite compromised. It's a wonder Ray can keep working with two of his agents at such risk,' Steward explains.

Ben scoops out chicken and chorizo from one of the dishes. He adds it to his plate, then takes a mouthful. He chews, staring ahead as though he's considering Steward's words.

'That's interesting. Especially as they are letting Michael work on, and not just insisting he goes to ground for a while,' Ben says.

'What do you deduce from that?' Steward asks.

'Ray isn't stupid. Michael is still walking around with a target on his back. But maybe that's the point. He hopes to draw out his enemies,' Ben says.

'You think Ray is capable of using Michael like that?' Steward says.

'He's a spy. What do you think?'

Steward looks down at the plate of food in front of him, he takes a mouthful of bread, chews and swallows. Then he sips at the soda water again while he considers Ben's words.

'I think you're right,' says Steward. 'The only thing I'm not sure of is whether Michael knows?'

'You're recording their conversations, so haven't they discussed it?' Ben asks.

Steward shakes his head. 'That doesn't mean he's not a part of the ruse. Ray may suspect we are monitoring them. Or fear someone else is.'

'Who else could?' Ben says.

Steward doesn't answer. Ben stops eating and looks at him.

'You think there's a mole?' Ben asks.

'There's been rumours for a while. Someone very trusted. My intel is usually reliable. But who knows? Misinformation is the weapon of our enemies.'

'But if there is… then Michael isn't safe. And Mia isn't either,' Ben says.

'We're keeping her safe,' Steward says. 'Even now there's eyes on her.'

Ben looks at Steward again. 'What eyes? The more

people who know where we are, the more in danger Mia and Freya are.'

'Don't worry. We have only the best on it and as always only on a need-to-know basis.'

Ben finishes his food. Steward's revelation makes him feel uncomfortable and he is itching to be on his way home. After all, it was MI5 who had relocated them. Steward wasn't supposed to know where that was, and Ben, despite keeping in touch with his boss, hasn't revealed their location. He finds himself questioning Steward for the first time since he started working for him ten years ago. How has Steward found them? And if he knows where they are, does anyone else? With the Network's reach, could anyone really be trusted?

Chapter Twenty

MICHAEL

'Her name was Nicole Sheridan,' I say.

I place Nicole's picture up on the investigation board next to Lizzie and Sinead's. Surrounding the previous two women is a series of white-board pen notes of things we've learned or leads we are chasing. I notice that Elsa has written a note on Lizzie's side saying 'No camera footage of poss perp'. And so, that course is closed to us as well.

'Nicole was 34 years old. Lived alone in East London. No family. Hobbies… a gym membership. Like clockwork she went on the same days, to the same classes, every week. She was found dead in the locker room of the gym late last night.'

I describe what I saw at the gym when I was called in after hours. Nicole was naked in the shower cubicle with fifteen knife wounds. The attack was brutal and frenzied which I know the autopsy will confirm. The killer had finished her off by slitting her throat. Such anger and violence and force had gone behind the knife that it makes me aware that the killer is losing control.

'The cleaning staff found her after closing time. She must have been the last person in the ladies' changing room and can't have been dead for more than half an hour at that point. Ray and I looked at the security footage of the last people to leave. There was a couple of women that left together. We have their details and plan to interview them today. There was also one man. He wasn't caught clearly on security, and that late at night, staff aren't always diligent on the checking-out system. This guy didn't sign out, or in either.'

'A starting point then,' says Beth. 'I'll have a closer look at the footage and see what I can pull up.'

'I'll have it sent to you,' I say.

'If it isn't anything to do with the mystery man, then we are drawing a blank. Footage of the corridor outside the changing rooms doesn't show anyone going in or out after the time that Nicole was left alone in there,' I point out.

'What did she do for a living?' Beth says.

'She had her own business. She's an interior designer. Very talented and successful by all accounts.'

'Relationships past and present?' asks Elsa.

'Unknown at this point,' I say. 'I'm going to interview people from the spin class she usually attends on Friday. See if she was friendly with any of them.'

'I'll interview her next-door neighbours and see if they know anything?' Beth says.

'I can do that if you want?' Elsa volunteers.

Beth glances at her, 'No it's okay. I'll take this.'

I see a frown appear on Elsa's forehead but she doesn't object. Perhaps she's feeling underused? And it's true that we aren't giving her much to do, but there's a period of settling in that I'd prefer for her to have for now.

'Elsa, could you set up some appointments for me? I'd do it myself but I'm going to be pretty full on today interviewing the last people who may have seen her,' I say. 'It would be a massive help if you could.'

'Sure,' she says, eager to please.

'I'll send over the list of members from the Friday class and their contact details. Thank you,' I say.

Beth catches my eye and she rolls her gaze to the office door. Then she walks away. I take the hint.

'Just fetching coffee,' I say to Elsa. 'Want one?'

'No thanks, I have water,' Elsa says. 'Caffeine makes me hyper.'

I follow in Beth's footsteps and fish out some coins to get my coffee from the machine located near Ray's office. Beth is waiting for me when I get there.

'Not getting along?' I say, keeping my voice low.

'She's a bit… needy,' Beth says.

'She's probably trying to make a good impression,' I say.

'It's just… *odd* having her around. Even with Leon gone, we don't really need her,' Beth says.

I pause before answering. I understand where Beth is coming from: there's something very irritating about Elsa, but I can't say it without being unprofessional. And as for Leon, the fact that we aren't missing him says a lot about how little he did. Neither of us elaborate on that part of Beth's comment though, as we try to remain professional.

'I know how you feel,' I say trying to be diplomatic. 'But Ray must have his reasons for bringing her into Archive. I think he's been working with her for a while and trusts her.'

'Let's work on this thing alone, Michael, please. We've been through a lot recently. I'm not sure I feel comfortable working with someone new right now, or giving them things I'd normally do.'

'Beth, Elsa's not here to replace you. Please don't think that,' I say.

'What is she here for then? I see her report to Ray every morning. God knows what she's telling him.'

'Report, how?' I ask.

'This morning when I came in, she was already in his office. They were talking and the door was closed. But I overheard him say something about her "keeping an eye out",' Beth says.

'You think she's spying on us for Ray?' I say.

Beth shrugs. 'Who knows. It wouldn't be the first time he's watched one of us. Leon was always his little spy before.'

I take this on board wondering what else Beth knows that I don't.

'Leon spied on us?' I say.

Beth glances down the corridor. 'Well, it's a periodic thing. Sometimes, he just checks all of us out. Watches our computer movements, studies reports for signs of omissions. As though he's searching to see if one of us has been compromised, or switched sides. Leon also used to watch us when he thought we didn't notice. Then I'm sure he fed back his observations to Ray.'

'How do you know this?' I ask.

'There were traces of his activity all over my reports. He'd try to remove it, but you know that computers are my expertise,' Beth says.

'Are you sure he was doing that for Ray?' I ask.

Beth looks surprised. 'I hadn't thought of that. But if not for Ray, then who?'

I shake my head. Then I get a coffee out of the machine.

'Let's talk again when we can,' I say.

This exchange has left me a lot to think about. Was Leon the mole that Neva mentioned? Or was that one of her lies? I find it difficult to imagine, given Leon's penchant for doing everything by the book, where Beth and I would often bend the rules. But maybe Beth is right and he was just watching us for Ray. After all, Ray turned a blind eye to most things if we got results, but perhaps he was concerned we'd overstep too much.

Beth follows me back to the office and we find Elsa studying the investigation board.

'I know it's been noted, but they do all look alike,' Elsa says.

'Yeah. The perp has a thing for that colour hair and blue eyes,' I say.

'What does that tell you about him?' Elsa asks.

'There's always a link between victims and how they are chosen,' Beth says. 'Sometimes it's location, or opportunity that defines why they are picked, but often there's a physical reason.'

'Is that right?' Elsa asks me and Beth bristles beside me because she hasn't been believed.

'Yes it is. Often there's a reason behind the physical type. Maybe the victims look like someone the killer knows or knew. Perhaps they are like the first person they killed or wanted to kill. That person could be a relative or friend. They act out the death over and over again – reliving how it felt, or they are exacting a revenge that they are unable to carry out on the original.'

'What about this one?' Beth asks.

I study the pictures again. 'The fury inside the killer is growing. It's getting more frantic. Which tells me there's a history that they are focused on. If these women are lookalikes, then our perp has a deep hatred for the original. Note Sinead. It was calmer. As though our perp thought they could relieve their frustration by taking this innocent girl's life. What it served to do, though, was release something in them. It freed up their inhibition but didn't ultimately satisfy the need it was trying to fulfil.'

'It showed skill, but you think this is the perp's first kill?' Beth says.

'There's no doubt this person knew what they were doing. The deaths were too well delivered. Sinead might not be their first kill, but it was probably the first one that meant something to the killer,' I explain.

'And now you think the killer is losing it?' Elsa says.

'How much do you know about the Network?' I ask.

'I know we are looking for links between them and the deaths we investigate – especially the cold cases,' Elsa says.

'We know that several assassins broke free of their handlers when we levelled our initial attack on them,' Beth says. 'The killer could be one of them. Breaking down. Losing their conditioning and therefore their focus.'

Elsa glances at me. 'Do you think that too?'

I don't answer. Instead I look past her to the board and the faces of the victims, all smiling and alive in photos taken long before they were singled out and killed. Do I agree with Beth? It's certainly a theory we've discussed. But there's a nagging doubt, a question that keeps floating around inside my head that I can't shake off. Is the resemblance of these victims to Neva merely a coincidence, or is there someone out there looking for her? And in lieu of finding her, are they wreaking their terrible revenge on innocent women?

This is a theory I keep to myself – for now. Though, knowing Beth as I do, I think she already suspects what I'm thinking.

Chapter Twenty-One

JANINE

Four years ago

Janine kicks out as Neva falls forward into a roll and then leaps to her feet. The kick misses its mark, much to the annoyance of Neva's protégé, and so Janine tries another tactic. She throws herself forward making a direct attack. Neva anticipates the move and once again ducks away, shy of the blow. They continue to fight, Neva always blocking or avoiding until she delivers a hard push to Janine's chest. Janine falls back, hitting the judo mat.

Neva holds out her hand and Janine takes it, knowing the sparring is at an end for the day. Janine is frustrated though. Neva always bests her and she can't imagine how she will ever have the same skill that her mentor patiently tries to give her.

They are in Janine's apartment, paid for by the retainer that Neva gives her. The sitting room is large, and, with the furniture pushed back into the corners, makes for a perfect sparring location.

'How do you always know my moves?' Janine asks.

'You move a fraction of a second too soon each time. It gives you away,' Neva says.

'I'm never going to match you,' Janine says.

'You're already better than most,' Neva says. 'But you're still too emotional. You have to quell the adrenaline. It makes you jumpy.'

Neva tells Janine how she might learn to still her emotions. 'It is a natural surge that was designed by nature to encourage flight when threatened, but to be an effective assassin you have to learn to control these impulses and use them to your advantage. When you master this, you'll be fully in control.'

She prompts Janine on breathing exercises and meditation. All of which she's studied with her over and over again. But Neva never loses her patience or reprimands her for not remembering, she merely reminds her about it again: she is as perfect as a mentor as she is as an assassin.

Janine has been training with her now for almost two years. She is physically strong, and an exceptional fighter. She has excellent sniper skills and Janine sometimes works a hit of this sort for Neva, freeing her up to do what she wants instead. Not that Janine ever knows what that is. It is peculiar, and she often questions how much Neva needs her, despite the fact that she insists she does. Even so, they aren't friends. It is an odd relationship, far from equal. Janine is aware of how much that is true. She is being groomed for some purpose that only Neva understands.

Janine has asked on occasion, but she feels guilty afterwards and frustrated when Neva won't explain herself. A frustration that sometimes turns to anger. She doesn't feel used, just uninformed. And because she knows that Neva works for some very powerful and very dangerous people, Janine prefers to know what she's letting herself in for.

'I have a job for you,' Neva says now.

'Sniper?' Janine asks.

'No. Something up close and personal,' Neva says.

Neva lets the blade in her holster slip down into her hand, and she passes it to Janine.

'I want you to pick up a man, take him back to his hotel room, and kill him,' Neva says.

'You think I'm ready?' Janine says.

'I know you are,' Neva says.

She holds out a brown A4-size envelope and Janine takes it. She opens the top and slides out the job file. A photograph greets her. It is *the general*. She hasn't thought of him for a long time. She tries not to think about the man that put a hit on her.

'You were asked to kill him?' Janine says. Her eyes are wide as she stares at the photograph.

'No. I'm employing *you* to.'

'Why?' she asks.

Neva blinks. 'Because I think you need it to consolidate your training.'

Janine nods.

'He's in Switzerland. A hotel not far from here. He's

brought with him a young female FSB operative, who has no doubt been coerced into sleeping with him,' Neva explains.

'You're an avenging angel,' says Janine.

'I'm death: I don't care about revenge,' Neva says.

Janine observes the coldness of Neva's answer and understands what this is all about. Janine needs to free herself from her old life in order to fully embrace her new one.

Neva doesn't confirm this. She rarely explains her motivations, something that Janine has learned to accept.

Janine's hand trembles as she pushes the paper and photograph back into the envelope.

'When shall I do it?' she asks.

'The girl flies back to Moscow today. He'll be alone tonight,' Janine says.

'What if he recognizes me?'

Neva's smile is cold. 'He won't.'

When she arrived earlier, Neva left a holdall in the corner of the room. She goes there now and opens it. Inside she has everything she needs to create Janine's disguise. But Janine is already different. She has her hair dyed strawberry blonde, just like Neva's. They could be sisters, but all of this is to ensure that Janine can be her at a minute's notice.

'Shower, and change into this,' she says.

She holds out a little black dress. Short, sexy and not something that Janine would usually wear. She takes it and goes into the bathroom.

When she's dressed, Janine comes back into her sitting room. The judo mat has been moved and a chair is placed in the centre. Neva is holding a black wig, cut into a bob with a fringe. Janine sits down. Neva pulls a hair net over Janine's hair then puts the wig over it. She secures it with hair clips. After this she makes Janine get up. She uses a tan makeup, and bright-red lipstick. She spends a lot of time around her eyes. When she's finished, she holds up a mirror and Janine can see the sexy smoky look. Neva has created a personality that suggests *availability*.

Janine doesn't recognize herself. She doesn't look anything like the girl she'd once been when she worked in the Kremlin. No, this is a sophisticated and confident woman. One that will appeal to men, not the women whom Janine prefers.

'You know what to do,' Neva says, fixing the wrist holster under the deliberately long sleeve of the dress.

'Should I take a gun as well?' she says.

'No. There's nowhere to hide it from him. And remember who he is. He may notice, even if we tried to.'

Janine nods.

She is nervous as she leaves her apartment. A rush of adrenaline curls up, stifling her as she steps into a taxi and makes her way to the hotel in question. She pushes it down as Neva has taught her, but it hides behind her calm exterior, picking at the edges like acid burning through flesh. By the time she reaches the hotel, Janine is trembling.

She pauses outside the building pulling her equilibrium back together. She runs the mantra that Neva has taught her through her mind. *I am death.*

Why am I like this? she wonders, for she has always done what Neva needed without question. And she's never been in such a state of nerves before a kill – normally there is a dizzying excitement.

It's him.

Once she identifies the source of her terror – fear of the general's power and anxiety that she will be recognized – she begins to regain control.

He tried to have her executed, and for that, Neva has given her an opportunity to take him out. To exact revenge – despite her declaration that she doesn't care about it. Janine explores the feeling of seeing the general die, of spilling his blood up close. Will this free her as Neva says?

When the rush of nerves recedes, it's replaced with a cold excitement. Janine goes inside the building.

The general has chosen an exclusive five-star hotel and therefore the reception is, of course, palatial. Marble tiles gleam on both floor and walls. The reception desk sparkles with polished brass fittings. There's a traditional, yet contemporary amalgamation of styles in the furniture, with plush green leather *chaise lounges* positioned around the walls and equally luxurious four-seater sofas placed at intervals in the centre of the space. To the right, Janine sees the cocktail lounge and she walks across and into the space, taking a seat by the bar.

As instructed, she buys herself a drink. She orders a strawberry daiquiri.

The bar area glitters. Expensive spirits line the mirror-backed shelves. Janine studies the cocktail bar through the glass. Behind her sits lavish furnishing and several luscious private booth areas. The place screams intimacy and would appeal to those with money who might not wish to be observed.

What business could a Russian general have here? she wonders as she casually glances around.

It's not long before the general arrives. It takes her a moment to recognize him because he is not in uniform.

Seeing him again brings a surge of anger and disgust. She watches him in the reflection of the mirror behind the bar.

There is a problem: the girl has not left and she joins him at one of the booths.

While the general orders drinks from a cocktail waitress in a short black skirt and white blouse, Janine is taken with how young the girl he's brought is. She can't be more than 18. Perhaps she's even younger.

Janine is sickened by the way he mauls her. The young girl doesn't appear to be enjoying it either. She wonders what he has over her to make her share his bed.

Feeling she will not get the opportunity she wished for, Janine decides to abandon the hit. She gets up from the barstool and starts to leave.

That's when she sees Neva, sitting at the back of the room in another booth with a young man.

Janine feels peculiar seeing Neva like this. She tells herself that this is not real, even as her mentor allows the man with her to run his hand over her bare thigh. Neva must have contrived the situation to watch over her. She has never thought of Neva in a sexual light before. Seeing her with this man gives Janine an emotion she hadn't realized she had for Neva. She feels… envy. Neva is allowing the contact but has never shown her any such affection at all. No. Janine is a commodity to Neva – nothing more.

She meets Neva's eyes over the shoulder of the man but she can gather nothing from her expression. Then Neva whispers something in the man's ear. He gets out of the booth and goes away. Janine approaches. She sits down with Neva.

'You said the girl would be gone,' she says.

'She will be. Watch.'

A few minutes later another man enters the bar. He walks up to the general and the girl. With a look of relief, the girl stands and scurries away with the other man.

'Don't let him be lonely,' Neva says.

Then she stands and leaves the booth, walking out of the bar.

Chapter Twenty-Two

JANINE

Janine watches the general order another drink, which the waitress brings to him. He gulps it down and then stands. As he exits the bar, Janine follows.

The general heads towards the lifts and she walks after him. He pauses at the reception desk, but Janine continues to the elevator. Her heart thuds in her chest. But she takes a deep breath and reaches out to press the call button.

The general comes to her side as the lift opens. Janine lets her clutch bag slip from her fingers. She bends to pick it up, relying on the general's lack of chivalry. He enters the lift and Janine scoops up her bag and scurries inside. By then the general has pressed the button for his floor. Janine presses the one for the floor above.

Then she opens her handbag and starts to rifle inside as though she's lost something.

'Mon dieu!'

She glances at the general and looks embarrassed.

'Parlez vous Francais?'

'*Oui*,' he says.

'I've lost my key. I will have to go down again! It is not my day!' she says. She smiles at him with the right amount of flirting.

The general smiles back. 'Why is that?'

'I hate to drink alone, for a start!' Janine says.

'So do I,' says the general.

When the doors open at his floor, he remains in the lift. The doors close and they go up to the next floor. Then as they open again the general presses the down button.

'Perhaps when you've sorted your room key, you'll meet me in the cocktail lounge?' he says.

Janine smiles again. 'Oh, for company on this boring trip!'

'Then it's settled?' the general says.

Janine nods and smiles again.

They reach the reception and the general walks back to the bar. Janine watches him go and then she walks over to the reception desk to feign getting a replacement key. There's a male receptionist in a smart black suit. He smiles at her.

'*Puis-je aider?*' asks the receptionist in French. *Can I help?*

'Do you have a spare room for the night?' Janine replies.

The receptionist looks at his computer.

'I'm afraid we're fully booked,' says the receptionist.

'Thank you,' Janine says.

She walks back to the bar and finds the general sitting in the same booth he occupied earlier.

Janine sits down opposite him, far enough away not to encourage his wandering hands, though she's facing the prospect of it in the near future if she is to coax him back to his room.

The waitress arrives with a strawberry daiquiri for her and a vodka for the general. The general looks smug as the woman places the glasses down in front of them. Janine smiles at him.

'I ordered us a drink,' he says. 'The bartender told me what you like.'

'That's kind of you,' she answers. She sips the drink. 'It's good.'

The general lifts his vodka glass to his lips. He doesn't knock it back as is traditional, instead he sips it.

'You're French, right?' he asks.

'*Oui*. I'm Parisian.'

'What are you doing in Switzerland?' he asks.

'Work. Boring meetings – they were cancelled today though, so here I am, alone in a hotel instead. What about you?'

The general looks away. 'A leisure trip,' he says.

Janine doesn't enquire more.

After several cocktails, the general invites her back to his room. By then she's sitting next to him and his hand is stroking up her thigh. She hides her disgust well, just as she feigns being drunker than she actually is. A lifetime of consuming neat vodka has made her as hardy as the general – who pays for all of the drinks.

They leave the bar and go back to the lift, this time together. As the doors close, Janine thinks she sees Neva in the reception. She looks away and back at the general. He's smiling in a very self-satisfied way.

They reach the general's floor and Janine giggles as he leads her to his room. She's aware that they haven't even exchanged names. It's as though Yahontov does this sort of thing so often he doesn't even care to know the woman's name.

He opens his door, steps back and encourages her inside.

'I can only stay for one drink,' Janine says. 'Early morning and more meetings tomorrow.'

'I understand,' the general says.

He closes the door behind them and Janine walks further into the room. He has a suite – equally decadent as the reception and bar of the hotel – with a lounge area including a bar and a kitchenette. The general takes a bottle of Champagne from the fridge. There's even an ice maker in the room and he fills a wine bucket with ice. After popping the cork and pouring two glasses he stows the bottle in the ice. Then he brings the glass to Janine. She's taken a seat on one of two sofas that are placed either side of an ornate mahogany coffee table.

Janine feels the weight of the knife, still in the wrist holster, as the general sits down beside her. A surge of adrenaline makes her cheeks redden.

The general doesn't waste any time coming onto her. Janine goes along with it for a short time and then she pushes him away. She is jittery and she lets it show because it would be abnormal if she wasn't nervous – a woman in the room of a stranger.

'The bathroom?' she asks.

The general points to the washroom by the bedroom door. Janine goes inside. She looks at herself in the mirror.

Her lipstick is smudged. She wants to wash her face and remove the makeup and wig. She wants Yahontov to recognize her.

She doesn't do it.

Instead she releases the knife from the holster. She stares at it in her hand feeling the weight of it. She knows how to use this knife, Neva has worked with her on it time and again, but still she doubts herself. That old fear and intimidation comes back. It weakens her until she quells the nerves and quietens the adrenaline. Her mantra flows through her brain and her lips move as she recites it in her head.

I am death.

She turns the knife back in her hand, holding it securely, but hidden in her palm and then she flushes the toilet, runs the tap in the sink and opens the door of the toilet.

The general is waiting for her outside. His eyes are clear as he looks at her.

'I hope you aren't teasing me?' he says.

Janine smiles and walks towards him. She lets him embrace and kiss her again. Then she steps back. There is a beat before she swings the knife, aiming for his throat.

The general traps her arm in his two hands. He pushes her away and then backhands her. Janine tries to block him but he catches her with a glancing blow. She stumbles back against the bathroom door.

'You think I didn't realize you were a spy?' he says with a smile.

The general advances even as Janine holds the knife up between them. He attempts to knock it from her fingers, but sparring with Neva has prepared her for this. She jumps the knife deftly into her other hand and wards off his attack with her now free arm. She punches her fist at his face while simultaneously stabbing the knife upwards with her left hand.

The knife slices into Yahontov's arm. He yelps, lashing out at her again. This time the back of his hand connects with Janine's face. Blinding pain bursts through her cheekbone and eye. The general presses his advantage and sweeps her feet from under her. Janine falls hard, rapping her head on the door frame of the bathroom.

Stunned, Janine feels the general pull her body into the room.

'Bitch!' he says, slapping her hard again. The same cheek screams with pain. 'Who sent you?'

Janine forces her mouth closed, cutting off the groan that almost escapes her lips. She pulls herself round. There's a ringing in her ears. *Neva's done worse than this during our workouts,* she thinks. But something about the general incapacitates her. And she feels as helpless as she did when she worked in the Kremlin.

His hand gropes her, reaching up her skirt between her legs. She heaves her body up against him, but he slams her down. Janine knows that he isn't stronger than her, his strength can be used against him, she just has to get the right leverage.

He stretches out over her, fingers grasping at her underwear. She struggles against him, *fight back fiercer*, she thinks as she smashes the hardest bone in her wrist against his face. The general grunts as the blow lands on the bridge of his nose.

He pulls his hand back to deliver another blow and that is when Janine sees Neva.

She emerges from the bedroom behind the general. Neva grabs his hair and yanks back his head. As her knife draws across the taut skin of his throat, blood explodes over Janine.

She yelps. Pulling herself free of the general's half-raised body, Janine propels herself back until her shoulder hits the sofa.

Neva drops the general's body. Then she goes into the bathroom and washes her knife and her hands. When Neva comes out of the bathroom, the general has bled out on the expensive carpet. Janine hasn't moved.

'Get cleaned up,' Neva says. 'We need to get away from here as soon as possible.'

Chapter Twenty-Three

BEN

Present day

'Someone is watching us,' Mia says as Ben arrives home.

'What's happened?' Ben says.

'I went to the park, and I'm sure someone followed me home.'

Ben takes her into his arms and holds her.

'You're safe, darling. No one knows we are here,' he says.

Mia pushes away from him. 'I'm telling you… I felt…'

'Okay,' says Ben. 'Let's start at the beginning. What happened?'

'In the park. They were all looking at me. I felt uncomfortable and then I saw a glint of light in a window.'

'A glint of light? Mia… I don't want to sound patronizing but let's just take a breath. Think about this rationally. What did you absolutely *see* that makes you think there's danger?' Ben says.

He pulls her into the living room and encourages her to sit down on the sofa by the window.

'I didn't see anything… it was a feeling. Like a prickle. In the back of my head. Like when you know someone is watching you. I'm not crazy,' Mia says.

Ben sighs. 'You're not going insane. MI6 do have someone looking out for you. So, it's probably just them you're sensing. You're very astute, Mia.'

'There is someone watching?' she says.

'It's for your own protection. Just try to ignore it,' Ben says.

'Oh thank god! I really thought I was losing it!' Mia says.

'No one is going to get near you while they are there. Okay?'

Mia trembles and the tears she's been holding back all day pour down her cheeks. Ben sits down beside her and wraps his arms around her.

'I'm… s… sorry,' she says. 'I'm just so tense. I keep feeling like any moment something is going to happen.'

'MI6 are keeping an eye on you, that's all it is. You just have to find some normality in this situation.'

'But the park was so weird… the women kept looking at me…'

'Why shouldn't they? You're gorgeous. And you're new to the area!' Ben says. 'Why not try saying hello next time? Make some new friends.'

Ben laughs.

'It's not funny,' Mia says pulling herself free.

'Sorry,' Ben says. 'I know this is difficult. I'm just trying to lighten the mood.'

'I might better understand why this has happened if you'd tell me what's going on.'

Ben sighs and shakes his head. 'It's best you don't know everything. I don't really think it would help you.'

'Try me,' Mia says.

'Where's Freya?' he asks.

'Kitchen,' says Mia. 'I just didn't want to put her in her cot until we were upstairs as well today.'

Ben gets up. He walks away into the kitchen where he finds Freya in her bouncy chair.

'Is Freya okay?' Mia asks.

'I'll bring her in,' he says.

He picks up Freya and the chair and carries her into the living room and places her down beside the sofa. Then he goes back into the kitchen.

'I need a drink,' he says.

He goes to the fridge and removes a bottle of Chardonnay. Then he takes two wine glasses from the cupboard. He pours the wine and brings it back into the living room.

He places one glass in Mia's hand and the other down on the coffee table.

Freya gurgles at him and then crams her fist into her mouth and begins to chew on it.

'She's teething, isn't she?' Ben says.

Mia nods.

'Drink your wine. You're going to need it.'

Mia takes a huge slug of the wine. 'I'm listening.'

'Do you remember the day Michael came to take you and Freya away?'

'Of course, I do. That's when I learned you worked for MI6…' Mia says.

'What else do you remember? About Michael? About you?'

Mia frowns. She thinks back to that day, just over a month ago, but it now feels like a lifetime. It's hazy in her memory. She recalls being scared.

'Michael's friend Neva told you some things. About a conglomerate called the Network,' Ben prompts.

Mia's frown deepens. 'Network?'

'Yes, and stuff about your parents…'

Mia shakes her head. 'My parents have vanished. Michael was there, and you… had a gun.'

Mia looks scared and confused. She glances at Freya.

'Mia, you remembered it all for twenty-four hours after the incident and then it just… disappeared. Since then I've only reminded you of some of it. When I've had to.'

'How can my memory *disappear*?' she says. 'You mean… I'm forgetting things?'

Ben sighs again. 'Yes. But it's not dementia. Mia, you and Michael aren't twins. You are brother and sister, born on the same day, but to different mothers. Your biological father was the man you thought was your uncle.'

Mia's expression changes as the memory of the revelations comes back. 'Oh my god, earlier today, I remembered it all. Then I forgot again.'

'Yes. The memory comes and goes. And I don't keep reminding you because it scares you,' Ben says. 'It's best you forget again and just accept my explanation that you're safe. But when you get like this, I'm forced to… prompt you. Freya is at the heart of this.'

Mia looks at Freya again.

'They'd take Freya. They'd turn her into… an assassin?'

Ben nods. 'It's why we are in hiding.'

Mia looks scared. 'But why do I forget? *Why?*'

'They… brainwashed you from childhood. It's not your fault.'

Mia starts to cry again as the memory of what she was told pours back into her conscious mind. 'I'm not safe! I could be turned against you… or Freya.'

'One thing I know about you, you'd never let anything happen to Freya,' he says. 'But what you need to remember is that you are being protected. By me or when I'm not here, by a highly trained operative. You're safe and so is our baby.'

Mia shakes her head in denial as the enormity of their situation hits her. Ben feels helpless as he watches the comprehension sinking in again.

'Drink the wine,' he says again.

Mia sips the wine automatically.

'And again,' Ben says. 'Have another sip.'

Mia does as he tells her, and then she blinks and smiles.

'Ben! You're home. And look at me… caught with a cheeky glass of wine!'

'Even better you poured one for me!' he says.

Ben picks up the wine and sips it. He looks calm, but he is shaky inside. These moments disturb him as much as Mia. But at least she has the luxury of forgetting them soon after. Ben doesn't know why a few sips of wine make her forget the horrors she's learned. He suspects it is her mind's defence mechanism as well as the conditioning. Every time she's faced with the truth, she has to blot it out and bury it back inside her subconscious. Now Mia will be calm and feel safe again. At least until the next little crack appears. And those cracks are becoming more frequent.

Ben's mind flies back to his conversation with Steward that day.

'Is she breaking down?' Steward had asked.

Ben looks at his wife and sighs again. 'No,' he says out loud. 'You're just trying to make sense of it all. One day maybe you will come to terms with what's happened.'

'Did you say something?' Mia says sipping the wine again. 'Oh look! My glass is empty.'

'I'll refill it. What about take-away tonight?' Ben says. 'We can have it delivered and just enjoy this wine.'

Mia smiles at him, 'That would be a nice change!'

Chapter Twenty-Four

ANNALISE

'I must admit you're tougher than I thought you'd be,' Annalise says.

Kritta lifts her head and meets Annalise's gaze. She tries to spit blood from her cracked lips but she barely has the energy, and the spittle and blood runs down her chin. Even so, Kritta grins and her mouth opens to reveal broken and missing teeth.

Annalise studies her. As a committee member, Kritta was afforded her own security detail. A team that Annalise had paid to capture her after she attempted to take Michael from his London home. Since then she had brought Kritta to the château, and stored her for a week or two, allowing her to sweat before she began work on her.

'You must understand that I don't enjoy hurting you,' Annalise says.

Kritta has borne all the torture that she has thrown at her. Waterboarding, beatings, teeth pulling, broken fingers, electrocution and even hallucinogenic drugs. Now Annalise is losing her patience and she's decided to resort to different tactics. She will see if Kritta is as tough as she appears or if there is something she can use as leverage to make her talk.

'The child you had for Beech. She now has her own baby. A girl,' Annalise says.

Kritta's face hardens.

'I'd like to show you something,' Annalise continues.

The door to Kritta's prison opens and one of her guards enters carrying a laptop. Another guard pulls Kritta to her feet. They push her down onto a wooden chair before a small table. The other guard places the laptop in front of her. He opens the lid and then sets a PowerPoint slideshow in motion.

Pictures of Mia flash onto the screen. Kritta tries to look away, but the guard that put her on the chair forces her face around. She watches. There are photographs of Mia walking down a suburban street pushing a pram. Pictures also of her hanging out washing in a pristine back garden while the little baby lies on a mat on the grass with a baby gym perched over her.

'A pretty child. And the mother is very attractive too. Clearly, she doesn't get her looks from you,' Annalise laughs. 'But the child interests me so much. She'll be such a clean slate and so useful as one of my trainees. And with her pedigree… I'll adopt her of course. She'll call me "Mother" like all the rest.'

Annalise bends over the laptop. She closes the PowerPoint and then pulls up a video from another file on the machine.

'We know exactly where they are. But, the mother – Mia

she's called – is no use to me as she is. She knows nothing. The conditioning has made her forget who and what she is. I think I'll just order her killed.'

The video shows Mia walking towards a local shop. She pauses outside, and then Kritta sees the red glow of a sniper laser resting on the back of Mia's head.

Kritta gasps.

Annalise closes the lid of the laptop.

'You were willing, weren't you?' Annalise says. 'Perhaps you were even a little in love with Beech. I know how it is to raise a child for a few years, only to have them taken away from you. But you have watched her progress haven't you, Kritta? He let you see her at times, didn't he?'

'No. I don't care about her,' Kritta says. 'I was just an incubator.'

'Really?' Annalise reaches into her pocket and removes a stack of old photographs. 'What about these?'

Kritta sees the pictures as Annalise scatters them on top of the laptop and table. Mia at various stages in her life. Playing in the park with the Kensingtons watching over her. At school during sports day. Later dressed for prom, a spotty boyfriend on her arm.

'She looks particularly pretty there,' Annalise says picking up a photograph of Mia and Ben on their wedding day. 'We found these in your apartment. I think you care, Kritta. I really do.'

'You bitch!' says Kritta. 'Fight me fair and square and we'll see who is the best. I'll mess up your pretty face and no amount of reconstruction will fix it.'

Annalise smiles. 'It's nothing personal, Kritta. You see, you have something I need. I want Mia's activation words.'

'I told you. I don't know. Beech never shared them with me,' Kritta says.

'And yet he shared Michael's with Subra? Come now, you don't expect me to believe that. Beech was intelligent enough to know you always had his back.'

Kritta shakes her head.

'Your refusal to cooperate just makes me surer that Mia has no value to me. And so, I shall probably tell my man to fire next time and then to bring me the child.'

Annalise turns and walks towards the door. The guard picks up the laptop but they leave the photographs of Mia and Freya behind. Kritta stares at the pictures.

'Wait!' says Kritta.

Annalise stops. She doesn't look at Kritta. But when she hears the tremor in the woman's voice, she knows she's won.

'What will you do if you activate her?' Kritta asks.

'Kill her brother Michael. He's lost to us.'

'And then?' asks Kritta.

'She'll be brought into my organisation and her skills will be used for me. I will even let her bring up the child. For the first five years anyway…'

'It's a detailed sequence, to avoid accidental activation…' Kritta says.

'Leave us,' Annalise says to the two guards.

The guards go, closing the door behind them. Annalise pulls a chair up to the table.

'I'm listening,' she says.

Chapter Twenty-Five

NEVA

I can confirm that the woman called Kritta is missing, Elbakitten says in a message.

Neva opens the hardback book and crosses Kritta off her list for possible committee members. In her world, 'missing' usually means 'dead'. She looks over the remaining names. *Banwick (Cardiff); Petters (Oslo); Conor (Edinburgh); Drake (Venice); Cruik (Madrid).*

There are so few of them remaining, Neva wonders which of them is now running the Network. Taking a chance of scaring her source away, she returns an enquiry to Elbakitten.

This will be a dangerous question to ask. Be careful. Who is the chairman of the Network?

Neva watches the messenger idle and then sees three dots that signify Elbakitten is replying. Then the dots disappear. Neva waits for half an hour but Elbakitten doesn't reply. She realizes that the hacker has been frightened off. She's about to give up when Elbakitten begins to reply again.

Sorry for delay. Confirming intel. Heard this one last week. Codename: Annalise was appointed Acting Chair.

Neva responds with another question. *'Acting Chair', what does that mean?*

Elbakitten replies. *My source wouldn't tell me.*

Neva stares at the message and then she shuts down her computer. Annalise is in charge. This must have been her plan all along. And, if Fracks told her the truth, Neva knows where to look for her.

Neva prowls around her small apartment. She feels caged and useless. This hide-out is a prison. She wants to return to London more than anything but such a move would be dangerous as she is sure she is on a watch list. With little else to do, Neva returns to her laptop. She opens it again and logs back on to the dark web. She is about to send Elbakitten another message when she sees further comments from her.

Rumour is Annalise took Kritta.

Neva sends a reply giving Elbakitten the other names on the committee. *Find them all for me. But don't take any personal risks. Wiring funds now.*

Elbakitten does not acknowledge receipt until fifteen minutes later. By then, Neva is deep in thought. What did Annalise want from Kritta?

She goes back to the web and hiding behind several IP addresses, she searches for 'Kritta'.

An image comes up of a screenshot of a woman. Neva examines the source of the picture and realizes it's attached to a few clone IP addresses from some months ago. Someone was searching 'Kritta' using this photograph. All of the links that it led to, or from, have been erased, but the picture has been missed from the apparent clean-up.

Neva saves it, and then she studies the face again. Is she familiar? Yes. She has a flash of memory. A burst of gunfire, and then Neva had thrown herself down at her enemy: Kritta was the woman she'd incapacitated in the stairwell. Kritta was the Network spy who'd come after Michael. But the police had captured Kritta and her colleague after Neva had left them both injured and unconscious, hadn't they?

Neva shakes her head – no, it's not just that. Something else makes Kritta familiar. The serious set of her jaw?

The image of Michael comes into Neva's mind, but she dismisses the thought that he's somehow linked to this woman in any other way than that failed attack. He's nothing like her.

Neva's brain becomes washed with detail as she pulls up her perfect-recall memory of Michael's sister, Mia, holding her child in the farmhouse when she learned the truth of her heritage. *Impossible!*

Neva looks back again at the picture she's found. Is this a coincidence? Could this really be Kritta? And is she Mia's biological mother?

Neva walks away from the laptop, frustrated with herself and her search. She's sure she's imagining the connection. Kritta is a plain woman, nothing like Mia who was very pretty. It can't be right.

Neva returns to the laptop once more. She copies Kritta's photo and puts it into Photoshop. There she manipulates the picture, turning the sour, downturned lips upwards. Even as she does this, the eyes show nothing. Kritta is a dark and humourless soul.

'It can't be,' Neva says aloud. 'I'm seeing connections where there aren't any.'

She closes the laptop a final time and then, because she can't stand her own company any longer, she leaves the flat and goes out for a long walk. But the feeling that she's right won't leave her. Instead it grows stronger and clearer in her mind along with the thought that Kritta isn't dead. Annalise has her, and there's only one reason why: she wants to activate Mia.

I need to warn Michael. But would he even listen to her?

Neva pauses at the water's edge and looks out at the Amstel. This river flows from Nieuwveen to Amsterdam and she always enjoys watching the movement of the water. But unlike other times when she's stood here, the flow of the river doesn't soothe her. The current pushes and pulls at the foliage and pebbles in the water, reminding Neva of life and how futile it is to struggle against it.

Neva is torn as she tries to decide what to do. She could go in search of Annalise. Finding a winery in Toulouse surely can't be that difficult? But what would she do once she came face to face with her possible birth-mother? What does she really want from Annalise?

Revenge.

No. Even though Neva had used it as an excuse when enlisting Michael's help, revenge was for other people. It wasn't what she wanted. She analyses her emotions. As time has passed, her original anger at being given to the house has faded. She's curious more than annoyed. She wants to know what sort of woman Annalise is. Who gives away their child to someone like Beech?

But her search for answers will have to wait. Neva has to warn Michael. No matter how he reacts to her and the news, she is compelled to try to help him anyway: even though it puts her at risk. After all, there is no more use denying to herself what she feels for him, even if Michael doesn't reciprocate.

Chapter Twenty-Six

MICHAEL

It is a very sad thing to distrust your colleagues, but after my conversation with Beth I feel hyper-sensitive to the fact that we might be being watched. I trust her instincts more than my own right now, and I think she's right. Even though I'm not doing anything wrong, the feeling of being studied by Ray, of him not trusting us, irritates and annoys me. For this reason, I remain behind at work, long after Elsa, Beth and Ray have gone for the day. If Ray is monitoring us, then I'd like to know for sure.

I comb my office for surveillance. The cameras and taps would have to be miniscule in order to go unnoticed in an MI5 office.

I open the top drawer in my desk and take out the magnifier that I occasionally use when studying redacted documents. Sometimes when the text is enhanced, I can make out the hidden words and learn something that my other colleagues have missed. I use the magnifier now as I search every surface of my desk, computer, keyboard and the door frame. I study the walls of my office, looking for anything that doesn't belong there. Even the clock above my desk.

I pick up the receiver on my phone and take it apart. I discover that the wiring is all as it should be: the phone hasn't been tapped. I'm about to give up and call myself paranoid when I discover a tiny black dot camouflaged on the outside of the receiver. It is easy to miss – black on black – and I only find it because my fingers feel the slightly raised edge of the area.

I scrape the dot away with my thumb nail. Then I turn it over. There is a microscopic circuit board on the other side.

My office has definitely been bugged and this gadget, small as it is, could also listen in to any conversations I have on the phone as well.

I widen the search after that, and discover more of these dots in Beth and Elsa's office because they are easier to find once I know what I'm looking for.

I gather all of the bugs into one plastic evidence bag. Then I go to Ray's office. I try his door and find it locked as usual. This isn't a problem because I have a lock-picking kit in my pocket. I always carry one. I use it now and soon I'm inside Ray's room. I don't turn on the lights.

The bugs I'd found in the central office had been hidden on the phones, like mine. I go to Ray's desk and switch on his desk lamp. Then I examine Ray's phone.

There's nothing there and it seems to confirm that he is the one monitoring us.

I place the plastic evidence wallet on Ray's desk so that he'll know I found the bugs and I'm aware he's spying on us. It's pointless searching his office under the circumstances and so I go to turn the lamp off. That is when my fingers feel the slight ridge of something that shouldn't be there on the base of the lamp.

I turn the main light on, fully lighting up the room, before examining the lamp. Yes – there is one of the same tiny bugs that I'd found in the other offices.

I comb Ray's office and find a few more of the devices. If Ray is behind this, why bug his own office? It doesn't make sense, and so the only conclusion I can draw is that someone else has been watching Archive as Neva had warned us. We'd been so distracted by her betrayal that any information she'd given didn't feel valid. Even Ray hadn't mentioned the intel that she'd shared since. But if this was true, then we'd dropped the ball by not investigating Neva's claims sooner. I find myself wondering who is behind this and what they may have learned. I also can't help thinking that this proves Neva wasn't all lies and deceit, but spies play games with truth and lies all the time. They give some provable information and hoodwink you once they have you believing them. But having found that her intel did have credence, it is enough to shed doubt on some of the things she was accused of.

I look around Ray's office one last time, then I leave the bugs all in the same bag on Ray's desk and then, locking the door behind me, I return to my office where I've left my mobile phone on the desk. I pick it up and call Ray.

Ray answers after a few rings. I tell him what I've discovered.

'I'm coming in,' Ray says. 'Stay there.'

When I put the phone down again, I find myself thinking about Neva, and the desperate way any confirmed truth from her can make me want to forgive her for her other transgressions. I bollock myself for being pathetic, but I can't help it. The feelings I have for her grow more complicated with every new revelation. Do I love or despise Neva? I only know that my life isn't the same without her in it. And the longer we are apart, the worse I feel. She is an addiction and cold turkey is torture.

It takes Ray an hour to get back to the office and he doesn't arrive alone. There is a whole security detail that sweeps our entire suite of rooms with specialist equipment. A few more bugs are found dotted around. They widen the search to the whole floor and they even find some in the bathrooms. After that, it's decided that the whole of the MI5 building will have to be swept.

'I don't understand this,' Ray says. 'We do regular sweeps.'

'Someone got in after the last one. Maybe that someone planned to return and remove these before the next?' I say.

'That would require prior knowledge of when they are going to happen. And even I don't know that,' Ray says.

'It's an inside job – but I just can't imagine who's behind it,' I say.

'How did you know?' Ray asks.

'I was working late. I was going to call for a car to take me to the safe house and felt something on my office phone. After that I thought I better check everywhere,' I lie, not wanting him to know that I suspected him of watching us.

'We'll let this lot finish up here,' Ray says. 'Maybe you should go home and get some rest now.'

It's nine o'clock in the evening and I'm feeling a bit tired. I'm glad to leave the professionals to do their job and make sure that nothing has been missed. It will make us all feel much safer tomorrow.

'Maybe we need to change your safe house,' Ray says. 'Just to make sure your location hasn't been compromised.'

'You really think it might be?'

'I don't know, Mike, but I'm not taking the chance.' Ray makes a call and a new security crew that I haven't seen before arrives to escort me out of the building.

As the other crew did, they lead me downstairs to the underground carpark, where three black SUVs are waiting. They put me in one. Then the first car in the convoy drives up to the barrier. I watch as it exits the car park and turns left. Heading back to the previous safe house, the car will follow the same route it's done, usually with me inside, for the last few weeks. When the outside surveillance announces the car is clear, they allow my car to leave. The third vehicle comes out of the car park and turns away towards a new direction. Then a fourth vehicle tags on and follows mine at a safe distance to the new location.

I don't know if all of these precautions are necessary, but I'm glad they are in place, especially until we find out who's been monitoring us.

Chapter Twenty-Seven

JANINE

Four years ago

They slip away from the hotel, leaving the general's body to be found by housekeeping.

Neva is at the wheel of an old Morris Minor that she has somehow procured. Janine has a strong sense that Neva has saved her again. If she hadn't been there, the general would have raped and killed her. Janine isn't just grateful, she feels something else, something deeper. She can't put a finger on what it is exactly.

'Go to ground for a while now,' Neva says. 'You're going to have to straighten this out in your head.'

'You always have my back, don't you?' Janine says.

'You always have mine too,' replies Neva.

They are driving to the Swiss town of Basel where they will part ways again for a while. Janine's Swiss flat is abandoned. Although this has been her home for the past two years, she isn't concerned about leaving the few possessions she has behind. She has a holdall containing money, various passports, and a few items she prefers to keep with her.

'I deposited your fee for killing the general,' Neva says.

'But… I didn't. You did,' Janine says.

'Without your seduction, it wouldn't have been possible,' Neva says. 'You did what I needed you to.'

'I wasn't good enough,' Janine says. 'I couldn't finish him. He was too strong.'

'Your past made you weak. You have the resources and the strength. You need to start believing in yourself. Now he's dead, nothing will hold you back. You have to use this as a way of divorcing yourself from the past.'

Janine looks at Neva. *How old is she?* Twenty-two, like herself? Yet she has so much maturity. Her grandmother would have called her an old soul.

Janine has never asked Neva how she came to be what she is. Like most spies, they don't talk about their personal lives. Yet Neva knows so much more about Janine than Janine knows about Neva. Now, Janine is curious about her mentor. What does she do with herself when she isn't working? Does Neva train daily as Janine does? Does she have a lover? Where does she live most of the time? These and many more questions go through Janine's mind. None of which she dares to ask.

They arrive at the Basel SBB train station and Neva gives Janine the keys to the car.

'I'll see you again soon,' Neva says.

She climbs out of the car and walks into the station without looking back.

On impulse, Janine abandons the car and follows Neva. From a distance she watches her buy a ticket. She's heading to Paris on the TGV train. Janine is familiar with the route as she's taken this one herself a few times: three hours and four minutes and she will be in Gare de Lyon, in Paris.

Janine buys herself a ticket and, hefting her holdall, she follows Neva onto the train.

This is a direct train with no other stops, for this reason the journey goes fast and Janine doesn't have to keep her eye on Neva in case she departs before Paris. On the train she remains hidden, several carriages away with the restaurant car between them. She begins to feel excited that Neva hasn't discovered her on board. It means she's doing a good job of not being noticed, just as Neva has taught her.

At Paris, Janine follows Neva onto the Metro. Neva gets off two stops later at Gare du Nord. Now, Janine is certain that Neva is returning to London via the Eurostar. She watches as her mentor buys another ticket and passes through the security checkpoint. Janine waits until the train starts to board before passing through herself. By then she's changed her clothing, and covered her hair with a hat. She boards the train, finds a seat and slumps down, hat over her eyes for the remainder of the journey. Anyone passing her seat will think she is sleeping.

In London, Janine picks up Neva's trail as she crosses the road from St Pancras to King's Cross. Once again, Neva boards a train. Confident she hasn't been noticed, Janine stays on her.

A few hours later Janine sees Neva's home for the first time.

Neva lives on a secluded country lane in a small detached cottage in rural Lincolnshire. Knowing she could be observed, Janine passes by the cottage in a stolen car, as Neva turns into her driveway. Once she knows where Neva resides, Janine drives away. She knows better than to push her luck now that her curiosity is satisfied.

She travels back to the nearest train station, discards the car, and catches a train back to London.

That night she receives a text from Neva.

Consider wisely how you use what you learned today.

Janine stares at the text, not knowing what to reply. Does Neva know that she followed her? What will she do when they next meet?

Janine sends back a basic message to appear benign.

Safe travels, wherever that might be.

The last person she would ever upset is Neva. Not only is Neva capable of killing her without a qualm, but Janine owes her life to her.

You too, my friend, Neva replies.

And that is the moment when Janine realizes, she and Neva are friends of a sort. They have shared so much and trust has been a part of this relationship from the beginning. And perhaps this means Janine's curiosity, if it's been discovered, is forgiven. At least this is what Janine hopes.

She tries not to think about it as she turns off the light in her hotel room. Tomorrow she will be out of England again, and finding herself this time a place that Neva doesn't pay for or know the location of.

The next morning, when Janine wakes, she finds an envelope of money beside her bed. She jumps up, shocked. It hadn't been there when she went to bed.

She searches the room and bathroom but finds she's alone.

She listens at the door but there is no sound, so she cracks it open and looks up and down the corridor beyond. Nothing. Silence.

She closes the door and returns to her bed.

She picks up the envelope. Opening it she discovers a wad of notes. Euros. She riffles through them: there are around twenty 500-euro notes there. Ten thousand euros. There's a hand-written note on the back of the envelope.

Take care, N x

Janine's hand trembles as she stows the money in her holdall.

Neva has been in her room as she slept. She knew where she was all the time.

She's not sure what Neva's message means. Is it a warning? Or a threat?

What it does confirm is that Neva can find her anytime, anywhere if she wants to. It's a lesson Janine never forgets.

Chapter Twenty-Eight

HILARY

Present day

Hilary Gillian runs the curry brush over the thoroughbred stallion's back, then taps the brush against the stall to clean it. When the dander is removed, she picks up the dandy brush and sweeps it over the horse until the sheen returns to his coat. The horse is irritable this evening, and she's tied him up in the stall making sure she keeps away from his back end. He's already slammed his back hooves against the rear of the stall and Hilary is determined he won't better her. It won't be the first time a highly strung horse kicked out and it won't be the last. The trick is to always make sure you aren't in the way when they do.

Hilary runs a livery yard near Newmarket and at 35 years old she is making a good name for herself in training race horses. Even so, she still likes to occasionally groom the horses herself, especially the difficult ones like Princely Sun here, who she's been paid a great deal of money to work with by his owner.

Hilary finishes grooming the horse and gives him some hay as a reward. She leaves the stall, securing the door with a sturdy bolt before making her way past the other horses out of the stable.

Outside she glances at her watch. It's late. But she doesn't mind. This job has always been a vocation, and something she has dreamed of doing ever since her parents bought her her very first horse when she was just 5 years old.

Hilary locks up the stable and walks across the yard to the office building. Inside she sees the old-fashioned answerphone flashing to indicate a new message. She presses play as she sits at her desk.

'Hi Hilary. It's Margot here. I'm in the area so I'd like to swing by and see Princely this evening. I should be there around eight.'

Hilary deletes the message, and looks at her watch. It's already 8:15pm and there's no sign of Margot.

She dials Margot's mobile number, but it goes through to voicemail.

'Hi Margot. I'll be here until 9pm if you're still around. But I have to go then,' Hilary says.

She hangs up just as a car turns into the yard outside. *Good.*

Hilary gets up. She's never met Margot, but she enjoyed receiving the first payment for the horse's care. Margot paid as much for one month as some owners pay for six and it was specifically requested that Hilary do all the training, and not one of the lesser employees. Now, Hilary hopes Margot is going to be pleased with the progress of the horse. She is sure that Princely's coat is gleaming with health at least, even if his temperament still needs to be dampened down a little. But it's early days and the horse has a long way to go before he'll be really ready for the race courses he's destined for.

Hilary opens the office door. A woman gets out of the car. She's younger than Hilary expected, around mid-twenties.

'Margot?' she says.

Margot's clipped tones come from the girl's mouth. 'Hilary? How is my horse?'

She leads Margot to the stable, unlocking the door again.

'He's here. I've just settled him for the night. He worked hard today.'

They walk to the stall and Princely Sun begins to neigh and becomes excited as they approach.

'He recognizes you,' Hilary says.

The horse lets Margot stroke his muzzle and is calmer than Hilary has ever seen him as Margot presses her forehead to his.

'He really loves you,' Hilary says.

'He fears me,' says Margot. 'Do you know why I picked you?'

'I thought I'd been recommended. By Sheik Imman,' Hilary says.

'You were with the sheik and his wife, showing off one of his race horses. That horse has won many races, hasn't it?' Margot says.

'Yes,' Hilary says.

'You look like her,' Margot says.

'Who?'

Margot straightens up. 'I was trying to think of a suitable tableau for you,' she says. 'And I realized this was already too magnificent for words.'

Hilary frowns. Margot is strange and she feels uncomfortable alone with her. She begins to wish she'd kept at least one of the stable hands back that evening.

'Anyway, if you're happy with Princely's progress, I need to close up for the night. We start very early in the morning here, and it's getting late.'

'I'm sorry,' Margot says. 'I should have thought this might be a bad time.'

Hilary notes how serious Margot is. She's difficult to read. Perhaps she isn't happy with her work after all?

They walk to the stable door. Hilary feels so tired, as though being around Margot is somehow draining all of her energy. Hilary is about to ask her if she's happy when she sees the knife in her hand. Hilary steps back, her shoulder connects with a bridle hook on the stall behind her. She feels the bruising pain of it, but that is nothing compared to when Margot stabs upwards with her knife.

There's a horrible grating feeling as the knife catches Hilary's rib cage, then plunges into her right lung. Hilary grunts then collapses against Margot, struggling to breathe. Margot pushes her back down onto the stable floor.

Around them the horses in the stalls, sensitive creatures that they are, begin to panic as Hilary's fear is conveyed to them. Princely Sun kicks and rears in his stall even as

Margot sits astride the mortally wounded Hilary as though she is the jockey and Hilary the horse.

The knife slashes down as Margot cuts and slices Hilary. Even though the knife shreds her hands and arms, Hilary still tries to ward off the blows. Adrenaline pumps through her ears blocking out the sound of chaos in the stable, even the sound of her own whimpering.

When she no longer has strength to fight back, Margot's words run through Hilary's fading mind… *you look like her…* before she slips down, sinking in a bloody mass to the concrete floor. Margot continues to slash the knife in a vicious arc across and over Hilary's torso. In her final moments, Hilary's mind clings onto the one question raised by Margot's insane declaration: *Who?*

Chapter Twenty-Nine

BETH

It takes an hour and forty-five minutes for Beth's security detail to drive her to the crime scene. By then, the local police have cordoned off the stables and are keeping all the employees in the small office until she can interview them.

After pulling on a crime-scene suit, Beth enters the stable. The horses are still in their stalls, cooped up to avoid any contamination until the forensics team do their work. The first thing Beth notices is the smell of hay and manure.

She sees Elliot at the far end of the stable. He's snapping photographs for future reference as he looks into the stall at the end. Beth's eyes scan the scene, she sees a severed finger next to a yellow marker to the right of the stable. Several other markers indicate other unrecognizable lumps of gore.

'Is it okay for me to come through?' she calls to Elliot.

He stops taking the pictures and looks at her.

'Stay left,' he says.

Beth hurries to his side. Then turns and looks directly into the stall: Hilary Gillian is not a pretty sight.

Beth feels the bile rising in the back of her throat.

Empty eye sockets.

Multiple stab wounds.

Blood.

The woman had been eviscerated too. It is almost an attempt to recreate a Jack the Ripper-style murder, but more horrific and less restrained than the Ripper had been known for.

'First blow happened at the stable door,' Elliot says. 'There's blood spatter that looks as though our perp struck upwards with an incapacitation blow. Then, she was attacked as she fell. Finally, she was dragged in here, dead or dying. Then laid out, like this. I think that's when the disembowelling happened and… the eyes.' Elliot swallows. He is usually composed but Beth can tell that this one has him rattled.

'My god. Is that barbed wire?' Beth says. 'She's tangled in it.'

'Razor wire. Dangerous stuff,' Elliot says.

Trying to divorce herself from the terrible sight by using her analytical training, Beth looks around the stall. There's a saddle resting over the partition between this stall and the next. Beth notes the victim's removed eyes sitting on top, facing the stall door as though watching them. It's the last straw. Beth gags, turns and runs. She makes it outside the stable and yanks off her mask, throwing up the McDonald's drive-through breakfast that the security detail had given her for the journey.

With her stomach empty, Beth takes a few minutes to breathe, before putting the mask back on. Then she returns inside.

'Sorry,' she says.

'No need to apologize. I did the same,' he says. 'This is the vilest thing I've ever seen.'

Beth leaves him to work while she goes away. Across the yard she sees a wooden-hut office. Inside is a girl and two boys.

Beth introduces herself to them.

'Which of you found her?' she asks.

'I did,' says the girl. 'I arrived first. Found the office open and the door to the stable was open. I assumed Hilary was inside so I went looking for her.'

Beth observes how green around the gills the poor kid looks. There'll be many nightmares before she gets over the trauma of what she's seen.

'What's your name?' she asks.

'Gemma White.'

Beth takes the names, addresses and details of the other stable hands. The two boys are Ritchie Campbell and Jonathan Deacon.

'Who was the last to leave last night?'

'I think I was,' says Ritchie. 'Around 7:30pm. She'd just tied up Princely and was about to groom him.'

Beth nods. 'Any of you know if she was expecting anyone last night?' Beth asks.

All three shake their heads.

'We need to let the horses out,' Gemma says. 'They are really distressed and they need mucking out.'

'You won't be allowed to do that for a while I'm afraid,' Beth says.

She sends the three of them outside for some fresh air while she looks around Hilary's office. There's a desk with a computer and telephone. A kettle and toaster sit on top of a small fridge and a filing cabinet by the door. On the walls are several framed pictures of a woman with different horses. One of which appears to be a magazine cutting. Beth reads the article and learns that this is Hilary with a sheik's racing horse. She takes the picture off the wall and looks closely at it. In the other photos it's hard to tell that Hilary has strawberry-blonde hair, but not in this one. Although she's in riding gear, she isn't wearing a hat and her hair looks as though it's been perfectly groomed for the photograph. She's pretty. She also looks a lot like the other murder victims.

Beth goes outside, taking the picture with her. She sees Gemma leaning on the paddock fence.

'Where was this taken?' she asks.

'Oh that was for *Hello* Magazine,' Gemma says. 'Sheik Imman and his wife at home. Hilary was asked to be part of the shoot. She said the Sheik was so pleased with how she'd trained his horse, he wanted to give the livery a boost.'

'Do you know where this was? The actual stable and yard?' Beth asks.

'The Grand National,' says Gemma. 'Last month.'

Beth looks back at the framed article. It says quite clearly where Hilary's livery yard is and under normal circumstances this would be a good advertisement. But Beth thinks in this case that possibly a bit of widely spread publicity could well have been the death of her.

Beth turns back to the office.

'She did get a new horse to train because of that,' says Gemma. 'Princely Sun.'

Beth stops and turns back. 'Is it in the stable?'

Gemma frowns, 'It should be. Stall four.'

Beth goes back to the stables. She's reluctant to go inside but pushes herself forward.

She reaches the fourth stall and looks inside. It's empty. She checks the horses in the other three and other than being slightly distressed, the animals look fine.

'Beth?' says Elliot.

'One of them's missing,' she says. 'A race horse called Princely Sun.'

Elliot frowns. 'Maybe this is about horse theft?'

'No,' Beth shakes her head.

She shows him the article and photograph.

'She's another lookalike then,' Elliot says.

'Yes. But the missing horse is strange,' says Beth.

Beth leaves the stable and returns again to the office. She opens the filing cabinet and sees files under several horse names. She flicks through until she finds Princely Sun. She pulls out the green folder and opens it. There are a few pictures inside of Hilary working with the horse. But nothing else.

'Gemma?' she calls from the office door.

Gemma comes to her.

'Where did Hilary keep records of the owners?'

'The filing cabinet. And probably on the computer too,' Gemma says.

'Do you have access?' Beth asks.

Gemma nods. She goes to the computer and tries to switch it on. Nothing happens.

They check that the machine is plugged in.

Beth goes to the security car and collects her bag. Inside she has a small canvas bag containing her lock picks and a few screwdrivers. She opens the back of the computer and discovers that the hard drive has been removed.

'What's wrong with it?' asks Gemma.

Beth doesn't answer.

Outside the mortuary van pulls up to take out the now bagged remains of Hilary Gillian. A further forensic team also stands by to bag and tag everything else they find. The computer will be taken, the files in the cabinet studied, but Beth already knows that any details of the horse's owner will have been removed.

Beth feels nauseous again. And an overwhelming sense of disgust and anger surges up into her chest. These deaths are getting out of hand, this is the worst yet. She wants to catch this killer. No one deserved to die like Hilary had. But how can they, when every way they turn evidence is going missing or was never left. Stifling down her wayward emotions, Beth goes outside. She sees one of Elliot's helpers standing by the van.

'We need to sweep the office,' she tells him. 'Take everything back with us for further scrutiny. Let's find something on this bastard. Please.'

The man nods, heading over to the office.

Beth watches as they load Hilary's remains into the van. Then she turns and walks away, pulling herself free of the crime-scene suit. Although her clothing was protected, Beth has an overpowering sensation of being contaminated. She can't wait to get back home to change her clothes and wash her hands several times, as if this will help to wash the sight of Hilary's corpse clean from her memory.

Chapter Thirty

MIA

With Freya in the front of the trolley, laughing and gurgling, Mia heads down the baby aisle. She finds the nappies she's looking for and slips a large pack of them under the trolley before moving on. The trolley is full with a week's worth of shopping and a few extra treats that they didn't need, but they all go towards making Mia feel a little more normal.

Mia pushes the trolley out of the aisle and makes her way to the nearest, and least busy, checkout. She joins the queue as the woman in front of her begins to load her shopping on the conveyor belt. There's a man on the checkout and he pulls the woman's shopping through the scanner so fast, that Mia begins to wonder if he's at the end of his shift and is in a hurry to close the till.

Mia starts to load the conveyor with her own shopping before she notices the woman behind her. The woman is stunning. She has white hair and tanned skin and is wearing a black linen jumpsuit. Mia observes that she is only carrying a basket with three items in.

'Would you like to go next?' Mia says. 'I've loads of shopping and I'm going to take ages.'

'That's so kind of you,' says the woman.

She has the trace of an accent. Mia can't place it but finds it sophisticated. She wonders how old she is because she has that classic, ageless beauty often found in mature models.

The woman moves around her, 'Are you sure?' she says.

'Of course. Please. It's not a problem,' Mia says.

'Your daughter is adorable,' the woman says.

'Thank you.'

'How old is she?' the woman asks.

'She's just over five months. Teething. But she's good at night,' Mia says, happy to talk about Freya.

The woman nods. She smiles at Freya.

'She's like you,' she says.

Mia smiles as this pleases her. She thanks the woman again. Ahead of them both, the checkout assistant is ringing up the final amount on the till for the first customer who is still loading her bags and refuses to be rushed.

'Can I help you pack?' asks the man on checkout.

'No thanks. I have a system!' says the woman.

Mia rolls her eyes at the white-haired woman, who shakes her head in silent agreement as she places her few items on the conveyor before Mia's shopping.

At last the first woman pays, and places her final bag into the trolley. But even then, she takes an extraordinarily long time to move away from the bottom of the till.

The white-haired woman is quicker. She pays and thanks Mia again, before hurrying away.

Mia continues to load the conveyor even as the overzealous checkout assistant gallops through her shopping.

Outside, Mia takes Freya out of the trolley and fastens her into her car seat, then she begins loading the shopping into the boot of her car. As she slams the boot closed, Mia notices a man standing by the trolley park. He looks over at her and then away again as though he doesn't wish to be observed.

Mia has a flash memory of worrying she had been followed the day before.

MI6 are watching over you.

Mia remembers Ben saying this, but not when. She quells the initial panic that the man brought up in her. *It's fine. He's MI6.* Then she locks the car, and pushes the trolley towards the bay. As she approaches the man walks away.

After stowing her trolley, Mia hurries back to the car.

'Are you all right?' a voice says.

Mia turns to see the white-haired woman standing near her car.

'Oh yes,' she glances at the retreating back of the man.

'He wasn't bothering you, was he?' the woman asks.

'No,' Mia says. 'It's fine.'

'I was just about to drive away and I saw you. I thought you looked… worried.'

'That's kind of you to check on me,' Mia says.

'Well one kindness deserves another,' she says.

'I'd better go. Freya needs feeding,' Mia says.

'What a lovely name,' says the woman. 'It's from Norse mythology, isn't it?'

Mia nods.

'Take care,' says the woman. Then she turns and walks away.

Mia gets into her car. She glances at Freya, safe and sound in her car seat.

'Yes. It is a lovely name for a very pretty girl,' she says to the baby.

Freya giggles as though Mia has just said the funniest thing in the world.

Chapter Thirty-One

MICHAEL

The new safe house is bigger than the last one and I'm not the only occupant. In fact, the place is a high-rise block of flats in a very run-down part of London.

'We'll set you up somewhere else tomorrow,' says one of the security men as they park the SUV outside the building. Not for the first time I wonder when I'll be able to return to my own apartment.

'This is a combined safe house. Sort of halfway until some of these people can be properly relocated,' explains the agent. 'This location is very "need to know" and so you have to forget being here after we leave tomorrow.'

'We? You guys are staying here tonight too?' I ask.

'Security Agent Martin's worried about you. Until we learn how much of a breach there's been, you're stuck with us.'

'Right. You'd better tell me your names then, since we are going to be mates for a while,' I say.

'I'm Steve. This is Den and the two guys in the front are Will and Joe.'

There are several other empty high rises. With doors and windows of the lower floors boarded up and warning signs plastered across them. The security team flank me as we get out of the car and walk to the building. It occurs to me how obvious they are being, but as I look around, I notice that this is the only occupied building in what appears to be a condemned area.

'There should be no one about, but we're even more cautious here, as by the empty location, we are somewhat exposed,' Steve says when he sees me looking around.

'When are they knocking it down?' I ask.

Steve shrugs.

'This building is secure. The small apartments are stocked for sudden arrivals and kept clean. It's not perfect, but the anonymity of the place works well for us.'

The reception area of the building is off-putting. Graffiti covers the walls and the lift doors. But when Den calls the lift using a key card that he waves before a scanner, the inside is clean and looks new.

'I take it the graffiti is a red herring,' I say.

Steve nods and as the lift ascends, I consider how much I don't know about what happens in other areas of MI5. Like witness protection programmes. But then, as Steve had said, a lot of this is 'need to know' and it wasn't an area I'd had to understand until I became at risk myself.

When we reach the tenth floor, Steve uses his card again on the scanner and the doors open onto a spotless corridor. I'm less surprised to see the passage looking clean and tidy, as the exterior of this building doesn't reflect the interior, which has been made very comfortable.

'Every floor requires a pass key to get onto it from the stairs,' Steve tells me. 'And of course, you need one to get in and out of the lift.'

He opens the door of the flat opposite the lift and ushers me inside.

The place is lit up with lamps in each room as though someone has come in and prepared it for my arrival. By the door is a small table and I see the pass key left for me there. Though it's unlikely I'll need it tonight.

'This is you for tonight. We'll give you your privacy but we'll be in the flat next door.'

Steve leaves, closing the door behind him.

I'm surprised to find all modern conveniences and nice furniture set out in this one-bedroom flat. I look at my watch and realize it's after ten. I'm tired and so, after getting a bottle of water from the fridge in the small galley kitchen, I make my way to the bedroom.

There I find the bedside lamp switched on and spare clothing – my size – left on top of the dresser. I look through the pile of clothes and find a T-shirt, two pairs of boxer shorts and a new white shirt still in the packaging. All of the clothing is new and still has labels inside.

In the bathroom, clean towels and some accessories have been left for me to use.

I strip off my suit and hang it up in the bedroom as I'll need it for tomorrow. Then I take a shower. Afterwards I drag the T-shirt and a new pair of boxers on.

I yawn. Then I climb into the bed. It's comfortable. And

despite being taken, once again, into a new environment, I feel safe. It's unlikely the Network or anyone else will be able to find me here.

On the bedside cabinet I notice that the lamp has a phone docking station. I place my phone on charge and switch off the lamp before turning over on my side.

Even though I'm tired, the events of the day encroach on my mind, pushing back the sleep that I really want. Bringing me here feels like something of an overreaction on Ray's part. Yet I know it's necessary until we bring down the Network once and for all. I hadn't argued with him about this move of location, because it had been one of Ray's stipulations when I declined to go into the witness protection programme with Mia and Ben. Ray had only agreed to allow me to continue working for Archive on the promise that I take the protection offered. I knew he hadn't wanted to lose me from the team even as I tried to bargain with him for my freedom. But Ray had been stubborn in his refusal to budge on this point. I'd been left with little choice but to defer to him in regards to my safety. And so far, the Network hadn't come after me. Or been able to find me thanks to these precautions. It also meant I was able to continue doing my job, which was still a very important part of my life.

Unable to sleep, I turn the lamp on again. I get out of the bed and go back into the kitchen. I haven't eaten since lunchtime and I find some fresh bread and make myself some toast.

Everything in the fridge is new and sealed, and I suspect, anything opened will have to be replaced for the next occupant of this apartment. For this reason, I don't open the jar of marmalade that's in there because it would be wasteful for just one night in this place.

In one of the cupboards I find some tumblers and some mini-bar bottles of whisky. I open one and pour it into a glass. In the living room there is a modestly sized flat-screen television. I switch it on and discover there are several free channels.

Sipping the whisky, I watch the end of the news until, feeling that pull of sleep tugging at the corners of my eyes again, I stumble off to bed.

Like most nights I dream of Neva.

We've just left Mendez's room, but the doctor wasn't present when Neva and I were there. We were talking to the trainer, Tracey. As I come out of the room the conversation slips from my mind and I can no longer remember it.

We are children, but we don't play, we don't scream. Instead we walk back down the corridor and to the large hallway.

At the door I see a man in a chauffeur's uniform. I should know his name but it eludes me that day, just like the reason I'm here at the house again. At the sight of the man, Neva takes my hand. I look at her. She's the only one here who ever touches me and it seems so important that she does.

'Come back to me,' she whispers. Then she releases my hand and turns and walks away.

There's a blur of time and another day at the house. I'm alone as I walk through the hallway. No chauffeur. No Mendez and no Tracey.

Mr Beech comes out of his office then. He's carrying a cake. Behind him, Tracey and Mendez smile and clap.

'Happy birthday, Michael,' Beech says.

There are fifteen candles on the cake. I blow them out like any normal teenager but I know I'm not normal. And neither is this house. No. There's something very wrong about all of it.

'This is your heritage,' Mr Beech says. 'One day soon, it will all be yours.'

Later, outside, Neva meets me. I've brought my piece of cake out to share with her. We nibble at it together, huddled at the back of the garage.

'You have to survive this place,' she tells me. 'We both do.'

I'm more afraid for her than I am for myself. I am, after all, chosen and Neva is merely one of Beech's cannon fodder assassins.

'You'll forget me when you've gone,' she says. 'You always do. And I'll forget you.'

I deny it but know it's the truth. Most of the time, away from here, I'm asleep. I'm only ever 'real' when I come back.

Another time slip leads me back home: Mum, with her trademark flour smudge. Dad with his passion for gardening.

'You have to work hard, Michael,' Dad says. 'You have to be recruited.'

I apply myself to my studies just as I'm supposed to. Opposite me, studying just as hard, is my sister Mia.

'You both have to be the best,' Mum says.

Chapter Thirty-Two

NEVA

Neva is in a dilemma. After investigating Kritta further, and with more feedback from Elbakitten, she's now certain that Mia and Michael are in danger. She contacts a source that can provide her with a new identity, but before she can go and take the pictures for another passport, she learns on the dark web that the forger she usually uses has been raided. He's now facing a long time in prison. There are others of course, but the delay will cost so much time that she decides to risk an alternative.

Neva spots a possible candidate laughing and drinking in a riverside bar. The girl is her height and build. She's in her early 20s and appears to be travelling with a group of people. The main attraction is the heavy goth make-up that Neva can replicate and will help her disguise who she really is on airport cameras. She watches who the girl interacts with and there is no obvious sexual attachment to any of the other members of her party. Then she follows them back to the hostel where they are staying.

After some enquires, she learns they are a group of students travelling from London. It all seems to be falling right into place. The trick, of course, will be to separate her from the others without causing alarm. After that she watches their movements at a distance, looking for the right moment to take the girl away from her friends and get possession of her passport.

After a few days of tracking them, Neva follows the group, a mixture of young men and women, to a known gay bar not far from the red-light district.

Neva has been studying how the girl moves, how she walks. With the right wig, Neva knows she could use her identity. At the club she watches her knocking back shots.

Neva buys herself a drink at the bar and then wanders through the crowd of people. The disguise she's wearing includes a fake septum ring and heavy sweeps of eyeliner along with black lipstick. Her fair hair is covered with a long black wig that's crimped and backcombed. She fits in at this club, because anything goes here.

As the evening progresses, Neva avoids contact with anyone in the girl's group as she observes them, keeping her distance. She plans to make a move on the girl when the moment is right and she's tipsy enough to make a new friend. Then she notices the girl accepting a drink from a woman in her 40s. Neva watches as they start hanging out together, dancing and drinking – all of which the woman pays for. They end the night with a full-on snog on the dance floor.

Later, the girl departs the club with the woman she's met. The group of students she's with barely notice her absence and this tells Neva it's not the first time she's abandoned them for a casual liaison. It gives her confidence in the decision she's made to choose her.

She follows the girl and the other woman back to a hotel. It's a lot nicer than the hostel the girl is staying in and she seems wowed by it as they enter the reception.

Neva follows them inside and gets in the lift as well. The woman takes the girl up to the third floor of the hotel. Neva exits behind them, and watches to see what room they go to. She passes them and pretends to look for her key for another room down the corridor. When they've gone into the room, she heads back downstairs and goes to the bar. There she asks for a bottle of Champagne, two glasses and a bucket of ice. She pays cash and takes them with her.

Back in the lift, Neva returns to the third floor. She makes her way to the service closet, picks the lock and goes inside. As she hoped, she finds one of the maid-service uniforms on a coat hanger. From her purse she removes face wipes and takes all of the make-up off her face as well as the fake septum ring. She removes the black wig, brushes her hair, and ties it up into a messy bun. Then she changes into the uniform.

She pops the cork of the Champagne and pours some of it away. From her bag she removes a flask and she pours some of its contents into the Champagne bottle.

Carrying the Champagne in the ice bucket, and the two glasses, she goes to the door of the woman's room and knocks. She's banking on them being too drunk and stoned to question why the bottle is already open, or the fact that she's in a cleaner's uniform and not a waitress's.

'Compliments of the manager,' Neva says holding out the bucket when the woman answers. She sways in the doorway; her pupils are dilated and Neva's assumption of the partying that's happening in the room is correct.

'Wow! That's kind of him,' slurs the woman. She takes the bucket and glasses from Neva.

'Look what I got us,' the woman says. 'Champagne!'

Neva smiles as the door closes.

The sedative will take a while to work but Neva is patient. She goes back to the service closet and changes back into her own clothing. Then she waits.

It's two in the morning before she enters the bedroom. Although all is quiet, the lamps are still on in the room. It looks as though they collapsed unconscious after downing the Champagne. *Good.*

Neva picks up the girl's discarded purse and rifles through it. As she knew would be the case, her passport is there. It's not the sort of item you leave in a hostel while you go out drinking.

Neva opens the passport and learns the girl's name for the first time. She's Adrienne Margaret Renfall. A very sophisticated name for what appears to be a rebellious student. She checks on Adrienne and the woman; they are unconscious and probably will be for hours. But Neva needs them to be unaware of the passport theft until she has reached London. She ponders giving them another dose of the drug because it's uncertain how long they will be under for.

In the bathroom she finds a line of cocaine on a small mirror. She brings it into the bedroom and places it on the woman's side of the bed. Hopefully the party will continue when they both wake up.

She takes out the flask again from her purse, and puts a few drops of the sedative in two glasses of water, which she places at each side of the bed as a precaution. A known side effect of the drug is thirst. She hopes this will send the pair of them back off when they come round and drink the water. But it feels like she's leaving everything to chance: something she doesn't like to do.

She contemplates killing them. The old her wouldn't have a problem with that, but the new her does: neither of these women deserve to die.

No. The best guarantee of her exit from Amsterdam and return to the United Kingdom is for her to get there as soon as possible.

She opens Adrienne's handbag again and takes out her credit card. Then she goes online on her burner phone and books the earliest flight she can find to London. She finds one at 8am to Luton. She hopes that this will give her enough time before Adrienne raises any alarm that her passport has been stolen and her card has been used fraudulently.

Neva places the 'Do Not Disturb' sign on the door. By then it is almost three in the morning.

She goes back to her apartment near the river. Changing her clothes, she then chops the long black wig down into the razor-cut style that the girl wears.

Once Neva's done this, she takes her time applying the make-up, copying Adrienne's look from some pictures she'd snapped of her on her phone.

When she's ready she packs a small overnight case with her laptop and a few essentials, as well as some English cash. At 5:30am she makes her way to the airport.

When she arrives at Luton, Neva abandons Adrienne's passport and her disguise in the airport toilet once she's through customs. Then she starts using her Dutch identity and cards again.

With her natural, strawberry-blonde hair scraped back into a ponytail, she makes her way into Central London via train to St Pancras. While she's travelling, she books herself a last-minute hotel in Soho because she needs a base to work from.

The journey from Luton only takes thirty-three minutes and so Neva is soon leaving the station, keeping her head down, and avoiding all of the cameras there that she knows about. Outside she joins the black-cab taxi-rank queue.

When she reaches the front of the line, she approaches the next black cab and tells the driver her destination. He gives her an odd look through his rear-view mirror as she climbs into the back. As they pull away the driver starts to ask her questions about her trip. Neva is deliberately vague in her answers.

'Look… be careful who you talk to here,' the taxi driver says. 'There's been a few murders.'

'Really?' Neva says, speaking with a Dutch accent.

'Yeah. Girls who… look a bit like you, to be honest,' he says. 'It's why I'm asking what you're doing here. I saw on the news that an Irish girl might have been groomed by the killer first…'

As they stop at some traffic lights, he passes her a newspaper through the screen between them. 'Front page,' he says.

Neva finds herself looking at the pictures of four women. The Irish girl the driver had mentioned had been visiting London for the first time. There was an older woman – a divorcee, a business woman and a livery stable owner. All of whom have nothing in common except for their physical appearance.

Neva speed reads the article and when they reach her destination, she thanks the driver, giving him an American-style tip of 20 per cent.

She registers at her accommodation. Then, because the driver knows the address, she immediately checks out. She goes on her app and finds alternative accommodation elsewhere. When she's finally settled, she changes into jeans, T-shirt and trainers. She places a woollen hat over her hair to disguise her appearance and then she heads off, looking for all intents and purposes like a tourist. By then it's late afternoon.

She makes her way to London Bridge and to the building where Michael works. At this point she isn't sure how she's going to get inside, but she knows she has to see Michael and try and talk to him face to face. For this reason, she plans to be around when he leaves work that night.

Chapter Thirty-Three

JEWEL

She sees her next kill from a distance. A shining beacon of golden hair that glows in the sunlight. Jewel's always detested the colour – how others rave about 'strawberry' blondes. There was a black-and-white movie once made called that. *The Strawberry Blonde.* Rita Hayworth starred in it, and the posters showed her with *red* hair, not the almost-blonde, not-quite-red colour strawberry is.

It is rare as a natural colour, Jewel knows that. But so many women choose to dye it in.

Perhaps this one erred more on the blonde and less on the red in truth. But finding that exact match was impossible. Jewel could only find close or near unless she came face to face with the original wearer and that only happened on one occasion. It was a bit of a shock being that close to *her* after so long. She hadn't recognized Jewel, which was a relief because then her cover would have been blown. Jewel was certain that *she* had not thought of her for a long time.

She hates her even now.

Fae they'd called her back then, later she'd become Neva. But Jewel had heard about the rename. It had happened after she'd been banished from the house. After she'd failed to prove she was the best. Then Jewel had been returned to Mother and her training had intensified as a punishment for that fiasco. Even now, she doesn't understand why Mother had tried her out in the house. Maybe she had wanted to test her prodigy against someone she considered the best.

But for now, Jewel has escaped the clutches of the château and Mother. Money has given her that autonomy. Like Neva had done before her, Jewel has saved her payments, living frugally as she accumulated her own wealth. Money was power. Money was independence.

Mother had wanted it all for herself, of course. She sent Jewel after the Syrian heir, Tehrin. He was another mark in a list of many that Jewel had played and stolen from for the sake of building the Almunazama's funds. Mother had spent years growing the conglomerate, hoping it would rival Beech's Network and ultimately take over his assets. That was all until Beech's death brought about the epiphany that Mother could take over the Network itself, merging the Almunazama with it to create an ultimate and unstoppable force.

Jewel had been working as an insider for Mother's enemies. She'd whored for her but she was smart and observant: she'd learned a lot about their dealings as well as Mother's. She'd taken it all on board. Hiding behind her calm veneer. Wearing the mask that Mother trusted. Until the time came for her to skip away. New identity. New life. Swiss bank full of the cash she'd skimmed off the top of the various thefts – bolstered up by the four million she'd obtained from Tehrin. It had been easy. And she deserved the money more than Mother did. She'd earned it.

But Mother hasn't come after her. So far. This is a surprise. Perhaps Mother thinks she is still working for her under cover. Or perhaps she just doesn't care. Whatever the reason, Jewel sees her new freedom as confirmation of the lies that Mother tells to all of her children. *She doesn't love us.* We aren't individuals. We are her personal army. Jewel is just one soldier among many. Not even worth chasing down when she goes AWOL. It's all so disappointing.

Jewel brings her mind back to the latest victim. She's a teacher at a primary school. Newly married. She reminds Jewel of an actress she once saw in a film – or a TV series. She can't remember which because it's not important. But she was pretty and perky and slender just like this one. Cassandra Clementine has that quality. Even her name sounds like it belongs to a film star. She's way too beautiful to spend all day with annoying children. No, she needs to become something else. An icon. A saint.

A corpse.

Jewel watches Cassandra from a car across the road from the woman's house. The husband left some time ago. Now, Cassandra comes out. She's carrying a rucksack and a lunch box. She climbs into her car and drives away.

Jewel doesn't follow. She already knows where Cassandra works. She gets out of her car and crosses the road.

On this street, several of the neighbours have cameras directed down their driveways. Jewel knows where all of them land. She's already hacked them through their various Wi-Fi networks. Security, for those who understand how it works, is one of the simplest things to disable especially when your target has no idea it can be done. And most ordinary people have no clue about these sorts of things beyond believing they are safe once the systems are installed.

She walks up Cassandra's drive, knowing that she isn't being observed.

She enters the house with a clone key. She'd copied it from Cassandra during an open day at the primary school. Jewel had been there, pretending to look around with a view to sending her daughter. No one had questioned the fact that a 26-year-old had a child of 4. Half the mothers there were younger than her.

Cassandra was the reception class teacher and she'd been warm and friendly. She'd left her house and car keys casually on the desk in her classroom. Jewel had taken them after Cassandra became distracted by another parent. Then she'd gone to the bathroom and pressed the house key into a ready prepared container of putty. After that, she returned the keys to the reception claiming she'd found them in the toilet.

Inside Cassandra's house, Jewel disables the alarm system and walks in. It's a character house, on an old street. Victorian and therefore big. The hallway is tiled in a tradition style that surprises Jewel – Cassandra appears modern in dress and behaviour.

Jewel walks around the house, admiring the character and looking at Cassandra and Ian's life together. Very cosy. Very normal.

It makes Jewel angry. In fact, it makes her furious but she holds it all inside, determined her rage won't leak out this time.

She goes upstairs and finds the couple's bedroom. It is far different from the rest of the house. There's a swan-style superking bed in the centre. The headboard is plush grey velvet with diamantes and seems decadent compared to the more ordinary furnishing downstairs. There's a dressing table with a Hollywood-style mirror and two matching mirrored chests of drawers. When Jewel opens the drawers in them, she discovers one contains Cassandra's lingerie, nightwear and sweats. The other is Ian's underwear, socks and T-shirts. There's an antique feel about the furniture, but all of these items are new and high end. It tells Jewel a lot about Cassandra and it matches the lifestyle Jewel thinks the woman should have.

Jewel knows that this stunning, expensive and beautiful room must be the stage where Cassandra will be set.

It will be many hours before Cassandra returns, she always leaves the school early on a Friday, and, like every other Friday, Ian will arrive home late after going for a drink with work colleagues. It all gives Jewel time to prepare the room.

In one of the other bedrooms, Jewel finds a free-standing antique mirror. She brings it into the master bedroom and positions it at the bottom of the bed. The bed is covered with a grey velvet duvet that seems to change colour in the light from the bedroom window and sometimes appears to have purple tones. But Jewel wants to see more colour on the future resting place of Cassandra Clementine. A beautiful death for a beautiful girl. She walks around the house looking for something that might work. Then she glances out of the window and into Cassandra's back garden. Her eyes fall on the rose beds. Yellow, white, pink and purple roses are in full bloom.

She goes downstairs, opens the back door and slips outside into the garden. She looks at the roses then goes back inside the house for something to put them in. In the kitchen she searches through the drawers until she finds a canvas bag with washing pegs inside. She tips the pegs into the drawer and takes the bag outside. There she systematically pulls the heads off all of the roses.

As she turns back towards the house, she catches sight of an old woman looking into the garden from the upstairs window of the house next door. She goes back inside the house, and places the canvas bag on the kitchen counter top.

After that she goes next door.

When Jewel has dealt with the witness to her presence at Cassandra's – a detail she barely thinks about because she doesn't want it to distract her from her plans – she goes back into Cassandra's house.

She takes the canvas bag upstairs and tears the petals off

the rose heads, scattering them in a flow of colour and scent onto the bed.

It looks gorgeous when she's finished and now, although she hasn't decided exactly how she will display Cassandra, she is excited for her return. She tries to envisage the final piece of art, all blending in with that last flash of red. It's going to be magnificent and this time she won't lose her concentration.

For a moment she recalls Hilary's death. It was not glorious. It was not well planned. Jewel had lost her cool too soon. She hadn't even been planning on killing her there and then. It just happened. Afterwards she'd tried to regroup. Tried to turn the mess back into art. She'd done a reasonable job, considering.

Jewel turns her mind back to Cassandra. How will she react when she sees the bed? Will she appreciate that Jewel is giving her a beautiful death? For surely someone as lovely as Cassandra must crave a magnificent end.

When she's finished, Jewel sits in a chair by the bed, as she's done in many hotel rooms. She switches on the television and finds a channel showing old movies while she waits. Not long now. Just a few hours. And then, Cassandra will belong to her.

Chapter Thirty-Four

CASSANDRA

Cassandra is tired as she pulls her car back into the driveway. It's been a long week and she's glad it's the weekend. Now she's looking forward to a quiet evening in, because Ian always eats out and goes for drinks with his work colleagues on Fridays. It's the one night she enjoys to herself in the week, and it's a good time to rest her mind so that she can enjoy the next two days off.

Half term is only a week away and Cassandra is looking forward to the time off the treadmill of the school year. Tired of concentrating, the reception children are already fractious, as they always are at this time of year. They need to be wild and free for a week, then there will be the final build-up to the summer holidays. Cassandra herself is as weary of this group of children as they are of her. There are always at least two children in every year group that test a teacher and Cassandra's tolerance is lower by the end of the school year. The final week will be exhausting, especially as the headmistress doesn't permit her teachers to put DVDs on until the last day.

Cassandra thinks about the class as she gets out of the car. She'll be glad to see this particular group move up to year one. The new reception kids always take at least the first term before they grow in confidence enough to be difficult. It's something of a reprieve that Cassandra enjoys year after year.

She retrieves her holdall and lunchbox from the boot and then locks the car.

As she walks towards the front door, she glances at the house on the left looking for Miss Mayberry: the old spinster next door is always curtain twitching in her somewhat run-down Victorian property. But for once, Cassandra doesn't see the old woman at the window. She shrugs. *Crazy old bat! She's always gawping at me!*

The alarm doesn't beep as she enters the house. Cassandra pauses in the hallway because she is certain she'd set it. She closes the door and takes a look at the alarm keypad under the stairs. The alarm is switched off.

She had been a little distracted that morning and it's not the first time she's forgotten to set the alarm. *At least Ian isn't home and won't know!* He wouldn't go on about it much, but he would remind her that only last week someone in the next street was broken into and robbed while they were at work.

She could hear him now, 'Our insurance will be null and void because the alarm wasn't set, Cas.'

Cassandra hangs her rucksack up on the hooks under the stairs. Then she makes her way down the long hallway, past the living room and dining room and goes into the kitchen.

She's unpacking her lunch box, throwing away the food she didn't get chance to eat as she was marking all lunchtime, when she notices that one of the kitchen drawers is slightly open. She likes her home tidy and drawers left like this are a pet hate. She pushes it closed. *It must have been Ian.* He often forgot to close doors and drawers and turn lights off.

Since they'd been married Cassandra was finding it a learning curve living with him full time. Before they bought this house, and finally tied the knot, they'd each had their own separate flats. Even though they were usually together at least four nights a week, it was funny how his untidiness hadn't bothered her much then. Perhaps she'd always thought it was because both of their places were a bit cluttered anyway. But now, with all this space, Ian still can't manage to put things away. Toolboxes were often left out for her to trip over, washing wasn't always dropped into the basket as it should be. His underwear drawer was frequently left untidy, even though Cassandra straightened it up once a week when she put the clean washing away. A job, she reminded him, she hadn't signed up for.

But for all of his untidy ways, Cassandra loved him and she was happy they were married. Most of the furnishings in the house were far from what she aspired to. Buying the place had stretched their finances, even after they'd sold both of their apartments. And so, they'd made do with most of their old furniture, keeping their best items and disposing of the rest. But one thing Cassandra had saved up for was the new bedroom furniture. Their bedroom had to be a lovely retreat. And she'd always liked the mirrored furniture, with its somewhat antique-looking chic.

Ian laughed when he saw what she'd bought.

'It's a boudoir!' he'd said.

But he didn't mind really and Cassandra always got what she wanted in the end because he really liked making her happy. Plus, he had to agree that the superking bed was comfortable and they slept better together now that they weren't squeezed into a standard double.

Cassandra washes her hands after stowing the lunchbox in the dishwasher. She always feels somewhat grubby after being in school and her habit is to shower and change into comfortable clothes when she gets home, throwing her school clothes into the washing basket. On Fridays she always runs a bath and soaks in it, reading a paperback because she rarely gets time for this during the week.

She goes upstairs now, and enters the main family bathroom. This room is probably the one that sold the house to her. It was already decorated in lovely black and white tiles, Victorian style, but modernized with a border of glittery pearlized tiles dividing the lower black from the upper white tiles. The bath is glorious, big and comfortable. The one addition that Cassandra had made was a small mirrored cabinet at the side of the bath. The drawers contain sweet-smelling soaps and Cassandra likes to place a glass of wine and her phone on the top while she bathes.

Now Cassandra tips a generous amount of bubble bath in and sets the water running into the bath. Then she goes back downstairs and pours a glass of chilled white wine into a glass. She takes a big sip of the wine before heading back upstairs.

When she opens the bedroom door and sees the bed full of petals, the alarm being off and the drawer left open in the kitchen starts to make sense. *Ian has been home. He's trying to be romantic.*

Cassandra finds herself smiling as she walks into the room. Then she frowns. *Why the mirror? Oh... he's trying to spice things up already!* That's not a good sign.

She approaches the bed, unaware that the door is closing behind her.

Cassandra looks in the mirror and sees the bed fully reflected in the glass, from the corner of her eye she notices a figure standing by the door. As she turns to look, a woman in black barrages into her. She's thrown down onto the bed. Some of the petals bounce away onto the floor and then the knife slashes down carving a line through Cassandra's cheek. She yelps as the knife withdraws. Frantic stabs pierce Cassandra over and over in a frenzied attack before she even has time to fight back, all she can do is raise her hands in an attempt to protect herself.

She's in shock as her attacker begins to position her on the bed. Blood loss and fear have made her too weak to move, but she can see herself, reflected in the mirror surrounded by the petals. Her blood adding another dimension to the collage.

American Beauty, she thinks as her assailant drapes more petals over her. She had watched the film with Ian the other month, and the DVD cover showed the strawberry-blonde star, Mena Suvari, lying on a bed of red rose petals.

'Why?' she croaks as the woman stands over her now.

'Because you look like *her*,' she says.

The knife comes down again: a tearing sweep across her throat. In the mirror Cassandra sees her life's blood splash upwards, over the pale-grey feature wall behind the bed that she'd tortured herself about. The red spray drips downwards towards the headboard, as though by artist's design.

'You look so perfect,' says the woman. 'Can you see it?'

Cassandra stares at herself. She feels cold, and scared and then, at last, numb enough to feel nothing more.

Chapter Thirty-Five

ANNALISE

After following her home from the supermarket, Annalise watches as Mia lifts Freya out of her car seat. Mia takes the baby inside, then comes out a few moments later. She opens the boot of the car and begins to remove shopping bags. She deposits the first few in the hallway, then comes back for more.

When Annalise is about to get out of the car, she notices a young man approaching Mia. Curious about the boy, and ever prepared, Annalise takes a listening device out of her glove box and directs it at Mia's house.

'Need help, Mrs Charter?' the boy asks.

'Hey Jack. No thanks, I've just finished.' Mia slams the boot shut.

'Let me know if you need anything,' he says.

'Be… Brody… mentioned getting you to do the lawn again,' Mia says. 'Are you free this afternoon as the weather is going to stay dry?'

Jack nods. 'I'll come over at two if that works for you, as I have Mr Bentley's to do first.'

'That's great!'

Mia goes inside and Annalise watches Jack walk away. She waits until the boy is out of sight before she gets out of the car and walks towards the house. Then she knocks on the door.

Mia opens the door a short time later, she has the chain on the door. She frowns when she recognizes Annalise from the supermarket.

'Why are you…?' Mia says.

'Hello,' Annalise says. 'It's time we had a talk. *Mangler. Manic. Network.*'

Mia goes still. Her eyelids flicker and a slight frown crosses her forehead. As the words sink in, her face relaxes and her eyes go blank.

'Step back, take off the chain and let me inside,' the woman says.

Mia opens the door properly and Annalise enters. Annalise closes the door behind her.

'Where's the baby?' Annalise says.

'In the living room,' Mia answers. Her mouth moves slowly and the words come out as though they are difficult to form.

Annalise walks to the living room. She finds Freya on a play mat with a baby gym over her. As though the little girl knows that something is wrong, she begins to cry.

'Fr… ey… a,' says Mia from the hallway but she doesn't come in and she doesn't move from where she's standing by the door.

'Your mothering instinct is strong,' Annalise says. 'But there's nothing to worry about. I'm not going to hurt her, or you. I'm just going to give you back your knowledge of the Network. Come in here and sit down.'

As though her limbs are semi-paralysed, Mia begins to walk towards the living room.

When she is inside, Annalise notices her turn her head and look at the baby.

'Sit down,' she says.

Mia sinks to the floor by Freya.

'Not there. Come and sit on the sofa,' Annalise says.

Mia gets up off the floor and goes over to the sofa. She sits down, but her eyes remain on Freya.

'Look at me,' says Annalise.

Mia turns her head to Annalise, but Annalise notices she is fighting her conditioning.

'Mangler. Manic. Network,' Annalise says again.

Mia's demeanour changes. Her body relaxes more and she looks directly now at Annalise.

'I'm listening,' she says.

'You belong to the Network and therefore me,' says Annalise. 'Do you remember your training?'

'Yes,' Mia answers.

'You are going to listen very carefully. I have a job for you.'

'I'm listening,' says Mia again.

Annalise sits down next to Mia and begins to give her instructions. After half an hour, she stands.

Mia follows Annalise into the hallway and opens the front door.

Annalise steps outside.

'Go about your day as normal now and forget I was here,' says Annalise. 'Network. Manic. Mangler,' she says.

Mia blinks and smiles at Annalise. 'How nice to see you again.'

Mia nods. She closes the door as Annalise turns and walks away to her car.

Back in the car, Annalise looks back at Mia's house. Then she takes out her mobile phone. She dials.

'Mother?' says a male voice on the other end of the phone.

'Jonah. It appears that Kritta has told me the truth. But don't kill her yet, I still have to see if Mia will carry out my instructions. Are your team in place?'

'Yes Mother,' says Jonah.

'Good. Continue surveillance.'

Annalise hangs up the phone and starts the engine of her car just as Jack Harman arrives at Mia's house with the lawn mower.

She watches the boy, wondering if he's someone to be concerned about. Then as she sees another neighbour pass him and stop to chat, she dismisses him as no one of importance. He's just a kid after all, trying to earn some spending money.

She drives away as Jack fires up the lawn mower and sets to work on Mia's front lawn.

As she drives out of the street, Annalise's phone rings. She pulls over and answers.

'Hello, Mother,' says a familiar female voice.

'How is your assignment going?' Annalise asks.

'I gave her Eldon Fracks,' the woman says. 'She went to him and I'm pretty certain that he pointed her in your direction. She gave me a list of names he'd provided. All the committee members and she's asked me to find their locations.'

'Excellent work!' Annalise says. 'I knew I could trust you.'

'What should I do about Fracks?' she asks.

'Nothing. I want you to stay on your assignment. Fracks' knowledge has been useful to us, but he knows too much. I'll send someone else to take care of him,' Annalise says.

'As you wish,' she says. 'What about Neva?'

'Keep helping her. Eventually curiosity or memory will bring her home,' Annalise says.

'And what then?' asks the operative. 'She doesn't know who she is. We mustn't forget she's dangerous.'

'Let me worry about that,' says Annalise.

Chapter Thirty-Six

BETH

Beth turns over in bed to find Elliot gone. She glances at her watch and notices it is almost midnight. He'd met her back at her house that night and they'd cooked together and eventually hit the sack around 10:30pm. Beth had indulged in half a bottle of wine, but was unusually tired. She'd drifted off while Elliot was still in the bathroom brushing his teeth.

Beth switches on the bedside lamp. She gets up, pulls on her robe and goes in search of Elliot. She hears his voice drift up the stairs as she reaches the landing.

'She's asleep,' Elliot says. 'No… not a thing…'

Beth pauses and listens at the top of the stairs. She finds herself frowning as she wonders who Elliot is talking to.

'There's another body,' he says. 'That's five now.'

There is a long silence while Elliot listens to the person on the other end of the phone.

When she returned to London from Newmarket a few days ago, Beth was told about the multiple bugs Michael found and the subsequent cleansing of their office that followed. After that there were a series of interviews. On Monday, all members of the team were subjected to polygraph tests to see if they could find the mole. Beth hadn't been concerned about this as she knew she hadn't done anything wrong, but one of the questions Ray asked was if she had any doubts about anyone else. She'd said 'no'. But she'd been lying because she openly accused Ray of spying on them all to Michael.

But it isn't just Ray she is worried about now.

As she listens to the one side of Elliot's call, a new anxiety creeps into Beth's mind. Who is Elliot anyway?

He's been in her life such a short time and he'd come on full pelt straight away. It isn't something she thinks about too much because when she does, she feels this same unease. Beth tries to dismiss these qualms again. It was, of course, a coincidence that the former pathologist had taken ill. Cancer she'd heard. When Elliot took over his job though, Beth fell straight into his arms with barely any hesitation. Elliot excited her and she liked feeling this way. Some would say she was rebounding following her split with Callum, but Beth knows this isn't true. Elliot is the most interesting person she's come across in a while, plus, she'd thought he was a safe relationship because they both work for MI5.

'I'll let you know what I find out, but I have to get over there now,' Elliot says.

She hears him hang up. Beth returns to the bedroom, gets back in bed and turns off the light before Elliot comes back upstairs.

'Beth?' he says from the doorway.

'Is something wrong?' she says sitting up as though she's just been jerked awake. She reaches again for the lamp.

'Just got the call to go to a crime scene. Ray asked if you could go over there too.'

'Sure,' Beth says. 'Do we know anything about it?'

'Another body. Looks like the same killer. As usual it'll be a need-to-know basis that MI5 are there, so the locals will appear to be running the show.'

'That's two in a matter of days,' Beth says. 'The killer is losing the plot.'

She gets out of the bed and begins to pull some clothes on. Elliot picks up his discarded jeans and T-shirt from her dressing table stool.

When they are both dressed, Elliot picks up his phone to make another call.

'Who're you ringing? Beth asks.

'Got to get the team motivated and over there,' he says. 'I don't have any equipment with me, so I need to make sure they bring it.'

'Oh, right,' she says.

She observes that he goes out of the room to make the call, but doesn't listen in. Instead she goes downstairs, opens the front door, and goes to talk to the security detail posted outside her house.

The driver in the vehicle gets out of his car when he sees her come out. 'Everything okay?' he asks.

Beth explains the call to the crime scene.

'We'll take you both,' he says. 'Safer that way.'

Beth goes back inside the house and finds Elliot on the phone in the kitchen.

'Hold on a second,' he says to the person on the line. 'Beth?'

'We've got a ride as they have to stay with me,' she says nodding towards the front door.

'Good,' says Elliot. 'Right, so we'll need crime-scene suits for myself and Security Agent Cane as well. Okay Pam. We're about forty minutes away.'

Elliot finishes his phone call and Beth picks up her house keys as they go back out to the security team outside. She sets her new house alarm and locks up. Then she joins Elliot in the back of the car.

'Sorry about this,' Beth says to the two security men.

'At least we have something to do,' the driver says. 'I'm always up for security on a crime scene.'

As the car sets off, Beth glances at Elliot who is staring at his phone as though reading a text message. He begins to tap a reply and then presses send.

She doesn't ask him who he's texting, but she experiences a nervous sickly feeling in the pit of her stomach. Can she really trust Elliot? They barely know each other in the scheme of things. And it's not the first time she's woken to find him gone in the night to take a call from someone.

'You're quiet,' Elliot says.

'Sorry. Still waking up. Tell me what Ray said about the crime scene,' Beth says.

Chapter Thirty-Seven

MICHAEL

'I didn't think you'd be here,' says Elliot as he and Beth pass through the wall of uniformed and plain-clothes police outside.

'I've just arrived,' I say.

I'm wearing my crime-scene suit but not a facemask as I was talking to the victim's husband in the kitchen. Ian Clementine is in such a state that we've sent for a family friend who plans to take him into their home while we do what needs to be done. It's no surprise he's in shock. Who wouldn't be when they come home and find their wife murdered?

'Have you seen the body yet?' Elliot asks.

'No one but homicide and the cop that responded to Clementine's hysterical 999 call has seen her. I was waiting for you,' I say.

Beth comes into the house suited up.

'Hi,' she says. 'I'm glad you're here Mike. I thought they'd want to keep you safe and locked away still, though.'

'They tried,' I say. 'I saw the Newmarket report. I wish I'd been at the scene too, but your account was great Beth.'

'Shall we go and have a look?' Elliot says.

I nod, and then put my surgical mask in place.

We climb the stairs and go into Ian and Cassandra's bedroom.

The first thing that greets me is colour. There is a red arc of blood splashed up above the headboard, and the bed is soaked. Cassandra's face has been mutilated on one side. Perhaps by accident, but it looks purposeful.

'Jesus,' says Beth beside me.

Her eyes are open. And as I advance, going around the free-standing mirror that's been posed at the bottom of the bed, it looks to me as though Cassandra is staring at herself in the glass from her position in the bed.

'Our perp has upped their game. This is something very different from the last one,' Elliot says.

'Is it though?' I say. 'This is a… display. All of the deaths have been that to a certain degree. Though the first two were less focused than this one and so it wasn't as obvious. Sinead was drugged, placed in the bath, and then her wrists were cut. The water was tainted by her blood. Lizzie was staked out in her shed. Her femoral artery cut. I had noticed the blood spatter in the shed, as though the perp had pulled back their arm and sent the blood from the knife raining down onto the wooden wall. Then there was Nicole. In the shower cubicle – several knife wounds. I saw that as frantic – and, yes it was – just like this attack. But that was the point of Nicole's murder. It was a bit like a scene from *Psycho*.'

'Did you see the pictures of Hilary?' Elliot asks.

'Yes. The kill was frenzied. As though the perp was really angry and couldn't help themselves. Then they tried to make it look like something else. Clawing back some of the urgency of the kill,' I say.

'What did it look like to you?' Beth asks.

'A tableau. Or an attempt at one. A mish-mash of horror movies and true crime. Jack the Ripper meets *Suspiria*,' I say.

'*Suspiria*?' Elliot asks.

'Mid-seventies Dario Argento film. Slash horror. There's a scene where a victim tries to escape the killer by crawling through a room of razor wire. Not a pretty sight,' I explain. 'This one doesn't quite add up though. It looks like...'

'*American Beauty*,' Beth says.

'Yeah,' I say. 'Only the girl wasn't killed in that. She was shown lying naked in a bed of petals as the sexual fantasy of the main male character. This isn't sexual though. At least I don't think it is,' I say.

'She's got the same hair colouring as the others, Mike,' Beth says. 'So, your theory that this is some kind of revenge kill is looking right to me.'

'It's a practice,' I say.

'Practice?' Elliot says. 'What do you mean?'

'The killer is gearing up to something bigger. This one took a lot of planning. They'd been watching this woman for a while. They knew when the husband wouldn't be home to interrupt,' I explain. 'The only thing I don't understand is how they found Cassandra in the first place. Surely she isn't on any dating site, as she's a newlywed.'

Beth starts to look a bit queasy and so I ask her if she'd go and sit with Ian Clementine in the kitchen until the friend arrives. She squeezes her eyes shut above her mask and nods her head, hurrying away to take her mind off this awful sight.

Elliot and I set to work.

'She was a very beautiful girl,' Elliot observes. 'Before that bastard sliced her face.'

I look at him and notice how clenched his fists are by his side. He's as appalled by this as I am.

'It's a horrible attack,' I say. 'And forcing her to watch… to see herself so damaged like that…'

'Sick,' says Elliot.

'Very.'

I take pictures as Elliot starts his onsite examination, talking all the while into a recorder to capture every single observation he makes.

'The cause of death was probably the severing of the carotid artery. But she was already weakened and dying by then as the assailant had stabbed her over twenty times.'

I take pictures of all of the knife wounds but don't comment as Elliot completes his report.

'Elliot?' says a woman at the door and I recognize her as the pathologist he left in charge at Lizzie Seacroft's house.

'Pam. Come in. You know Michael Kensington?'

'We didn't officially meet, but yes,' says Pam.

'Pam's working with me while we have all of these extra investigations. She's on loan from MI6,' Elliot says. 'You can bring your team in now, because Mike and I are done here. Bag and tag her and then see if you can find any trace of evidence left by our perp. I want fibres that don't belong here, I want fingerprints. You know the drill.'

Pam nods.

Maybe keep your mind on the job, this time, I nearly say but moderate myself before I do.

'We need to make sure all evidence is kept clean,' I say instead.

Pam nods. Her eyes skitter to Elliot but I don't say anything else. I hope she's learned her lesson not to be distracted during working hours.

I follow Elliot downstairs but my mind is on Cassandra and her similarity to Neva.

'This is horrifying,' I mutter.

'Yes,' says Elliot overhearing me even as he reaches the hallway and I'm only halfway down the stairs.

'It's only going to get worse,' I say. 'Until our perp finds the woman they are really looking for.'

Elliot meets my gaze as though he understands who I'm talking about, though he can't know I mean Neva.

'Well,' he says. 'Let's hope she doesn't find her. Have you any idea who it might be?'

'A few ideas,' I say. 'But it's all a bit need to know at this stage.'

'Fair enough,' says Elliot.

As Elliot walks away, I replay his words. He'd said *she*. As though he already knows more than he should. This knowledge makes me feel uncomfortable until I realize Beth and Elliot must have been discussing the case, and the few bits of evidence we've kept out of the press.

A few days ago, Beth had broached the subject about the

dead women, and their similarity to Neva's photofit. We hadn't discussed it before then, but she'd seen it as soon as I had.

'You're right. All the women do resemble Neva. Not perfect, but close enough,' I'd admitted.

'Which means that the killer is looking for her just as we are,' Beth said.

I'd nodded. 'We need to do something. Find her before they do.'

'I have some sources on the dark web,' Beth had said. 'I wouldn't usually use them in a Network linked search for information as it's too dangerous for all concerned, but I'll put some subtle feelers out.'

True to her word, Beth had set some searches in motion and her sources came back with some good intel. There had been some more sightings reported of a woman who sounded like Neva. Also, the British Embassy in Amsterdam reported the stolen passport of a student on holiday there.

'The passport was used and I've seen airport footage of the thief using it to enter the country,' Beth had told me. 'It could be Neva.'

All of this pointed to Neva having returned to the UK. Even though we knew we needed to report this to Ray, Beth suggested we continued our own searches for now. I hadn't been sure if she was testing me to see if I was happy to cover up for Neva, but in the end, I let her persuade me to keep it between us until our spy was found. It made sense to keep what we knew close to our chests just in case the wrong person got access to the information.

All of this brings me back to Elliot's apparent knowledge. Yes, Beth and I suspected a woman was the killer because in the first two cases there'd been one, mysterious enough to leave no trace of themselves, but who we believed had met up with Sinead and Lizzie. But we'd agreed not to share this information with anyone. Beth shouldn't have told Elliot, if indeed she had. I plan to ask her, just to clarify if Elliot was, in her eyes, safe to be in the know. But of course her relationship with him may well be clouding her judgement.

While Beth had been briefed by Ray about the bugs in the office, I'd gone with my security detail to the gym where Nicole had been found and interviewed the entire spin class. There was mention again of a woman. Mousy haired, and not particularly memorable. But it had confirmed the profile that was shaping up around our killer. A profile that I'd so far only shared with Beth.

As I remove my crime-scene suit and dispose of it in a black bin bag, I find myself wondering more about Elliot. He and Beth have grown very close. I couldn't really blame her for talking shop with him, since he was so important within the department. After all, we relied on his autopsy information and nothing he'd given us so far suggested that he couldn't be trusted. Even so, I was determined to find out just what they had discussed. If Beth felt him safe then maybe we could use his help in learning more about the killer and their association with Neva. No resource was unusable.

My mind is taken away from Elliot as I leave the house. The lead detective assigned to the case on paper is making a brief statement. I make sure to avoid being caught on camera by the ever-present news crews. No matter how hard we try to keep the details out of the press, someone always leaks something. It's unfortunate that this serial killer case has caught their attention, because it makes it harder for us to do our job.

'Oh my god!'

I turn to see a man running from the house next door. He's in his early fifties, with greying hair and he's hysterical.

'It's my mother! Help! Someone!'

A young PC ducks under the cordon and hurries towards him. Wondering what's happening, I follow and join the cop outside the house next door.

'My mother's dead,' says the man.

And that's when I learn, with a firm slash across the throat, our killer silenced their only witness.

Chapter Thirty-Eight

JANINE

One year ago

Janine didn't see Neva again for a couple of years. By then she'd decided she never would. She worked the dark web, taking hits, honing her skills alone and she grew in confidence. Her stash of money was slowly building. She hid in plain sight as Neva had taught her. But there wasn't a day when she didn't think about her mentor and wonder where she was and what she was doing. She'd been tempted a few times to go back to Neva's house. But she remembered Neva's reaction to her spying and didn't want to repeat the mistake she'd made. She was sure it was why Neva had severed contact. And Neva's burner phone was no longer in play.

Neva's absence in her life hurt Janine more than she ever thought it could do. She'd thrown herself into her work, it was a diversion and it paid well, after all. As her life settled down into a pattern of death juxtaposed with normality,

Janine began to wonder more and more what it would be like to have a relationship with someone. She wanted to know what it would be like to truly walk away from killing and become a regular person.

Not knowing how to meet people under normal circumstances, she tried a few dating sites. But after a few dates she realized that she just wasn't attracted to anyone she met. They all seemed to expect her to jump into bed with them, and after breaking the nose of one of them who came on too strong, Janine deleted her account.

That's when she met Kady.

It wasn't a fling; it was something more. Kady was young, beautiful and flirty. In a way, Janine hadn't stood a chance. It was as though Kady had searched her out. And Janine was ripe for the picking. Of course, she'd considered what her sexuality was. On the whole she'd thought herself frigid. The general's aggressive pursuit of her had been enough to put her off men initially and then his death and the near-miss *that* had become also played a big part in how Janine felt about the opposite sex.

Kady started working in a local coffee shop that Janine frequented. Going in once or twice a month, it was one of the few routines Janine allowed herself. As soon as Kady started there, Janine felt an impulse to go more often. The girl's smile always dialled up when Janine came in, and it wasn't long before Janine realized Kady was as interested in her as she was in Kady.

'Do you drink anything other than coffee?' Kady asked her one morning, when she rushed to wipe the table Janine was sitting at.

'Vodka,' said Janine.

'You're Russian, right?' said Kady.

Janine looked around to see if they were being overheard. No one else in the coffee shop was paying attention to them.

'Yes,' she said finally.

'I like vodka too,' said Kady. 'I finish at six.'

It took Janine a moment to realize that Kady was telling her this for a reason.

'Don't leave me hanging,' said Kady. 'Go for a drink with me?'

Janine found herself blushing.

'Jeez. Sorry. I thought you were like me. I didn't mean to offend you,' Kady said.

'You didn't offend me,' Janine answered. 'I don't know if I'm…'

Kady smiled again. 'But you had a crush on a girl once?'

Janine's blush deepened. 'I think so.'

'We can just go for a drink,' Kady said. 'Just be friends?'

Janine felt a rush of excitement at the thought of spending time with Kady. Even a simple friendship would break up the monotony and loneliness that her world revolved around. She didn't say anything and Kady walked away looking disappointed, but at 6pm Janine was waiting for her outside the coffee shop.

They'd gone for a drink together and it was the start of a long affair. One that Janine couldn't walk away from too easily, but when she learnt of Kady's betrayal with another woman, Janine had to end it.

Being with Kady had made her vulnerable. It had

stopped her working, and now Janine had to get back to the world she knew the best. But it had also taught her who she was as a woman.

That's when Neva came back into her life.

Neva is standing on a corner outside a cake shop as though she's arrived there by complete accident.

By then Janine has her own permanent home. A small flat in Cardiff. She lives frugally, retaining as much money as she can. She even has a regular job by which she pays all of her bills.

Janine is afraid even as she hurries to Neva's side. Perhaps this is the moment when Neva will take back the life she's given her.

Neva has barely changed. Without hesitation Janine holds out her arms to hug her.

'I thought I wouldn't see you again,' says Janine.

Neva blinks, surprised by the show of affection. She doesn't respond to it. That is when Janine understands that the passage of time is irrelevant to Neva. She has not been missed at all during this long hiatus. She realizes that the absence means she just wasn't needed.

'I have a job for you,' Neva says as Janine's arms fall back awkwardly to her sides.

'I need to be you again?' Janine asks.

'No. You need to be Ingrid Rouille,' she says.

Janine doesn't know what Neva is planning, but she takes the details of who and what Rouille should be. She walks away from the life she's established, dropping the boring office job, and with money Neva provides, she buys clothes and styles her hair as instructed.

In London she rents an apartment for Neva under Rouille's name.

They meet there once the rental agreement is signed. Janine watches Neva as, wearing another disguise, she examines the flat, leaving some possessions behind that Rouille's identity will need.

'You won't be needed again for a while,' Neva tells her.

Then she wires Janine fifty thousand pounds for the trouble she's gone to.

'Take this. I'll be in touch,' Neva says, giving her a new burner phone.

Janine takes it, thrilled to be back in. She has questions about where Neva has been. How she is, but she doesn't ask them. Any such behaviour might make Neva cut her off. She can't risk being out in the cold again.

As she and Neva part again a growing excitement of rebuilding their relationship surges into Janine's mind. It takes her thoughts away from the promiscuous Kady, and back to why she'd followed Neva from the start: she loves her. How, and in what way, Janine still isn't certain. But for now, her confused feelings have a focus and all Janine wants is to show Neva that she can be trusted again.

Chapter Thirty-Nine

NEVA

Present day

Michael's security detail is good, but Neva picks up on them on her second night in London. They have a routine of moving SUVs around, one of which takes Michael and two more are decoys, with a fourth one following Michael's vehicle. This is the giveaway. Even so, Neva is pleased to see so much effort being put into Michael's protection.

Since they'd parted, she had wondered if Ray would insist on putting him into witness protection. It's more than likely that they tried. But she's not surprised that Michael refused to go to ground, even though he's still in danger. He wouldn't want that. After all, he revels in his work.

She follows the fourth SUV now at a distance and on a motorbike she's procured to make it easier to go unnoticed.

The SUV heads from Central London and out towards Wembley. Neva stays back as far as she can until the car joins the North Circular. Then she speeds up and keeps the car in her sight.

They end up in Richmond. A small house on a little street not far from the park. All of which is familiar to Neva as she spent many months in the past hiding out in and around areas of London.

She speeds past the SUV as they park up, then she takes a turning at the end of the road and drives away. She dumps the bike a few streets away and then returns to continue her surveillance on foot. When she reaches the house, the SUVs have gone and another car sits conspicuously outside. Michael is nowhere to be seen, but she assumes he's inside, tucked away, safe for another night.

Neva uses this opportunity to examine the other houses on the street, looking for either an empty property or one whose occupants have gone away but her luck isn't in on either count. She turns her attention to the street behind this one instead, and the house that backs onto the one that Michael is in. She counts the number of houses that lead to Michael's, then she goes to the next street and does the same. After that, and unobserved, she focuses her attention on this house. It's a clone of the one Michael is in but, as Neva knows, the exterior won't reflect the interior of the other house, as Michael's one is likely to have security cameras everywhere and a panic room.

This house however is currently empty as, judging by the lack of lights on inside, no one is home yet. Making sure she isn't observed, she slips into the small front garden and goes around the back, wending her way into the yard. As she'd hoped, it backs up onto the house Michael is in.

From the safety of the trees and bushes that divide the two gardens, along with a four-foot fence, Neva examines the safe house's back garden and takes note of the motion sensor security lights at the back. She can see two cameras, moving as they pan the whole plot.

The lights come on as another security guard walks around the garden. He's smoking a cigarette and Neva thinks this is more of an opportunity to take a break than a necessary breach check. But the light gives her the opportunity to see the back door and windows. It also confirms how difficult it will be to get to Michael here.

Neva hears a car pulling into the drive at the front of the house she's in. She ducks back around the side, watching from the darkness as a man in his early 20s gets out and goes inside the house. Once he's gone in, she hurries down the small drive and back onto the street unobserved.

Even though she'd easily found the safe house, Neva understands that the only way she can get to Michael is if she encourages him to ditch his security to meet her.

She turns on her phone and dials the last number she has for him, which was the burner phone that Ray had given him in the safe house that they'd shared together.

She pauses before pressing the call button. Will Michael still be angry with her? Or has he calmed down enough to hear her side? Neva mulls over again how she feels about Michael's acceptance that she lied to him. In his shoes would she have thought the same about her? His lack of belief in her is a betrayal because trust was crucial between them. Neva has struggled with it ever since she divorced herself from the Network. But Michael had been some form of stability from the moment they met. If he agrees to meet her, she knows she can trust him. But will he trust her again? And if he doesn't, how will she feel? Angry? Hurt? Disappointed? Neva will feel all of these emotions: they are a waterfall inside her now, hard to stop from flowing in and around her. Even harder to process. She's afraid: another rejection from Michael will bring the delicate balance of her equilibrium crashing down once more. She doesn't know how much more of her can break down before there's nothing left.

Neva sighs. Remembering the connection they'd once shared, she makes the decision to risk his rebuff and calls the number. It is the bravest thing she's ever done. Her heart leaps with adrenaline as the phone rings out then goes onto a messaging service. She's both relieved and disappointed as she listens to Michael's voice telling her to leave a message.

Chapter Forty

JACK

As Ben leaves for work Jack Harman wheels his mower to the house across the road. From there he has the perfect vantage point to watch the Charters' house. Of course, he knows that this couple are not Brody and Mica Charter really. They are Mia and Ben Cusick and they are in an MI5 witness protection programme.

As Ben's car drives from the street, another vehicle enters. It's a black van, with tinted windows. But Jack notices the two men sat in the front. Black suited, with sunglasses, even though it's a dull day. He knows immediately that they shouldn't be here.

At the arrival of the van, Jack stops mowing the lawn and takes a sip from the water bottle he has in a pouch attached to his belt. The driver of the van glances at him. Then he carries on past the Charters' house and off to another street.

Jack watches it go. He stows his water bottle away and resumes his mowing. When he's finished the front of this house, Jack moves onto the next. That's when he notices the van has returned. He leaves the mower inside the gate of the next house, and taking cover behind one of the cars parked on the street, he watches the van stop outside the Charters' house.

The side of the van opens and another man gets out. The passenger in the front joins him. They are wearing identical black suits. Jack observes that they both have an earpiece in their left ears. One of the men waits by the open van, while the other goes and knocks on the door.

Mia opens the door and looks at him. Then she follows the man back to the van, leaving her front door wide open. She walks slowly as though her feet are heavy.

Realizing something is wrong, Jack comes out of his hiding place and crosses the road. He walks towards the van.

The driver watches him as he approaches.

'Mrs Charter. Is everything all right?' he says.

Mia doesn't look at him. She's like a sleepwalker, unaware of her surroundings. She moves to the side door as though she is going to climb into the back of the van.

'Mrs Charter! No!' Jack shouts.

He hurries towards them. The man waiting by the open door turns as Jack reaches them. Before the man has time to react Jack kicks him hard in the testicles as his first attack. The first man goes down, screaming in pain.

Jack grabs Mia's arm and pulls her back from the van.

'Go inside with your baby,' Jack says.

Mia doesn't move.

The second man circles Jack and then attacks. Jack fights

back with expert skill. They exchange blows using a variety of fighting techniques while Mia watches through dull, emotionless eyes. Jack is strong and a trained fighter but as he starts to overcome the second man, the driver of the van gets out and joins in. Jack is now fighting off two men. Even so, he holds his own, kicking and punching at the two men alternately. He almost wins too.

Recovering from the kick he'd received, the first man pulls himself off the floor. He watches as his colleagues begin to overpower Jack. Then he goes and takes Mia's arm and leads her back to the van.

'Run Mia!' Jack yells. He receives a hard punch in the face that stuns him. The second man sweeps his feet from under him. Jack lands hard on the ground. The second man and the driver deliver kicks and blows to his side to keep him down. All Jack can do is try to defend himself.

The blows stop raining down and winded, Jack is helpless as he watches Mia get in the van. The three men stop hitting him and hurry into the van, leaving Jack on the ground outside the house.

They drive away.

When he can breathe again, Jack pulls himself up from the pavement. He takes out his mobile phone to call in the incident. His first real job with MI5 has been a failure. But he was only supposed to watch and observe, none of them thought that Mia and Ben's position was compromised. As he dials the number, Jack begins to wonder how they've been found when their location was known to so few people. It suggests to him that someone must have betrayed them. Someone in MI5. There can be no other explanation.

He hears the baby crying now inside, and as he reports to Ray Martin, giving the licence plate of the van, he goes inside to make sure the child is all right. After all, she's just as much in his care as Mia was.

'At least they didn't take the kid,' Ray says. 'That's something.'

Ben returns with a security detail in tow a few minutes later. They pour into the house to find Jack feeding Freya with a bottle of expressed milk he'd found in the fridge.

'She was screaming the place down,' Jack says.

'What the fuck happened?' Ben asks. He takes Freya from Jack's arms and holds her to him as though he's afraid someone will come back and take her away too. He can see the tears still wet on her cheeks and he kisses her forehead as he soothes his daughter.

'Your wife went with them willingly,' Jack explains. 'She didn't even try to escape when I gave her the chance.'

'That's impossible,' says Ben. 'She wouldn't…'

'She looked like she was hypnotized,' Jack says. 'I'm sorry. I let you down. I tried to fight them off but there were three of them and they were all as trained as I am.'

'You didn't let anyone down, Jack. You kept my daughter safe. That's a major result under the circumstances,' Ben says. 'You're a fucking hero in my eyes.'

'Can I do anything else to help?' Jack asks. His eyes tear up slightly, but he hides it with an awkward rub of a hand over his face.

'Ray is on his way. He'll need to question you. I'll get a medic here to look at your injuries.'

'I'm bruised but it's not as bad as it looks,' Jack says.

'Either way, let's get you checked out. We aren't the Network, Jack. We look after our assets.'

Jack nods. 'Can I go and wash my face?' he asks.

'Sure. Bathroom is in the hallway.'

Jack goes out of the living room, leaving Ben holding his daughter. In the small bathroom he looks at his bruised and battered face in the mirror. He barely feels the injuries. He's had worse when he was in the hands of the Network. Jack was grateful that MI5 had rescued him several months ago from a mansion in Alderley Edge, where he'd spent the last ten years being turned into an assassin. Being in the house had been hell and up until that point he'd never believed he could be free of the Network. But once they'd taken him from there Jack had volunteered to work for MI5 instead.

Retraining had taken him past his seventeenth birthday and after much therapy, Ray had finally trusted him with something important. Jack had been willing to help protect Mia and Freya. He never wanted any child to go through what he'd been through. And now, Mia has been taken by the Network. Jack feels sick at the thought of them controlling her, and using her for their own ends.

He washes the dried blood from his face and examines his bruises again. *I deserve every one of them for failing Mia,* he thinks. Jack shakes his head. *No, that isn't true.* He had done his best and his best was good enough for MI5 – even if it wouldn't have been for the Network.

Jack counts himself lucky again that he'd been found that day. Another week and he'd have been shipped away to start his career as a killer for the Network. And then, he'd never have freed himself from them. No one ever did.

Chapter Forty-One

MICHAEL

I wake up that morning to find a missed call on the old burner phone that I've been keeping in the hope that Neva will contact me. There's no message on the answering service and so I send a text to the number asking who they are. Then I put the phone back down at the side of the bed. A few minutes later it vibrates as another call comes in from the same number. I answer it.

'Michael?'

It's Neva. The sound of her voice, after all of these weeks, takes my breath away. *I can't fall for her tricks again. She can't be trusted. She played me,* I remind myself. But I'm not really prepared for how hearing from her makes me feel.

'What do you want?' I ask, making my voice sound hard.

I resist the urge to ask her how she is. It's as if the last few weeks haven't happened, and I hadn't seen Granger accuse her of murdering Angela Carter. I wish I could unhear, unsee, unfeel all of those terrible moments of doubt and betrayal.

Neva sighs down the phone. I can almost visualize her, hesitant to speak, ready perhaps to tell me something that can change my mind about her. I ache for any excuse, any explanation.

'Mia isn't safe,' she says. 'They are coming for her.'

'She's in witness protection. Even the Network can't find her,' I say.

'They've known all along where she is. I told you. There's a mole in Archive.'

'Neva, don't lie to me. I have no intention of falling for your rubbish again,' I say even though I know she's right. Didn't the bugging prove she hadn't lied about this?

I feel tired and old then, as if I've given her every drop of my energy and she's thrown it away, along with my feelings for her. Despite my attempt at sounding hardened to her, I yearn for her to redeem herself. I take a breath after realizing I'd been holding it too long. *Tell me what I need to hear,* I think. *Tell me something that makes me believe in you again.*

'Michael. Please. I'm not lying. Meet me face to face and I'll prove it. I have information from a very trusted source. The woman who tried to kidnap you for the Network was called Kritta. I bet you'd remember her voice. She was German, wasn't she?'

I don't answer, but I remember the woman well. She did have a German accent. An accent that Neva hadn't heard when she'd surprised her, and me, in the stairwell and rescued me from her clutches. This at least I know is a truth.

'I know you don't trust me, but please just let me explain. Kritta was Mia's mother, as Subra was yours.'

'Go on,' I say. *Give me something to hold onto!*

'She was taken by my mother, Annalise. Annalise is now running the Network after she took out half of the committee using an assassin called Vasquez. I don't have to be a genius to work out what Annalise wanted with Kritta. Like Subra, Kritta has the trigger words that will activate Mia. Which means that Annalise now has them. It won't be long before they'll make a move on Mia. And through her, they'll make an attempt again on you.'

I think for a moment. My rational mind wants to believe this is a lie: everything Neva has said plays into my fears for Mia and my niece, Freya. I know the Network don't give up their assets and both Mia and I belonged to them once. If I'm unwilling to belong to them, then they will kill me if they get the chance. It's the only thing they can do. Thanks to Ray that chance has been denied them so far.

My regular phone rings then, and I see Ray's number come up.

'Just stay on the line,' I say to Neva. 'I have to take this.'

'No. I'll call you back in ten minutes,' she hangs up, no doubt suspecting me of trying to trace her call.

I answer Ray's call.

'Michael. I've some bad news. The Network have taken Mia,' Ray says.

'*Fuck!* How did this happen? You said she was safe…'

'I don't know, but all I can say is we are interrogating

everyone who had any access to that knowledge. We'll find that mole if it's the last thing we do,' Ray says.

He explains the attack and Jack's report of Mia going with them without putting up a fight. I see Mia in my mind's eye and I know that she was trapped inside her own body and mind, unable to fight the commands they'd conditioned her to obey – as I had once been in the same position. I find it hard to imagine her leaving Freya alone in the house, regardless. This makes me once more aware of how strong the Network's hold can be, especially if you don't know how to fight them. I curse under my breath again. *I should have warned her*.

'Did the vehicle plates show up anything?' I ask.

Ray hesitates for a moment as though he's afraid to tell me this part.

'The van is registered to MI6,' he confides.

'*What?*'

'I'm looking into who was using it, but honestly I'm expecting it to be a deliberate clone of one they have and not their actual van. It'll be some kind of sick Network joke on us. The interesting thing is, they could have killed Jack, or pulled a gun on him but they didn't. They tried to get out and away as clean as possible without casualties.'

'I wonder why? That's not their usual M.O. and Jack has seen them now. So, you'd think they'd have killed him rather than incapacitate him.'

'I know,' says Ray. 'My first thought was he was in on it. But the security footage shows him genuinely putting up a fight and being overpowered. The kid is mortified. And so am I. I thought Mia was hidden, but it seems as though they knew where she was all along.'

'It's an inside job. Neva warned us about the mole and we didn't believe her,' I say.

'I know. I should have listened to her, Mike. But this whole thing with Granger…'

'What if Neva didn't do it? What if Granger set her up, and then someone else silenced him? This mole perhaps,' I suggest.

'I know you want to believe in Neva. I get that. But Granger wasn't lying. We polygraphed him. You know this,' Ray says. 'But I do accept that she probably didn't kill him. I'm starting to realize it had to be one of our own. How else did the perp get through our security unseen?'

I don't reply as Ray works out everything I've been suspecting for a while for himself. But I'd been too afraid to believe it because of my feelings for Neva.

'Ben tells me Erik Steward at MI6 said they had eyes on Mia and Ben too. He'd argued it was for their own safety, but if there is a leak, maybe it's in MI6 and not Archive,' Ray tells me. 'But I just don't know. All I know is anyone could be involved. And we're screwed if we can't trust our own people.'

Everything he's saying reinforces the decision I'm about to make regarding Neva. No, we can't trust anyone at MI5 or MI6. This much is becoming clear. Even so, can I trust Neva?

'Any sightings of the van since?' I ask.

'None. But we're still working on it.'

'I'm coming into the office,' I say.

'Best to stay where you are for now,' Ray says. 'I've sent extra detail to make sure you're safe.'

I try to argue but Ray won't listen. He hangs up and I find myself staring at the phone.

True to her word and on the dot, Neva calls me back on the other phone. As I see her anonymous number flashing up on the screen I make up my mind: I'm going to give her one final chance.

'Ray just called me,' I say. 'They've taken Mia.'

'I wasn't expecting them to act so soon,' Neva says, 'I'm sorry, Michael.'

'What does Annalise want with her?'

Neva sighs again. 'I don't know. I've been wracking my brains wondering what this is all about. But I *knew* she would take her. She'll want the child too.'

'Ray's sending extra detail to protect me. I need to get out of here before they arrive or I'll be in lockdown. Will you meet me?' I ask and I feel a rush of relief: I've made the right choice in putting the past behind us. At least for now. How I'll deal with it later I'm not sure.

'You know I will,' she says. 'But what are you planning to do?'

'We go after Mia. And we take down Annalise at the same time. Are you with me Neva? Because now's the time that you really need to take sides.'

'I've always been on your side,' she says and I feel that jolt again inside me, that firm belief in her. *She's not lying.*

'Do you know how to find Annalise?'

'Yes,' she says.

'Then we go after her directly,' I say.

'Michael, I have to tell you something. When Granger said I was Angie…' Neva says.

'I don't care. All that matters is saving Mia,' I say.

I want to trust Neva, even though I shouldn't. I know better than to put myself in her hands, but Ray's revelations have made her my only conceivable ally. After all, who can I trust at MI5 and MI6? Anyone could be behind Mia's kidnap. Even Ray.

'I care. Because I don't *think* I was Angie. But the truth is, I don't *know*. The Network messed with my head for years. I have no idea if they also have trigger words that can turn me back into their puppet again,' she says, her voice breaking.

I hear her anguish and fear. It must have been hard for her to admit this to me. That in the end she doesn't know if she can even trust herself. I know how she feels. Our whole world is nothing but doubt and paranoia. Even so, I hear absolute truth in her voice. I understand more than anyone where she is right now. How awful it is to think you have control and yet someone can come along and take it from you with just a few words.

'Have you remembered something that might make you think this is the case?' I ask her now, my voice soft.

'No. But I've been trying to. If there's something there, it's buried very deep inside me.'

'Okay,' I say. 'Look, I have to figure out a way to sneak out of here… then I'll call you to meet. But if you're going to betray me, know this Neva. I'll kill you.'

'That's fair. But Michael, if I turn, and I'm not the person you knew, I'd be grateful if you would put me out of my misery. I don't want to belong to anyone but myself. I can't be their pawn anymore. And if I did that to Angela Carter. If I put that poor woman in that car, trussed up and left to die like that, then I don't deserve to live. I don't know how I could forgive myself for turning her child over to them.'

Then she tells me exactly how to escape the safe house, right under the noses of my bodyguards and I learn just how easy it was for her to find me and surely too, for the Network to do the same. I have a momentary wobble, a second of questioning her motives. But I push it aside. If she's working for them I'll soon find out, and since I'm confident that we've broken all of my conditioning, maybe I too will play a double game. Anything to get me closer to saving Mia. As much as I hate what the Network did to me, I can't help feeling grateful for my knowledge now of them. They may be one step ahead of us, but soon I'll take that lead from them. I feel the assassin in me rearing again, eager for the deliverance of a cold, but revenge-filled, death.

When I hang up the phone from Neva, I pull some clothes on. Then I load my Glock and stow several cartridges in the pockets of my jeans. After that I place the Glock in my belt holster, covering it with a casual zip-up black jacket.

As Neva suggested, I go out into the back garden, and without pause, climb over the fence into the garden backing up onto the safe house. As the security detail aren't worried about my movements, no one comes to stop me. It's almost too easy and does give me momentary pause that someone other than Neva will be waiting for me.

I walk around to the front of the neighbouring house

and head down the road. I have the burner phone with me so that Neva can contact me, but not my regular phone as I don't want Ray to be able to trace me. Any minute he'll open the email I sent him, telling him that I'm going after Mia and he isn't to try to find me.

I wait at the agreed meeting point but I'm nervous that the security detail will realize I'm gone and come looking for me. So it's a relief when Neva pulls up at the kerb in an innocuous Ford Focus.

I get in the passenger seat, trembling at the nearness of her. Neva drives off as soon as I close the door, and before I can fasten my seat belt.

I stare ahead at the road, trying not to look at her, because just a glimpse has been enough to remind me that I still want her.

'Check out that bag by your feet,' she says. I look down into the footwell and see a plastic bag. I pick it up and open it. Inside are passports, and clothing.

'We'll ditch your clothes,' she says. 'Change everything. I know how tricky Ray Martin can be with trackers.'

We approach Euston station and Neva parks the car in a nearby street on double yellow lines. Then she takes my hand and we walk across the road and into the station. She glances at me as her skin touches mine, as though she feels the same desperate rush of electricity coursing through her hand as I do through mine.

Taking the carrier bag with me, I go into the men's toilets and change. I leave the bag full of my old clothing in the toilets. I even ditch my wallet, after removing cash and cards from it, just in case.

Neva is waiting for me outside when I come out of the gents. Even without make-up she's breath-taking. I have a flash of Cassandra/Sinead/Lizzie/Nicole/Hilary... faces distorted and crying as they died. Their resemblance to Neva makes me feel sick. Should I tell her about the deaths? Will she know who the killer is?

'You got rid of everything?' she says.

I nod.

Pushing the faces of the dead women away from my mind, I need to focus on now, and Neva is here, safe. Even if a killer is on the lookout for her. Telling her perhaps will just distract us from what we have to do.

'I've booked us a flight to Toulouse early tomorrow,' she says.

'What's in Toulouse?' I ask.

'Hopefully some answers for us both,' she says.

'I have to find Mia,' I say. 'That was the deal.'

'I know. And I promise we will. Come on,' she says.

'Where to now?' I ask.

'My hotel. We have to lay low. I guarantee MI5 will be looking for you,' she says.

I follow her down towards the tube station. My mind is full of doubts and worries. Now I'm free of my security detail I'm raring to get to the bottom of what's going on. I'm anxious to learn what has become of Mia. And more important – to learn if I can I trust Neva. This whole protection thing has been holding me back from getting to the truth.

Neva's nearness is making me feel unstable and the illusion of control is rapidly slipping away as I put myself more into her hands. Foolish or not, I have no choice but to follow the path I've chosen. Wherever it leads. I have to find my sister and, if I can, destroy the heart of the Network once and for all. And to do that, I have to risk everything, and that includes Neva as well as myself.

Chapter Forty-Two

BETH

'I need everyone on task. Beth, search the street cameras near the safe house. Elsa, I want you manning the phone in case Michael calls. He left his phone at the house, and ditched the burner I gave him a while back so there's no way of tracing him by that means. I just hope he hasn't done anything foolish,' Ray says.

'What will you be doing?' asks Elsa.

Beth gives Elsa a sharp look, surprised that she feels she can question Ray, but Ray doesn't get annoyed with her despite the fact that he's in such a bad mood.

'I have a meeting with Erik Steward,' Ray says. 'I'm going to find out how he knew where Mia and Ben had been relocated.'

Beth opens her access portals as Ray leaves for his meeting and begins to look at the footage around Michael's safe house. A place that now can't be used again because too many people know where it is.

'Do you think Steward is involved?' asks Elsa.

Beth shrugs, she's never seen Ray so pissed off. He'd told her about the black van, and it appears the vehicle was missing from storage which implies that someone in MI6 is playing a double game. That same person may well be the one who bugged Archive's offices. The thought of having a spy among them doesn't please Beth anymore than it does Ray. She'd rather trust her colleagues but now they are all looking at each other and wondering who deceived them.

As the newbie in the group, Elsa is looking particularly suspicious to Beth too. For this reason, and until she's proven to be innocent, Beth is reluctant to confide anything Ray has told her.

Beth is feeling uneasy about a lot of people right now. She frowns as she scans the images on the camera footage as she tries not to think about Elliot. He was at her house more than his own apartment these days and they'd even begun to talk about making this a permanent move when Elliot's tenancy agreement is up for renewal.

'It seems insane to have two homes, when clearly we are getting on so well together,' Elliot had said.

Beth agreed it was practical. Though now she wonders what her mother will say about her moving someone into her home, so soon after her divorce.

Recently, she'd got back into a routine of seeing her boys again and they were staying overnight on occasion. With the security detail on hand, and no further attempts made to take her, Beth was starting to feel much safer again. And she missed the boys. On those nights, she told Elliot he can't come over, it gave her time to think and she wasn't sure the timing was right for them to meet her new boyfriend just yet. Especially with all of the upheaval of going to live permanently with their dad, Callum.

Beth finds herself zoning out from the camera footage and so she pauses it, while her mind wanders. She's worried about Michael, and suspects that he has taken off with Neva. Any idiot could see that he was completely gone on the girl. No one gets that haunted look in their eyes unless betrayed and truly hurt by someone they care about. He'd been used. Beth understands it and she wonders now if Elliot is using her in the same way too.

There are just too many moments that Beth finds herself questioning. Like last night after she and Elliot made love. Beth had feigned sleep and Elliot got up and went downstairs. She'd heard his voice, muted but still drifting upstairs as he spoke to someone. Whoever it was, the receiver of his late-night calls was expecting him to ring.

As she'd done previously, Beth crept to the top of the stairs and tried to listen. But Elliot's voice was too soft for her make out more than a few words. The impression she got was that Elliot was reporting to someone. And that person might well be at the Network. Or maybe he was working for MI6 on the side, reporting to Steward what Archive were doing. That would fit in with Ray's suspicions that Steward was behind the bugging of their offices and that there was a mole, not in Archive, but in MI6.

But Elliot isn't the only one Beth has suspicions about.

Leon Tchaikovsky's sudden 'promotion' into MI6 had made her suspicious. Even though she and Mike hadn't discussed it, they both knew Leon was a bit of a slacker. He always left her and Mike to do the work, and sometimes had taken credit for Beth's successes, though he'd never tried that with Michael. Beth often thought that Ray must have been aware that Leon was cruising in the job. Sometimes heads of departments got together and discussed colleagues: the office grapevine often came up with gossip of that sort. Affairs in house, mis-usage of MI5 and MI6 resources. Steward had to have known that Leon was deadweight in Archive. It's why Beth knew that Leon hadn't earned any such promotion with his track record. Steward owed no loyalty to Leon, not unless he'd done him a huge favour. So why give him a job?

Now she thought about it, Leon had been acting weird before his departure. When he left, Beth had put it down to the fact that he had been schmoozing with Steward and knew he was being promoted. But maybe he'd been working for Steward all along?

Even so, Beth can't make random accusations. She needs to find out more before she accuses anyone of anything, especially Leon.

Right now, with the paranoia in the Archive ramped right up, anyone could be the traitor. And sometimes it is those closest to you that you have to watch.

Now, Beth explores her feelings for Elliot as she sits and stares at her computer screen. She loves him, but she'll give him up in a heartbeat if she discovers he is a spy. *Damn*. She will even shoot him. But she hopes her suspicions are nothing more than her fears of commitment.

Beth tries to reconcile her thoughts in the light of day. What does she really have to worry about with Elliot? She considers again what she'd heard him saying on those few occasions he'd made late night calls. *He was talking about the murder case.* He hadn't said anything about Archive that she'd heard. Or anything that could really be seen as illegal, if she was honest. But why did his behaviour make her wary?

He could be getting advice on the case from another colleague, she reasons. Maybe to back up his own theories. There are so many excuses she can make to justify his behaviour... Except there aren't really. Not when it comes down to it. Beth knows that Elliot isn't getting advice from another expert. If he was, he'd call them during the daytime.

No matter how much benefit of the doubt she gives him, there's only two real questions that she can't answer. Why are the calls always at night? Why are they always when he believes Beth is asleep and can't hear him?

Even if she can convince herself that Elliot is just working late, then why hide it from her? It's conspicuous. And Beth, as a Security Agent, is trained to observe atypical behaviour. It all comes down to getting proof of wrongdoing. And she doesn't have any. All she has is this gut feeling that something is wrong. And Beth has always been big on fact and not on suspicion.

Beth restarts the camera footage and forces herself to concentrate on the images on the screen. She manages this for a few moments before the idea of how to put her mind at rest comes into her head. *I can clone his phone,* she thinks.

She catches herself. To do this without the proper warrant would be illegal. But did whoever had been spying on them even consider the legality of their position?

I'm a spy, she thinks. *I'm trusted when there's judicious doubt. And this is reasonable, isn't it?* Beth goes through the pros and cons of doing something like this. MI5, under other circumstances, would probably investigate and spy on any new boyfriend she has. Elliot's position in MI5 almost negates this. Unless there is a reason to suspect him of something. And Beth can truly say there is.

It might prove I'm imagining things and I can put all these thoughts away, she thinks, trying to justify it.

After concluding this is the way to go on a professional and personal level, Beth leaves Elsa in the office and goes downstairs to Equipment Acquisitions. She knows what she needs and she rehearses her lie all the way down in the lift.

When she returns to the office, she has an innocuous-looking device that resembles a pen drive in her pocket and a spare iPhone, the same model as Elliot's.

If there's nothing unusual on Elliot's phone, Beth will return the erased cloning device and the phone back to Acquisitions. But if there is something wrong, she'll own up to her use of MI5 equipment to Ray and take the consequences. If Elliot is their mole, Ray will only praise her for her initiative anyway.

'You okay?' asks Elsa, studying her from her desk on the other side of the room.

'Yes,' Beth says. 'Needed a bit of fresh air. Watching this footage does your head in.'

'Right,' says Elsa.

With her personal situation organized, Beth goes back to the footage with better concentration. Almost immediately she sees Michael coming out onto the street that runs parallel with the one from the safe house. She tracks him to the end of the road. Then she sees a pale-blue Ford Focus pull up next to him.

Beth tries to zoom in on the driver but the camera angle is wrong and the picture is too grainy.

She takes some snaps of the car. Picks up the registration and puts it in her computer to search for ownership on DVLA records. The search soon reveals the car was stolen and then recovered near Euston station that morning. So, no leads through the owner.

'Elsa? Can you help me please?' she says.

'What do you need?' Elsa asks.

'Check out the footage around Euston station around 9:30am this morning. See if you can spot Michael and find out if he's alone.'

Elsa looks at Beth for a long moment and then nods. She turns to her computer and logs on to the camera systems. She scoots down the alphabetical list until she finds Euston station. Then she flicks through various cameras and views looking for the time she wants.

Though Elsa doesn't know she's doing this, at the same time, Beth is watching Elsa's movements on the system: tracking her all the way through the camera footage. It's a test to see what she does and how she does it. And if she admits seeing Michael too.

'I found him,' Elsa says after ten minutes or so. 'He's not alone.'

Beth drops her computer into standby mode and goes over to Elsa's desk to pretend she's seeing the footage for the first time. Michael is talking to someone. He's facing the camera, but the person with him is deliberately keeping their face hidden.

'It's a woman,' Beth says. 'But I can't tell who she is.'

'I can,' says Elsa. 'It's Neva.'

Beth looks at Elsa. 'How do you know?'

'I met her. That day at the Tower Bridge Hotel. She talked to me for a while – right before Granger accused her of being Angie. I noticed we were the same height. I'm tall for a girl so I don't meet many women my size.'

'Oh yes!' says Beth. 'I hadn't thought of it. And I didn't realize you were there as well.'

'She's back in London…' Elsa says.

'Yes. And she came for Michael. I have to wonder if they've continued to stay in touch, even though he'd said they hadn't,' Beth says, then she bites her lip.

'Maybe he's our spy?' Elsa says.

Beth stares at the screen but doesn't answer. Could Michael be the one who'd been spying on them, then 'miraculously' found the bugs? It certainly removed all suspicion from him and cast doubt on everyone else when he did.

Beth feels the weight of the phone and cloning device in her pocket. It's never been easy working for MI5.

She returns to her desk and puts her screen back on.

Elsa is zooming in on Neva and taking screen shots of her at different angles. She doesn't take any of Michael except for a distance shot of him with Neva. Beth glances at her and she sees the intensity with which Elsa watches the woman.

'They are into each other,' Elsa mouths.

Her expression changes but it's brief because she looks

up and sees Beth watching her. Afterwards, Beth is sure she imagined the whole thing. But she does think, just for a second, Elsa looked as though she wanted to kill. Maybe she resents traitors just as much as Beth does?

Chapter Forty-Three

MICHAEL

When we get back to Neva's hotel, I feel awkward. I haven't forgiven her, but I believe she might *not* know what she's done. I know how that feels better than anyone. But now we are alone it doesn't seem like such a great idea that we are together. There's a dynamic tension in the air. I smell the subtle perfume of her skin and the aroma makes me feel crazy again. I'm fighting the urge to touch her, for if I do, I know I'll be lost.

'Perhaps we should go out to eat?' I say. 'Lunch somewhere.'

'We'd have to keep avoiding cameras every time we step out. So, it's not a good idea. But if you're hungry I'll order room service,' she says.

She's right of course, and my suggestion was stupid, but I'm struggling to be alone with her like this. I'm hyper-aware of her as she switches on the television, sits down on the bed, kicks off her shoes and stretches out to watch the news. Her long legs are enticing. I remember them bare. I think of her under me, but my memories of her are more than just the casual lust we sometimes shared. There was a comfort in being in the same room, and now I'm fighting against slipping back into that same sense of ease. She makes me feel safe. Insane as that is.

I sit down in the chair by the dressing table and try to distract myself by watching the television as well.

On the TV, the camera switches from the studio to a location and I sit upright, recognizing Cassandra's house behind the reporter.

'Primary school teacher, Cassandra Clementine, is the latest victim of what the press are calling the Redhead Murders…' the reporter says.

I glance at Neva as pictures of the victims come up on the screen. Her likeness to them is more obvious now I'm in her company. She pays careful attention to the report and listens to the sparse information that we've released to the press. They don't know about the staging of the bodies, just the similarity between the victims.

'Have you been working on this?' she asks.

I meet her gaze. 'Yes.'

She turns the television down and asks me to tell her the details of the case and I weigh up how much I want to tell her. I'm worried that this will distract her from our current mission. Plus, I don't feel comfortable with sharing what I know from a case I've been working on. I admit this to her.

'Just tell me what you told the reporters then,' she says.

As this seems like an okay compromise I fill her in.

'They don't have red hair,' she says. 'It's strawberry blonde.'

'The Strawberry-Blonde Murders doesn't quite have the same ring as Redhead Murders…' I comment. 'It's the way the media thinks: it's all about selling the story to those vultures.'

I glance at the screen and see that they have different reporters at each of the locations. I feel sick again. These deaths will stay with me a long time. I look at Neva again, hyper aware that this case is connected to her, but unwilling to admit it.

'You think it's linked to me, don't you?' she asks then as though reading my mind, and I catch myself wondering if she actually can.

'Do you?' I say.

'I don't know,' she says. 'They look like me.'

I nod.

'But I don't see the point in killing someone who looks like me, if they want to kill me. Why not just come after me and kill me?'

'Maybe it's because you're so hard to find,' I say. 'Or maybe they are doing it to draw you out.'

She looks down at the hand holding the TV remote. She turns the TV off. She stands up, wanders around the room. Her movements are languid. I find it provocative. She sits back on the bed and moves her long legs again, deliberately drawing my eye to them. I feel her eyes on me and raise them to her face. She smiles and it's subtle and seductive.

What is she playing at?

'Come and make love to me,' she says.

I gape at her.

'*Seriously?* You think we are just picking right up where

we left off?' I'm so shocked by her suggestion that I can't stop myself from shaking my head at her. 'Really Neva. You've got some nerve.'

'You are tense,' she says. 'And so am I. It makes sense we relieve each other.'

And now I have no need to distract my raging libido because her cold and calculated summation of our physical attraction to each other is enough to make me aware that it means nothing to her other than fulfilling a need. Can she be as frozen inside as she appears? We are complete opposites. *Yin and Yang.* I feel a jolt as I find that name sitting there in my head in reference to us two. On that dating site, we'd probably be a perfect match.

'Have you heard of *Yin and Yang*?' I ask her now.

'Yes, it means—'

'No, not the definition. The dating site,' I say.

Neva shakes her head.

'You've never heard of it?' I ask again.

'No. Why would I? I'm hardly the sort to look for long-term romance,' she says.

I weigh up what to tell her without betraying my colleagues. I decide I need to come clean with my suspicions at least.

'I think whoever this person is, they know you. Or did know you.'

'What else do you think?' she asks.

'How about you tell me what you know?'

'I don't know anything. This has only come to my attention since I returned to London.'

I look down at my hands, thinking through my next

question. I want to ask her about the things I suspect about the killer, without giving away information that's confidential.

'Do you know anyone who is fanatical about old films. Horror ones especially. Like *Psycho* for example?'

Neva meets my eyes, she frowns slightly as she explores my question.

'Not obsessed, no. But we were subjected to films that showed death all the time in the house. It was part of the conditioning, a way of making us disassociate from the ones we caused. Our life was like a film unfolding around us, and sometimes we took the role of the killer,' she says.

'Did any of your former associates have a grudge against you?' I ask.

Neva shrugs. 'We were encouraged to be competitive. That doesn't inspire friendship. But resentment… grudges. Not really,' she answers.

I know what she says is true, even though my own recollection of the house is shady. I think for a moment. 'No enemies among them then?'

Neva looks away as she thinks about this. 'The Network are hunting me. Any one of their assassins could be responsible for this mess. But if one of them is breaking like this, and has turned sociopathic, then their handler would usually take them out of the field and have them reconditioned at the very least.'

'That's what I thought,' I say. 'So, it might just be that this one is a rogue and has ditched both handler and the Network as they pursue their path for revenge.'

Neva pulls her knees up to her chest on the bed. She

drops her head down on them and closes her eyes. She looks vulnerable and confused. I want to go to her. Hold her. But I don't move.

Is she scared by the prospect of a possible stalker? Is she even capable of fear?

As always, her change of mood surprises me. She goes from cold-hearted seductress to vulnerable child in a matter of seconds.

I'm drawn to her again, and this time I don't resist. I get up off my chair and join her on the bed. Even as I sit beside her, I wonder, is this some ruse to misdirect and reel me in again? I don't know. And part of me doesn't care.

I run my hand over her back as a way to offer comfort. She doesn't move or object. She remains still and allows me to touch her. And all the time my mind is screaming, *You idiot Michael! She knows exactly how to manipulate you!*

But I can't help it: I'm an addict and she's my drug. I try to force back the memory of my anger against her, but it doesn't come. It's gone: washed away on the wave of my susceptibility. I forget all about going cold turkey. All it's taken her is to crook her finger my way and I'm running back to her. It's as if she has some kind of invisible cord looped around my heart: one tug and I'm under her spell. Only this rope is more like razor wire and it cuts into me until I think my heart will split in two.

She raises her head and looks into my eyes.

I'm a spy and you'd think I would be able to tell when I'm being used, but I see no guile in Neva's eyes. What is there, is a reflection of my own raw emotion. Does this mean she feels it too? Can she feel anything at all? If not, then why did she risk capture to come and warn me of the danger?

And that's when I understand: I love her.

This is a trap, I tell myself, but I know it isn't.

She takes my hand in hers and I'm plummeted back to the house, where two once-innocent children held hands and found a kinship. We've shared these secrets so long – some I still can't hold in my mind – that maybe, just maybe this is all meant to be.

I feel her hesitate. There's nothing clumsy now about the way I move closer: something I wanted to do the moment I saw her again. She lets me place kisses over her face and neck. Her eyes are wide and full of emotion. It's a wonder to see it there mixed in with our mutual lust. Then she's in my arms and we are wrapped in each other. I kiss her mouth, pushing my tongue possessively between her lips. She gives herself over to the kiss.

I make love to her. It's not just a mutual relieving of tension as she'd suggested we might give each other. It is intense. Beautiful. A joining that any poet might write better words about than I can.

I bite back the words that threaten to tumble from my lips as I enter her. But my eyes are still on hers and I try to convey it anyway. She rolls back her head, eyes hooded as though she can't bear to see my defenceless expression. I should be put off by this, but it makes me love her more. When I know she loves me back it will be the biggest victory.

I almost lose my stride as she lets go, crying out. She's always been controlled before. Then, I'm lost too, grunting and heaving and exploding into her as though it's been months and not weeks since we were last together.

Neither of us speaks as I roll away from her. Then Neva straightens her clothes, reaches for the hotel phone, and orders room service.

By the time the food and drink arrive, she's acting like nothing has happened between us. I follow her with my eyes, but now she won't meet mine. Have I given away too much? Can't she bear the knowledge that I love her and I'm completely hers? Oh god. I am such a fool to be this much in love.

Chapter Forty-Four

MIA

Confusing images float behind her eyes. She sees herself boarding a private jet. On board the plane, there are offers of drinks and refreshments which she takes as she sits down in a plush armchair and fastens her seat belt. *This is how the other half live,* Mia thinks. A part of her delights in and recognizes the luxury, as though she's always known she deserves it too. She is relaxed and unafraid throughout the trip. Wasn't she once promised glory? Perhaps this is her time?

It's a short journey, a couple of hours, and then she exits into brilliant sunshine and a dry heat.

In this dream she is someone else, travelling to see an important person.

She's waved through passport control on a French passport. She glances at it, seeing her face but not her name there. But she knows her name is Florence Bisset. There are others with her. The bodyguards: three men in black suits. The guards are there for her protection, not to imprison her.

It is an important distinction that ensures her cooperation. They escort her from the airport to a long sleek black limousine.

She gets inside with the men, and one of them opens a bottle of Champagne.

'To the return of your memory,' he says in French, and Mia understands him perfectly though she's never studied any languages.

She sips the Champagne and, after one glass, she knows who she is.

She is the daughter of the Network's former CEO, Andrew Beech, and a German assassin known as Kritta. She was raised by the Kensingtons to keep her hidden. And at weekends she went to the house with her brother Michael and they trained together so that one day, one or both of them would take over their father's empire. All of this comes to her with alarming clarity as they drive through a stunning landscape towards a beautiful château that lies in the middle of a vineyard.

The limo passes through a gateway that is monitored by an armed guard. Then it approaches the château via a mile-long driveway. Mia looks out at the imposing house as they draw nearer. She feels as though she knows this place: she hasn't been here but someone once told her about it. The car pulls up at the impressive double doors. One of the guards opens the door: he holds out his hand to help Mia step out onto the driveway.

She looks up at the front steps and sees the door open ahead. Several uniformed staff pour out and line the steps as though they are there just to greet her. Mia realizes that this is exactly what they are there for. It's a mark of respect for her status.

As she ascends the steps the maidservants and butler and footmen all applaud.

She takes their applause with a modest smile. It feels as though she is coming home after a long absence.

Mia reaches the top of the steps, still flanked by the three guards. There she sees a beautiful white-haired woman waiting for her in the doorway.

'Welcome,' she says.

'Thank you, Annalise,' Mia says, knowing instantly who this is. 'How can I assist you?'

Annalise smiles. 'I want to help you to secure your birthright.'

Mia nods. 'I'm listening.'

Mia feels as though she is fully in control and this is merely a meeting for business that had to happen sooner rather than later.

'Come inside. Let my people make you comfortable. Then, when we dine, we can discuss my plans.'

Now Mia is lying in a comfortable four-poster bed. She turns over, reluctant to let this empowering dream fade. She sees herself being escorted upstairs and led to a beautiful chamber. The room is full of preserved antique French furniture and it adds to the fairytale that Mia is imagining.

She's given a bath, helped by two of the maidservants. They bow and scrape to her as though she is from royalty. And perhaps to these people her heritage makes her so.

Mia wakes now, and opening her eyes she realizes that she has not been dreaming after all. She is indeed in a château in the South of France and she is the daughter of someone important. But she's also Mia, wife to Ben and mother of Freya.

She sits up so fast that she feels dizzy.

'What's going on?' she says.

Her mind is assaulted by memories. Her head hurts so much she feels it is going to explode. A rush of recollections, dreamlike at first, and then swarming and attacking like flying ants. She feels nauseous and she gets up from the bed and runs into the ensuite bathroom. Dropping to her knees by the toilet she throws up the entire contents of her stomach.

When the sickness subsides, Mia gets up off the floor and washes her face in the sink. The bathroom is black and white and elegant, but she feels woozy and can barely focus on her surroundings. She stares at herself in the mirror, seeing the bags under her eyes and the bloodshot whites that suggest she was drinking heavily the night before, something she is unused to doing.

Feeling a fraction steadier, she staggers back into the bedroom. She can't shape her thoughts into total coherence, there are too many details and images that loop around like an annoying stress dream. Everything has changed. Her life is no longer simple, and with the return of so much that has been suppressed, Mia isn't sure she wants it to be anymore.

She lies back down on the bed and begins to focus on the room as she tries to bring her mind back to the present. *Period but contemporary.* The décor is fresh and clean even as the furniture is renaissance. A perfect pairing of the good things about the present and the past and it shows magnificent taste, and wealth. Something that doesn't always go together in Mia's opinion.

'Annalise…' she says.

Yes. Annalise is an important and influential figure. She is the current chair of the Network. That was what she told her last night over a supper of chateaubriand and fresh vegetables. 'All grown,' Annalise had said, 'on the château's grounds.'

There's another flashback of memory that laps over the recollection of the night before. A lunch date with Uncle Andrew… no, not uncle. He was her father and she knew it as they sat opposite each other in the conservatory of his home in Lincolnshire. She'd often visited him there and they'd talked. When she was… *activated*… was that the right word? No. When she was allowed to remember, her father had told her all about Annalise.

'I don't trust her, of course. If anything happens to me, she'll make a move to control. But then she'll find that she can't do it without you.'

'Why?' Mia had asked.

'You hold the keys to my kingdom, Mia. You and Michael combined will be unstoppable. You could reshape the world. Buy governments,' he explained.

'Why would we want to?' Mia asked.

'Because power is freedom,' Beech had said.

He had made it seem so simple. Mia had listened and she understood now, how Annalise needed her. It was obvious really. There'd always been a Beech running the Network. Male or female, it didn't matter, they were always known as 'Mr Beech'. And the figurehead was what kept the Network together. As well as the fear of the current Mr Beech's wrath.

Annalise hadn't told her, but Mia knows that this is why she has been brought here, and why her memories have been returned. But it's no temporary transition and that is why it hurts so much. This time she remembers who she is – and it's permanent. It can't be taken from her, thanks to the codewords that her mother, Kritta, must have revealed to Annalise. As a result, Mia understands that she has to take over the reins or the Network will fall apart. All because Michael has failed to do so. Beech had known what he was doing with his children, even though the conditioning, the dual personalities and lives, were an experiment. As children they would switch from one personality to the other and their alter egos were totally unaware of each other.

That's why the two merging is so confusing and painful, Mia thinks. Just as Beech had warned her it would be.

Mia's mind settles. So much information is inside her that it's hard to focus on what is important. *The Network is designed to fail without its rightful leader.* Beech has never explained how or why this was. Perhaps it was something that his father had instilled to make sure his reign would never be challenged. It doesn't matter because now Mia recognizes it's time to take back control.

She sits up now on the bed. Her mind and body once more within her full possession. Annalise will ask her later why she didn't bring her daughter when she had requested it. Mia must have the answer ready.

Freya will one day take over the empire, and she must

never be given into the hands of Annalise. Even in her activated state, Mia knows that. Despite appearances, Annalise's 'invitation' was more of an order. But Mia understands that Annalise can't make a move against her. She'll be looking for an alliance. The cards are all in Mia's hands, as long as her daughter remains safe.

Chapter Forty-Five

JANINE

Janine searches through her encrypted email in search of news from Neva. It's been weeks since she helped Neva hide Michael and they've had no contact since. She doesn't know where Neva is or if she is still with Michael.

At the thought of Michael, Janine feels a burst of intense anger and frustration. Neva has feelings for the man: it is obvious. If Michael hadn't come along, if he wasn't around, perhaps Neva would have been able to see another place her heart could lie.

Part of her now wishes that she'd let the Network take him. But despite how she feels, Janine knows it is irrational to hold it against Neva that she doesn't feel the same: Neva was never hers. But on some level, she'd hoped that her loyalty and admiration would be noticed. It hadn't been. The thought stirs something in her that she is unused to: anger, jealousy and an onslaught of grief.

Janine is about to close her email when she finds

something in her junk mail that shouldn't be there. *It's from Kady.*

Despite believing she is over this period in her life, there is a tight lurch in Janine's chest. Kady had been important once. They'd shared so much, and Janine had thought she loved her. She stares at the subject line, *Hi Babe*, for a short time and then out of curiosity she opens the email.

Thought I'd catch up with you, Kady's email says. *What are you up to these days? Heard you quit your job and moved away.*

Janine reads the email again. It's a simple enquiry that could mean nothing at all. It's been over a year since they last spoke, and Janine found her with another girl. At the time she'd been devastated. She'd never expected Kady to betray her like that. Even now, the thought of it still hurts. For a time the whole affair had run around her brain until she short circuited, got drunk and then picked up a man on a one-night stand. The breakdown hadn't lasted long, and Janine had regretted the drunken fumbling and had soon forgotten the name of the man in question.

She reads Kady's message again. Without contact with Neva she feels isolated. *What harm can it do?*

I'm in London now, she replies. *Have another job. What are you doing?*

Kady answers almost immediately. *I'm in London too. Want to meet for a drink?*

Janine stares at the screen. Her mind goes over the good and the bad and the intense loneliness she'd felt when Neva had disappeared from her life before. Kady had once stepped in and filled the breach. Despite how that had turned out, Janine is still open to friendship with her. After all, Neva might not be in touch for months or even years. If ever again. She just doesn't know. But one thing she does understand is that she will be thrown back into that empty void with no friends, no home and no lover once Neva uses her again for whatever intrigue she's involved with. It is all more depressing than it should be to someone in her position.

She emails Kady her new phone number. Known only by Neva. Within seconds the phone rings.

'Hey,' Janine says.

'Hi beautiful. I missed you. Can you forgive a stupid tart for her mistakes?' Kady says.

Janine feels breathless as she hears Kady's voice. Yes, she still is under her skin. Perhaps as much as Neva is. But Janine holds back her giddy emotions: she doesn't want to be hurt again. Not by Neva and not by Kady. Even so, curiosity gets the better of her. What does Kady look like now? Maybe she won't find her attractive anymore? Surely then she can put this part of her life aside for good?

'I'm up for a drink,' Janine says, hoping that she doesn't sound too interested.

After arranging to meet, Janine puts her phone down and closes her laptop.

She dresses, making more effort than usual. Her hair is dyed Neva's colour at the moment, just in case she needs to double for her. It's longer than usual, and she wears it down, over her shoulders. After she applies make-up, she finds a short, sexy dress to wear. She holds the dress up against her body and looks at herself in the mirror.

'What are you doing?' she says to her reflection. 'She cheated on you, remember?'

The thought of seeing Kady again is such a diversion that Janine pulls the dress on anyway, enjoying the feeling as it hugs her curves. She could do with some relaxation after the last job with Neva, and Kady was always good at helping her do that. What real harm could it do?

Chapter Forty-Six

BEN

Feeling suspicious of Steward, Ben doesn't contact his boss when they move him and Freya back to RAF Digby. Instead he destroys his mobile phone and leaves the remnants of it in the old house. He also doesn't take his work laptop, passing it instead to Ray Martin to return to MI6.

His mind is a mess. He can't believe that Mia has been taken, nor that she appeared to go willingly. It was just as Michael had warned, back when they were first in protective custody. Now he wishes he'd listened harder. He hadn't really believed the things Michael had said about Mia being triggered. It just wasn't possible that she could become someone else. But Ben knows it had been the same with Michael for a time too, he had just hoped that it wouldn't work on her, or, better still, that the Network would never find her.

Now, back in the family apartments at the barracks, Ben feels helpless. All he wants to do is find Mia and bring her back home to safety, but Ray has ordered him to stay with Freya.

Ben feeds Freya some baby food followed by formula milk because she's fractious. After she's eaten, he places her down on the floor on her baby mat. In the last few hours since they'd arrived at the barracks, Freya has begun to flip herself over onto her front. Ben watches her do it again and his heart hurts because he knows that Mia would be so thrilled to see this progress. The thought brings tears to his eyes and makes him feel even more useless. What kind of agent was he that he couldn't protect his own wife?

Ben feels responsible for what's happened. He'd known that Steward was spying on Archive, but not why. Though he suspected it was some sort of pissing contest between Steward and Ray Martin. If it hadn't been for the fact that he hadn't wanted to give up his career, Ben and Mia would have been off the radar. He'd have been with her all the time too, ready to defend her, and Jack Harman wouldn't have had to fight off three of the Network's thugs alone. Ben is sure he had been followed after one of the meetings Steward had insisted on having. He's always known Steward to be a prick. Now he is paying for ignoring his instincts. He should have stayed away from Steward and MI6.

For the first time since they'd had their daughter, Ben regrets their decision to become a family. Not because he doesn't love Freya – he does, and it is agony – but because he can't help wondering if Mia was somehow activated into desiring motherhood and becoming a breeder for the Network. From the point when Mia left their home, leaving

Freya behind, it feels to Ben like nothing in his life is genuine: a thought that sinks inside him and causes deep regret. Hadn't Mia once felt the same when she'd learned that Ben had pursued her in his attempts to take down Beech? He can't help believing that this was all karma.

A knock at the door of the flat brings him away from his dark thoughts.

No one is supposed to know they're there, so he checks the spyhole in the door first. It's Ray Martin. He opens the door.

'Can I come in?' Ray says.

Ben steps back and allows Ray to enter.

'Can I get you a drink?' Ben asks, remembering his manners.

'I'm not here for a social call. I received this today,' Ray says.

Ray holds out a letter that is addressed to Ben. Ben looks at it, recognizing Mia's handwriting. His heart begins to beat harder as a rush of fear-soaked adrenaline races through his body.

'It came in an envelope that was postmarked three days ago,' Ray says. 'There was a letter to me, asking me to give this to you unopened. As it's addressed to you, I didn't open it until Mia went missing. I had to then. I hope you understand. It's from Mia. You need to read this now.'

Ben's hand is shaking as he takes the envelope. He looks down at the handwriting again. His wife has a particular scrawl, often hurried and untidy, and his name on the front has those usual rushed curves. Ben pulls the letter from the already opened envelope to see a handwritten note. Unlike the urgent penmanship on the front, the handwriting inside is neater and appears to be carefully considered.

Ben,

Today I began to remember something very important. I'm going to be gone soon and you'll want to come looking for me, but this is what I need you to do. You have to stay with Freya and keep her safe. They want her Ben. You know who I'm talking about and I don't need to spell it out here. But they can't have her and you must be that last line of defence.

I know what I'm asking will be difficult for you to do. But don't leave Freya in the care of anyone else. Not even for a moment.

You can't trust anyone now. Especially me.

I love you.

Mia xxx

Ben lets Ray take the letter from his trembling fingers. The blood has surged into his face. He feels hot and feverish and very scared.

'I guess she finally remembered who she is,' Ray says.

'But what does this mean? Even if she remembers she can't forget who she has been. She can't forget our life together,' Ben says. 'She can't want to be parted from Freya!'

He slumps down onto the sofa near Freya. The little girl

is on her stomach again and rocking back and forth as though she's working out how to crawl for the first time. Ben is in shock. He feels alone and afraid. An emotion he's unused to. He stares down at his daughter and his mind tries to anticipate a future as a single parent.

'We'll find her,' Ray says.

Ben looks up at him. His eyes are wet with unshed tears.

'But what then? She's changed now and forever lost to us as who she was,' Ben says.

'Not necessarily. Michael was able to combat his conditioning. He remembered his real self and chose to be true to it,' Ray says.

'What if we speak to Michael? Maybe he'll remember something that could help,' Ben says.

'Michael has gone AWOL. He's looking for Mia himself,' Ray says.

'Oh my god, that idiot. It's exactly what they'll want him to do. And when they have them both we'll never find them again,' Ben says.

'I know this is hard to hear,' Ray says. 'But you need to concentrate on Freya's safety now. We're going to keep you both on base for the foreseeable future. No excursions without security. And, as Mia said, don't leave the baby with anyone. She just isn't safe.'

Ben looks down at his daughter again and then the tears finally come. He feels like he's breaking apart as, like a cavern that both he and Freya may topple into, the very real possibility of a future without Mia looms before him.

Ray pats his back in an awkward gesture of sympathy,

then he turns and leaves the apartment without another word.

He's just as shell-shocked as me, Ben thinks.

When the door closes behind Ray, Ben picks up Freya and holds her. She's so like Mia that he feels the urge to cry again. But instead he tries to smile at the baby.

'We'll be okay,' he says. 'Uncle Ray will get Mummy back for us. Just you wait and see.'

He doesn't believe the words that he uses to soothe Freya, but he hopes that somehow, by some miracle, they will come true. Because Ben doesn't want to do this alone. He's a spy, not a single parent, and has never seen himself in any other role, even as he'd fallen in love with Mia and started their 'normal' life together.

His heart aches and the confusion and stress of the situation gives him the urge to run away from it all, as Mia appears to have done.

'I'm not cut out for this,' he says to Freya.

But then, Mia's words come back to him. *You can't trust anyone. Especially me.*

'But I'll do my best to make sure you're safe,' he says. 'Not matter how hard it is.'

Freya gurgles and giggles and Ben smiles despite how heartbroken he's feeling. At least he has the unconditional love of his daughter. And Freya needs him. It's the most important job he's ever had in his life.

Chapter Forty-Seven

MICHAEL

'Have you brought me on a wild goose chase?' I ask as we sit in a small patisserie in Toulouse, drinking coffee with two pastries on a plate to share.

'My source says Annalise is here. And if that's the case, then Mia is more than likely with her,' Neva says.

'Where here? We don't even have a proper location,' I say.

I'm frustrated because we've been here two days now and know nothing more.

'You don't understand. The information I'm waiting for has to be found discreetly. It will be dangerous for my source to blatantly search for it. But she's one of the best hackers I've ever worked with. And we're here because she's narrowing down the location using a lot of subtlety,' Neva explains.

Despite spending every waking moment together for over sixty hours, we haven't been intimate again. Neva hasn't even broached the subject. I'm going through a range of emotions from confusion to relief. As if she's afraid of how she feels about me, Neva has shut me out. I am teetering on the edge of my nerves all the time, torn as I am between my feelings for her and the need to find Mia as soon as possible. Part of me thinks this divorcing of her emotions is down to Neva's conditioning: she's in work mode and therefore wants to keep her mind on the job. If so, I applaud it, but I can't help feeling insecure anyway. It's too easy for her to lapse back into the cold calculator operative, though really I shouldn't be surprised. I'm capable of doing the same thing myself. At least I was, until Neva came back into my life and changed me. Now, I wish I too could keep my mind solely on our search. Life is complicated enough without my seesawing emotions.

After breakfast we go back to the hotel and check Neva's encrypted laptop for messages again. But nothing has come from Elbakitten and I'm beginning to wonder if this person is just stringing Neva along. Beyond telling her Annalise is in Toulouse, we have no other information, and this town has too many occupants to make it possible for us to come across her by accident.

Toulouse is a beautiful place though, and if we were here for romantic reasons there'd be much to do. As the capital of France's southern Occitanie region, Toulouse is near the Spanish border. There is an impressive river – the Garonne – that passes through the centre of the town. Locally the town is known as *La Ville Rose* (The Pink City) and Neva points out to me that it's because of the beautiful terra-cotta bricks that most of the buildings are made from.

From our hotel room I look out on the Garonne and

appreciate the charm of this place, while Neva searches the dark web again for any further signs of Elbakitten or Annalise.

'I think Elbakitten has had to go to ground,' Neva says now. 'It's not like her to be offline this long. She must have been compromised.'

'We may have to begin our own searches,' I say. 'Are you sure there was nothing else she could give you?'

'It wasn't her that told me to come here,' Neva admits. 'She's merely been trying to narrow the search.'

'Who was it then?' I ask.

'Eldon Fracks,' she says. 'I caught up with him in Belgium. He told me Annalise had a château attached to a vineyard. But I wanted to be sure before I go in, guns blazing.'

'A château? Maybe that won't be too difficult to find after all,' I say, though I wish she'd told me this sooner and I'd have begun to do my own searches of the area. I wonder why she would want to delay and then it occurs to me that Annalise is Neva's birth mother. Maybe that is why she is hesitant: she's afraid to meet her for the first time. Annalise and revenge are so close, what must Neva be going through right now?

For the first time I begin to consider that Neva's shutting down has nothing whatsoever to do with me after all. It's a defence mechanism: she's preparing for this meeting. She's defending herself against the certainty that she must kill her own mother.

Down below our window I see a stretch limousine pull up at the patisserie we'd just eaten in. The driver gets out, goes inside. I frown. There's something about the uniform he's wearing that scratches at my brain with sickening familiarity.

'Neva. Come here,' I say.

Understanding the urgency in my voice, she comes to the window and looks down.

'The limo,' I say.

At that moment the chauffeur comes out of the patisserie holding a large bag of pastries. He gets back in the driving seat and pulls away.

'The Network are here. And I'm sure that means so is Annalise.'

I'm shocked to realize that the suited appearance of the driver was the Network's standard uniform. But I don't know what it is about the black suit that makes him belong to them.

'How do you know it's definitely one of theirs?' I ask. 'Any driver might wear a black suit.'

'The tie,' Neva says. 'They always wear a red tie.'

I remember then, something that Beech had once said to me about the uniform of his minions. He could always recognize his own at a distance.

'You're right,' I say.

'We're too late to follow, but let's see if this is a standard trip for that driver. Maybe Annalise has a sweet tooth,' she says. 'And that patisserie *is* the best one in the area.'

Chapter Forty-Eight

MIA

Annalise shows Mia the estate with much pride. As well as the main château she discovers the training school building next door that has been purpose-built for Annalise's students.

'Over five hundred children have passed through this school,' Annalise says, 'and none of them have been a failure.'

Some of the students put on a display for Mia. She feels like she is watching a rehearsal for *The Karate Kid* and that this place is a dojo of the most exclusive order. It makes her somewhat uncomfortable to see the boys and girls hammering each other until one of them wins the battle, but it also brings back memories of her own training and induction into the Network. She and Michael had fought often together, and sometimes they'd also battled with other children in the house.

In her mind's eye she remembers the blonde girl the most. She was tall, but waiflike. She and Michael were often exchanging looks. Was this the woman that Michael had later almost lost his career over? Something jogs in her mind, a painful bump that shoots a shard of lightning into her brain. When it subsides, Mia remembers Neva. She has a distinct vision of her and Michael standing side by side. She sees the slight touch of their fingers entwining, then pulling apart as Beech barks orders at them all. Only Mia had seen it, or maybe Beech had chosen to ignore it. Was Neva Michael's first love? Was she the reason he'd never settled with the myriad of girlfriends that had passed through his life?

When the school demonstration is over, Annalise takes her to the nursery. Mia keeps her face blank as Annalise outlines her plan for future generations of operatives who will be procured and trained, a legacy that Annalise feels worthy of her time and effort.

'These are my children,' Annalise says. 'I want the best for them, and they want the best for me.'

Mia doesn't question her on this, but she sees the subtle brainwashing and radicalization in one of the classrooms in a group of 3-year-olds playing in a situational environment that is almost role play.

When Annalise enters, the children form a line and stand with their hands behind their backs like young soldiers. Then with one command, they 'fall out', and become like ordinary kids once more. After that the children surround Annalise and vie for her attention. Showing her their artwork, and scribbled writings, all of which are advanced for their age. What imprints itself most on Mia is how they all call her 'Mother'.

They stay in the nursery a long time, and Mia watches the subtle manipulation Annalise uses with each of the children, as she rewards them with hugs and pats and kisses for their hard work. She is the single person in the room that gives them affection. The teachers remain cold and passive as though they too are conditioned to behave a certain way.

When she's shown her everything, Annalise leads Mia from the nursery back to the château and outside onto a garden terrace.

A small mosaic table is set out with coffee and a plateful of the pastries under a gazebo.

'Please, let us breakfast,' Annalise says.

Feeling dazed and drained by all she's seen, Mia sits at the table and allows Annalise's butler to pour steaming-hot coffee into her cup. He places a napkin on her lap and then puts a plate down in front of her. He serves her one of the pastries from the plate in the middle.

'I'll serve myself,' Annalise says and she dismisses him.

When he's gone, and they are alone in the glorious gardens of the château, Mia sips the coffee and waits for Annalise to speak. So far, Annalise has not told her why she's here, and even though Mia already suspects, she keeps her knowledge to herself. But Annalise is in no hurry to speak as she drinks her coffee, pulling one of the pastries apart with her fingers and eating each piece.

'When I arrived,' Mia says, 'you told me you had a proposition for me.'

'You must try the pastries,' Annalise says.

'I don't wish to be rude, but I'd like to understand where

we are right now. Am I, despite your reassurances, your prisoner?'

Annalise puts down the remains of her food and dabs her lips with the napkin.

'My dear Mia, I wanted to show you what I've built here. And you most certainly aren't a prisoner. You're my guest. Haven't you been free to roam these last few days?'

'Yes. But I haven't tried to leave. What will happen if I do?'

Annalise sips her coffee again. 'You really should try the pastries. They are most delicious.'

Mia picks up the croissant from her plate and takes a small bite. The sweet-tasting pastry melts in her mouth and is every bit as good as Annalise has said but she doesn't feel hungry: she feels impatient.

'I do have a proposal,' Annalise says now.

Mia nods. 'Okay.'

'I'm informed by Kritta that you should have your memory back now,' Annalise says with a tight smile as though this is not the news she had hoped for, but is coming to terms with.

Mia doesn't answer.

'And for that reason,' Annalise continues, 'I am ready to talk to you.'

'Go on,' Mia says.

'As you know, Beech is dead. I have been elected chair. We need a woman in charge. One who will see the vision I have for the future. A woman who is also a mother and understands what it is to give up their child for this cause. As I have done, and many before me did.'

'Freya is not up for grabs,' Mia says now, all thought of making an excuse gone with the possibility that Annalise wishes to use her. 'No matter what my father tried to brainwash me to do.'

'I don't ask for her,' Annalise says. 'Initially it was what I wanted. But since we've spent time together, I've reconsidered my position. You see, I am mother to many children and many generations. I understand that bond more than most. What I ask… what I suggest… is that we form an alliance.'

Mia sighs. It's as expected, but the terms will be the make or break on this deal. 'In what way?'

'I will rule the Network with you. But you will be, to all intents and purposes, the figurehead.'

'You already have the Network at your command. Why do you need me?' Mia asks.

'So, we are playing *that* game?' Annalise says. 'All right. I'll spell it out for you, since you wish to pretend you don't know. It was brought to my attention that the Network can only be *owned* by a Beech. You're that Beech, Mia. It was going to be your brother, but I soon realized how wrong that was. It has to be you. You will be Mr Beech and any division that is happening within the organization will end.'

Mia nibbles again at the pastry to give herself time to think. She remembers well her father's instructions. Beech had told her Annalise wanted power, and he'd placed it beyond her reach.

'What's in it for me, if I am "Mr Beech" in name only?' Mia says.

'Safety,' Annalise says. 'No one would dare harm you

for fear of their own undoing. Didn't you ever wonder why the other committee members didn't rise against Beech? They couldn't, their conditioning wouldn't allow it. Also, you will still be the most powerful woman in the world. You'll have access to all of Beech's wealth, naturally. Anything you want for you and your family.'

Mia glances back towards the training building. 'But you are building a new army who don't have that conditioning. So, what's to stop you taking everything the Network has when you're strong enough?'

'My own organization, the Almunazama, is new and does not have the long history that the Network has. As you know, the Network has been around now for generations. Always ruled by one Mr Beech or another. I don't want to destroy everything the Network has. I want… a future for my own child within it. When I step back, my biological daughter will partner with you. When both of you are done, then her child and yours will rule hand in hand. It will be the perfect pairing. The growing strength of the Almunazama along with the empire that is the Network. And my people will be taught ultimate loyalty to both as we combine our strengths.'

Mia is thoughtful. This is not what she expected. She remembers Beech's warning to protect herself from Annalise, who he believed would betray him. If he could have foreseen an alliance of this magnitude though, would he have joined forces with her himself?

Mia thinks not, but her safety is still on the line and so she decides to give Annalise's proposal serious consideration. After all, the Network is powerful, and *power is freedom*. Would it be so bad to join forces with this strong, determined and charismatic woman in order to guarantee Freya's future? But Mia is a Beech and ultimately Annalise's terms only offer her a name badge and not full control of her birthright. Even with her life on the line, she knows she has to broker this deal and twist it to her own advantage.

Mia sees herself as holding all the cards, while Annalise frantically does the leg work. And then, Freya would hold the same enviable position later on. It was what Beech had wanted ultimately, though his methods of raising his children were questionable. Mia knew she could change things there for the better too, just as Annalise had.

'I agree that it's time for a woman to take action now. I'll give you an alliance but I won't just be a figurehead. I run the Network, you run the Almunazama, but we work together to strengthen our grip on our territories,' Mia says.

Annalise stops eating and studies her.

'You really *are* Mr Beech,' she says. 'Will you work with me, Mia?'

'The way I see it, this way we all win,' Mia says.

'What about your brother?' Annalise asks. 'What if he comes after you? He's sworn loyalty to MI5 and his precious Archive.'

Now Mia feels the pull of everything Beech had secretly prepared her for: Beech had taught her well. Mia recalls every lesson, every battle and every detail that as a child she'd craved to know. Now she recognizes the Beech inside herself. All along, even as Mia Cusick, she'd craved it, yearned for it, and never understood what it was that she always felt so dissatisfied about with her life. She thinks now of Ben. Part of her, the Mia Beech part, had always known he worked for MI6. She'd reeled him in, nurturing the love he had for the woman he thought was Mia Kensington.

She sees and remembers all of her conditioning, but unlike Michael she doesn't feel a need to fight it. Instead, she embraces who she is, preparing as she does to step into the role of Mr Beech. After all, this is her destiny.

'If Michael gets in my way, I'll take care of him,' Mia says in answer to Annalise's question.

'And what about your daughter?' Annalise asks.

'She'll be brought up knowing her birthright,' Mia says. 'Just as I did.'

Chapter Forty-Nine

BETH

It takes Beth a few days before she manages to separate Elliot from his phone. Putting a ban on it at the dinner table, she takes it from him and stows it in his coat pocket.

'I've turned mine off,' she tells him, 'and I want no work talk tonight. I just want "us" time. Open that bottle of wine for me, will you? I'll hang your coat up in the hall.'

Beth takes the coat out of the kitchen and then quickly removes the phone from Elliot's pocket. She activates the hacking device and gives permission from Elliot's phone to connect via Bluetooth, which allows her to copy the sim card and everything that's on it. Then she puts the phone back in the coat pocket and returns to Elliot in the kitchen. The wine is open and he's pouring it into their glasses.

Beth takes a casserole out of the oven and puts it on a heat-proof plate on the table.

'It's hot. Be careful,' she says.

The device takes half an hour and Beth makes every effort not to appear jittery as it does its work. Serving up warm baguettes with the casserole and some lavish salty butter, Beth continues to top up Elliot's glass until he's so relaxed, she's sure he isn't thinking about his phone.

When the first bottle is downed, Beth gets up.

'Let's live a little,' she says. 'There's another bottle in the wine rack, if you'll take care of it. I just need the loo.'

Beth hurries out to the hallway again and takes Elliot's phone from his pocket. The device shows green, which indicates that the copy is complete. She puts his phone back in the pocket and goes in the bathroom. She hides the hacking device in a bottle of aspirin. After flushing and washing her hands she comes into the hallway to find Elliot looking at his phone.

'Hey you! I said no phones tonight!'

'I'm just turning it off,' he says. Then he grabs her to him. 'How about we leave that wine to breathe for a while?'

She lets him take her upstairs.

They make love and afterwards, because of the wine and the food, not to mention a very intense orgasm, Elliot nods off.

Beth listens to his breathing level out before getting up. She pulls on her dressing gown and goes back downstairs. She takes the device from its hiding place and retrieves the other iPhone from her handbag. She activates the transfer into the new phone, it starts to overlay Elliot's details onto the new sim card.

She places the phone and stick in her robe pocket, then starts tidying up the kitchen, putting a lid on the remains of the casserole and the cork back into the second bottle of wine. After she's done this, she checks the phone. It's not quite done and she doesn't want to risk it being interrupted.

She pours herself another glass of wine while she waits.

The device takes longer to clone than it did to copy but when it's finally done, Beth looks at Elliot's apps. All of which are normal for any smart phone. She opens his text messages and sees a lot from his mother. She skips in and out of a few and there's nothing abnormal about any of the communications. The only thing that's odd is, Elliot has rarely mentioned her. It was weird considering how much Beth talked about her own mother to him, that he had never come back with any reference to his own. No, that wasn't strictly true. He'd talked about her once, not long after they first met. It was a casual comment, about having to do something for her.

Satisfied for now. She turns the phone off, swigs down the last of the wine in her glass and goes back upstairs.

In the room she removes the robe, taking the phone with her as she approaches the bed.

Elliot is snoring loudly. Beth opens the drawer at the side of the bed and places the clone phone inside it. She gets in beside him. Then she lies back and stares up at the ceiling. It is peculiar that he doesn't talk about his mum, but then Beth had never asked him about her or his father. From the texts she's read, his mother is rather needy. But all of this isn't a sign of any wrongdoing and so Beth closes her eyes.

I've overreacted, she tells herself. And then she feels guilty for her deceitful and untrusting behaviour. Elliot has been a sweetheart from the day they met. She has no right to question him: omission is not a lie.

Despite feeling anxious about her own actions, Beth drifts off to sleep feeling more confident that she's made the right decision in getting involved with Elliot. Perhaps it is time for him to meet the boys, after all.

Chapter Fifty

JEWEL

When she checks her email in an internet café Jewel finds the first message in a while from Mother.

Keep Kozem's money if it makes you happy. Our dreams are almost a reality. It's time to come home, little one.

Jewel feels the swirl of Mother's love come over her as she reads these words. Mother wants her home. She is not to be punished for the theft. She can return. But still she has to find the one thing that has always been between them.

Neva.

She had hoped the beautiful deaths she'd delivered would bring her out from wherever she was hiding. But it appears that Neva is oblivious to them. Of course, Jewel had been banking on Michael to share information about them because Neva was being brought into MI5. But Jewel hadn't predicted that Neva and he would be parted so abruptly. Damn Granger and his accusation. It almost ruined everything. She's annoyed even now about it. She should have had access to Neva. She shouldn't need to still be trying to grab her attention from a distance.

The same intense fury she'd rained on her victims rises up inside her, and it pushes away the warmth of Mother's summons. She casts a gaze around the place, noting the other users of the computers around her – mostly teenagers, and one man that looks like an itinerant. No one is paying particular attention to her activities or her anger which is on the brink of exploding from her.

She reads Mother's email again and this time sees the command for what it is. 'Little one' is a trigger she's built into them all. A way to bring them right back to the days spent in the nursery. She takes a deep breath, then slowly exhales, centring herself, bringing back all calm and control.

Returning her attention to the computer again, she uses a VPN to mask her movements and logs on to the dark web. She goes back to the forum where she touches base with Neva as Elbakitten. She's spent months building her trust, and now, after sending her to be near Mother, she has left her to sweat for a few days. Neva is ripe for picking and Jewel will make one final triumph before she kills her. The most glorious and extravagant death of all.

She falls into a reverie about her last kill. Cassandra – named after a Greek prophet whose predictions were never believed. In the end Cassandra saw her own death and she too was unable to avoid it.

Jewel brings her mind back to the present and types a message to Neva. Though Neva goes under several different names in onionland, Jewel has been able to recognize her new handles each time. But she sends the message to the GloriaBoo identity because this is the one that Elbakitten has always worked with.

Sorry for delay. Think I was being tracked for a while but managed to lose them.

Neva replies almost in an instant. Yes, she's been waiting for her.

In Toulouse. Where is my mark? she asks.

Jewel takes a breath. She feels excited and adrenaline pumps into her like always when she's speaking to Neva. She can almost touch her – just like that day when they stood side by side! Jewel often thinks about it. That moment when they were briefly together, exchanging pleasantries. And Neva hadn't recognized her.

Jewel sends Neva the location of the château with no explanation. Then she logs off the borrowed computer knowing that she has just set wheels in motion that will gather momentum and end with her final revenge.

She looks at her watch. *It's time.*

She gets up and leaves the internet café, then walks down the street towards the bar where she's arranged to meet Janine. Her revenge has been gestating for a long time. Long enough to have used Neva's prodigy as a pawn. But now she will be the ultimate sacrifice.

She reaches the bar and goes inside.

Janine, ever punctual and so desperate for attention, is waiting at the bar, a shot of neat vodka already in her hand, and a tight-fitting *fuck me* dress clinging to her body.

Janine turns and again Jewel sees how close to Neva's double she really is. The tones in the hair are perfect. Jewel flushes with excitement and anger as Janine stands to greet her.

'Kady,' Janine says. 'It was nice to hear from you.'

Jewel kisses Janine on the lips, then she pulls her into her embrace. She's trembling as she tries to hold herself in check. She sees it all behind her eyes. The victims, all in a tableau with Neva at its core.

'I'm such an idiot,' Jewel says. 'I've missed you so much.'

Janine's arms linger around her and when they pull away, Jewel can see the pathetic vulnerability shining through a confident veneer.

Yes, Jewel thinks, *you're very needy, Janine. I must cure you of that trait.*

Chapter Fifty-One

MICHAEL

When Neva receives the note from Elbakitten, with the address where Annalise lives, I want to go there straight away and find Mia. Neva takes my arm and pulls me down onto the bed. She holds me in an uncharacteristic display of sensitivity.

'No, Michael. No. Listen to me,' she says as I try to pull away.

The smell of her hair is enticing and too distracting. I have to save my sister from the clutches of Annalise.

'Annalise is no fool,' Neva whispers in my ear. 'The place will be surrounded by security.'

I feel her hot breath on my neck and I shudder. I'm torn between desire and resentment. As I stop fighting and start listening, I've never been so divided about anyone before. Neva brings out such emotion in me. Rage, anger, lust. I don't want to resist her any longer. From the moment we met as children, and our fingers reached for each other, I'd belonged to Neva. That's why I listen to her now and don't rush away though every instinct makes me want to.

'Then how will we get to Mia?' I ask.

I nuzzle her neck. She takes a breath as she feels the change in my mood.

'Recon,' she says. 'We have to check out the perimeter first. At a safe distance, because they'll have security for miles around that place.'

Once she's certain that I won't just walk out, she lets me go. Now we are no longer touching I'm spiralling down into a pit of frustration.

'Neva…' I say.

I pull her back to me and kiss her. She allows it, and just when I think we are at the point of no return, she pushes me aside and gets up off the bed.

'Let's check this place out, shall we?' she says.

She leaves me hanging and I'm thrown again by that sudden coldness that she puts on and takes off as though it's a piece of clothing. It takes a minute for me to switch my libido off. I'm only human, after all.

I focus my energy on the idea that we may soon find Mia.

Neva opens her laptop. She Googles the château and vineyard: D'Aragon Wines are held in high regard, especially with local bars and restaurants. They operate a tasting house on the premises that's open to the public, with tours of the winery included.

'We've probably even had some of her wine since we've been here,' Neva says, taking us back to the problem at hand.

She studies the location on Google Maps, zooming in to see three main buildings, one of which is the seventeenth-century château at the heart of the hundred or so acres of land. As Neva focuses on gaining information, I watch her, wondering what she is feeling about the prospect of coming face to face with her real mother. Though Neva has always suspected her mother gave her to the house, we have never discussed what she hopes will happen when this reunion occurs.

'Do you know this place?' I ask her as she frowns down at the still image.

'I probably do, but I don't recall it,' Neva says.

She doesn't need to say more. I suspect the first five years of her life were spent here until the Network took Neva. Was Annalise willing to let her child go? Or did she resent Beech's power to take her away?

Neva continues to search around the perimeter of the château and vineyard, working out a possible access point to the place.

'Look at this,' she says.

She zooms in on an aerial shot of a courtyard.

'One of the buildings has this as its centre. It looks like… an arena,' she says.

'This is a kill house?' I ask.

'Very likely,' Neva says. 'Which means there will be more than a few trained assassins on the complex.'

'Come on,' I say.

'Where?'

'We'll go and hire a car and take a drive to the place. It's open to the public, right?' I say.

'I need to change my look,' she says. 'And so do you. That bristle you've grown over the last few days will help.'

I run my hand over my chin and nod.

'Different hair then?' I ask.

'Wait here. I'll be back soon,' she says. 'Don't go anywhere without me.'

I nod. My moment of insanity has passed and I know I can't do this without Neva or a viable plan.

'Don't be long,' I say.

Neva comes back a couple of hours later with wigs, make-up and clothing that will transform us both.

She makes me sit at the dressing table and then she cuts and changes the style of my hair, making it shorter at the sides than usual. She leaves the bristle on my face, and then hands me a pair of contact lenses. They are brown to cover my blue. I put them in my eyes and blink until they settle down. Then she gives me a bag containing new clothing. A pair of charcoal-coloured chinos and a black polo shirt. There is also a pair of brown leather loafers which are my size. I change as Neva sets about transforming herself.

She pulls on a brunette bobbed wig, and puts green lenses in her eyes, covered by a pair of metal-rimmed glasses. Her make-up is light and natural, browns around her eyes and a pale-pink lipstick to finish the look. These small touches make her look completely different.

The clothing she's chosen is simple. A pair of jodhpurs, with a polo-neck shirt and a sleeveless padded tabard.

Added to this look is a pair of low-heeled, brown leather boots which she pulls on over the jodhpurs.

'We're looking for wine to ship home to England to our country estate,' she says.

And I realize our somewhat understated country look is exactly the image she was going for.

In another bag, Neva has a Glock 17, and several cartridges. I check the safety is on, and place the gun in the waistband of the chinos. I cover it with a jacket. Neva puts a knife in her boot, and a gun in the back of her jodhpurs. The tabard hides the bulge of the weapon.

Online I hire a car, opting for an Audi R8 V10 sportscar, reasoning that a couple with money wouldn't drive a boring Fiat. When the hire company arrive with the car it's bright red. It suits the image we are trying to put across.

Using Neva's phone, I put the address into Maps and drive the car away from the hotel towards our destination.

Chapter Fifty-Two

JEWEL

As she gets on the Paris Métro and heads to Charles de Gaulle Airport, Jewel's mind drifts back to the years spent at the château. And the brief time that Mother sent her away to England to further her education.

She'd arrived there, confident that she knew what she had to do. They'd called her Elizabeth for the sake of the visit – though that wasn't her real name. Then the woman known as Tracey changed her name to Jewel. She'd liked it much better than her real name. 'Jewel' implied that she was unique and precious and above all valuable.

Mother had briefed her before the visit. It was like their other exercises when they pretended to be soldiers and fought to win Mother's approval. Only this time, these other children, they'd all be several months into a different kind of training from the château children. Some of them had even forgotten who they once were. Like Fae. Jewel knew who she really was but she wasn't allowed to say anything. Fae was Mother's missing daughter and they called her Neva.

Jewel had been pleased to see her. But Neva behaved like they'd never met. She behaved as though she hated Jewel on sight, treating her like a usurper.

She realized it was impossible to befriend any of the other children – they weren't comrades like in the château and they didn't 'play' – they were pitted against each other instead like dogs in a ring. Jewel had tried so hard to prove herself worthy, mimicking their behaviour: a perfect chameleon. But then Neva had ruined it all for her when she'd started that fight in the dormitory.

Jewel hadn't wanted to hurt her, Mother wouldn't like that, she was sure, but as the sparring began to get personal, Jewel fought back as hard as she could.

The others had surrounded them. They watched Neva beat Jewel, without raising a hand to help. They were feral creatures, craving violence as much as they craved food or sleep.

Jewel understood later that it was a rite of passage. One of them had to lose. One had to win. And Neva had overpowered her because she wanted it more: taking away Mother's love when Jewel failed to prove herself the best.

She remembers now Mother's disdainful expression when she collected her. She went inside the house, and there was an argument between Tracey and Mother that Jewel didn't understand. It wasn't supposed to happen. The two of them had not been meant to fight each other. Mother blamed Tracey for it.

Back then though, all Jewel saw was how Mother stayed

inside and sat with Neva, holding her on her lap, showering the kisses on her that Jewel deserved.

Jewel waited by the door and listened to the words of love that poured from Mother's lips. Words that had never been said to her in such a way. Mother showed Neva a different side than her other children saw. She told Neva how proud she was of her – there was to be no punishment for her vicious turning on Jewel, even though she hadn't merited it. Neva was absolved of fault.

'You are what they are making you,' Mother had said. 'No one can blame you for that.'

Jewel was taken back to the château in disgrace. Her wounds were tended by the nurse in the medical room. But Mother never hugged or comforted her while she healed. She never said words that took away Jewel's guilt. It was as if she was a major disappointment to Mother. And she was returned instead to the training school with instructions that she must work harder.

She never considered that Mother was the one who really had something to prove by putting her in the house in the first place. No, the blame was all Jewel's to bear.

Jewel worked harder than the others after that. She rose in rank among Mother's children. She became the most trusted, the strongest, and above all the most dangerous of her operatives.

When she graduated from the school, and was sent out on her first assignment, she killed her mark with emotionless skill. She hadn't been alone, but the others with her were under instruction not to interfere. She had to win or lose on her own. It was a final test and this time she passed it.

She returned to the château immediately afterwards where Mother waited for her.

'I'm so proud of you,' she said. 'Come and embrace me. My little one. My brave and strong child. You will lead my army. You will make the Network stand up and take notice. One day, the kingdom will be mine.'

Jewel had melted in her arms breathing in her musky perfume. *Mother. Mother. I love you,* she wanted to say. But the words wouldn't come. *I do everything for you.*

And then Mother said, 'One day Neva will return to us and then she will inherit my empire. And we will once again be a complete family.'

Jewel's heart broke into a million pieces. The pain was worse than the physical beating she'd endured from Neva. No one had done more than Jewel to prove her devotion to Mother. But in that moment, she knew that as long as Neva lived, Mother would never love her the same. Neva was the sacrificial lamb. She was the prodigal daughter that would one day return. She was the ultimate weapon. Neva was everything to Mother that Jewel wasn't.

Jewel had hidden her feelings. She'd let Mother hold her for as long as she wished. Then, when Mother let her go, she stepped to the door and took up the inspection stance.

'Fall out, soldier,' said Mother. 'Do something fun tonight. Have sex with one of the boys if you like. You're a woman now and can chose from any of them you wish.'

'Thank you, Mother,' Jewel had said.

She left her then, and went for a walk around the

perimeter, checking that Mother's other soldiers were doing the job they were meant to. She didn't take any of them to her bed though. Jewel didn't want the touch of anyone other than Mother, and certainly never some sweaty boy who she could beat in the arena anytime she wished.

No, it was not for her, despite Mother's permission to indulge: such liaisons should only be used for real gain. Jewel had learned that sex and love were for the weak.

Chapter Fifty-Three

BETH

It's just after five in the morning when Beth wakes. She reaches out her hand and discovers that Elliot's side of the bed, though still warm, is empty again. Light filters into the bedroom from the landing window because Elliot has left the door ajar. Beth lies in the gloom and listens. Even though he's speaking in hushed tones, she can hear his voice drift upstairs.

Beth turns to the bedside cabinet and opens the drawer. Taking the clone phone out, she looks at it. She can see he's on a call and the recipient is once again his mother. Beth fights with herself not to listen in. It would be so easy to press the phone to her ear but before she does, Elliot hangs up the call. Beth puts the phone back in her drawer and waits for him to return.

When Elliot comes into the room, Beth turns the light on beside the bed. He's shocked to see her awake.

'What's wrong?' she asks.

'Oh nothing, just went for a glass of water,' he says.

Beth blinks. She's hurt by the obvious lie. She decides to take the bull by the horns.

'You were on the phone,' she says. 'Who were you talking to?'

'It was just a work thing,' Elliot lies again.

Beth sighs. She doesn't know what to say or how to reveal she knows this is a lie without admitting to cloning his phone. Something they'd probably never be able to recover from as a couple.

'It's not the first time you've made calls in the night. Tell me what's going on.'

Elliot loiters by the bedroom door, uncertain what to say.

'It's my mother,' he says. 'She suffers from insomnia sometimes.'

'Your mother? You've never told me anything about her,' Beth points out. 'Where does she live?'

'She's in a care home in Manchester,' Elliot explains. 'I did mention her once. She's got dementia. I don't talk about her much because… I feel guilty about leaving her there. I thought you'd think bad of me.'

Beth folds her arms.

'Why would I think bad of you?'

Elliot shakes his head, reluctant to talk.

'You might as well tell me because I'm not going back to sleep until you do,' Beth says.

'I tried to look after her, but she needed twenty-four-hour care,' he says. 'The weirdest thing is, she's mostly okay and remembers everything, but then she gets these episodes. The doctors say, one day she won't remember who I am and that will be it. So, when she wants to talk to me, I let her.'

Beth processes this information but she still has doubts. Why would he talk about work to his ailing mother? And because she can't think of a reason, she asks him.

'I thought I heard you talk about the murder case to someone, a few nights ago. Were you talking to her?'

'Beth, my mother is the only person I talk to about anything other than you. You know what this job is like. We can't tell anyone anything. But sometimes, when she's not being very lucid and she's all confused, I talk shop just to have something to say. I know it's odd. But she never remembers our chats anyway. She just knows she's talked to me and it settles her down.' Elliot holds out his phone. 'Look at it if you want to. You'll see her texts and the calls I make.'

Beth shakes her head, refusing the phone.

'I'm sorry,' Beth says. 'It must be awful for you that she's fading.'

Elliot closes the bedroom door. He gets into the bed beside her.

'I was going to tell you about her. But… I didn't want it to be something we talk about. I really want it to be about our life when we're together. Mum's condition is a bit of a downer, and I try avoid thinking about it when I can.'

'I understand,' says Beth. 'I won't ask, but I want you to feel you can talk to me about her if you want to.'

The cloned phone is on her mind as she turns off the light and cuddles up to Elliot. She feels terrible that she hadn't just asked him what was going on sooner. She blames the current situation at Archive for her constant state of paranoia, but it doesn't excuse her suspicion of him. She closes her eyes, determined to return the phone and hacking device to Acquisitions the next day, both duly erased and reset.

When Elliot leaves for work the next day, Beth takes the phone out of the drawer. She switches it on and looks at the screen. Determined not to spy on him anymore, she is about to reset the phone back to factory settings when she sees that Elliot is writing a text to his mother.

Might be compromised, Elliot types. *Beth questioning our late-night calls.*

Time to come home? Mother replies.

Not quite yet, Elliot says. *Haven't got what we need.*

Hope you're not falling for the girl… Mother says.

Never in a million years, Elliot answers.

Make a move soon and get out of there! comes the reply.

Elliot replies that he is *On it* and the text exchange ends. Elliot then erases the conversation from his phone.

Beth stares at the message even as it disappears.

Elliot isn't who he says he is and even worse, he's using her. This is Beth's worst nightmare.

Beth turns the phone off. Putting it back in the bedside drawer once more, she sits down on the bed staring into space. She wants to cry but she holds it all in.

Elliot had been the one to say he loved her first. He'd instigated every step they'd taken to advance their relationship and he didn't fake his lust for her. That was genuine. But then, these things were easy for men to do. Beth knew she wasn't unattractive. She worked out, keeping herself fit to do her job and her body was toned. Yes, she was lust-worthy and Elliot may have seen that part as a perk of the job.

All of those romantic talks we've had, she thinks. How he must have laughed at her behind her back. Looking back at everything he'd said and done, Beth finds the deceit almost too hard to conceive. But on the text, Elliot had said he could never love her 'in a million years'. Beth feels sick to her stomach. She runs into the bathroom and dry heaves into the toilet bowl.

She's shaking and crying when she returns to the bedroom. She sees the ruffled sheets and her mind flashes back to the night before. The heady sex. Always so unselfish on Elliot's part as he made sure she was taken care of. Could someone really fake that?

She tries to reconcile what she's experienced with him and what she now knows about how he really feels and it's a hard pill to swallow.

He's a liar. No… he's a spy. Probably the mole that placed the bugs in their office. But how? He'd never been left alone when he visited her. Beth dismisses this as soon as she considers it. Elliot couldn't have planted the bugs.

She dries her eyes and tries to bring her mind back to what's important, taking the emotion out of it and looking at the situation as an agent. According to the text from 'Mother', he had a task to do. What was it?

Beth picks up her phone and searches for Ray's number.

She pauses, then presses cancel. What proof does she really have that Elliot isn't who he says he is? Ray will question why Beth suspected him in the first place. He'll tell her she shouldn't have acted alone, and he would be right. What she'd done was dangerous. And really, a few late-night calls weren't that suspicious, were they? Maybe she'd been looking for a way out of this relationship all along. At least, Ray might see it that way, and that would mean 'misuse' of MI5 equipment. A sackable offence. She can't afford to lose her job, not after all she's worked for.

Beth decides to keep her findings to herself for now. But it's not a decision she makes lightly. She's been an idiot in every sense. She's shown a serious lack of judgement in getting involved with Elliot, and in cloning his phone just to prove something to herself. Ray will not understand. Not unless she goes to him with something tangible. It is important to discover what Elliot is up to first, and next time to make sure that she screenshots any conversations he has with 'Mother' – whoever that really is. That way, she'll be covering her own back and hopefully bringing a spy in their midst to much-deserved justice. This is the only way she'll come out of this with both her reputation and her job still intact.

After confronting him for his late-night phone calls, she's sure he won't make any again when he's with her, but that doesn't mean she can't monitor others he makes during the day.

Feeling as though she's taking back control, Beth showers and changes. She removes the phone from the drawer and places it in her handbag, determined to keep checking it at intervals throughout the day. She's a spy. This is her job and she's damn well going to find out what Elliot is up to.

When she gets to work, Beth finds an email from Elsa saying she's been pulled away for a 'family emergency'. This means the office is only being manned by Beth and Ray. And Ray is out, having yet another meeting with MI6.

Beth curses under her breath. Some people just don't have the same work ethic as others. The girl hasn't been there long and she's already giving excuses not to come in. Beth had learned early on that you don't put family before this job. Beth finds herself wishing Michael was there. They'd at least be able to bounce ideas off each other, and maybe Beth would even ask his opinion about Elliot. He was after all the one person she'd feel safe to confide in.

On her own and trying to field calls as well as do her own job, Beth's day is swamped, and she only gets a chance to look at the phone at lunchtime and at 5:30 in the evening when she finally calls it a day. She sees that Elliot's phone has been silent all day. Beth begins to worry that he knows what she did.

She sends Elliot a text and tells him she's tired and needs a night alone. On the clone phone, she sees the words pop up as he sends the text.

Not upset with me, are you? he asks.

Beth has been expecting this and so she responds, *Think I'm coming down with something and just wouldn't want to give it you.*

Okay. Rest up. Let's talk tomorrow.

Beth wishes him a relaxing evening and then she studies his phone to see if he contacts anyone.

He doesn't.

She packs the phone away and picks up her handbag. Then on her own phone she sends a message to her security detail to arrange collection in the car park.

Beth locks up Archive's office and walks towards the lifts. She wasn't lying when she said she was tired. A night away from Elliot might help her get some perspective. She knows she'll have to face him again soon though. If she is to learn what he's up to, she has to be a better spy than him.

Beth gives a bitter smile. First and foremost, this is what she was trained for. She's a spy, Michael is a spy and so is Ray. Why should it surprise her that Elliot, MI5 pathologist, was anything else?

A night alone, that's all I need, Beth thinks. *And then I'm going to string that bastard along, just like he's been doing to me.*

Chapter Fifty-Four

BETH

After saying goodnight to her security detail, Beth closes the front door and walks down the hallway. In the kitchen, she drops her handbag down on the table. The house feels quiet: she realizes how used to having Elliot around she has become.

'That shitbag,' she murmurs.

She opens the fridge and pulls out a bottle of Sauvignon Blanc. Pouring herself a glass, Beth takes a long swig and then places it down on the kitchen table.

She returns the bottle to its spot in the fridge door. She's hungry but she doesn't feel like making herself hot food to eat alone. That too was something that she and Elliot had started doing together. Beth takes a block of cheese and some butter from the fridge. She puts them down on the worktop, opens a cupboard and takes out a packet of cream crackers. Then she puts a dinner plate on the worktop and she proceeds to make herself a snack.

Even now, as Beth butters the crackers, she can't believe how the past few months have been a lie. *He sure had me fooled.*

She sits down at the table and sips the wine. Then she takes a mouthful of cheese and cracker, choking it down. After a few more bites, she pushes the plate aside, finding it too difficult to eat. Beth is nauseated and only the wine makes her feel any better.

She gets up and takes the bottle back out of the fridge and tops up her glass.

Her phone rings then, and she sees her ex-husband's number come up. She hesitates to answer, imagining that he's calling just to tell her how foolish she was to let him go. But she and Callum are on good terms now and she's sure he no longer wants a reconciliation. In fact, her son, Callum junior, had let it slip that his dad had a new 'friend'. It had grated a little to know Callum was getting over her so soon, but hadn't she fallen into bed with Elliot not long after the split? To criticize Callum now would be hypocritical.

She answers the phone.

'Hi,' she says. 'Are the boys okay?'

'Yeah. Just wanted to see if you can make the school play next week? Phil has a lead part and he'd like you to be there.'

'I'll make sure I am,' she says. 'What day and time?'

Beth writes the details on the kitchen wall calendar and then Callum puts her on the phone to Phil.

'Hey Phil,' she says. 'What part are you playing then?'

Phil chatters about the play and Beth listens. Talking to her son at least takes her mind off Elliot and their current situation. She almost wishes she had never cloned his phone. That way, she would be ignorant of his lack of real love for her and maybe tonight she'd be enjoying his amazing tongue exploring her instead. But such benefits don't outweigh what she knows, and Beth can never go back to that time of innocence. He is a liar and a fraud. All she needs now is to learn who he's working for and what he wants.

When Phil's conversation dries up, Beth asks to speak to Cal.

'He's on a sleepover tonight,' Phil says. 'But he's got his phone with him so you can call him there.'

'Okay, honey. Love you,' she says. 'You guys are coming here at the weekend still, aren't you?'

'Yeah. See you Friday,' he says.

Beth hangs up the phone and tops up the glass she's been sipping from. Then she goes into the living room and turns on the television.

She flicks through the channels but nothing grabs her. She's down and doesn't know how to get herself back up again.

Going back to the kitchen for another refill, Beth's eyes fall on her handbag, still on the table where she left it. She opens it up and searches for the clone phone. *What is Elliot doing this evening?*

She pulls the phone from her bag and takes it into the living room. She checks the text messages and doesn't find any new ones. Then she notices that Elliot is actually on a call.

She opens it up and listens in, something she shouldn't

be able to do unless they were both using the same network tower. He must be close by. The call is once again made to 'Mother'.

'Beth's given me the heave-ho tonight,' she hears Elliot say.

'I thought she couldn't get enough of you,' says a female voice.

Elliot laughs. 'You taught me well. She's been having a great time.'

Beth feels sick at his words. Whoever he's talking to, can't be his real mother but the thought of Elliot sleeping with another woman disgusts and hurts her. She takes a sharp breath.

Beth hears a thump upstairs. She looks up to the ceiling frowning.

'What was that?' says the woman.

'Sounds like noise on the line,' Elliot says.

'You'd better check your phone,' the woman says. 'It might have been hacked.'

Beth feels the blood rush into her face with guilt.

'Beth was suspicious but probably thought I was chatting up some other woman. She's clueless really. I told her I was speaking to my mother and she accepted it.'

Beth almost blurts out her anger at his words. She bites her lip to stop herself making any noise. Then she mutes the phone, kicking herself that she hadn't done that in the first place.

'Have there been any more murders?' asks the woman.

'No,' Elliot says.

'There won't be any more for now,' the woman says.

'You know who it is, don't you?' asks Elliot.

The woman doesn't answer right away and Elliot waits. Beth can hear his breathing as he does.

'Yes. But I'll take care of the problem in house,' the woman says eventually.

'Yes, Mother,' says Elliot.

Elliot hangs up the call. Beth puts the phone down and then picks up her glass of wine again.

The conversation she's just heard confirms Elliot is a double agent of some sort, it doesn't tell her who for.

She goes upstairs, taking the phone with her. She looks in the bathroom, feeling nervous after hearing the noise that seemed to come from there. She sees a bar of soap in the centre of the bath and realizes it's slipped down. This explains the heavy thump she's heard. Feeling relieved she goes out onto the landing and closes the bathroom door behind her. In Phil's bedroom, she switches on his desktop computer. Then she types up all of the conversation she's overheard for future reference. She saves the document on her own Dropbox account and then shuts down.

In the bedroom she puts the clone phone on charge. She strips off, throwing her clothes into the washing basket and heads to the bathroom. She switches the shower on and gets in before it warms up. Beth scrubs herself clean, wishing she could remove the last few months of Elliot from her skin. Her skin is red when she finally gets out of the shower. She wraps a towel around herself and goes into the bedroom.

Elliot is lying on the bed.

'What the fuck…? You scared me!' she says.

'I thought I'd surprise you,' he says. 'And it's purely selfish, as I didn't want to miss out on a night together when I know you have the boys this weekend.'

'Elliot. I'm tired. I thought you understood that. Have you been hiding in the house? Because security is supposed to let me know if they let anyone through,' she says.

'You got me,' he says. 'I thought you rumbled me when I knocked something over in the bathroom. So, I went and hid in the spare room until you came up. I really did want to surprise you.'

Beth glances past him at the clone phone charging on her side of the bed.

'Okay. That's sweet of you,' she says. 'I need a glass of wine. Let's go downstairs and get one together?'

'I've a better idea. Why don't I go down and get a bottle and two glasses and bring it up?' he suggests.

Beth smiles at him. 'That's a great idea.' She drops the towel. 'I'll wait for you in bed.'

Elliot smirks and gets up off the bed. He leaves the room and goes downstairs.

Beth runs to her side of the bed, unplugs the phone and puts it in the top drawer of the bedside cabinet again. She gets in the bed and pulls the covers up over herself.

Elliot returns. He places the glasses on top of the dresser and pours them both a large glass of red wine.

Beth is trembling as she takes the glass from his fingers.

'I noticed you have a new phone,' he says.

'No…'

'It was on the side, charging when I came in before,' he says.

'Oh. That was just my work phone. I turned it off so that we won't be disturbed,' she says.

Elliot gets in the bed and slides over to her. 'I was just speaking to my mother again,' he says.

'Were you?'

Elliot nods. 'She has a very suspicious mind and not surprising really. She was right, what she said, of course.'

Beth tries to keep her face blank. 'Right about what?' she says.

'That someone had cloned my phone. You see, I didn't accidentally knock something over. I did it to see if there would be an echo of it on the copy you have.'

'What are you…?' Beth says.

'Shush,' he says. 'Eavesdroppers never hear good of themselves.'

'Elliot?' Beth says.

'Where is the phone now?'

'I don't…'

'I know you're lying. You're really bad at it. No poker face at all. I guess that's why they gave you an office job instead of, after all that training, letting you out in the field.'

Beth stares at him. Her heart is beating so hard she can hear the blood pounding through her ears.

'I do like you. A lot. Despite what you may have heard or seen. Mother is a control freak. She never lets us have our own lives, even when we are out working for her,' Elliot continues.

'You're scaring me Elliot,' she says. 'Please…'

'I just need the phone, Beth, and then I'll be leaving. I'd hoped I could stay on here. You know, I'm good at my job. And we really did have something nice going on together. I mean, I made you happy, didn't I?'

Beth doesn't answer.

'But now you suspect me, I'm no use to Mother and I can't continue with our little… courtship,' he continues. 'It was fun while it lasted though. Maybe we can fuck just one more time before I go?'

Something snaps inside Beth's head as Elliot admits his guilt and makes this revolting suggestion. She'd been prepared to fake it that night, just to stop him being suspicious, but the thought of letting him use her one last time after his admission, makes her see red.

'What have you been doing here?' she asks and her voice is cold.

'You know I'm not going to tell you that,' Elliot says.

'You're one of them. You work for the Network,' she says.

'No. I'm a different breed from Neva and Michael,' Elliot says. 'Now… Give. Me. The. Phone.'

Beth opens the drawer at the side of the bed and reaches in, but it isn't the phone that she picks up. Ever since her kidnapping she's slept with her service revolver in close proximity. She pulls it free, and throwing herself out of the bed and out of reach, she rolls expertly and comes to her knees. She points the gun at Elliot.

Elliot leaps off the bed and backs up.

'It was you, wasn't it?' she says. 'You kidnapped me?'

Elliot's silence confirms her suspicions.

'It had to be you. You knew all about me by then. You came in here and chloroformed me, and then dumped me in that hospital. You had access to all of the right forms to do it.'

'Clever girl,' he says. He steps towards her. 'You weren't in any danger though, Beth. I made sure. You have to listen. I really do care about you.'

'Come any closer and I'll shoot you,' Beth says.

'I just want the phone. And then I'll leave,' Elliot says again.

'You're not having the phone,' Beth says. 'Now fuck off out of my house before I shoot you.'

'You're not going to shoot me Beth. You're not a killer. I could have taken it... while you were in the shower,' he points out.

'Why didn't you?'

'Beth... I love you,' he says. 'I wanted you to know it wasn't all a lie.'

'Really? "Never in a million years" comes to mind.'

Elliot dives at her then. Beth doesn't blink as she fires two shots directly into his chest. He drops to the floor and doesn't move.

When the security detail burst into the house and run upstairs, they find Elliot dead on Beth's bedroom floor.

Beth, still naked, continues to point the gun at the corpse until the security men take it from her trembling fingers.

'He was a spy,' she says. 'He was a fucking spy.'

One of the security guards picks up her robe from the back of the bedroom door and wraps it around her.

Shaking, Beth pulls on the robe. She glances back at Elliot's prone body and then bursts into tears.

'Don't worry,' says the security guard. 'We'll take care of everything.'

He leads her from the bedroom, as the other guard makes the necessary phone call. Downstairs, Beth sits at her kitchen table, staring into space.

I've fixed that lying bastard, she thinks. *He can't spy on us anymore.*

A strange calm comes over her. Ever since she was kidnapped, she's lived in fear of being taken again. With Elliot dead, and his admission of guilt, Beth no longer has to be afraid. Even with the questions she will inevitably be required to answer, Beth isn't worried. She can tell them of Elliot's confession. After years of being a loyal employee, Ray should have no reason to doubt her. Besides, she was already getting her story straight about her suspicion of Elliot. No one had been closer to him than her, she was bound to catch him out eventually. She has no doubt that she will be believed.

As Beth plans her report, the enormity of what's happened sinks in. Beth's calm disappears. The tears come again along with a raging sadness that Elliot is dead, despite all of his lies and deception. She'd really cared about him and now she understood just how Michael must have felt about Neva's betrayal.

She sees her life spanning out before her: working at

Archive; coming home to an empty house; *never trusting anyone again.*

What kind of future is that?

When the tears dry up, she goes to the fridge, withdraws the half-drunk Sauvignon Blanc bottle and pours herself another glass.

Chapter Fifty-Five

JEWEL

Jewel arrives at the château by late afternoon, a taxi bringing her straight from Toulouse Airport. She is nervous as she approaches the gates. All of her life she's done everything Mother asked of her but what will she say to her about her recent transgressions now that she's home?

The guard at the gate smiles at her and waves her through. 'You've been missed around here,' he says.

'Is Mother home?' she asks.

He nods. 'She has a guest too.'

Jewel's taxi passes through the gates and she instructs the driver to take her up to the front of the château. Then she pays him and watches the taxi go, tempted to call him back and get inside, leaving this place behind her for good, but she can't do it. This is home, despite everything and she *must* answer Mother's call. Refusal to do so will bring about repercussions that even Jewel fears.

She walks up the front steps and enters the house,

passing into the huge hallway. There's a central staircase that goes upwards and then divides into two, then travels upwards to meet the landings on either side of the main hall. The château has five storeys including a cellar. And on each landing the building divides into north and south wings. Jewel stands in the hallway looking upwards, almost overwhelmed by the family residence even though she grew up here.

Mother's loyal butler, Jeremy, greets her as he comes into the hallway from the service corridor.

'Miss Annalise is in the vegetable garden,' he says. 'But she has a visitor.'

'I know,' says Jewel.

The thought of meeting Mia sets Jewel's teeth on edge and brings an unreasonable urge to cut the woman's throat for just being there. She forces a smile for Jeremy.

'And how is Mother?' she asks.

'Very upbeat,' says Jeremy. 'I think this partnership will be good for us all.'

Jewel nods. 'Good. Good.'

'It's very nice to have you home,' Jeremy says.

Instead of going to the garden, Jewel goes upstairs to her own room which is on the same level as Mother's, just a few doors down. Other privileged children of the training school have also been granted their own space in the château, instead of sharing with their operative brothers and sisters in the barracks attached to the school. Jewel's room has always been her pride and joy. When she goes inside it now, she finds it is ready for her arrival.

The room has a balcony, just like Mother's and the doors

are open. Fresh warm air filters into the room. Jewel glances outside at the peaceful scenery. She overlooks a landscaped garden with a magnificent old fountain as its centrepiece.

Jewel lies on her four-poster bed, smelling the fresh sheets, perfumed with fabric softener and the smell of the outdoors that she's always loved since childhood. She is more confident that Mother has no negative plans for her. But is she glad to be home? She's not sure.

There is a knock at the door and Jewel gets off the bed and opens it. Jeremy is outside and he holds a tray out to her.

'I thought you'd need this,' he says.

Jewel takes the tray and thanks him. After closing the door again, she places the tray down on her dressing table. The tray holds a half carafe of red wine, and a beautifully dressed crab salad. It's one of her favourite dishes. She knows Mother has instructed the cook to prepare it for her welcome home. Even though she hadn't confirmed she would be coming back today. But Mother expected her to obey and it was impossible for Jewel not to. Mother likes to bestow gifts on her children when she feels they deserve it. The food tray is a reward for her obedience.

Normally she would take such a lunch outside on the balcony to eat, but Jewel is enjoying being back in the haven of her room so much that she sits at the dressing table and begins to eat instead.

After she's eaten and sipped at the red wine, Jewel goes downstairs. In the hallway she follows the path right around the staircase and goes into the estate office. There is a whole room full of computers here. This is where the operatives learn their hacking skills. She glances inside to see some of the operatives hard at work. Then she walks past and out through the kitchen to the back of the house.

She goes outside and takes a stroll down to the guard post and from there she begins the long walk of the land, checking the perimeter to calm herself, as she always does when she's home.

Chapter Fifty-Six

ANNALISE

Annalise has just concluded her business with Mia when she sees Fleur. They are in the grounds of the château as she approaches. Annalise looks at her wayward daughter, assessing signs of deterioration. She's been told of her activities and is concerned that she is breaking down in a more catastrophic manner than Neva did, some months back, when she broke away from the Network. But Fleur's prompt return is a good sign. It shows that Annalise still has enough control to command her.

'This is my daughter, Fleur,' she says, introducing her to Mia for the first time. 'You've arrived at a fortunate time. We've agreed terms.'

'What terms, Mother?' asks Fleur.

Mother gives her 'the look', and Fleur falls quiet. Another sign that she is not irredeemable. Annalise smiles at her, and gives her a pat on the arm as silent praise.

'Goodbye, my dear,' says Annalise to Mia. She and Mia hug as though they are old friends. Then the security detail

– Annalise's personal bodyguards – come and escort Mia away.

'She's returning to England to take her place as Mr Beech,' Annalise says.

'And what about you, Mother?' Fleur asks. 'I thought you wanted the keys to the kingdom.'

They follow Mia and the guards around to the front of the château. The limousine is waiting, and Mia gets inside. She waves and Annalise can see the excitement in the woman's face as she leaves the château with a full understanding of who and what she is. A few weeks ago, Annalise had thought it a shame she never got to Michael before Subra interfered with him. What a powerful force the brother-and-sister team would have made. But now, she is pleased she has restored Mia to her real self, even though it hadn't been her intention to do so. But Kritta had tricked her, not explaining that once triggered in this way, Mia would eventually regain all of the information Beech had given her. She'd hoped to be able to control what Mia knew, but soon learned that wasn't possible. In the end it had all worked out for the best though. Mia had confirmed she didn't need Michael and she and Annalise had formed a formidable alliance.

Annalise glances at Fleur. Though she's a good agent, the girl is always lacking. Now Annalise wonders what Valentin would have made of his two daughters. As twins went, they were chalk and cheese. Had he lived, Annalise might never have built her empire, distracted as she was with her feelings for the man. In the end, his death had been for the best.

'I'm glad you are home,' Annalise says. 'Don't go missing again.'

'You said I could keep the money,' Fleur says. Annalise sees the petulant child Fleur has always been. She sighs.

'The money means nothing Fleur; your prolonged absence was the betrayal. What have you been doing while you were gone?' Annalise asks.

Fleur's face drops as she plummets from adulthood to childhood in an instant. Annalise studies her. This daughter does not always please her, even though she is of her own blood.

'I was resting. Sometimes I need time alone Mother. I had to put up with that man pawing me. I needed downtime after that,' Fleur says. 'And I prefer to be called Jewel.'

Annalise has tried so hard to shape Fleur. Pushing her also into having relationships when she was so reluctant to share physical contact with anyone. Like the job with Tehrin. It was more about making Fleur rounded than getting access to his pitiful inheritance. She wanted Fleur to learn to enjoy the art of seduction like Annalise did, because such control over another was a great power to possess.

'Don't be pathetic,' she says now. 'You did a good job on him. Even if men aren't to your taste, you convinced him he was. And as for "Jewel", you need to prove yourself deserving of such a name. But no matter, what of the *other* task I set you? Did you manage that?'

Fleur's face is guarded, but Annalise sees the stubborn twist of her jaw, always Fleur's tell that she's on the verge of rebellion. So far, she has never acted on this urge, but Annalise will knock her to the floor if she ever does.

'I did what you asked me to do. I always do what you say,' Fleur says.

Annalise looks back at the limo as it wends its way down the long driveway and approaches the gates. She signals the guard to open up and let them through. The limo drives away.

'A big change is approaching,' Annalise says. 'Mia is going to be so useful to me.'

'How Mother? I thought you wanted the Network for yourself?'

'My plans have changed, but ultimately the result will be the same. Through Mia I will control the Network. I may send you out on another task soon,' Annalise says.

'What task?' Fleur says.

'We need to get our hands on the child. Then we can ensure that Mia is *controlled*.'

Fleur turns away without a word.

'Where are you going now?' Annalise asks.

She already has her suspicions as to what the girl was doing while she was away, but the question is why was she doing it?

'I'm walking the perimeter,' Fleur says. 'Like I always do Mother. I'm making sure everyone is on task.'

'Good. When you've finished, we will dine together, and you will tell me then, everything you've done in your absence.'

'Yes, Mother,' says Fleur.

Annalise watches as Fleur walks away. Not for the first

time she wonders if she made a mistake parting with Fae instead of Fleur. After all, as Neva, Fae continues to work towards her mother's goals, even when she doesn't know she's doing it. Would Fleur have even survived out there, alone, this long, even as Jewel? Annalise doubts it.

Chapter Fifty-Seven

MICHAEL

After driving around the perimeter, I approach the winery with confidence. It's late afternoon. Unlike most of the wineries we've passed, the D'Aragon Winery has security at the gate. I pull the car up to the barrier and wind down my window.

'Hello,' I say. 'My wife and I are wondering if we can have a wine tasting. We'd like to order a shipment of your finest wines.'

'Usually tastings are prearranged, *Monsieur*,' says the guard.

'Really?' asks Neva. 'Can't you make an exception?'

'One moment. I will see if there is anyone available to help you,' says the guard.

He picks up the phone in his booth and makes a call. Then he begins speaking low in rapid French. When he hangs up, he gives us a smile.

'You are in luck,' he says. 'The winery manager is available and can do the tour.'

'Wonderful!' I say.

'Just follow the road and it takes you straight to the building,' the man says.

The barrier begins to rise as I wind up the window and then I drive through and onto the signposted road.

'That was too easy,' says Neva. She looks around as we drive up a tree-lined driveway.

As we approach the winery building, we take in our surroundings. We can see the château to our right and a further two buildings. One has the appearance of a hospital. The other is clearly the training school building that holds the arena in the centre.

'Do you recognize this place now?' I ask Neva.

She shakes her head. 'If this was my home, then they took the memory from me at the house.'

I feel her frustration as I drive up to the building and park in one of the bays at the front. I look up at the tall brick building which is large and functional but not attractive, despite the rural setting.

'It might come back,' I say.

Neva doesn't answer, instead she looks back at the dense trees as though she expects an assault at any moment. She runs her hand over her boot in an unconscious gesture. She's ready to reach for her knife if needed.

As we get out of the car, a short man comes out of the building to greet us.

'*Bonjour Madame et Monsieur,*' he says. 'I am Louis and I'm going to be your guide this day.'

Louis gestures towards the building. I glance over my shoulder back at the château.

'Lovely château. Who lives there?' I ask.

'Ah yes, the estate owner. It has been in the family for a few centuries,' Louis says. 'This way if you please.'

'How long does the tour usually take?' I ask.

'For a private visit like this, as long as you wish,' Louis says.

We follow him into the building.

'We have a quiet day today,' Louis says. 'It is Sunday and our vintners do not work this day. And so, you will see us on a rare visit. Nevertheless, I hope you will enjoy the experience and I can answer all of your questions and especially let you taste our fine wines.'

'So, you're alone here today?' Neva asks.

'*Oui*,' says Louis.

As he closes the door behind us, Neva chops her hand down on his neck. Louis slumps forward, smacking his head on the door. He slides down the wood, landing hard on the stone-tiled floor. We pick the unconscious man up and carry him into the office. Then Neva pulls cable ties from her pocket (I hadn't even realized that she had them with her) and she secures Louis to the chair. From the office drawer she gets a roll of brown tape and covers Louis's mouth.

'This couldn't have worked out better,' I say. 'The absence of staff today…'

Neva shakes her head. 'It's too convenient, Michael. We need to keep our guard up.'

I agree with her. It's all just too easy. Our timing can't be this good by accident.

'Maybe Elbakitten knew they'd have less people on hand today?' I suggest.

'Maybe she did. Or maybe she is setting us up,' Neva says.

'You're suspicious of everyone,' I say.

'It's kept me alive so far,' she comments.

I take my Glock out and check the cartridge is full. Neva does the same with her gun.

'We need to avoid shooting anyone if we can. They'll hear the gunfire,' I say.

Neva takes a silencer out of her bag and tosses it to me. She always thinks of everything. Then she puts her gun away, and removes the knife from her boot.

'I'm happier with this, anyway,' she says.

I screw the silencer onto my Glock as we walk back out of the winery building and start making our way through the vineyard towards the château. I glance at my watch: it's just gone 5pm.

'Should we wait here for nightfall?' I ask.

Neva shakes her head. 'The guard on the gate will become suspicious if we aren't out in two hours. We need to do what we came for, as quietly as possible.'

Neva leads the way through the grape plants towards the château, as though, despite her denial, she does remember this place. I'm about to ask her again if she recalls anything but she silences me. She crouches down and pulls me with her. We hear the crunch of feet as someone moves through the vineyard a few lanes left of us. We remain quiet and still as they pass by.

Once the coast is clear, Neva stands again. 'We need to be quick,' she whispers.

We hurry on now, being less quiet but getting closer to the château with every step.

The plan is to get in, find Mia and get out again. Neva will not look to engage with Annalise at this time. Once Mia is safe, I've promised to help her confront her mother. But today isn't the right time or place for such a meeting. But this is all so ad hoc that I'm concerned we'll fall at the first hurdle. What were we thinking, taking on this place alone? But then, it isn't as if I can call in help from Ray who has no jurisdiction in France and they'd see him coming a mile off anyway. No, our only option is this direct action and now we have to get inside that building, find Mia, and get away without being noticed.

I try to anticipate how this will go down. There has to be security around Mia, otherwise I believe she would have attempted to escape. As I think about this, my mind flashes back to some of the moments I now remember when Beech had activated me. I hadn't been desperate to escape on any of those occasions. I'd been more than willing to stay and do his bidding. Will Mia be in that mind-set too? The dilemma we face is this main insecurity. Will Mia fight us to remain, or remember who she is and let us rescue her? Knowing how the conditioning can affect us, I have no idea which Mia we will find, and for this reason I'm very nervous as we reach the end of the vineyard.

Chapter Fifty-Eight

JEWEL

Jewel walks back around the château and heads towards the vineyard. On what should have been a loving return home, Jewel finds herself still more frustrated with Mother. Why can't she call her by the name she prefers? Why does she always make her feel so useless? Why can't Jewel ever please her?

Jewel enters the vineyard and makes her way towards the winery, stomping through the trees like a spoilt child. All she wants is Mother's love. Is that too much to ask? She feels like screaming. But the walk does her good and soon the rage subsides inside her, and as she comes out of the vineyard and walks around the ugly redbrick building, she sees a red sports car parked outside. She hurries to the front and goes into the winery.

'Louis?' she calls as she traverses the rooms containing barrels of wine.

Louis enjoys his private tours, and the wineries' finest wines, which he can drink any time he wishes. He always makes Jewel welcome when she does her inspections. Jewel likes to see him, and enjoys it when he brags to visitors how Jewel is the heir to the D'Aragon Estate. Even if Jewel doesn't believe it herself, everyone else sees her that way, as Annalise's biological daughter. Now Jewel goes into the tasting room, expecting Louis and his visitors to be there. But the winery manager is nowhere to be found and she hadn't seen him out in the vineyard during her approach.

She feels a prickle of suspicion. Could the assault have already started? Neva was smart and knew all about stealth. Could she already be here? But of course! The winery was always the weakest point on the estate. It had to remain accessible to the public, but others could get to the château so easily from there.

Jewel comes back to the front of the building and opens the office door. She finds Louis trussed up. There is dried blood on his forehead and his head lolls down to his chest. She checks if he is still alive and when she discovers that he's just unconscious, Jewel leaves him where he is. She's not concerned for his safety; she doesn't want him to raise the alarm. She doesn't want anyone to know that Neva is here until it is too late. Why didn't Neva just kill him? Jewel would have. Perhaps she is weaker than Jewel thinks?

Her head buzzes with excitement, pushing away thoughts of Louis, because she has no real loyalty or emotion for the man despite his obvious consideration towards her. Jewel isn't wired that way. The only person she cares about is Mother.

Neva is here! That's all that matters now. Jewel is ready for this final showdown. How wonderful it will be when she ends Neva. Of course, she won't have come alone, and Michael, if he gets in the way, will be collateral damage. He's Neva's Achilles heel, a thing she can use to bring her down.

And Mother will just have to deal with the consequences!

Jewel comes out of the winery and looks around. Which way would they go? She glances at the château beyond the vineyard. Neva and Michael must have passed her.

Some of the plants have been snapped or damaged. Now she's looking closely, she sees their entry point but Neva and Michael have been careful and it isn't that obvious.

Jewel follows. There is a subtle trail left by them that Jewel is able to track. The odd bend of a vine here, the crushing of some budding grapes there. They are all signs that someone has made their way through, desperate to reach the house.

Jewel takes her time, remaining far behind them; she wants the element of surprise to be hers. As a result, she reaches the end of the vineyard in time to see both Neva and Michael entering the château by the back entrance.

She pauses, allowing them time to get inside, and then she strolls across the lawns and sneaks into the house behind them. She feels tremendous satisfaction as she follows them unseen.

After that she trails them through the kitchen, remaining hidden as they avoid the kitchen staff and move on into the main house. She sees Michael and Neva slip into one of the smaller side rooms used for storage as Jeremy makes his way back down the corridor carrying her tray back to the kitchen. Once the butler has passed, Neva comes out of the room and she and Michael head towards the hallway.

As they begin their search of the château, starting upstairs, Jewel hides under the expansive staircase until they have climbed the stairs. She doesn't want either of them to see her until she has the advantage. Jewel waits, knowing that at some point they will have to split up and then she will make her move, taking down her much-hated sister first.

Chapter Fifty-Nine

NEVA

As they reach the top of the stairs, Neva sees that the landing goes in two different directions. *One north wing, one south wing,* she thinks.

'We need to split up and search before our presence is discovered,' Neva says. 'I'll try this side. You take the other.'

Michael nods but she can see he isn't happy that they are parting.

Neva turns and walks away. As she reaches the first door, she glances back at the stairs and sees Michael at the door on the opposite side. She turns her attention away from him and back to her search. She listens at the first door, then opens it and goes inside. The room is a basic bedroom, and not as lavish as the rest of the house. It has very little in the way of personal possessions and has two single beds inside, both neatly made. It reminds her of a barracks. Something twitches in Neva's brain. A recollection that this corridor and these rooms are used by other employees of

Annalise. But she doesn't know where the memory comes from.

She tries the next room, finding it equally empty, then she's plummeted into a memory that was once suppressed somewhere deep inside her.

'Coming ready or not!'

Neva staggers against the door frame of the second door.

'I know where you're hiding, Fae!'

The little girl giggles as she runs from room to room. 'I'll find you!' she yells.

And Neva knows who this is as the memory comes flooding back. *Fleur!*

Neva pulls her mind back to the present. She looks back up the corridor towards the stairs as though she expects that same little girl to come running towards her now.

I was here, she thinks. Neva had half-believed her similarity to Annalise had just been a coincidence. But her own memories confirm that Annalise is her mother.

Shaken, she continues down the corridor, passing several rooms without checking them. She reaches the end of the corridor and the final door on the right as though drawn there.

When she tries the door, Neva finds that it is locked. She is confused for a second as she sees the two little girls in her mind's eye running along the corridor again, yelping in excitement. She tugs at the handle again. Like an automaton, Neva takes the lock-pick set she carries from her pocket. She prods the lock until she hears that satisfying click and then she opens the door.

Chapter Sixty

ANNALISE

After seeing Mia off, and the brief and irritating exchange of words she'd had with Fleur, Annalise seeks the haven of her bedroom. She has a strict beauty regimen which she now begins. She cleanses her skin and puts on a face mask and then she lies down on the bed and closes her eyes.

The last few months have been challenging, sometimes draining, especially with Fleur going rogue.

Then there is her operative Elliot. A promising man, with good abilities. Beth Cane was just Elliot's type, which was why Annalise had picked him for the job. Submerged in his pathologist role – a career he'd trained for with her money – Elliot had lost his way. He'd begun to believe he could keep the job and just feed Annalise scraps of information. He'd begun to fall for Beth. Annalise had recognized the signs. Since their phone call last night, he hadn't been in touch. In the end even the best of spies could make stupid choices. Elliot wasn't the first and wouldn't be the last, but Annalise hoped his training would kick in and spur him to make the right choice in the end and kill Beth Cane like she'd ordered him to do.

Life is full of hard choices, Annalise thinks.

She gets up out of the bed and goes to the laptop on her dressing table. Elliot had sent her the autopsy reports of the killings he was working on with Archive.

She opens the folder now and looks at the photo gallery of the women: each before and after death. Even with Annalise's constitution the murders are hard to look at. Especially the woman in the stable. Annalise knows death: sometimes for necessity but never for pleasure. These kills serve a purpose only the killer can understand.

She scans the autopsy report. Elliot was supposed to send her Michael's profiling on the killer too, but so far, he hasn't been able to gain access.

Annalise looks at the photographs again. Then she closes the laptop. It looks to her as though Fleur is pursuing a goal that doesn't suit Annalise's plans.

Annalise's mind follows a path of memory. One she tries not to recall too often, but today it's somehow important to draw on. It reminds her that difficult decisions are sometimes crucial and that she has more to make herself soon regarding both of her daughters.

Chapter Sixty-One

ANNALISE

Forty-three years ago

Annalise was 17 when she met Mr Beech for the first time. She'd graduated from the house, top of her class, and already had several professional hits to her credit.

Annalise observed that this Mr Beech was young. He was barely a few years older than herself, in fact. She'd heard rumours that the old one had died. Or been executed. She wasn't sure which and it didn't matter anyway. What did matter was that this young man now owned the Network, and all of the handlers were bowing and scraping to him which meant that he was a very powerful man.

'You've exceeded all expectations, Annalise,' Mr Beech said. 'And for this reason, I'm going to give you a rare gift.'

'A gift, *Monsieur*?'

'Do you know how you came to be here, my dear?' Beech asked.

Annalise shook her head.

'I'm going to give you your parents,' Beech said. 'Would you like that?'

Annalise stared ahead; she showed no excitement at the prospect of meeting her parents.

'I'll give you a choice,' Beech said. 'You can kill them, or you can kill your twin sister.'

Annalise's curiosity spiked at the mention of a sister.

'I have a sister?' she said.

'Did you know that your parents gave you to the Network?' Beech said.

Annalise didn't react as Beech revealed this. She was not broken and did not rebel. She was fully trained to do as Mr Beech ordered her to.

'It would be a revenge killing. Payback. Would you like that?' Beech continued.

'I will kill whichever of them you wish,' Annalise said.

'I want you to choose. Your mother and father? Or you sister?' Beech said.

Annalise was unable to respond. She couldn't make such a decision herself. She killed if her situation was jeopardized. She killed witnesses, and anyone who got in her way when on a mission. There was no thought necessary for these deaths, they were all logical calculations. But to be given the choice of her own mission? Her conditioned mind spiralled with the unfathomable idea of such choice and freedom.

'I… can't…' Annalise said.

'You don't want to kill them?' Beech had said.

'Their deaths mean nothing to me,' Annalise said. 'I will do what *you* want me to do. But I can't choose.'

Beech sent her away after this response, and Annalise had thought she'd failed some important test. But she didn't have to undergo further conditioning, and she was sent on her way a few days later to the halfway house.

But Annalise never forgot Beech's offer to tell her who her parents were. And, as she matured, she began to wonder who they were, and why they'd chosen to send her away, instead of her sister. It was several years until she discovered the truth for herself. By then, Annalise was in her late twenties. She had a string of successful jobs behind her, and a large accumulation of wealth. She was also an expert on infiltration and seduction. Skills that she used to gain leverage for the Network.

Then Beech sent her on a new assignment. She was to work for a fashion photographer, called Henri D'Gault. Her mission was to infiltrate D'Gault's circle and learn secrets that Beech could use as leverage against the man. Annalise disguised her looks, taking on the appearance of a dowdy secretary. She hid her red-blonde hair and her demeanour matched the mousiness of the wig she wore.

After a few months working at the photographer's studio, she was called to go to a photoshoot on location. She travelled with the crew to Paris.

At the last minute, the model got sick and Annalise was asked to search the books of a local agency to find someone else suitable. Annalise went through the pictures and then, to her surprise, she found a model who not only resembled Annalise's true appearance but was identical to it. Her name was Zuria D'Aragon. Annalise called the agency and they told her Zuria wasn't available: she was visiting her family in Toulouse. She hired another of the models and the shoot went on, but now Annalise was curious about Zuria and the D'Aragon family in general.

Then, Annalise remembered the offer that Mr Beech had made her. Did that offer still stand?

When the shoot in Paris finished, Annalise hired a car and took a few days off from the assistant job. By then she had a lot of dirt on D'Gault, particularly his procuring of underage girls for his own private photoshoots and more. She sent this information on to Beech before she left Paris and then she took herself off radar.

She drove to Toulouse and stayed in a five-star hotel. It didn't take her long to find D'Aragon wines and to learn the location of the winery.

From the archives of a local newspaper she discovered an article about the family and the loss of their daughter Zaphire. Annalise knew then that her life was about to change.

Removing her dowdy disguise, Annalise dressed in a long, chic maxi-dress and took a walk along the side of the Garonne. Though she had no active memory of the city, she felt an innate familiarity.

At the house any regional accent had been eradicated, and she spoke a neutral French, and a similarly neutral English as well as being able to emulate other accents when necessary – speech, languages and dialects were taught as part of their curriculum.

As Annalise paused by the river, she considered how different her life should have been. She didn't feel angry, just curious as to why she was picked and not Zuria. She wasn't even sure what she gained by coming to the area.

'Zuria?' a voice said behind her.

Annalise turned. It was a man. Young, very handsome. She expected him to realize his mistake, but to her surprise he walked towards her.

'I thought you'd returned to Paris,' he said.

Annalise let him kiss her on both cheeks.

'Come for a drink with me,' he said. 'We need to talk.'

Curious, Annalise followed him away from the river and across the road to a café. He ordered a decent bottle of wine and they sat outside, looking out at the busy city street.

'So, what happened? You were supposed to come back to me.'

Annalise looked away, she was good at being others, but she didn't know how her sister talked and just one word could give away that she wasn't Zuria. At that moment, she was saved from answering as the café owner came out to speak to the man.

'Valentin! And Zuria. I'm so happy to see you both here,' he said.

Annalise took in the local twang of the man, rolling the name Valentin around in her head as her tongue moved to shape it.

Annalise smiled at the man, hoping it was warm enough to be from someone he knew. Neither man questioned her identity. When the owner left them, Annalise looked at Valentin and waited once more for him to speak.

'You know I love you. Why do you torture me, Zuria?'

Understanding the relationship now, Annalise rested her hand on Valentin's leg.

'Are you going to give me your answer, or make me wait longer?' he said.

Annalise shrugged, 'What answer do you want, Valentin?'

He was shocked by her words.

'Have you been stringing me along?'

'No,' said Annalise.

'Then, tell me you'll marry me,' Valentin said.

Annalise thought for a moment. 'But we must see my parents.'

Valentin's face erupted into a smile that Annalise found endearing. As she considered the life she could have had if she had been the one to remain with her parents, she wondered if Zuria was stringing this sweet and sensual man along. After all, her sister had left him with his question unanswered.

'When?' Valentin asked then. 'When shall I meet your parents?'

'Soon,' Annalise said. 'Now, take me back to your place and make love to me.'

Annalise was amused that Valentin had been shocked by her suggestion that they make love. Old fashioned as he was, he had merely kissed and held her. Annalise didn't pursue it; she didn't want Valentin to realize just yet that she wasn't Zuria.

Annalise was curious to see if her parents would also think she was Zuria or if they'd recognize her as the daughter they sold to Beech, when Valentin, Zuria's boyfriend, had been unable to tell the difference. She had driven to the house with Valentin that night.

It was the oddest thing to recall Zuria. Other memories had come back into the mix at the same time, memories that even Beech's prompting years earlier hadn't surfaced. Not until that day when she saw herself in a modelling catalogue and realized this was the life she could have had.

Annalise had analysed those emotions – something she wasn't used to having – and decided that she would make her parents pay for choosing Zuria over her. It wasn't anger exactly that she felt: she'd been taught never to indulge in that area as it weakened you. It was a feeling of jealousy mixed with resentment and the underlying depression that is sparked by rejection. But she didn't understand all of this until much later, when she got her revenge.

As Valentin had driven into the driveway and up towards the house, Annalise had experienced a sensation of elation. She was coming home! Not only had she survived all that they'd done to her at the house, but she'd excelled there. She was the best in her year group. Beech had favoured her many times and she was on her way to becoming immune from retirement, perhaps even establishing herself on the committee. All she had to do was keep her head down and do the work. The irony of this was not lost on her.

As she got out of the car, and her parents' butler opened the front door, Annalise began to see the possibilities of the château and its amazing vineyard. She studied the house for the first time, searching her mind for any residual memories that may help fool her parents now.

'*Ma cherie?*' Valentin said. 'Should we go in?'

Annalise looked at him, trying to see Valentin through Zuria's eyes. Why had she hesitated to say 'yes' to his proposal? Why had she run away instead to Paris? And then she knew what it was: Zuria craved excitement. Valentin was safe and loving. He'd be an attentive husband, but it wasn't what Zuria wanted.

Annalise understood that this was exactly why she found Valentin so appealing. Valentin was everything that Annalise was not permitted to have because she was an asset of the Network. Just as she couldn't have her parents, or any semblance of a normal life.

She walked up the steps holding Valentin's hand. It was such an ordinary thing to do but it thrilled her.

'Are my parents home?' she asked the butler.

He didn't challenge her claim to be there and instead turned and led her and Valentin to the drawing room.

'I'll let the *Madame* and *Monsieur* know you are home,' he said. 'Shall I organize refreshments for you and your… friend?'

Annalise nodded and the butler left them alone in the room. She indulged herself in casually looking around. The room was awash with beautiful regency furniture. Expensive artwork adorned the walls. The sofa that she and Valentin sunk down onto was plush and expensive. Her parents had untold wealth. Probably more money than they knew what to do with. Annalise wondered where this wealth had come from.

She had a flashback moment. A man and a woman arguing. *Mère et Père.*

'We'll lose everything!' her father said.

'We're talking about sacrificing our child!' her mother, Estelle D'Aragon, said.

Estelle had cried then. But she'd let him do it anyway, and only a few short hours later, Annalise was on her way to Paris to begin her training.

I was called Zaphire.

'Zuria? Are you all right?' Valentin asked.

Annalise smiled at him. His eyes were wide as he looked at her, and Annalise knew he was confused by her behaviour. She was different from her sister, after all.

Estelle and Anton D'Aragon came into the room. Neither of them tried to hug her. Annalise didn't know how to feel about that: on the one side something inside her craved it, on the other the idea disgusted her. They were older versions of her memory of them, but essentially the same pompous father and the same weak-as-water mother. Annalise despised them.

It was a strange encounter; one Annalise would remember years later when she was faced with a similar decision to let one of her own daughters go to Beech's house in England.

Her parents didn't *recognize* her; they accepted Annalise as the daughter they'd brought up: it spoke volumes about the relationship they'd had for the past few years with Zuria. Annalise knew there must be differences, there had to be. Zuria would have affectations that Annalise didn't. And what of the local dialect? Had Zuria rubbed off all those edges as she'd built her career in Paris? Or was she so estranged that her parents didn't really know her at all?

'This is Valentin,' Annalise said. 'We're getting married.'

Anton's disdain for Valentin became obvious as he remained standing and glared at the man.

'Zuria, you know what I told you,' Anton said.

'Anton…' her mother said. 'Can't you see she's in love…?'

'She gives up on this, or she's cut from my will!' Anton said.

Annalise found herself frowning. Was this the problem? Her parents didn't like Valentin as a prospect? *Why?*

'You're a grown woman. You can make your own decisions,' Valentin said. 'Let's go…'

He stood and took her hand but she stopped him.

'Let's talk later,' Annalise said. 'Leave me with them. I can fix this.'

Valentin looked worried but he did as she asked. She walked him to the door.

'I'll come to you later,' she said.

True to her word, she found Valentin again that night. By then her parents were no more: a freak accident that brought the real Zuria back to Toulouse and within easy reaching distance of Annalise.

Chapter Sixty-Two

NEVA

Present day

The shutters are closed and the room is in darkness. Neva stretches out her hand and searches for the light switch by the door. In a glare of illumination, the room lights up. Neva stops in the doorway, shocked by what she sees: a child's room fully preserved from the day she left it.

Except for the pictures.

Photographs cover one entire wall interspersed with newspaper clippings, all of which show details of times and places that Neva remembers. Kills. Her kills. On a small patch on another wall, Neva sees the death shots – pictures she took and sent to her handler as proof that she'd completed each job. That handler had always been Tracey and so she knows she had to have passed them on to Annalise.

Neva walks further into the room, distracted by the graveyard of toys that are covered with a thick layer of dust.

There is a child's bed, turned down ready for use, and a small moth-eaten pile of clothing waiting on top of the dresser for their tiny owner to return.

Memories hit her like a bolt of lightning in the chest. Her heart hurts: a dull homesick longing. She runs her hand over the musty fur of a once-loved teddy, remembering it clutched in her arms as she lay in the tiny bed, looking up at that one person she most trusted. *Mother.*

Rest, my little one.

A crack inside her brings her to her knees. Neva doesn't notice the dust that puffs up into the air as the wrenching pain of leaving Mother and Fleur hits her again.

And Mother's words. 'She's only a baby. Be kind to her, please…'

It was the moment she first saw Tracey. Thereafter, Fae died and Neva was born. A child's life and destiny were forever changed.

'I'm Fae,' she says. And the crack in her sanity widens. 'No. I'm Neva.'

The room around her swirls and writhes as Neva tears herself from one identity to another in bursts of cohesive recollection. Layer upon layer of memories fall back into place. One moment she's playing in this very room, the next she's honing her gymnastics skills in the kill house. Each memory overlap blurs together, as she grows and changes under Tracey's direction. A vision of Fae in the château grounds, holding her mother's hand, erases Neva. While in another moment, Neva plunging her knife into Kurt, eradicates Fae. Over and over, memories and moments pour into Neva's conscious mind, dragged as they are from her subconscious. Until, unable to take in any more, her mind short circuits and Neva breaks.

Collapsing forward onto the neglected carpet, Neva's mind shuts down, plummeting her into welcome darkness until her memories can reshape and find a place to hold it all within.

Chapter Sixty-Three

ANNALISE

As she lies on the bed, Annalise continues to think back to her early days at the château.

On the night she killed her parents Annalise had made sure that the château staff had seen 'Zuria' leave. By then Annalise had established her knowledge of the place and knew exactly how to get inside again without being seen. She'd returned later with another assassin she knew. This man helped her heft her drugged parents into her father's Bentley. Disguised as her mother and father, they'd driven the car from the property, making sure the security guard saw them leave. It was late, but no one questioned it.

After that, rigging the car crash, along with the explosion of the petrol tank, had all been easy.

Annalise paid her colleague off: a silence she later made permanent when the man wasn't expecting it, and then she went to Valentin. He would be her alibi in the coming days.

On hearing of her parents' sudden death, Zuria returned to Toulouse. Annalise had used her sources to learn of the girl's movements and so she was ready and waiting when the girl arrived at the château.

She waited in one of the unused rooms while Zuria settled back in at home. And because she didn't want her contacting Valentin, she cut the phone line to stop her using it. It would be a few days before the telephone company would come out and fix it and so this bought her all the time she needed. She let Zuria make all of the funeral arrangements and deal with the invitations, all information that would have been challenging for Annalise to deal with, as she knew so little about her parents and their family and friends.

Then, one night, when all of the staff had retired, she went into Zuria's room and killed her. It wasn't messy but it was strange: looking at Zuria was like looking at the mirror image of herself. And as she pressed the plush pillow down on Zuria's face, it felt as though she was killing herself.

Zuria was very underweight and it wasn't too difficult for Annalise to move her body, especially with Annalise's lifetime of training and fitness. She was strong, because she had to be. So, she'd carried Zuria over her shoulder, out into the vineyard. Always prepared, Annalise had left herself a shovel and she spent the next few hours digging a deep grave under the grapevines.

When she finished this labour, she pushed the lifeless body of Zuria into the hole and covered her over. Patting down the earth to make it appear undisturbed.

Muddy and tired, she returned to the château.

In Zuria's bathroom Annalise took a shower, washing away the death along with the mud. Afterwards, she dressed in Zuria's clothing. She sat at her dressing table, combing out her wet hair as she familiarized herself more with Zuria's life by trying her beauty products.

Eventually, growing tired, Annalise got into the bed her sister had died in. She turned off the light and slept, taking on in this one evening the life and identity of her sister.

Just one week after she arrived in Toulouse, Annalise's life had changed: she became Zuria, the heir to the D'Aragon fortune. The irony of it didn't escape her that this same money had been given to her parents to buy Annalise from them.

Annalise married Valentin soon after her parents' funeral. He never asked her about Zuria, but she knew that he suspected that she wasn't really her. By then they were lovers in more than just words. It didn't change Annalise's world too much, but gave her a home to come back to after her kills as she continued to work for the Network, her absence from the château explained as modelling assignments.

She thought she could juggle it all. Then she received a message from Beech asking her to be the mother of a child for the Network. She refused. She was pregnant at the time and by then knew that she was having twins. She'd promised herself she would never give either of them up, and she wouldn't have, but for Tracey.

Though Beech had taken her refusal in good spirit, eighteen months later Valentin was killed as he drove from the château to Toulouse. It appeared to be a tragic accident, Annalise never knew for sure, but she'd suspected that

Beech had discovered she'd taken over Zuria's life, and punished her for it.

Annalise understood vengeance as much as she did murder. That was why she'd triggered Neva's first break, knowing that her daughter would exact her revenge. And she had executed Tracey magnificently.

Annalise was prepared for Neva to come after her too one day, which was why her contingency also included a way to bring her daughter back home in mind and body.

But then, Annalise hadn't banked on Fleur breaking down like she had. Annalise doesn't know why or how this has happened.

In the bathroom, Annalise removes the facemask and slips on a new brilliant turquoise kaftan. The comfortable clothing looks wonderful with her white hair.

She'd been looking forward to a peaceful dinner, a last supper if you like, with Fleur before she did what any mother in her position would do. *I had to get her help*, she thinks as she justifies what she's done.

Doctors and orderlies would be here to take Fleur in the morning to a private clinic in Switzerland that Annalise has been funding for her own reasons for years. Her operatives are in charge, Fleur would be in safe hands. Maybe they could even help her. But one thing Annalise knows for certain: Fleur can't be allowed to have her own agenda. Not now that Annalise is so close to her goals. Not now that Neva is due home.

Chapter Sixty-Four

JEWEL

It's as though Neva is calling her and they are playing once again that silly game of hide and seek that Neva always won. Neva always knew where to find Jewel. Now that same sixth sense pulls Jewel down the corridor, passing the numerous closed doors on the way, until she reaches the room at the end. *Fae's room.* Mother had locked the door the day she left.

Jewel had believed that no one came in here. And then, years later, she'd seen Mother entering the room, locking the door behind her.

Jewel had crept to the door and listened. All was silent within. She thought perhaps this room was used for some secret only Mother knew. A secret she wanted to share.

When Mother had retired for the night, Jewel came back. She'd picked the lock and gone inside. That was when she learned how Mother really felt about her other daughter. That was when she knew that she had lost her Mother forever and it was all Fae's – no, Neva's – fault.

The whole room was a shrine given over to that lost child at first. Then it became a place where Mother celebrated Neva's many successes, even as she left the rest of the room to rot. Jewel had never earned that same love and respect, no matter how hard she tried. Sometimes she felt she was a painful reminder of the favoured child, a runner-up prize. Second best. Though Jewel had pined for Fae at first, she'd grown to resent, and then hate, her missing sibling. Her departure had somehow stopped Mother from loving Jewel.

Jewel's bitterness increased with time, spurred on from the moment when Mother had pitted them both against each other. Jewel had revisited the room often. She studied Neva's many achievements as Mother had displayed them on the wall. The deaths were always so simple and clean, yet never rushed. Jewel took up the knife as her favoured weapon. She honed her use of it. Killed with it, emulating Neva to perfection.

Mother didn't notice. Jewel's fury grew.

Now, the moment of her ultimate retribution has arrived.

Neva is unconscious when Jewel enters the room. Jewel turns her over, sees the carpet-burn smudge on Neva's cheek, signposting the suddenness of her collapse.

It is a dream come true that she is here, vulnerable, right in the place where Jewel can stage her perfectly. A present for Mother that she'll have to accept.

Taking her by the wrists, Jewel pulls Neva towards the small bed. Then she goes to the door and closes it.

She pulls the rotting cotton sheet from the bed then rips it into strips. She ties Neva's wrists to the footboard. Neva doesn't wake as Jewel stretches her body along the floor. Her arms are pulled up and over her head in an uncomfortable position.

Jewel steps back. She tries to visualize what she wants to show Mother but the inspiration she's had with previous kills evades her. She turns around in the room looking for the props. Her eyes fall on the teddy bear, a one-time favourite of Fae's. Jewel blinks as she's plummeted back again into childhood.

'Your sister won't be back,' Mother had said.

'But why? Where is she?' Fleur had asked.

'She doesn't belong to us anymore.'

From the day she left everything changed.

Mother was cold to Fleur's tears. If she ever cried over the loss of her daughter, Fleur never saw it. But sometimes she'd find Mother alone, a faraway look in her eyes that confirmed that Fleur had lost both sibling and parent on that one day.

Now Jewel looks at her sister and sees the entity that took away her mother's love and turned Fleur into the killer that is Jewel.

She doesn't regret who she's become, for now it will give her the ultimate ascension.

She will prove she's better than Neva.

'Fleur?'

Jewel turns to look at Neva.

She observes the confused expression on Neva's face and recognizes that she has yet to fully understand her plight.

'Good. You're awake.'

Chapter Sixty-Five

MICHAEL

Gun in hand, I turn right and start to walk down the corridor to begin my search of the château. A door opens ahead of me and someone steps out into the corridor. There is nowhere I can go.

I am face to face with Annalise.

'I did not expect you,' she says as though I'm a surprise guest in her house and not an invader of it.

'I'm sure you didn't. Where is my sister?' I say.

'Of course. I should have known that you would throw away everything to come for her. How did you find us?'

'You're not as anonymous as you think you are,' I say. 'But when Neva's source told us about this place, I knew you'd be here. This was your parents' house wasn't it?'

Annalise's expression tells Michael all he needs to know about her parents even though she tries to hide her emotions under a frown.

'Where is she?' I say, pointing my Glock directly at her.

Annalise shakes her head.

A slow smile plays on her lips as she looks at me.

'You won't kill me, Michael. You had the chance when Subra had you under her control. I've brought Mia up to speed with who and what she is. I suspect she will be rather annoyed with you for keeping her in the dark. Especially when she takes over the Network.'

'What are you talking about?' I say. 'Mia would never…'

'I've made an alliance with her. If you've any sense, you'll do the same,' Annalise says.

I don't want to believe her but there's a nagging memory in the back of my head. Something that Beech had told me, months ago, in the English kill house. How only a Beech can take control of the Network. I hadn't thought about it since. I'd been dealing with all the information my mind had had to absorb once I'd been activated and now, Annalise's words take me back to that fateful conversation.

Beech was calm as he spoke those special words that made sure he had me fully in control.

'You're my heir, Michael,' he said. 'But, in the event that you are dead, or compromised, Mia will be activated. Now, let me warn you about Annalise…'

Beech's words ring in my head as I watch Annalise. She's going to try to blindside me. She wants to get to Neva, and I remember why. Neva can be compromised. Tracey and Annalise were working together and they'd really done a number on her. But how Beech had known all this, I couldn't remember.

'You have to kill Neva,' Beech had said after he triggered me.

And I'd been going to, until the door opened and I'd come face to face with her. I couldn't do it. I'd remembered too much. I knew she was the little girl that held my hand when I was scared and who shared this horrible experience with me. The connection we'd had from the beginning had led me to her over a year ago in a busy London street. I'd been there for her, just as she had been for me.

'Where's Neva?' Annalise asks and the sharpness in her voice focuses me back on her.

'She's looking for Mia, and probably you too, to take her revenge on you,' I say. 'You deserve it for what you've done to her.'

'She's alone? *Here?*' Annalise's face shows concern as the assassin façade drops away.

'*Fleur,*' she says. 'I have to find Fleur!'

'You're not going anywhere until I find Mia.'

'Mia's gone. She's probably already on my jet flying back to London!' Annalise says. 'Look, we can deal with your hatred of me another time. I have to find my daughters.'

The reason for Annalise's concern occurs to me: she's worried that Neva will hurt her twin.

'Don't worry, I doubt Neva will kill her. It's you she wants revenge on,' I say.

Annalise's irritation slips away as her eyes dart past me.

'It's Fae – Neva – I'm concerned for, not Fleur,' she says.

'Why would you care? You gave her away to be made into a murderer,' I say.

'You can judge me all you want when… Look, Michael. This is serious. You've been investigating some murders, haven't you? The victims all looked like Neva, didn't they?'

'What do you know about that?' I ask.

'I don't know, but I suspect… We have to find them both. *Now!*'

'You're really worried, aren't you?' I say.

Annalise hurries towards me and taken by the sincerity of her alarm, I let her pass me as she heads towards the stairs. She stops at the top, looking down the landing that Neva had taken.

'Did she…?'

I nod.

'How long have you been on the property?' she says.

'Why?' I ask.

'We don't have time to lose,' she says. 'She'll be vulnerable and that's when Fleur will press her advantage.'

I hear rising hysteria now in her voice and it translates over to my already taut nerves. Despite myself I'm pulled along by it. I don't know Annalise, but somehow I believe she really is worried. Whether that is for Neva or Fleur, I just don't know. And it doesn't really matter. It's enough to make me concerned for Neva either way.

In a matter of seconds I have to decide what I'm going to do. Do I believe her that Mia is no longer here? Do I believe that Neva is in danger – and knowing how resilient Neva is, that one is hard to believe. Or do I just kill Annalise now and end this once and for all?

'Lead on and don't try anything stupid,' I say. 'I'll have no problem shooting you.'

Annalise glares at me, then turns and hurries off down the corridor. I follow, keeping my gun trained on her and my finger on the trigger. The killer in me rears again. One false move and I will happily put a bullet in her.

Chapter Sixty-Six

NEVA

Neva's head hurts as she opens her eyes. For a moment she can't place where she is. Then the void begins to fill and her whole world twists and turns, threatening to overwhelm her once more. She's Fae D'Aragon. She's Neva. She's both. A burst of more agonizing memory brings her back to consciousness. The irony of this recollection is not lost on her. It explains so much about her life. Mother had given her away, but she had also helped her. She'd worked with Tracey. They were both involved in Neva's conditioning. Neva remembers it all.

She feels her mother's arms around her, and accepts the cold caresses with the distance and unfeeling of the assassin she's become. Fae is inside still but it's far more complex than just having a dual personality, or being a sleeper. No – the sleeper is her 'real' self, trapped inside the killer of the Network Tracey and Annalise had made. She's fragments of a whole that now merges into one cohesive being.

Her eyes fall on the back of a tall slender woman standing a few feet away. She searches her memory and the recollection returns with a painful vengeance.

'Fleur?'

The woman turns, Neva knows now she's right. It is her sister, fully grown. But she's familiar. They've met recently and she can't quite remember where. She feels that sense of disjointed confusion as her mind searches for the pieces of the puzzle, a jigsaw that slots together to bring all the details and knowledge into her control.

Fleur's eyes are cold as she looks at Neva. This is not a happy reunion for either of them.

Neva's arms ache and she realizes she's in an unnatural position. She tugs at the bonds.

'I'm not here to hurt you. We came for Mia,' Neva says, remembering their mission. 'Do you know who I am?'

'You're Neva,' Fleur says.

'Fleur… I…'

'I'm Jewel now,' she says.

Jewel. Neva remembers a Jewel. Yes. She remembers a war, an attempted coup to take over her reign in the house. Jewel had tried to undermine her – Neva had taught her a lesson. She'd triumphed over her. She sees the resentment that this caused, left inside Jewel all these years, festering like a pus-filled sore that is now ready to burst.

'My sister… you were her and I didn't recognize you. I'm sorry. I wasn't myself… the house…'

Jewel gives a harsh laugh. 'Your death is going to be beautiful, Neva. I think I'll place the photograph of it in a frame, above your achievements.'

Neva looks at the wall and the kill photographs. She recalls them now, remembers once more entering the room just a short time ago and the agony of her psyche breaking down. This break, worse than the first, had taken torture to a whole new level. Neva craves revenge now for all that was done to her. All that she's been forced to endure. She lapses back into her cold killer self as her default mechanism kicks in.

'This is your work?' she asks and her voice is calm. Her pulse is steady. She has expected her own demise for years, and her mortality holds no fear for her now. Instead, she feels alert. Strong. Ready.

'Mine. Oh no. This is Mother's doing. She's been following your *career* all along.'

Neva tests the bonds again; she can feel a slight give on the wooden bedpost she's tied to. A hard tug might free her. She watches Jewel as she stalks around the room.

'You're my gift to Mother,' Jewel says. 'She'll have to notice me then.'

Neva looks into her sister's face and sees that her black pupils are dilated, threatening to take over the whole of her eye. There is darkness in there, but not the cold and calculated workings of a professional killer. There is something more, that leads Neva to wonder what Jewel has been through at the hands of her mother. Jewel is broken. But it's more than that. A break can be recovered from, it's more about establishing self and freedom. But not in Jewel's case.

Even as Neva is struggling to bring the pieces of her own collapse back together, she feels Jewel's anxiety. She senses the swirling void, the rage, the absolute abject loneliness that has brought this all to the fore. And more than anything else, she sees the pure insanity that might mean her once loved sister is now completely lost in a mind full of hate.

Chapter Sixty-Seven

NEVA

As Jewel approaches, Neva sees a blade drop into her hand. She's wearing an identical wrist holster to hers, and the knife is the same size and make as Neva's own blade. She begins to work out how she can escape.

'I could kill you now,' Jewel says. 'But I want you to see *my* work first.'

Jewel pushes the blade back into the holster, then goes to a dresser near the door and opens the top drawer. She retrieves a box and brings it to Neva.

'I brought this here earlier today. Ready for you. Even though I didn't expect you quite so soon. I suppose it was the man… pushing you to come and take Mother on. To rescue his sister.'

'What do you know of Mia?' Neva asks.

'She will be a strong leader. Not like the… Michael. His compassion is his weakness,' Jewel says.

Neva doesn't respond: Michael's empathy is a strength to her. Though of course, Jewel would never see that. She watches her now, wary of what she will do next, but waiting for the right moment to free herself and to bring down Jewel more dramatically than she did all those years ago when they were both children of the house.

Jewel opens the lid of the box and starts to lay photographs at Neva's feet, and around her body as though she is creating a collage with Neva as the centrepiece. Neva sees the content of the photographs as Jewel lays them out beside her. They are all duplicates of the same five kills: all women in various bloody scenarios; wrists cut in a bath; staked out on the floor; multiple stab wounds in a shower; a body wrapped in razor wire; another on a bed covered with petals. She recognizes that these were the women from news reports she's seen.

Neva appreciates what is happening. Jewel was the killer of all these innocent victims and now she is being staged. The victims all looked like her: it makes sense why Jewel felt they had to die.

Neva tests the bonds and feels the width of the footboard spokes she's tied to while simultaneously stretching her arms to relieve the cramping discomfort.

Once she's placed the photographs around Neva, Jewel steps back. She studies her display. Then removing her phone from her pocket, she takes a photograph of Neva among them.

'It's not quite right,' Jewel says.

She picks up the teddy and places it on the bed behind Neva.

Then she takes another picture.

'Better.'

She stops to look through her phone. Then she frowns again.

'I forgot this one,' she says. 'I didn't get a chance to have a print made.'

She bends down and holds the phone out for Neva to see.

There's a photograph of another victim: Janine is naked and tied to a bed in a hotel room. Her throat has been cut. On the wall behind her is written, presumably in Janine's blood, 'Our Beloved Daughter'. Neva's expression remains cold. She doesn't give Jewel the satisfaction of seeing her shocked or upset. But she feels a terrible regret that her friend has been killed and all because she doubled for her. A burst of emotion erupts inside her, breaking down the assassin training once again. Neva pushes back. She removes the image of Janine from her mind. She runs her mantra in its place instead. *I am death…*

'I knew she'd see you in my smile. She was besotted with you. Just like Mother. I played with her for months in the hope she'd lead me to you. When she didn't, I decided to save her for last. Her death was very satisfying.'

Neva looks at Jewel and says nothing. Her mantra continues to flow over her mind, pushing away the shocking hurt that Janine's death brings. She'd saved her life and in some way felt she owned it. It was not Jewel's or anyone else's to take. Neva's world was better with Janine in it, even when they were apart.

'Clever, don't you think? Using the scenarios from films to celebrate the deaths. I decided on that after the first kill… there was something not quite right about that one. It lacked *finesse* and needed a proper stage on which to be celebrated.'

She drops the phone, picture face up, onto Neva's stomach. Then she takes a step back.

'Perfect. Mother will appreciate this,' she says.

The knife drops back into Jewel's hand. Neva tenses, pulling against the restraints as Jewel approaches. Then, the bedroom door bursts open.

Jewel spins around to face the door and with her attention diverted, Neva gives the bonds a hard tug. The wooden spokes on the footboard give way with a loud crack. She pulls one arm free, while catching hold of the spoke and gripping it, sharp end pointed outwards as a makeshift weapon.

'Fleur!' says Annalise. 'What are you doing?'

Chapter Sixty-Eight

JEWEL

With Mother standing before her Jewel finds herself in a quandary. She wanted to surprise her with the dead and presented Neva. She pulls against Mother's control on her, fighting hard to not let herself be plummeted back into her subservient role.

'I have a present for you Mother,' Jewel says.

'Put the knife away, Fleur,' Annalise says.

Jewel frowns. Why won't she call her Jewel? Then she remembers Neva. She has to do this before Mother tries to stop her. She looks behind her and sees that Neva has freed one of her arms. Good, then this won't be too easy. She needs to have the war again and win this time. She needs to beat Neva down until she's blood and pulp and nothing more.

'What are you doing, Mother?' Jewel says as Mother moves into the room.

'She's not your enemy, Fleur,' Mother says. 'You had

everything, she's the one I gave up. She should want to kill you and me.'

'No one needs to die today,' says Michael from the doorway.

Jewel's face goes blank when she sees him there, but her eyes glare at him. *Neva's lover.* Are he and Mother now plotting for the ownership of the Network? Nothing would surprise her.

Michael looks back at her, shocked. His eyes show his recognition of who and what Jewel is.

'*Elsa?*' Michael says.

Jewel laughs and then slips into the voice she used as his colleague at Archive. 'Oh Michael, I just want to help.'

'How?' Michael says.

'I took over the identity of the real Elsa once we knew she was likely to be recruited. Mother's plan was years and years in the making,' Jewel says. She casts Annalise a proud glance.

'I sent you to Archive before I knew you had your own agenda,' Annalise comments.

Neva moves behind Jewel. There's a piercing crack as another spindle breaks and Neva pulls herself free. She gets to her feet. She looms tall and regal. Jewel casts a glance Neva's way.

No, Neva won't take this moment from her.

Jewel is in the centre of the three of them now, like the core of a trinity, the heart of everything. She turns from one to the other. Michael. Mother. Neva.

'She's your sister,' Mother says. 'Do you remember?'

'Yes,' says Neva. 'I remember everything. Especially what you and Herod did to me.'

'I had no choice. Fae…'

'I'm not Fae. Anymore than she is Fleur. You changed us both and there's no going back,' Neva says.

'Neva?' says Michael.

'I broke again, Michael. I'm no longer the Neva you knew. I'm a… I'm… Fae *and* Neva. With joint knowledge of who and what I am. I know my real purpose,' Neva says.

'My child!' Annalise says, smiling and proud. 'I knew you would evolve.'

'I'm not your child,' Neva says coldly. 'I'm a child of the house.'

'She's my gift…' says Jewel. '*Mine*. I wanted to make her beautiful for you.'

Annalise's attention switches to the photographs on the floor.

'I hoped it wasn't you…' Annalise says. 'Fleur…'

'I wanted to make you proud of me, like you are of Neva,' Jewel says. She smiles looking down at the photographs.

Annalise looks at the wall of death as though realizing that she has created a monster in both of her daughters.

'You could *never* be *her*, Fleur,' Annalise says.

Annalise's rejection sends Jewel tipping over that final edge of sanity. She falls into the precipice of madness, consumed by her urge for revenge. Knife between them, Jewel turns on Neva. The hatred inside her overflows. She sees blood spilling red as she anticipates the coming fight that this time she will win. She runs through every move that Mother's school taught her. In her mind's eye she is stronger, faster and more powerful than her sibling. And Neva's weakness is the man; if all else fails, she'll take him down to cripple Neva further.

Neva lashes out first, the wooden spoke in her hand crashes against Jewel's wrist, but she holds onto the knife. Jewel comes back at Neva, the knife flashes through the air, barely missing her face in a vicious attempt to spoil her. Neva ducks away, but uses the wood again to whack Jewel hard on the back of her calf. Jewel stumbles, then rounds on Neva.

Jewel focuses her attention on the enemy, even as she feels Annalise and Michael moving around them both. Each looking for a safe opportunity to intervene. The bedroom is their arena and only one of them will leave it. The sisters circle each other. And as Neva moves forward, attacking first again, Jewel tracks backwards, keeping distance between them as she assesses what her next move should be. But patience is not Jewel's best virtue, even though she tries to adhere to the training, her need to see Neva's blood splashed over the faded room, pushes her to leap forward. Just as the cracks in her mind widen and take away the last vestiges of good judgement.

The knife flickers through the air in a series of cuts. Neva fends her off with the piece of wood and then the knife slices through her sleeve, cutting her arm. There is a splash of red as Jewel pulls back the knife and then spots of blood fall down onto the pictures. The spilling of Neva's blood sets free a torrent of emotion. Jewel throws herself forward, feral, wanting more. She aims for Neva's throat.

Jewel hears Mother cry out but ignores it as she sees the beauty of Neva's death almost realized. Then Annalise is between them and the knife hits home: a clean stab in the jugular.

Jewel pulls back in shock. Blood spurts. The same way she wanted but not from Mother. The turquoise kaftan darkens, turning purple as Mother slumps down between them. Jewel finds herself facing Neva again. They look at each other in equal shock. Jewel looks down at the body.

Mother is dead. And nothing else matters. She raises the knife and swings at Neva.

There is a muffled crack and a hard thump hits her in the back, sending Jewel to her knees.

Chapter Sixty-Nine

NEVA

The knife falls from Jewel's fingers. She pitches forward and Neva catches her. They both sink to the floor. Neva holds Jewel as a patch of blood widens on her back. Michael's aim was true, the bullet had penetrated her back and had buried itself in her heart. She wasn't dead yet, but she was dying.

Neva turns Jewel around, looking down into her familiar face. Then Michael comes closer.

'I couldn't find the killer because she was right under my nose,' Michael says. 'Elsa. I should have recognized she was your sister but she was wearing a wig and contacts. My god, she was insane and yet she played the part of Elsa to perfection. She was so… controlled.'

'I remember her now. Brown bob. She was talking to me at the hotel when Solomon Granger accused me of—'

'Jesus! He meant *her*! Not you,' Michael says.

Neva's mind flicks back to that moment as a flash of perfect memory clarifies the situation behind her eyes.

'It's her,' Granger said. 'Angie! I thought you were dead!'

Neva looked at Granger, shocked.

'You killed her! She killed my Angela!' Solomon said, looking directly at Elsa.

'*I didn't do it.* I didn't kill Angela Carter or steal Granger's child. She did. For her mother,' Neva said. 'For a while I doubted my own sanity. I thought that I had done these things under another personality, one I knew nothing about. It's the sort of mind-fuck that these people do to the kids.'

There is a sense of euphoria as Neva realizes she is not guilty. Such a small thing, in the scheme of all of the deaths she has delivered. But she hadn't wanted Carter's blood on her hands.

Michael looks around the room and nods. 'This is fucked up.'

'Tell me about it. You're not the only one with a weird family. She killed Janine.' Neva glances over at the mobile phone. Discarded among the photographs and blood on the floor. She lets the grief and loss come out for one brief moment. A tear slips down her cheek. She looks up at Michael and lets him see the raw emotion inside her. No more hiding. No more pretending. She can feel and she wants to, even when it hurts this much.

'I'm sorry,' Michael says.

They look at each other for a beat.

'We have to get out of here,' Michael says, as if attempting to break the spell.

'I can't,' Neva says. 'This is where I belong. I have to take over from Annalise. I'm the only heir.'

'Neva? You don't *have* to do anything. You're free. You can just walk away from this shit,' Michael says.

Neva strokes Jewel's hair as the last breath hisses from the girl's lips. She wipes away the stray tear. Then she pushes Jewel's body away. She stands up.

'She was fragile. Mother's methods drove her insane. She was right to send me to the house and not Fleur,' Neva says. 'I wish I could leave. But it's far more complicated than that. It's time we both faced the truth, Michael.'

'What are you talking about?' Michael says.

'If you don't take over the Network, and I don't take on the Almunazama, then someone else will.'

'Neva…?'

'She told me. She told me everything. Every visit she made at the house, she brought me back to being Fae and my duty was instilled in me. Mother wanted an alliance of the two most powerful cabals in the world. We can do that, Michael. And *our* children will bring it all together.'

Chapter Seventy

MICHAEL

'If you don't take control, Mia will,' Neva says. 'We can't have that.'

'No, Neva. The Network is evil. It's everything that both of us have fought against. How can we…?'

I feel myself shattering inside as more of Beech's secrets come crashing back into my mind. I fall to my knees, head shaking from side to side in silent denial of everything that Neva says. Inside me I try to fight it. But deep down, I know that she's right.

She kneels down beside me, pulling me into her embrace as if she understands the inner turmoil that now threatens to eat me up from the inside.

'You know what we have to do,' she says.

But still I fight on. I see my career at Archive, the life I'd wanted for myself fade as if my inner vision has become myopic. But I know the truth: Neva and I have always been set on this journey. We are the creation of our own parents as well as of the house. Moulded in their image to maintain a legacy. I even remember the three words to say to Mia to make her stand down. This revelation soaks in as I free myself from Neva's arms. *I can save Mia* – she can have a normal life. But it will take one final sacrifice to make it happen.

Neva and I remain kneeling. I stare at her without seeing her. I see Mia now instead, running back towards Ben, taking Freya into her arms. They have a chance.

I take Neva's hand and we both stand.

I've been fighting my inheritance ever since Beech was shot in the kill house at Alderley Edge. I'm a child of the house of killers. And beside me, as we walk downstairs, is the one person who understands. She, like me, must take up a mantle: a poisoned chalice if we make it so. But we don't have to. It's a discussion we will both have when we start our full and new life together as heads of our respective families.

In the hallway the young Almunazama assassins wait for us as we descend the staircase.

We pause before we take the final steps to the hallway, maintaining an elevated position, that shows our status among them. I can't remember how I know to do this, but it feels right.

'Mother is dead,' Neva says to the assembled children and adults that make up Annalise's household. 'And Jewel… Fleur… had to be retired for her part in that. I am Fae D'Aragon: codename Neva. I am the rightful heir and leader of the Almunazama.'

The butler steps forward. I expect a challenge but instead he bows before Neva. The other warriors and trainees follow suit with a murmur of '*Namaste*' as they bow to Neva.

'Annalise told us to follow you in the event that this happened. I am Jeremy,' the butler says.

Neva shows no surprise that Annalise has prepared them for her coming as she accepts their pledges of allegiance one by one. It is odd seeing her in this role, but also right.

'This is Michael. He's Mr Beech,' says Neva. 'He's my consort.'

Her words baffle me as they seem so archaic. But the assassins bow to me now and Neva takes my hand. I feel as though I've been plummeted back into a different age, not the tech-driven world I live in. But her hand… feels like it always belonged there.

Neva turns now to Jeremy. He looks like an old retainer to me, but I see such character in his face. He's seen much in Annalise's house of killers. I know he is a force to reckon with.

'Have the crew return with the jet as soon as possible. If they are still with Mia, have them detain her. Michael needs to go to England and claim his position.'

'Yes, Mother,' says Jeremy.

Neva blinks. She's shocked by the label. She looks at me for reassurance. I nod. I see the burden landing on her strong shoulders. I squeeze her hand to remind her she has me beside her. We are never going to be alone again. She accepts my silent promise to be her rock, just as she will be mine.

'Upstairs,' I say. 'The bodies need to be disposed of. That room… strip it of everything and clean it.'

Jeremy looks at Neva for her approval of everything I've said.

'Do it,' she says. 'Always obey Mr Beech as you do me.'

Jeremy turns and indicates to two men, who take to the stairs to do our bidding.

Neva turns then to the waiting assassins and staff of the château.

'It's business as usual,' she says. 'Back to work.'

The crowd disperses on her command.

We watch them go in silence, and then I raise Neva's hand to my lips. Never have two people been more suited than us.

'The car will take you to the airport,' she says. 'Go. Claim your crown. Then come back to me.'

Again, her words summarize our reign, but I know I'm no king and so the weight of what's to come sits heavily on my shoulders.

'What will you do here?' I ask.

'See how it all works. Change things. *Maybe,*' she shrugs. 'I don't want to be parted from you for long. Those days are gone Michael,' she says.

I pull her into my arms. Heart swelling with pride and joy and a tinge of anxiety, as I know we will be taking on the world. I stare off into space. Thinking of how morally wrong the Almunazama and the Network are. And how we might improve that for the better. Or how we might not. But I do know this: we have a legacy to take on and neither of us can shake our duty now. It's the way we were made.

And in doing so we will have a life together. We will be able to love each other. Has any other Beech ever done that?

I release her again and kiss her hand one more time before I let her go. For now, we'll part, but on my return, we'll take on what we know we must, for the future of all concerned is now in our hands. Even the future, as she'd said, of our own children.

Four suited men escort me to a limousine. I cast Neva a last glance before I leave the château and get into the car. She stands tall, bearing the burden of her thorned crown well. I don't look back as we drive to the airport and to my future.

THE END

Acknowledgments

As always, huge thanks go to my agent Camilla Shestopal for her guidance, support and friendship. She often listens to my ramblings of ideas during the writing process and it really helps me to focus and shape them into a whole coherent piece.

A massive thank you to Tom Irwin, a director of Accuracy International, for his really informative discussion with me about their sniper weapons. In the height of lockdown, Tom very kindly called me all the way from the USA and ran through the features of their weapons and how they could be effectively deployed on a target. All of which helped me a great deal to bring the believability to Neva's use of the AX308 in order to fake Talia's death. I'm definitely going to take him up on the offer to visit their factory too!

Huge thanks to the actor Frazer Hines for his knowledge on horses and livery stable practices, which became a wonderful backdrop for a murder. Thanks also to Linda

Compagnoni Walther for helping me get to grips with locations and travel in Switzerland. Much appreciation has to go, once again, to Colin Paul Renouf who helps me massively to focus on technical details – all of which adds to the content used in the world of my spies.

Thanks to my editor Bethan Morgan, who keeps me on track and catches me if I fall. Wow, how she guided me on this one! I know her words of wisdom have pushed me hard to deliver the best I can to bring *The House of Killers* to this final conclusion.

Applause as always to the crew at One More Chapter for working so hard to get the word out all the time about my books. Thanks as always to Lucy for this stunning cover design and for the amazing support of all of the publishing team.

And last, but definitely not least, love, thanks and adoration for my rock David who puts up with losing me to a novel every time I embark on writing one. Without David, none of this would be possible. 'Never have two people been more suited.'